DYING TO TELL

A Wild Fens Murder Mystery

JACK CARTWRIGHT

DYING TO TELL

JACK CARTWRIGHT

PROLOGUE

A SINGLE ROBIN REDBREAST EYEBALLED HER FROM WHERE IT WAS perched on a fence post. Beyond it, in one direction, the wild Lincolnshire Fens roamed for miles. Behind her, in the other direction, Lincoln Cathedral dominated the horizon. But in between those beautiful vistas was chaos.

Winter had drawn to a close. The first signs of spring were evident in the fields and on the verges. Yet the cold air lingered, and Poppy Gray bent double to catch her breath.

It wasn't the sound of footsteps that roused her, like she had been expecting. It was a whistle. The bird. Angered by her presence perhaps.

Or was it a warning?

It glared at her then whistled again. But it didn't move or flinch at Poppy's company.

Poppy stared back at the robin through bloodshot eyes, still wet from the tears she had spent. Her chest heaved from the exertion of running. She had no idea how far she had run, but she was sure she was safe now. Almost sure, at least. *Ninety-nine per cent certain*, her stepmother would have said. *As near as damn it positive*, her father might have voiced.

But there was the robin, defying her confidence.

She tried to piece the events together. The bend in the road. The screeching tyres. The little boy and those big, wide eyes.

And then that scream.

What a mess.

Should she turn back? It was all her fault. She should come clean. Yes, she should tell them all what happened. That would show them.

She knew the thoughts were futile. And when she heard the footsteps coming up the track, she knew she would never be given the chance to say what she had to say.

Preparing to run, Poppy pulled off her boots and looked down at her bare feet. She had two options – climb the gate and run through the field, or go further up the track. The field was open ground. She could be seen. And there was no clear way out. She would be trapped.

No. The path is best. Stay on the track. Find somewhere to hide. Stay there. Until it's dark. Until it's safe to go for help.

A figure rounded the corner while she debated, stopping to enjoy Poppy's quandary, equally breathless.

"There you are."

"Why are you doing this?" Poppy screamed, which only seemed to raise delight. "Please. I won't say a thing. Not to anyone. I promise."

They took two steps forward.

Blinded by tears and fright, Poppy ran, not daring to look back. She cast her boots into the bushes and sought the soft patches of spring grass for every step, though often the way was paved with sharp stones, and only her fear drove her forward, hoping, praying to find somewhere safe. A hole. A road. A house. Anything.

She ran until her legs were not her own and her feet were bloodied, broken, and bruised. She ran until her lungs could take no more and her vision succumbed to her tears.

It had been a bright, sunny morning. She remembered opening her curtains and taking in the view. One of those spring days where blue skies gave hope to the long depression of winter and the fresh air bit at her bare ankles. Fresh leaves clung to boughs, and long grass that had been flattened by winter now stood tall, erect with the warmth of the sun, concealing the deep ditch beyond.

She stumbled forward, expecting to find solid ground, but there was none. She reached out instinctively for a branch, but it snapped and she fell. A few moments passed. Time enough for her to question her injuries, and time enough for her to regret the life that still ran through her. To regret what she had done, what she had seen, what she knew.

Who she was.

A cool stream of water soaked her dress, but she cared little for the discomfort.

She rolled onto her back, pulling herself up into a seated position, and considered the fall fortuitous. Out of sight, but not out of mind. She could wait there. Beside the long grass and the trees, the sky above was all she needed. How long had it been since she had stared at it? How long had it been since she and her only friend had made shapes from the clouds? And how long had it been since she had felt the warmth of the sun on her bare skin?

She smiled, genuinely. The flow of tears stopped and dried, and for the first time, there was hope. True hope. Not the charade that her mind had convinced her with. True hope. Escape.

No more secrets. No more self-loathing.

A flutter of wings caught her eye. A familiar face stared at her from the tree above. He whistled then glanced around nervously.

She closed her eyes on her old friends – the robin and the sun – and slipped into a dream she had long since forgotten. But the dream was short-lived. A shadow passed over her. The heat on her face dropped by a degree or two. Enough to rouse her from her slumber. Enough for her to open her eyes and stare up. Enough for her to know escape meant death, and that death was imminent.

A silhouette stared down at her, the face masked by shadow. And above. Out of reach. Untouchable. Poppy's friend whistled once.

And she smiled.

"A robin redbreast in a cage puts all heaven in a rage," she said.

And the secrets she carried died with her.

CHAPTER ONE

SEARING HOT WATER SCALDED FREYA BLOOM'S SKIN, BUT SHE lingered beneath the spray for a moment longer, savouring her success. For three days, she had been forced to wait for heating oil to be delivered to her little farmworker's cottage, and she had managed to get the boiler working without any help from her colleague and friend, Ben.

Savouring those final few moments, Freya gave thought to how she'd spend that evening after work. She would have an early night. Maybe do her nails and watch a film? Something quiet, something girlie.

That would be bliss, she thought.

She switched off the shower, groped for a towel, and stepped blindly through the misty bathroom. Whacking her toe on the door when she slipped on the tiled floor had little effect on her elation. Three days without hot water. Three days of enduring freezing-cold showers, of towelling off as fast as she could before hypothermia set in. Now she leaned on the bathroom sink, wiped away the condensation, and stared at herself.

The last time she had run out of oil, she hadn't even known the old cottage heating system ran on oil. She had called Ben and asked for help, and he had diagnosed it in an instant. That had been three months ago, and this time, not only had she diagnosed the issue herself but she had called an oil supplier, booked a delivery, and had even managed to bleed the system of air, and fire the old boiler up. To be fair, the man who had delivered the oil had helped her do that part, but Ben didn't have to know that. All he needed to know was that Freya Bloom, the posh, hoity-toity city girl with the public schoolgirl accent, as he called her, was mastering the country life.

"It's a doddle," she said to her reflection, as she inspected the lines around her eyes. For a moment, she thought there were fewer than before. Fewer than when she had arrived in Lincolnshire, that was for sure. Was it the country air? Or was it that there were fewer investigations? In London, she was notorious for working simultaneous enquiries and producing results. But here, even in the major crimes unit, there was just no need.

She blew herself a kiss, then winked, then made her way along the upstairs landing. The heating was on full and the steam from the shower had been so fierce it had reached her bedroom. Even the little mirror she had bought to do her makeup was clouding over.

She cast open the curtains with a little too much vigour, knocking over a small vase of wild flowers she had picked at the weekend. She caught them and replaced them on the window ledge, rubbing out the wet patch on the floor with a bare toe. With her towel wrapped around her, she gazed out at the view and deemed herself lucky to have met Ben. In all her years, never had somebody done so much for her and asked for so little in return.

Her first week in Lincolnshire had been at the beginning of the previous winter. Her final investigation in London had been particularly brutal. She pondered those days like they had been another lifetime. Captured, like the girls she had been trying to save, Freya had spent three days in captivity. Three whole days had been lost from her memory, resulting in a six-month sabbatical during which she had lain in bed, wallowing in self-pity and guilt. The inevitable divorce had followed and Freya had driven away in the family motorhome. A new start. A new place. Fresh air and new adventures. Her secondment had developed into a full-time position, and she had been so successful that the original structure of two major investigations teams had been merged into one, spearheaded by her.

She smiled at the thought of her newfound success. The view wasn't bad either.

Her closest colleague, Detective Sergeant Ben Savage, was from farming stock. His family had worked the land for generations, and although he was police through and through, he still lived in the house his father had given him for his twenty-first birthday. Freya lived across the field in one of the old farmworker's cottages, and from her bedroom window, she could see all three of the Savage houses in the distance. It had been Ben who had not only convinced her to stay but convinced his father to rent the cottage to her, allowing her to move out of the motorhome until she was on her feet.

The truth was that she was already on her feet but couldn't imagine not having Ben on the other side of that field. She hadn't conquered the countryside *that* much. Not yet anyway.

Reaching for her phone, she found her music and selected an upbeat song she had listened to as a teenager. It was a classic. Timeless. Much like the view she enjoyed every morning.

The teasing intro to *Material Girl* began and she hit the button on the side of the phone to crank it up to full volume, then tossed it onto the bed. It took a few moments for her to get into the swing of the tune. Her hips swayed at first, then she sidestepped into her moves and began to sing. A little shuffle was all it took for her towel to fall to the floor, and using the mirror as an audience, she worked her way through the first verse. She danced and sang her way to the chorus as she descended the stairs, three steps down, two steps up, putting her own flavour on the powerful woman Madonna had portrayed in the video. Finally, she reached the bottom of the stairs, and with a sweeping sidestep, emerged in the kitchen doorway – where she screamed.

Her hands flailed trying to cover herself, and all thoughts of the sexy and powerful woman she had conjured in what she had thought was a private dance routine vanished.

"What the bloody hell are you doing?" she screamed, bent double with one arm covering her chest and the other her groin.

Ever the gentleman, Ben turned away, holding a hand up. "What am I doing?" he said. "What the bloody hell are you doing? Put some bloody clothes on."

"I'm in my bloody house," she said, moving to hide behind the door frame. She peeked out at him, clutching onto the wooden architrave, then finished, "You're in *my* bloody house."

"You told me to come over for coffee before work."

"Most people knock on the door," she said, furious that he had almost certainly seen everything. "They don't just let themselves in."

"The keys were in the door, Freya," he said. "I thought you had left them there for me. You know. To save you coming down and letting me in."

"Why the bloody hell would I want you to come in while I'm naked?" she said, waving at the closed door to support her argument.

"I didn't know you'd be naked, did I?" he replied, then sheepishly, gestured that one of her feminine charms had broken free of the door frame and was hanging in full view.

She screamed again, then ran upstairs, with one hand clutching her behind in case he decided to peer up at her.

He wouldn't though. Of course he wouldn't. Even if she had wanted him to. She slammed the bedroom door. The exclamation mark to her rant. Then she fell onto the bed, the embarrassment giving way to something altogether different.

If only he did try to look up the stairs to catch a glimpse of her backside. If only he did ever show a sign he felt something. God knows she had given him enough chances.

Unsure if it was the thought of him seeing her like that, or her imagination dreaming up ideas of what he could have, should have, and what any other red-blooded male would have done, but she found herself reaching for the top drawer of her dressing table.

She bit down on her lower lip, unsure if she should, or if she even had time, or if she could get through an entire day with him if she didn't.

CHAPTER TWO

It was forty-five minutes later when Freya opened her bedroom door. She was dressed, her hair was done, and for the first time in a long while, she had used only a smidgen of face cream around her eyes. To see if anybody noticed more than anything. She listened for movement downstairs and heard Ben's rumbling voice from the kitchen, then reddened at the embarrassment that was sure to come.

She coughed, making her presence known, and he told whoever it was that he had to go and that he'd call them back.

Then, defiant as ever, she told herself she would put the embarrassment on him. It would be him that wouldn't be able to look her in the eye. It would be him that blushed, and fumbled with an apology.

She smoothed her jacket, pulled her hair from her collar for the third time in under five minutes, and, with her chest out, she stepped forward and kicked a mug of hot coffee down the stairs.

"What the bloody hell?" she said, seeing coffee spray up the walls like blood at a crime scene. The mug at least bounced all the way to the ground floor in one piece, slid a little, then broke when it hit the kitchen door frame.

Ben poked his head out cautiously.

"Everything alright?" he asked.

"Is everything alright?" she said, her voice lowering to almost a growl. "No every-bloody-thing is not alright, Ben. What the hell was that? You could have killed me."

"Coffee?" he said. "What do you think it was?"

"On my doorstep?"

"Well, I didn't want to come in," he said, blushing a little. "Not after... Well, you know."

"You came to my door?"

"Yeah."

"When?"

"Fifteen minutes ago? Just after you flashed me."

"I did not flash you."

"Looked that way to me," he said, grinning.

"You broke into my house."

"You left the key in the lock. Technically, that isn't breaking and entering. Negligence on the home owner's behalf, I'd say."

"I must have left them there when I came home last night. I was carrying shopping. It's not exactly Piccadilly Circus out there, is it? It's nearly a mile to the nearest road. Nobody is going to walk by and see it."

"Okay, well, I made you a coffee to apologise," he said. "What have you been doing anyway? That was ages ago."

Clearly, he hadn't noticed the effort she had made.

"What was I doing?"

"Yeah? It's been nearly an hour."

"Has it?" she said, glancing at her watch.

He leaned against the door frame, an eyebrow raised expectantly.

"I was epilating, if you must pry," she said, thinking on her feet. She carefully made her way down the stairs in her new boots, hoping, of course, that he'd spot them and make a comment.

"Epilating?"

"Yes, Ben," she said.

"What's epilating?"

She stopped midway down and searched his face for a sign he was winding her up.

He wasn't.

"You really don't know what epilating is?" she asked. "An epilator? You know? The buzzing thing women use."

"Is that a posh word for–"

"It's bloody hair removal, Ben. To get rid of unwanted hair!"

"Oh."

"Would you like a demonstration? Because right now, I'd be glad to epilate your bloody head."

"Alright, alright," he said, holding his hands up in defence. He looked a little confused as she made her way down the final few steps, and she came to stand before him, unwilling to let her own embarrassment get the better of her.

"What?" she said, as he reached to open the front door.

"I didn't see much that needed epilating myself," he said, and he leaped over the broken mug and escaped through the door before she could swing for him.

CHAPTER THREE

"It doesn't matter what I saw," Ben explained, as he waited for Freya to fasten her seat belt, then pulled away. "You've seen me naked, and I've seen you. We're equal."

"Oh god. How did I know you were going to bring that up? You flashed me, and if you remember rightly, you even scared your would-be-girlfriend away."

"What?" he said. "You were looking up my towel."

"You sat down on the stairs and–"

"You even complimented me. You said I had a nice–"

"I know what I said, and you're taking this completely out of context, Ben."

"And you said it was–"

"Ben, stop. Please. I don't want to be reminded of your..." She gesticulated, as she often did when she was embarrassed. "Thing."

"We're even, anyway," he said. "And if I might add, that's a lovely pair of–"

"Ben!"

"Alright, alright," he said, edging as far from her as he could. "Boots. I was going to say boots. They're a lovely pair of boots, that's all. Are they new?"

"They are, as it happens," she said, in that sulky way he enjoyed so much. She raised a leg to bring them into view.

"Did you get them in a sale?"

"A sale? No. Why? What's wrong with them?"

"Nothing. There's nothing wrong with them. I just asked because..." It was his turn to fumble over his words. "Because that's what women do, isn't it? Buy stuff then boast how much money they saved."

"*I* don't."

"No, that doesn't surprise me. Go on then."

"Go on then, what?" she said, clearly not following.

"How much were they?"

"What an odd thing to ask."

"What? I thought you girls loved to tell each other how much you saved."

"I didn't save anything. I saw them. I liked them. I bought them. What's the big deal?"

He waited, smiling to himself.

"Three hundred pounds, if you must know."

"What?" Ben exclaimed, and he brought the car to a stop at the end of the farm track before they turned onto the road. "You paid three hundred quid for a pair of boots?"

"So?"

"Are they waterproof?"

"No, of course not."

"Insulated?"

"No, it's spring. It'll be warm soon."

"Do they have diamonds in the heels?"

"What? No. They're just boots, Ben. Knee-length boots. Confidence-boosting boots. Sexy boots," she said, finishing with her best husky flourish.

"Why are you wearing them to work then?" he asked, and she shook her head to look out of the window.

She sighed audibly. "I honestly don't know, Ben. I honestly

don't know. Maybe I'll meet Mister Right, and maybe he'll sweep me off my feet today?"

"Mister Right?"

"Yeah. It could happen."

"Right," he said, and he was just about to mention the fact that the only people she met were either criminals or police officers when the screen on the dashboard lit up, displaying one of the incident room phone numbers.

"DS Savage," he said, eyeing Freya, who had dropped her sulking act and was staring at the screen in anticipation.

"Ben, it's Jackie. We've had a call come through from the front desk. Are you on your way in?"

"Yep, we're about five minutes out. What's happened?"

"It's a hit and run. A little boy. Uniform are on scene and I've asked Gillespie to swing by."

"Is he alive?" Freya asked.

"He is, yes," DC Jackie Gold replied. "But only just."

CHAPTER FOUR

The location pin DC Gold had sent to Ben's phone placed an arrow on the map. But for the life of her, Freya couldn't tell where it was. She zoomed out, holding the phone at arm's length to read the tiny writing.

"Stixwould?" she said. "Does that sound familiar?"

"Out towards Bardney," he replied, and she saw his expression alter as he decided if they were going in the right direction.

They were.

"Past Woodhall Spa. There's not much out there though."

"No, you're right," she said, seeing the empty space depicted as green on the map. "There's not much at all."

Ben drove fast, but not so fast that Freya couldn't find Gillespie's number on Ben's phone. The ring tone came over the car's speakers and they both waited for the gruff tones of their Glaswegian colleague.

"Aye, Ben," he said, by way of a greeting, then sighed audibly. "You've heard then, I suppose?"

"We've heard, yes. We're on our way. What do we have?"

"Ah. From what I can tell, the little boy ran across the road–"

"How old?" Freya asked.

"Ten, boss," he said, then continued relaying all he had learnt. "Car came around the corner driving too fast. Knocked him off his feet. Poor bugger didn't stand a chance."

"Bloody hell," Ben muttered.

"Aye. It gets worse. The car ploughed through the hedgerow. The boy's mother heard the crash and came running out of the house just as the driver ran off. Female. Late teens, Early twenties."

"Did she go after her?"

"No, she saw her boy lying there. I mean, what would you have done?"

"That's just it, Gillespie," Freya said. "We don't know until it happens, do we? Where's the boy now?"

"The ambulance just left. He's breathing, and all that, but unconscious. Paramedic suggested there might be some internal bleeding."

"And the mother?"

"She's with him."

"Did you get a statement?" Freya asked.

"She just watched her ten-year-old boy get loaded into an ambulance, boss. She wasn't really in the speaking mood, if you know what I mean?"

"Right. I'll get DC Gold to go and speak to her there," Freya said. "In the meantime, we need to locate the runner. Have uniform arrived?"

"Aye, boss. I've got Griffiths at one end of the road, Jacobs at the other end, and I'm in the middle of them waiting for a recovery truck."

"Jacobs?" Freya said, trying to put a face to the name.

Then she wished she hadn't.

"Aye, boss. You know the one. Tall fella. He's got a face like the moon. You know? Like he's just been spanked with a cartoon shovel."

"Nice image, Gillespie," Freya mumbled. "Well, if more

uniforms turn up, pass the car on for them to deal with. I want that runner found."

"Aye, boss. Will do," Gillespie said, sounding a little demoralised. "Makes a change though, eh?"

Freya glanced up at Ben, who offered her a quizzical look.

"What's that, Gillespie? What makes a change?"

"Well, you know? We're not all standing round a bloody body scratching our heads, are we?"

"Not yet we're not. Have you run the car registration?"

"Aye, did that just now. Belongs to a bloke in Kings Lynn. That's Norfolk way. It was reported stolen about twenty minutes ago."

"So some poor sod just lost his car. I'll let you deliver that particular piece of good news to the owner. Get in touch with him. We're coming into Stixwould now, so we'll see you in a few minutes."

"Aye, boss. Will do. I'm going to take a wee look around."

Freya ended the call and glanced Ben's way. She knew exactly what he was going to say.

"Is this really a job for us?" he asked.

"I knew it," she said. "I can read you like a book."

"What?"

"You've had a few murder enquiries and now you're baulking at a measly hit and run."

"Well, it's not exactly a major crime, is it? A stolen car. A hit and run. It's for traffic, surely–"

"Surely, nothing," Freya said. "Hit and run. A ten-year-old boy in hospital. Sounds pretty serious to me."

"Whatever," he said, in that tone he often used when he couldn't be bothered to argue.

"Alright," she said, as Jacobs raised the cordon for them to pass beneath and waved them through. She noted his round face, and though she would never admit it to him, Gillespie's description hadn't been far off. "I'll make a bet with you. I'll bet there's more to this than just a hit and run, and that we'll still be working on this investigation in two days from now."

"Oh god, no. The last time I bet with you, I had to cook you bloody dinner."

"So what? We're always having dinner. It's just a bit of fun."

"Yeah, but it's one thing to invite you over for dinner every now and then, but *having* to cook you dinner is a completely different story."

"How is it?"

"It just is. It's an obligation is what it is."

"An obligation?" Freya spat.

"Yeah. I mean, let's say I was to cook you dinner tonight, randomly. We work late, we go home, we might as well eat together, right?"

"Yeah, so?"

"Just as we've done dozens of times."

"Right."

"Then it's no bother," Ben said, as they rounded a bend and saw the back end of the old car sticking out of the hedge. "But if I *have* to do it, if I *have* to cook you something nice, then it takes the fun out of it."

"So you're scared of losing," she said.

"I'm not scared of losing," Ben said. He came to a stop in the safest place he could find, with all four wheels up on a grass verge. "We need to up the odds, that's all."

"What's your suggestion?" Freya asked. "You can't up the odds if you don't have anything to bargain with, Ben."

"Okay, I've got it," he said, losing confidence in his own idea with every passing millisecond. "The loser cooks the other one dinner..."

"Eh? That's what we said in the first place."

"Naked," Ben added, then opened the car door.

"Naked?" Freya hissed.

"You've seen me. I've seen you. What's the big deal? You can wear a pinny. How does that sound?" Ben said, as he climbed from the car. He leaned on the roof and waited for the eruption.

The passenger door was flung open and Freya climbed out, meeting him across the roof of the car, as was usual for them.

"This morning, Ben," she began, index finger fully extended, "was the first and last time you ever see me naked."

"Morning, guys," Gillespie said, gazing wide-eyed from one to the other, and clearly very surprised at what he'd just heard. "Did I miss something?"

"No," Freya said, eyeballing Ben, who was grinning from ear to ear.

"Right. Of course," Gillespie said disbelievingly. He jabbed a thumb over his shoulder towards a track that ran between two fields. "She ran this way."

CHAPTER FIVE

THE AREA CONSISTED OF A SINGLE HOUSE ON A BEND IN A narrow lane. The patch of road containing the skid marks from where the car had braked had been cordoned off.

A familiar white van parked a little further away on the tight bend in the road, and upon seeing the driver get out and tie her hair back into a ponytail, Ben suddenly felt the urge to investigate the track the runners had disappeared into.

"Shall we, erm..." he began, nodding toward the track.

"Don't you want to stay and talk to CSI?" Freya asked, knowing full well why he didn't.

"Aye, it's Michaela, Ben. I thought you and her were, you know? Getting it on, as it were."

Freya, clearly enjoying the situation, put her hands in her pockets and nodded in agreement with Gillespie.

"Yes. Come on. Let's stay and have a little word with Michaela before we set off. I mean, we might even need her to come."

A hundred yards away, Michaela was standing at the back of her little van, pulling on her white coveralls. It had been a few months since Ben had dramatically cocked-up his chances of taking her to dinner. In fact, he hadn't just blown his chance of taking her out, he'd blown his chance of ever being able to look her in the eye again.

"Jim," Ben said, using Gillespie's first name, "help us out, will you? Stay and give her the lowdown on what happened and what we need?"

"You want me to get you out of bother?"

"Personal favour, mate."

"I mean, the way I see it, and I don't know about you, DI Bloom, but you're a Detective Sergeant and I'm a Detective Sergeant. So, by rights, you can't really pull rank here. Am I right there, boss?"

Freya nodded, playing along with Gillespie's game.

"Yes, it's a stalemate," she said.

"That's why it's a personal favour, Jim," Ben said, as Michaela slammed the van doors, picked up a heavy case, and began walking in their direction. "I'll buy you a beer."

It wasn't unusual for Ben to get embarrassed around women he liked. He'd had very little experience and found himself at a loss as to what to do with his hands, and nearly always said the wrong thing. But with Michaela in particular, his embarrassment was monumental. Having spent an entire investigation trying to coax her to dinner, messing it up by accidentally flashing her, then convincing her to give him another try on the basis that he'd injured his legs, she had arrived unannounced at his house one night. That was when she had peered through the living room window and seen Ben relaxing in his armchair. And it was moments after that she had spotted Freya kneeling before Ben tending his wounded shins. Of course, Michaela hadn't seen his shins, or what Freya was doing, and had come to the conclusion that she was surplus to Ben's requirements.

"Three beers," Gillespie said.

"Done," Ben replied without hesitation.

"And a pizza."

"A pizza?"

"Aye, a pizza. You can't have a beer and not go home with a pizza or something."

"Whatever. No problem. Let's go," Ben said, and he turned to start his search of the track. He stopped when he realised Freya hadn't moved.

"You coming?" he asked.

"In a minute," she replied, then turned to greet Michaela without a morsel of embarrassment. "Good morning, Michaela. How are you?"

"DI Bloom," Michaela replied stiffly. She found Ben staring at her, nodded once at him, then smiled enthusiastically at Gillespie. "Good to see you, DS Gillespie."

"Aye, likewise. Call me Jim, please."

"What are we looking at?" she asked.

It was hard not to admire the woman with two PhDs and a career as unblemished as the skin on her face. She held her head high, doing her best to remain professional. Even in her oversized, white suit, Ben was drawn to her. Her hair looked soft and her hands were well-manicured with her nails cut short. She refused to look in Ben's direction, giving him ample opportunity to study her from afar.

"It's a hit and run. The victim has been rushed to hospital unconscious," Freya said, though Michaela could barely look at her. "I'd like you to dust the car for prints and anything else you can find."

"Has the car been searched?"

"Not yet," Gillespie said. "I didn't really want to disturb anything until you'd worked your magic."

"Well, that's something, at least."

"We'll be back shortly. Do you need anything from us?"

"I'm on my own. Perhaps you can leave me, DS Gillespie?" Michaela replied. "I'll check what I can in situ, and if need be, we can get the car back to a more sterile environment to take a deeper look."

"Over to you, Gillespie," Freya said, then turned to Ben, who was still a few metres away on the track. "Call us if you need anything."

"Don't hurry back," Michaela said, eyeing Ben with what he could only describe as extreme distaste. "At least, not on my account."

The mood was, at the very least, fractious, and Ben was glad to get out of there. Freya caught up with him and they worked their way along the track, checking hedges and ditches.

"That was awkward," Freya said at last.

"I don't know how you can even look her in the eye. Especially after what she saw."

"She saw nothing, Ben. It was me tending your wounds. If she chooses to misinterpret the situation then I for one am not going to bow to meet her at gutter level."

Ben considered what she said. "Is that your posh way of saying you don't care what she thinks?"

"In a nutshell, yes," Freya replied. "Do you still like her, Ben?"

He shrugged. "I mean, she's pretty. But if she's going to jump to conclusions like that, then I can only imagine what a relationship would be like."

"Too emotional for you?"

"Hard bloody work," Ben said. "That's half the reason I'm single. I honestly can't be bothered with the arguments. You see it all the time. Couples arguing over the smallest things. I mean, how many houses do we go into and have to stand there and watch couples bickering? Seriously, I'd rather be on my own."

"Or with a friend?" Freya suggested.

"Yeah. Someone who isn't going to jump to the wrong conclusions and freak out about anything and everything."

"Good luck with that," Freya said. "I believe people have been searching for that person for centuries."

They came to a break in the hedge where a five-bar gate led

into the adjacent field. The grass before the gate had been flattened, like somebody had trodden it down.

"You see that?" Ben asked, and nodded at the patch of grass. "They stopped here."

"But then where did they go?" Freya mused aloud. "Over the gate and across the field? Or did they carry on up the track?"

"What would you have done?"

"Stayed and helped the boy, of course," she replied, offering him her 'holier than thou' smile.

"Yeah, right. You'd have waited for him to come around just so could shout at him for being in the road."

She laughed, but they both weighed the options, putting themselves in the mind of the runner.

"She's scared. Worried she's killed the boy. She'll have run as far away as she could," Ben said. "The field is a trap. There's no way out. She ran up the track."

"Let's go a little further and see then, shall we?"

She took a few steps, but Ben stayed where he was.

"Are you coming?" she asked.

"Listen, I, erm..." he began, and took a deep breath. "I'm sorry I saw you. You know? Earlier. I should have called up or something."

"Yes, you probably should have. But we can't change the past, can we?"

"Sadly, no."

"And we can't forget what we saw, can we?" Freya said, giving him a knowing look.

"If it makes you feel better, I'll try."

"Don't bother," she said, as she made her way past him, and ventured further up the track. "I don't."

CHAPTER SIX

Michaela Fell, in DS Jim Gillespie's opinion, was the very epitome of his ideal woman. Physically, at least. She was intelligent, witty, and undeniably without fear. Yet she had this way of looking down her nose at him that he just couldn't stand.

She was pretty though. He'd give her that. And not afraid to get her hands dirty. On her hands and knees, she was peering under the driver's seat of the Vauxhall when she suddenly turned and caught him staring.

"Find anything interesting yet?" she asked.

"Oh aye," he said. "Plenty."

"I meant in the car, DS Gillespie."

"Ah, right. I'll start in the back, shall I?"

"That would be helpful, unless you want to still be here when it gets dark."

Gillespie opened the rear door with a gloved hand. The inside had a musty odour, how he would imagine a garden shed to smell. But there was something tucked behind the passenger seat that interested him – a sports bag, zipped up but bursting at the seams.

"Here we go," he said, and he reached inside for the handles of the bag.

Michaela said nothing; clearly it would take more of an effort to pique her interest.

"Let's see what we have in here then," he said, as he unzipped the bag, making sure that Michaela would hear the zip.

She didn't look up or comment. In fact, it was as if Gillespie wasn't even there. He could hear her, tapping away with her brush and opening little plastic evidence bags. But she seemed lost in her own world.

He'd have to up the ante.

"How's it going with Ben?" he asked, as he rifled through the bag of clothes for anything that might have been tucked down the sides.

"Ben who?" she said finally.

So, she does speak then.

"Ah come on. I thought you two were sweet."

"Nope. Never have been. Never will be."

"But I spoke to you before. You said you'd give him another chance."

"You did," she said, pulling herself out of the car and resting back on her haunches. "And I did."

"And he blew it?"

She didn't look impressed to be reminded of whatever it was that had happened.

"How bad did he blow it?" he asked.

"On a scale of one to ten? Hiroshima. Atom bomb. Devastating."

"Like an eight or a nine then?"

"A ten, Gillespie. A ten. Undoubtedly, a ten."

Feeling as if he'd just kicked a wasps nest, then insulted the wasp queen, Gillespie put a little more effort into searching the bag. It was just full of scrunched-up men's clothes, and he grimaced as he pulled out a pair of boxer shorts.

"Why do you ask, anyway?"

"Oh, no reason," he mumbled, hoping she would climb back into the car and resume that awkward silence she had perfected.

"No. You don't just start a conversation like that, pry into my feelings, then close off. You don't get to do that." She watched him still searching the bag. "DS Gillespie, will you listen to me while I'm talking?"

He peered through the car at her, finding her glaring at him.

"Aye," he said.

"Well?"

"Well, what?"

"Why did you ask?"

"I was just curious, is all."

"No, you weren't. You're up to something. He asked you to spy on me, didn't he? Is that what this is about? You're doing that disgusting pig's dirty work for him?"

"No way. I wouldn't do that if he asked."

"You're insufferable. You did this to me before. You put on this charade of innocence and idiocy to lull me into a false sense of security, in the hope that I open up and tell you how I'm feeling."

"Eh?"

"Don't play dumb with me."

"I'm not. I wasn't. I was just making conversation, that's all."

"So why not ask me what I like to do in my spare time? Why not ask me what music I enjoy? Hmmm?"

"You don't do a lot in your spare time. You have a cat or a small dog. Probably a cat. You listen to classical music and anything that relaxes you, or helps you forget what you've seen that day. You're studying. Always studying."

She stared at him while he felt the edges of the bag but found nothing.

"Are you analysing me?" she asked.

"No. They're just my observations," he replied coolly.

"Is that it? You think I'm just a sad loner who reads books and plays with my cat?"

"So you do have a cat?"

"Yes, I have a cat. But so do about fifteen per cent of the population."

He sighed, dropped a wallet into an evidence bag, then set it down atop the holdall.

"You go to the gym. Religiously. You don't eat meat, but you do eat fish. You house is neat and tidy, with a little garden because you don't have the time to keep on top of anything larger, and each night before you go to bed, you spend around ten minutes brushing your hair and applying creams and lotions, and whatnot."

"That's beyond an observation, Gillespie," she said, her voice low. "What are you, some kind of stalker or something?"

"I'm a detective," he said, grabbing the sports bag and closing the boot lid. "You're single, which puts you in with fifty per cent of the population. And you're wrong. It's not fifteen per cent of the population that have cats, it's closer to thirty. The majority of which are single females, I might add. Which means that I stand a roughly seventy-five per cent chance of being right. And I was."

"I don't know where you learnt mathematics, but–"

"But I was right, wasn't I?"

She nodded, uncertain of him, but intrigued.

"Why is my house small?"

"Because you're hoping that one day you'll meet a man and buy a larger house together so you can raise a family. You're a strong, independent female, and you want to make sure that, A, you have a home until then, and B, when you do meet him, he sees you for who you are. Independent. Successful. Strong."

Although she was clearly miffed that he'd given her situation this much thought, she nodded, happy with his analysis.

"What about the creams and lotions?" she asked. "How would you know my bedtime routine? Don't tell me. Seventy-five per cent of single women cat owners apply some kind of cream before going to bed?"

"No," he said, with a slight shake of his head, and he left it there.

"Well?" she asked. He fully had her on the line now. She pushed herself up to her feet and strode over to him, stopping just out of reach. "What makes you so confident?"

"You're what? Late twenties?"

She nodded, her eyebrows raised in anticipation of being overwhelmed with statistics.

"I found a wallet with a bank card. I'm going to radio through and have it checked."

He turned with the bag in his hand and took a single step before...

"You're going to leave me hanging, are you?"

He stopped, then cursed himself for showing off, and opened the boot by way of a distraction. And if he was seeking a way to bring the conversation to a close, he'd found it.

She insulted him. Of that he was sure. But her words were muffled, distant, and irrelevant, and it was all he could do to stop himself from crying out.

"Gillespie?" she said, and she came to his side. "Gillespie, what's wrong?"

CHAPTER SEVEN

LESS THAN A HUNDRED YARDS FROM THE GATE, A SPLASH OF colour caught Freya's eye. Deep in the hedge, a single red boot hung by its lace from a thin branch.

"Ben?" she said, and found him peering into the narrow dyke that ran alongside the track. "I found something."

He wandered over as casually as he might if Freya had announced that she had spotted a rare bird or flower.

"A boot?" he said.

"Not just any boot. It's clean. Almost new, in fact. Think you can reach it?"

He appraised the hedge with all its spikes and thorns, searching for a way to reach in. He took a wide step over the bank of stinging nettles and brambles, leaving himself in rather a precarious position. Once committed, he took a cautious glance down at his groin, gave Freya a slightly concerned look, then forced his arm into the inviting hawthorn.

"Can you reach it?" she asked, but he was too preoccupied to reply. "Can I help at all?"

Extending his full six-foot-something length, Ben's entire upper half was now buried in the hawthorn, with one leg on the track, the other beside the hedge, and a whole host of sharp brambles clinging to his thin trousers.

"If I might say," she said, "you probably want to be a little careful as you come out."

The comment was met with what Freya could only describe as abuse, and ended with a suggestion as to where he might put the boot when he finally reached it.

His fingers groped and the boot swung a little, threatening to fall deeper in the hedge.

"Don't let it fall," Freya said.

"Oh really?" he snapped. "You know, I did wonder."

"You really are quite an angry man, aren't you, Ben?"

He gave a final reach, his shirt pulling free to reveal his taut abdomen, and the brambles tightened their grip on the fabric of his trousers.

"Got it," he said, and he pulled the boot free, holding it out for Freya to take. The second she took the boot from him, he opened and closed his hand. "Pull me out."

"Pull you out?" She laughed.

"I'm in quite a delicate situation, Freya."

She removed her phone from her pocket, opened the camera app, and framed the photo. She had to admit, it was pretty funny to see half of a Ben sticking out of a bush.

"Freya, bloody hurry up."

"Alright, alright," she said, as she gripped his hand. "On three. One, two, three."

She heaved on his arm and felt him pulling against her to pull himself upright. And then it happened. The sound he had been dreading and Freya knew was inevitable. Thankfully, the tear in his trousers was on the inside of his leg, leaving the crotch part intact.

"Oh, for crying out loud," he said, pulling at the fabric. "Do you have a safety pin?"

"A safety pin? What is this, nineteen-thirty? Nobody carries safety pins anymore."

"Well, I can't go around like this."

"It could be worse," Freya suggested, holding the boot by the end of the lace. "But then, I don't suppose that would bother you, would it? You're used to exposing yourself."

"Oh right. That's rich, coming from London's Material Girl," Ben said. "Are you going to bag that?"

"Yeah, when you get the other one."

"What other one?"

She pointed a little higher up in the bush. "There. See it?"

He stared at her, incredulous.

"What?" she said.

"You didn't think to tell me about it when I was already in the hedge?"

"I've just seen it," she said, feeling her phone vibrate in her pocket.

"You liar. You just want to watch me struggle."

Laughing at him, she pulled her phone out, frowned at the name on the screen, and hit the button to answer it. With her free hand, she pointed at the boot, gesturing for Ben to get to it.

"DI Bloom," she said, admiring the amused yet hostile expression on Ben's face. It was a play fight, and those were what she most enjoyed about working with him.

"Boss, it's Gillespie."

"I know, it said so on my phone. How are you getting on with the leggy blonde? Has she sunk her teeth into you yet?"

"Boss, we found something. Well, someone, really. In the boot of the car."

"A body?"

"Aye. Dead as you like. Female. Middle-aged. No ID. Looks like she's headbutted a mountain."

"We'll be there as soon as we can. Call DC Gold. Have her

arrange the medical examiner, and tell Michaela she'll need some help."

"Aye, boss. We're already on it."

"Good," she said, ending the call.

"That doesn't sound promising," Ben said, preparing to step back over the brambles and stinging nettles while holding the new hole in his trousers together.

"Two things. When this investigation is over, you're cooking me a dinner in nothing but a pinny."

"Eh?"

"Secondly, leave the other boot for forensics. This so-called hit and run just took a turn for the worse."

CHAPTER EIGHT

THEY HAD LEFT THE SCENE OF THE ACCIDENT WITH JUST A handful of uniforms, Gillespie, and Michaela Fell. When they returned from their foray up the track, however, Ben and Freya found an army of uniforms, half a dozen white suits, and a private ambulance, not to mention the tow truck that could be seen parked up close to where Jacobs was stationed.

"You've been busy," Freya said to Gillespie, admiring the melee of activity.

"I'd rather not be," he replied. "Took me by surprise, let me tell you."

"You okay?"

"Aye. I will be."

"I'll find some water for you," Ben said, and he made toward the line of police cars.

Freya surveyed the scene.

"Let's work out what happened here, Gillespie," she said, hoping the distraction might make him feel better. "From the direction the car is facing, it must have followed the lane down from Edlington Moor, and then just as it came around this sharp left-hand bend, right in front of the only house in sight, it swerved."

"That's the boy's house. The mother came running from there when she heard the screech of tyres."

"The boy must have been about to cross the road. Which means he must have been coming from the track."

"Maybe he was out playing or something?"

"Maybe," Freya agreed. "A girl climbed from the car? Is that right?"

"Aye," Gillespie said. "Jacobs spoke to the mother. He said she heard the car tyres, then came running out and saw the girl as she was climbing out of the car. She ran off somewhere, and the mother ran to her boy."

"So who is the woman in the boot?"

"It might explain why the driver was speeding. I mean, you don't have to be a pathologist to know those wounds are fresh."

"I haven't looked yet. What do you make of it?"

"Blunt object. Brutal."

"So, whoever our runner is made a mistake, stole a car, loaded a body into it, then hit a boy."

"Not having a good day, is she?"

"Explain that to Ben. It might give him perspective."

"Eh?"

"Don't worry. He's had a little accident in the trouser department."

"Eh?" he said again. "He's wet himself?"

"No. He's torn them."

"Ah, right."

"Where does this road lead to?" Freya asked.

"Stixwould. It's a wee village about half a mile away."

"I thought this was Stixwould?"

"It might fall under Stixwould, but look at the place. You can't see another building in any direction. The village is that way."

"And after Stixwould?"

"Bardney. Then Lincoln. She could have been heading anywhere, boss."

"In which case, she was coming from somewhere. Where? Why come this way, down this lane? There's a B-road less than half a mile away. With a dead body in the boot of a stolen car? No. There's something we're missing," Freya said.

"Catch," Ben said, as he approached, and he tossed Gillespie a bottle of water. "Uniform carry them in the back of their cars."

"Thanks, Ben," Gillespie said gratefully, as he twisted the lid off and downed half the bottle. He wiped his mouth with the back of his hand and then downed the rest. "We were just trying to work out why the runner drove down here with a dead body in the boot of a stolen car. Any ideas?"

"There's nothing down here," Ben said. "The lane only serves this old house, plus that track. It used to be a farm. It was sold off years ago."

"Sold off?" Freya said, not following.

"The land got sold to another local farmer. Massive organisation. Bigger than my dad's. The house would have been sold to private buyers."

"The boy's parents," Freya suggested.

"Mother," Gillespie corrected her. "She mentioned to Jacobs that it's just her and the boy."

"Does this boy actually have a name, or are we going just call him 'the boy?'" Freya asked.

Gillespie pulled his little notebook out of his jacket pocket. The pages were scrunched up and he felt every one of his pockets at least twice before he found his pen in his breast pocket. "Lee," he said.

"Lee?" Freya repeated.

"Aye. Lee Sanders," Gillespie continued. "Ten years old. Head injuries, likely from the car. Unconscious. Left in an ambulance with his mother, Teresa Sanders."

"Right. I'll see how Gold is getting on with the mother. Gillespie, find the owner of the car. I want to know where it was stolen from. And see if you can get an ID on the woman in the boot, she might be able to unlock a few of these closed doors. Ben, coordinate with Sergeant Priest. Whoever our runner is, she's missing her shoes, so she can't have got far."

"She probably took them off to run faster," Gillespie said. "You'd break your bloody neck running in those."

"Probably, Gillespie. But we'll see. I want a full-scale search. What time was the accident?"

"Ah, she didn't say. It's ten a.m. now, and we've been here an hour. Stick another half hour on, I'd say."

"This isn't a guessing game. Have Chapman contact the desk to see what time the 999 call was put in."

"Aye, boss. I'm all over it."

"Michaela?" Freya called out, and the CSI she had referred to earlier as a leggy blonde emerged from where she was leaning into the car. A mask and goggles covered most of her face. "Anything to report yet?"

She pulled her mask down to speak. "So far, nothing," she replied. "I'll need to get it back to base for a closer look though. I could be wrong."

"Wouldn't be the first time," Ben muttered.

"Thank you," Freya said, ignoring Ben's comment for the sake of keeping Michaela on board. "Ben, Gillespie, come on. We've got work to do. I want that bloody girl found."

"Ma'am?" a voice called from the end of the track. It was one of the uniforms she had sent to search the rest of the track, and he was breathless from running.

"What?" she snapped, then regretted her tone.

"I think you should see this," he said, and jabbed his finger back up the track. "We found the runner."

CHAPTER NINE

Michaela was clearly in her element, Freya thought. She'd let her have this little moment of glory taking ownership of the crime scene. It wasn't often CSI got their hands on a scene before anybody else, and she was clearly making the most of it.

"Poppy Edwina Gray," Michaela read out from the bank card she found in the dead girl's wallet. The girl was lying in a ditch, face-down, and her head was at an unnatural angle.

Michaela had requested that neither Ben nor Gillespie jump down there, stating that if anybody was going to touch the body, it should be her. Ben and Gillespie didn't seem to mind, and within a few moments, when Michaela had complained her feet were getting soaked, they seemed quite happy with the arrangement.

"Cause of death?" Freya asked.

"Hard to say for sure," Michaela continued, and, to her credit, she got on all fours and peered all around the body. "We'll need to wait for the FME. There's some bruising around her neck. Her nose seems to be bloodied. There's no visible signs of bleeding anywhere else, and she's wearing a dress, so we can't rule out crimes of a sexual nature. But we won't really know for sure until we get her out."

"Poor thing," Gillespie muttered.

"Poor thing?" Freya said. "She's nearly killed a small boy and god knows what she'd done to that woman."

"Aye, well. Still... Nobody deserves to go like that."

"Ben?" Freya said. "What do you make of this?"

"Somebody hated her," he said flatly.

"I agree," Gillespie added.

"Yes, so do I, sadly," Freya said.

"What makes you think that?" Michaela asked her. "We've only just found the body. I need to examine this girl properly, as does the pathologist. She could have been killed elsewhere and dumped here. Who are you to decide on anything until we give you the facts?"

"I'm a detective with years of experience, Michaela. And you'll notice I'm not on my hands and knees in mud. Besides, she's dead in a ditch," Freya said, nodding at the body. "You don't leave someone you love like that."

Michaela shook her head and carefully pulled at the girl's clothing to search for injuries, probably in an effort to prove Freya wrong.

"Could have been the boy's mother," Gillespie suggested.

"Can we start using his actual name, please?" Freya said. "It's Lee Sanders. He's the victim here."

"Aye, well. Could have been his mother. She could have chased her up the track. It's pretty much a dead end. She would have been trapped."

"Let's not start casting our aspersions on the mother just yet. We need to find Poppy's family. Do we have an address, Michaela?"

"You're the detective, why don't you have a look?" Michaela said. She extended a gloved hand for Gillespie to take the wallet from her, then pass it to Freya.

Turning to one of the uniforms, Freya retrieved the bank card from the wallet and held it up for him to see. "Write this name down, please. Radio through and see if you can find an address."

The uniform scribbled the girl's name down, then walked away to talk on his radio.

"Right, so we found our runner," Freya said. "It doesn't help Lee Sanders or his mother, but it does help us. All we need to do now is work out who the woman in the car is and piece this lot together."

"Shall I call off the search, boss?" Gillespie asked.

"Unless you think there may be another girl of this age running around this place with no shoes or socks on, then yes. I think it's a safe bet. If we're wrong, then I'll take the hit."

"Ma'am?" the uniform said, and he returned with an address written in his pad, then held it up for Ben to snap a photo of it on his phone. Taking a photo was a far more reliable method of recording data. Handwriting could be mistaken. Pieces of paper could be lost.

"It's local," Ben said, staring at the address. "Just up the road in Stixwould."

"That's where she was coming from," Freya said. "I wonder where she was going. Ben, you and I will go and see the parents. Gillespie, can you talk to Chapman, and then see the owner of the car? In the meantime, DC Gold is on her way to the hospital." She checked her watch. "It's ten-thirty now. We'll debrief back at the station at three p.m. Michaela, do you need anything from us?"

"Nope, I just need you lot to stop trampling all over the grass," she said from inside the ditch, glaring at Ben but unable to meet Freya's stare. "This is a crime scene, you know."

"You really are something else, aren't you?" Ben said, shaking his head.

"Ben, come on, mate," Gillespie said, giving him a polite tug on his sleeve.

"*I'm* something else? Look at you two, bowing down to her like she's some kind of queen."

"She's the boss, Michaela. It's kind of what you do, right?" Gillespie said, defending himself. "Besides, you're the one who jumped down there. I don't think we should be arguing about who did more damage to the crime scene. You're lying next to the body for crying out loud."

"DI Bloom, are all your team this unprofessional? Or is it just you three?"

Freya exchanged glances with Ben, who shrugged and held his hands up as if refusing any further involvement.

"Let me see," Freya said. "There's DC Cruz, who spends more time either messaging his girlfriend or in the washroom than he does actually working. I'm not entirely sure what he does in there. Then there's DC Gold. She's quite professional, but she is a bit ditzy, and she enjoys those dating apps. Always swiping left or right, or something. She sends pictures of her breasts to random men. I caught her doing it in the washroom once, but don't tell her I told you that."

Michaela shook her head in disbelief, but Freya wasn't going to let her make an offhand comment about her team like that without giving the jumped-up, leggy blonde something to think about.

"Then there's DC Chapman," Freya continued. "Now, you'd be forgiven for thinking that Denise Chapman really likes to be in the office at her desk, as opposed to out here in the action, dealing with uptight people so far up their own arses they can't see where they've been let alone where they're going. But if you ask her nicely, she'll openly admit that she's into dogging. You'd never believe it to look at her. But I've seen the videos. We all have. Shocking really. But, if anything, it's a demonstration of her ability to multi-task. Who else is there?"

"Anna?" Gillespie suggested, unable to conceal the grin that was spreading across his face.

"Ah yes, DC Nillson. Now, *she's* a professional," Freya said with a nod. "Flawless career that one. She'll go far. Why do you ask?"

Michaela stood aghast at Freya's description of the team. It was exactly the response she had hoped for.

"Please get off my crime scene," she said.

"With pleasure, Michaela," Freya said, as she turned and walked back down the track. She called her closing statement over her shoulder as Ben and Gillespie took their places either side of her. "I look forward to seeing your report first thing in the morning."

CHAPTER TEN

"That was a bit harsh," Ben said, as Freya pulled her seat belt on.

"Well, she got what she deserved."

"I hope that wasn't for my benefit."

"Nope. It was for my own. I'm not having her insult the team like that, Ben. What kind of boss would I be if I let that go? Besides, she needs to learn that two PhDs mean nothing when you're lying in a ditch beside a dead body. Where are we going anyway?"

"Just into Stixwould," Ben replied, double-checking the photo he snapped of the uniform's pad. He pulled a confused expression. "It's just up the road."

"So?"

"Well, if she stole a car, she didn't get very far, did she?"

"It's definitely not her day, that's for sure."

They drove in silence for the remainder of the five-minute journey, each of them contemplating their own versions of what they thought might have happened, and each of them very aware that to jump to conclusions before they had spoken to the parents would hinder their abilities to approach the investigation with an open mind.

Ben pulled the car up on the driveway of a very large, Edwardian looking house. The front boasted two bay windows and the central doorway was as grand as they came. The front door itself was at least twice as wide as Freya's front door, with coloured glass depicting a vague pattern of Lincoln Cathedral outlined in lead.

"Is this it?" Freya said, spying a sign above the doorway, concealed by ivy, that read, *Witham Valley Guest House*. "It's a hotel?"

"Guest house," Ben corrected her.

Freya gave him what she knew was a very judgemental look. "It's a jumped-up bed and breakfast."

"Call it what you like," Ben said, as he climbed from the car. "One of us has some very bad news to deliver."

They strode up the driveway and Freya noted the relatively empty street. It was as if anybody going to and from Lincoln bypassed the place. It was silent, idyllic, and with the views across the Fens, Freya could see the appeal of staying in the village. Two wheelie bins were lying on their sides, and Ben nudged her then gestured at them. "A fiver says Poppy knocked them over."

She didn't reply. She was more interested in the rundown, old guest house, which, call it what you like, she thought, a guest house, a bed and breakfast, a hotel, whatever it was, it was an absolute tip. From the driveway, it had appeared grand enough that guests might be pleasantly surprised. But when they saw the cracked windows, the pile of rubbish bags beside the front door, and the flaking paintwork, she imagined they would get back in their car and find somewhere else.

The doorbell worked, at least, which Freya guessed was a must when your business relied on people coming to the door. Freya followed a crack in the render from the front door, all the way across the front of the building, where another car arriving caught her eye. From inside, a familiar face waved.

"What the bloody hell is Gillespie doing here?" Freya said, and Ben turned to see. Now was not the time for a chit-chat about the investigation.

The front door opened and a man appeared in what was once clearly a beautiful hallway but was now fit for demolishing. He was in his late sixties or early seventies, using the door as support. His head was shaved, perhaps owning his hair loss, as opposed to pretending it wasn't happening. Not like some men Freya knew, Detective Superintendent Harper being the one closest to her mind, who refused to admit that age was getting the better of him, and hoped that by dragging what remained across his bald patch, he might trick his friends and family into believing he was still young and virile.

"Can I help?" he said, his voice sounding tired and weak.

Freya showed him her warrant card. "Detective Inspector Bloom. This is Detective Sergeant Savage. We're looking for Mr Gray."

"You're looking for me?" he asked. "Not Mr Harringer?"

"Mr Harringer?"

"He reported his car stolen a couple of hours ago," Gray explained. "He's one of our guests."

"Ah, I see," Freya said, and she turned to find Gillespie walking from where he'd parked beside Ben, tucking the tails of his shirt into his trousers as he strode up the drive.

"Hi there," he said, leaning in between Freya and Ben to shake the man's hand. He checked his notes quickly. "Roy Harringer?"

"No, I'm Desmond Gray."

"Oh," Gillespie said, once more looking at his notes. Then he looked to Ben, and then to Freya, hoping for some support.

"What the bloody hell is going on here?" Gray demanded, though his voice lacked conviction.

"It's okay, Mr Gray," Freya said. "I see what's happened here.

Perhaps you and I can speak inside, and my colleague here, DS Gillespie, can talk to Mr Harringer?"

"Talk to me? What for? I didn't bloody steal it."

"I know. It's okay. You're not in any kind of trouble, but I think we should perhaps go inside. Is there somewhere quiet?"

"Quiet?" he said, as a voice called down the stairs.

"Is that them, Des?"

Gray turned and peered up the stairs.

"Yes. It's half the bloody police force on my doorstep."

Offering Gillespie a stern look for him to get inside and control Harringer, Freya then stepped into the hallway.

"Mr Harringer, I believe my colleague DS Gillespie would like a few words with you," she said to the grey-haired man who was halfway down the broad staircase. He wore a smart shirt, a waistcoat with matching trousers, and his hair was slicked back with some kind of wax. "Mr Gray, shall we go through to the kitchen?"

"What for? What's this about?" he asked, suddenly becoming quite concerned.

"Is it this way?" she asked, keeping her voice calm and doing her best to control the situation. She didn't wait for him to answer. She walked to the end of the hallway and pushed open the door. It led out into a conservatory overlooking an unkempt garden that some might have called mature. Freya, however, considered it to be as much of a hole as the house.

She was joined by Mr Gray, and Ben followed, closing the door behind him and taking in the surroundings. A small set of wicker furniture had been positioned at one end of the space, and after moving a few plastic bags and some newspapers, Freya managed to clear a space for them all to sit.

She took a place in one of the two armchairs and Ben took the other, leaving Mr Gray the little, two-seater sofa. Despite the cushions, something sharp had nestled itself into Freya's backside, and she wriggled a little to get comfortable. But that only made it worse.

"Please," she said, offering him the seat opposite them.

"I don't like the look of this," he said slowly. "It's Izzie, isn't it?"

"Is there a Mrs Gray?" she asked.

"I am married, yes, but the wife's out. Whatever you have to say, you can say it to me."

"Mr Gray, I'm afraid I have some bad news," Freya said, opting to rip the plaster off, as opposed to dragging it out and listen to him guess why they had visited. "We've found the body of a young woman. It's your daughter. Poppy."

"Poppy?" he said, staring her straight in the eye. "No. No, I don't–"

"I know this is very hard to hear–"

"My Poppy?"

"I'm afraid so."

"She were just here," he said, offering Freya a thick Yorkshire twang, which reminded her of Sergeant Priest. It was a strong accent yet suited the gentle, mature type, she thought. "She were just here this morning. Home early, she was. Just popped upstairs to get changed. She said she'd make a tea when she comes down. You've got it wrong."

"I'm very sorry, Mr Gray. She was carrying this." Freya showed him the evidence bag containing the girl's purse.

"How?" he said. "I don't understand. She's fine. She was fine this morning. She said we'd have tea."

"I'm afraid Poppy was the victim of an attack. We're investigating now, but I'm afraid we can't do much until we've formally identified her."

"Identified her?"

"What's this?" a voice said from the end of the room. A door opened to another part of the huge building and a woman stepped inside, removing her coat and hanging it over the back of an old, wooden chair. She was a tall lady, curvy, in her forties, and what

Freya's mother might have called 'well-maintained'. "What's happening, Desmond?"

"Dear, they're police," Mr Gray said, and with considerable effort, he got up and stumbled the few steps to her. "It's Poppy. They've found her."

"Found her?" she said. "What on earth are you talking about, Desmond?"

"She's dead," Freya said, matter-of-factly. No holds barred. She said it as it was. "We found her body an hour ago, not far from here."

"Oh my," she said, and she hugged the man. "Oh, Desmond, you poor thing."

"May I ask who you are?" Freya asked, assertive, but respectful nonetheless.

"I'm Izzie. I'm Poppy's stepmother," she replied, still reeling from the news and clinging to her husband. "How?" she asked.

"We're investigating now. I'm afraid we can't really say much else, other than Poppy was sadly the victim of a terrible attack."

"Oh my god." She breathed the words rather than spoke them, then found a tissue in her sleeve to wipe her eye. Mr Gray clung to her, almost lifeless.

"I'll be arranging for you to see her tomorrow–"

"No," he said. "No, I can't. I couldn't. Not possibly."

"I'm afraid somebody needs to formally identify her, Mr Gray."

"Then I'll do it," Izzie said, and her husband took his head from where it rested on her chest and looked up at her.

"You'd do that for me?"

"Of course I would. God knows, it'll be a terrible thing to see, but no parent should ever have to see their child..." She choked on her words then regained some strength. "Just tell me where and when, and I'll be there."

"Thank you, Mrs Gray," said Ben.

"It's Brand," she said. "Mrs Brand. I didn't take my husband's name."

"I see. Well, thank you, Mrs Brand."

"I have to ask," said Freya. "Is there anybody who might have wanted to hurt Poppy? Someone she was arguing with, maybe? Or perhaps owed money to?"

Mr Gray shook his head, refusing to believe that anybody could have disliked his precious daughter. "She didn't have many friends."

"There's Grant," Izzie suggested, her tone soft as if she was trying to coax him into the idea.

"Grant?" Ben said.

"Her boyfriend."

"He wasn't her boyfriend," Mr Gray snapped, then hung his head. "Oh, what does it matter?"

"Is he local?" Ben asked.

"There's a foster home on the other side of the village," Izzie explained. "Lovely couple run it. I can't think of their names now."

"A home for children?" asked Freya.

"No, it's a normal house, with a normal family, but they foster children with nowhere to go. Big hearts, you know?"

"And he lives there, does he? This Grant?"

She nodded. "He's a troubled boy, if you ask me. Kind enough, and he's always good to Poppy. But he is troubled. Doesn't say much. Actually, I've never heard him utter a single word. But they're good people. The parents. I'd want to take them all home if I could. A good meal. Some love. Maybe a little hard work. That's what they need. Give them a glimpse of what they can achieve in life."

Freya glanced across at Ben, who was making notes. He looked up, and although neither said anything or made any kind of gesture, they both agreed that would be their next port of call.

"I'm afraid I do have to mention something else," Freya said, and she took a deep breath in preparation.

Desmond Gray peered up from his wife's grasp. His eyes were red and he looked as though he might collapse at any moment.

"Usually, I wouldn't say anything. But given the circumstances," she said, "I think you should know that we believe Poppy was driving a stolen car before the attack happened."

"A stolen car..." Mr Gray began, then he fell in. "Harringer's?"

"That's why my colleague is with him now. Unfortunately, it appears she hit a small boy and was seen running from the scene. Her body was found a little way away."

"But my Poppy wouldn't..." he began, and his shoulders slumped. "She's a good girl. She wouldn't–"

"My colleague will discuss the matter with Mr Harringer. I'll make sure this doesn't come back to you. You need time to grieve, Mr Gray."

He nodded his thanks, the way the older generation does, whatever the hardship they're enduring.

"I'd like to look at her room, if I may?" Freya said, directing the question to Izzie, who seemed more able to deal with the questions than the girl's father.

"Is that really necessary?"

"It's not a search. It'll just give us an idea of Poppy's character, and maybe help us find who attacked her. Often, if we know what the victim's last few days were like, we can get a pretty good picture."

"She's been away," Izzie said. "She stayed with her mother for a few days. The mother lives in Spain, you see. Poppy said she needed some time away from this place."

"Thank you. That's very helpful. Can we see her room?"

Izzie searched her husband's eyes for approval, and he nodded reluctantly.

"I'll take you up," she said, and guided Mr Gray back toward the wicker sofa.

"And if you give your number to my colleague here, please, Mrs Brand. Just while I remember. I'll be in touch tomorrow to arrange the viewing."

Reluctantly, the woman let her husband go and took Ben's pen off him to note her number down. Together, Ben and Freya moved toward the door, and then stopped on the threshold when Mr Gray called out. He was standing by the wicker sofa with no strength left to hold him upright save for the bones in his ageing body.

"The boy," he said. "You said there was a boy. Is he hurt?"

"I'm afraid so. He's alive though. His mother is with him."

"That's something then," he said, as Ben left the room. "I'm sorry," Desmond Gray mumbled, then cleared his throat, as Freya turned for the last time to look at him. "For whatever it was she might have done. I'm so terribly sorry. There's nothing I can do to make it better, is there?"

"Not right now, Mr Gray," Freya said. "You rest now."

CHAPTER ELEVEN

"I'M AFRAID MY HUSBAND HAS TAKEN THE NEWS QUITE BADLY," Izzie said, as she pulled the hallway door closed behind her. "It's a tragedy. A bloody tragedy. You'll find them, won't you? Whoever did this?"

"Usually," Freya said, not wanting to commit with both feet.

She stepped aside for Izzie to pass and led the way back through the hallway, allowing Freya a moment to appraise the woman. She was tall. Much taller than her husband, and she wore a long, flowing dress that didn't quite suit her personality. Floral pattern and loose fit had a hippy vibe to it, yet the taut expression she wore, and indeed had been wearing since she had first walked through the door, was not one of an easygoing, happy-go-lucky type. It was like she was trying to be someone she wasn't. Trying to be younger perhaps? Freya could relate to that, but there were ways for a mature lady to dress that complemented her years, rather than live a life in denial.

The empty hallway seemed sparse and Freya took the opportunity to look around. It was as she would have expected a guest house to be – devoid of large furniture, leaving plenty of room for heavy bags to be carried through and up the stairs, and a tiled floor to make regular cleaning easier. Although, however easy the tiled floor made it, it clearly did not clean itself. The tiles were black and white in a chequer-board style, but the white tiles had a thin veneer of grime, making them yellowish-brown, like bad teeth.

A small frame hung on the wall less than two meters from the wide front door. It was a fire escape plan, which Freya presumed was part of a requirement for the business to operate, yet clearly it hadn't dawned on anybody that the fire escape for that particular part of the building was less than two metres away and far more obvious than the six-by-ten-inch frame.

On the opposite wall, placed where guests would see it as they descended on their first morning of holiday bliss, was a small rack containing tourist leaflets. There were pamphlets on Lincoln Cathedral, Lincoln Castle, and the old Victorian prison. Plus there were less professional-looking leaflets advertising attractions in the immediate area, such as Tupholme Abbey, with a photo of what looked to be the ruins of the old building.

The rack, however, was not really up to the job. Several leaflets had fallen through the gaps and lay scattered on the floor at the foot of the stairs.

Izzie stepped over them and led them up the stairs.

"How's business been?" Freya asked. "Do you get many tourists?"

"Not as many as we'd like," she admitted. "Used to. Not now though. It's that Airbnb website. Do you know it?"

"Of course. It's very convenient, from what I hear."

"Convenient for who? Not us, I can assure you. Desmond always tells me about the good old days. Before I came along. Him and his ex-wife used to run it and they were always full by all accounts. Nowadays people don't want a hotel like this. They want quaint, little converted sheds, or whatnot. I keep telling him we should sell up while we can. The place is worth a fortune. Twelve bedrooms," she said, and stopped on the stairs, turning to exaggerate the point. "Twelve. That's not including our suite. But no. He wants to keep it going. He said he made it work once, he'll make it work again. The problem is, the only way he'll ever get his hands on the fortune it'll take to get this place looking nice is by selling it. Ironic, isn't it?"

"But you do have guests," Freya said, referring to Mr Harringer.

"Oh yes, we have guests still. Regulars mostly. Come from all over. Business trips mostly. We get the odd old couple passing through on their way to somewhere else. But they don't like the stairs," she said, as she reached the top of the first flight and made her way across the landing to a second flight. "Nor do I, if I'm honest. Takes me a week to clean the place. As soon as I've finished, I have to start again."

"I would have thought you'd have a cleaner," Ben said.

"You'd think, wouldn't you? Desmond says his ex-wife used to clean and she managed, so there's no reason why I shouldn't."

"And you didn't try to bring Poppy into the business? Give her a little pocket money?" Freya asked.

"I tried. Lord knows I tried. I shouldn't say really," she said, stopping again on the stairs and peering down at them both. "She was... how do I say it? Reluctant."

"To help?"

"She was a teenager. Had other things on her mind, I suppose. Can't blame her really," she said, then she dropped her face into her hands. "Oh god, I can't believe she's gone. What are we going to do?"

Freya and Ben exchanged glances but said nothing.

"I'm sorry," Izzie said with a big sniff. "I don't think it's really hit home yet. The place will be empty without her."

She stared down at them both, her eyes moist and red. Then she tightened her lips as if to push on through it.

"It's such a big house to clean. And Desmond, well, he's in no fit state to help anymore. We've had to move him downstairs. He can barely climb the stairs now. That just leaves me."

There were just five rooms on the second floor, as opposed to the seven Freya had counted on the first. Plus, there was a small doorway, which Izzie led them through into a narrow corridor. Freya imagined that a century ago, the corridor gave access to the servant quarters.

Ahead of them, a large space opened up with couches and a TV. But Izzie stopped at a small door on the right. "This is it," she said. "This is Poppy's room."

"Thank you," Freya said, and without asking turned the round, brass handle and pushed the door open. She stopped before entering and met Izzie's gaze. "It's usually best if we do this alone."

"Oh," Izzie exclaimed. "I thought perhaps I could help."

"It's okay. We won't touch anything. We'll just be a few minutes."

Freya stayed there until the message had sunk in. The minds of the grieving were often dysfunctional and slow to react.

"I've got to get out, you see. I'm supposed to meet somebody."

"We can show ourselves out," Ben explained.

"No. I'll stay a few minutes. Desmond doesn't like strangers in our space."

Freya glanced along the hallway to the lounge area.

"Is this where you all live? The three of you?"

Izzie nodded. "Hard to believe, isn't it? Big house like this and we're couped up here like chickens. Now that Desmond is downstairs, this is just me and Poppy." She thought about what she said for a second. "Just me now."

"And you don't sleep downstairs with your husband?"

"Oh no. Too cold for me down there. Besides," she said, "we've never had what you might call a physical relationship. He calls when he needs me. We're happy."

"Indeed," Freya said, waiting for the woman to leave them. "We'll just be a few minutes."

The room wasn't unlike the bedrooms of other teenage girls Freya had been in. Some girls' bedrooms were messy but clean. Others were tidy and organised. Poppy's was exactly the opposite of what Freya had been expecting. She had expected a filthy hole to complement the rest of the grubby, old house. But it was immaculate. It was small, but it was neat and tidy, and the soft furnishings were a girlish pink. The only stain on the appearance was the movie posters that she had pinned to the walls, which Freya assumed she had used to cover the ghastly floral wallpaper that seemed to have spread across the entire house like some kind of fungus.

"Looks normal to me," Ben said, as he flicked through a few photos on a small desk. He held one up. "This must be Grant."

Freya nodded, then peered inside the wardrobe. Again, it was neat and tidy. Then came the part Freya did not enjoy. It was time to search the little hiding places teenagers often used. She checked under the bed, under the bottom drawer of the bedside table, inside an empty tissue box, and finally in the pockets of the few coats that were hanging in the wardrobe.

"She had no secrets," Freya whispered.

"None that we know of," Ben replied.

She stared at the photo Ben was holding. It showed Poppy and who they presumed to be Grant by the seaside. Following her gaze, Ben eyed the photo.

"Skegness," he said.

"Are you sure?"

"Positive. I spent many a school day in those amusements."

"Take that, will you?" she said, then called out to Izzie who she knew wouldn't be far away. "We're done here, Izzie."

The door opened almost immediately and Izzie stood in the doorway, her eyes redder than before. She blew her nose with a fresh tissue, and then peered up at Freya. "It's hard," she said.

"Nobody ever thinks the stepmum loves the children, do they? But she was everything we had. She was the life and soul of this place."

Freya considered her words carefully. It was too easy to be sucked into being somebody's rock when in actual fact they needed you to get out there and do your job.

"May I ask," Freya said, "did Poppy have a job, or was she studying?"

She shook her head. "No. Not really. She had no real ambition. Not that she ever mentioned anyway."

"And her friends?"

"Grant, you mean?"

"Were there any others?" Freya asked.

"When she was a little younger. But not since she left school. I often wonder if she had gone to college, then maybe she would have had more. But no. There was some interest from another lad. Local boy. But I don't think he was Poppy's cup of tea. Had to send him on his way a couple of weeks ago."

"Was she unhappy?"

"No. Complacent, I think. Content with what she had."

"Thank you," Freya said. "I hope you don't mind. I'm just trying to build a picture of her. Talking of pictures. Do you mind if we use this?" She pointed to the photo Ben was holding, and a warm smile spread across Izzie's face.

"Of course. If you think it'll help."

"It will," Freya said. "We have a team working on this. It's good for them to be able to picture her."

"Humanise her, you mean?"

"Well..." Freya said. "It helps. We've got your number, Izzie. I'll call you tomorrow to arrange the viewing. I can have a car collect you, if you need it?"

"No. No, I'll be fine. I'll be there," she said, offering Freya a weak smile of gratitude. "I'll do it for Desmond and Poppy. It's the least I can do."

"You're a kind woman, Izzie," Freya said gratefully. "We'll be paying a visit to Grant when we leave here. Do you happen to know his last name?"

She shook her head. "Sorry. He's always been just Grant to us," Izzie replied. "But do me a favour, will you? Go easy on the boy. He's had a pretty tough time already. I don't know how he'll react."

"We will, Izzie," Ben said. "Thanks for the warning. You said you were off out somewhere?"

"Yes," Izzie said. "I'm a nurse. Well, a manager really. Care homes. We've three in Lincolnshire, you know? I'll need to find someone to step in for a few days. I don't want to leave Desmond for too long. He'll need my shoulder as much as I'll need his."

"I'm sure," Freya agreed. "And where are you based?"

"Based?" she said with a little laugh. "From my car most of the time. I flit from one to the other, putting out fires as I go."

"That must be challenging," Freya said. "The next few weeks will be difficult. If there's anything we can do–"

"I'll let you know. Thank you, Detective..." She waited for Freya to repeat her name.

"Bloom. Detective Inspector Freya Bloom," Freya said, offering her a card. "Do call, if you feel the need. I can arrange a Family Liaison Officer."

"That's lovely," Izzie replied, studying the card. She looked up and stared Freya in the eye. "Frost."

"Sorry?"

"That's their name. Frost. Grant's foster parents."

CHAPTER TWELVE

Gillespie's car had gone when Freya and Ben left the old guest house. They walked to the car in silence. It wasn't until they were inside, belted up, and Ben was pulling out onto the main road that Freya spoke.

"As far as delivering bad news goes, that was one of the easier times," she said. "Still awful, but not as heart-wrenching as it could have been."

"Because Izzie's the stepmum, you mean?" Ben asked.

"I think so. It's not a disconnect, as such. It's more the lack of maternal connection. There's nothing worse than listening to a grieving mother. Always makes me feel guilty."

"Yeah, I know what you mean. It's good that she can go and identify the body too. I'm not sure Mr Gray has it in him."

"That's what I was thinking. I'd like to get her to look at our mystery woman too, if we can."

"Eh? Izzie Brand?"

"Yes, why not? If the woman is local, then she'll know. Might help us out a bit."

"You don't think that's a bit much to ask?" Ben said. "Regardless of the lack of maternal connection, she's still going to be cut up about seeing Poppy. You can't then ask her to have a quick gander at some other bodies we found."

"I won't be asking her. I'll make it sound like her idea. She seems like a strong woman," Freya replied. "I won't explain where we found the woman. Not until she's seen her."

"Christ, Freya. You're bloody heartless sometimes."

"I'm afraid we have to be. Unless of course you'd be happy to let the family of our unknown woman spend the rest of their lives not knowing what happened to their mum, sister, aunt, or whatever she was to them."

"Right," Ben said, not really paying attention. He was looking at the house numbers they passed. "I get it. Just seems a bit harsh, that's all."

"So does killing a woman and stuffing her into the boot of a car," Freya said, as Ben stopped the car outside a detached house. It was another large property. Not quite as large as the Gray's guest house, but large still.

"Ready for this?" Ben asked.

"If I say no, can I go home early?" Freya joked, letting her head fall back onto the headrest.

"Come on," Ben said, and he shoved himself from the car.

By the time Freya had summoned the willpower to do the same, he was waiting for her across the roof of the car.

"How about we get the team together after this? Brief them, then call it a day. Something tells me we'll have some long nights ahead of us."

"Oh, so you're calling the shots now, are you?" Freya said, teasing him. "It makes sense. By the time we get back to the station, it'll be getting dark. With any luck, what Gillespie and Gold have to report will give us some direction. Failing that, we'll have to hope the pathology reports point us somewhere."

They strode up the narrow footpath, having to edge sideways at one point to avoid the rose bushes from getting caught on their clothes.

"Mind your trousers, Ben," Freya said. "Wouldn't want to rip them on a thorn."

He looked down and opened the hole up, giving Freya a view of the inside of his thigh. "I'd completely forgot about that."

"Oh, don't worry about it," Freya said, leaning past him to push the doorbell. "I won't be letting you forget about it for a very long time."

The door opened and a middle-aged lady answered. She wore an old-fashioned gingham apron and her hair had been arranged in a timeless bob that fell just shy of her shoulders. A short woman, who gave more weight to creature comforts than calories burned in the gym, she waited for one of them to speak.

"I'm sorry to bother you," Freya began, flashing the lady her warrant card. "Detective Inspector Bloom. This is Detective Sergeant Savage. We're looking for Grant."

"Grant who?" the lady said, with a heavy Northern Irish accent.

"I'm sorry, we don't have a last name yet. Do you have more than one Grant here?"

"No," she said, as if the idea was ridiculous.

"So can we speak to whichever Grant you do have?"

"Pestering him, are you?" she said, in a manner that parents often used that irritated Freya. It was almost as if it was Freya's fault that their child, be that blood relative, fostered, adopted, or whatever, was regularly in trouble.

"No, we'd just like a word with him if we could. He's not in any trouble."

"A word with him?" she said, as if there was some kind of hidden joke in there.

"If we could, Mrs Frost," Freya said.

"Are you sure you've got the right Grant?"

"He's friends with Poppy Gray?" Ben said, pointing back up the road. "From the guest house?"

"Aye, that's him. That's our Grant."

"Good, well, maybe we could just have a quick word?"

"You can have a word with him, if you like," she said. "As long as you don't expect a word in return."

"I'm sorry?" Freya said, tiring of the charade, especially after the debacle at the front of the guest house.

"Hasn't said a word in months," she said. "Didn't you know?"

"This is your home, is it, Mrs Frost?"

She nodded.

"May we come in and speak to him? He might be able to offer some insight into an investigation."

"Insight?" she said, almost laughing to herself at the idea. She stepped to one side. "If you can get him to talk then you're a better woman than I am. Thought I'd seen it all, I did. But you never have. He always gives us fresh things to challenge us."

"Who does?" Ben asked, as he stepped in behind Freya.

"Him upstairs," she said, flicking her head upward.

"Grant?" Ben asked.

It was only when Freya saw the wooden cross on the hallway wall that she realised what Mrs Frost was talking about. "You're right," Freya said. "He certainly keeps us on our toes."

The front door closed and, politely edging between Freya and Ben, the rotund lady stopped at the foot of the stairs, cleared her throat, and called up, "Grant, dear. There's some people here to see you, love." She turned back to Freya. "He's probably reading. He's always got his head in a book, that one."

"Shall I go up?" Ben suggested, and he was already on the stairs before Mrs Frost could complain.

"Well," she said, "I suppose, if you think. It's the white door at the end. At the front of the house. You can't miss it."

"Got it," he called, and Freya heard Ben's trademark three raps on the door a few moments later.

"Troubled, is he?" Freya asked.

"Poor lad. Been through it, he has. What with that lot a couple of weeks ago. He must be going out of his mind. It doesn't help, you know? I wish you people would just leave him alone."

Ben knocked again. "Grant? It's Ben Savage. I'm with the police. Can I have a quick word, please?"

"Two weeks ago?" Freya asked. "What happened two weeks ago?"

"What do you mean? You don't know?"

"No. We're here to talk to him about an investigation. Until twenty minutes ago, we didn't even know Grant existed. We don't even have his last name, Mrs Frost. It was Poppy's stepmother who told us about him."

"You don't know his last name? It was you lot who took him away," Mrs Frost said, almost insulted at Freya's lack of knowledge. "It's Sayer. Grant Sayer."

"Took him away? You mean he was arrested?"

"Locked him up, you did. Well, not you, of course. Four of them, there were. In uniforms. Big lads. Dragged him out on his knees. He doesn't deserve that. Not our Grant. He's a sweet boy."

"Freya," Ben called down with urgency in his voice. She looked up and found him leaning over the banister. "Window's open. He's done a runner."

CHAPTER THIRTEEN

"Aren't you going to go after him?" Mrs Frost asked.

"Does he often run away?" Freya replied.

"He always comes back."

"In which case, no," Freya replied, turning to watch Ben as he stopped at the end of the footpath. "DS Savage here will alert the team. I wonder if we might have a word with you."

"Well, I don't know how much I can tell you."

"Oh, you'd be surprised, Mrs Frost," Freya said, guiding her through to the kitchen, following the smell of home baking. "It's amazing what insights you can give us. Do you mind if my colleague has a quick look in Grant's room?"

"Whatever for?"

"It might help our investigation," Freya said, then in light of Mrs Frost's lack of objection, Freya gave Ben the nod.

The kitchen was clearly the centre of the house. The room was split into a large dining space with a six-seater pine table and chairs and the business end of the kitchen, where Mrs Frost had been busy. Flour had been scattered over the work surface, three large baking trays had been lined with greaseproof paper, and a large bowl filled with dough or pastry, or something, was covered with cling film.

"You're baking cakes," Freya said. "How lovely."

"Cakes? This is pastry, dear."

"Even better," Freya replied, dragging one of the pine chairs from under the table. "Shall we?"

Mrs Frost looked hesitant. She stared at the bowl with the pastry in, and then quizzically at Freya as if she was mad. Then, dutifully, she checked the timer on the oven. "I've got about ten minutes."

"Plenty," Freya said.

"Will I make tea?"

"Not for me. But thank you. Tell me about this incident, if you would, Mrs Frost," said Freya, inviting her to take a seat.

"It's Rose. Please," she said, and busied her hands with unfastening her gingham apron and hanging it on a hook on the back of the door. Then she came and sat opposite Freya. "You'd have to know a little about Grant first."

"Okay," Freya said, adjusting the way she sat to indicate she was ready to start listening. "Let's start from the beginning then, shall we?"

"He hasn't been here long. Two years or so."

"Two years is a long time," Freya said.

"Not when you know all my others have been here since they were babies."

"How many do you have?"

"Three, plus Grant. There's Jake. His mother died before he was one. He's seven now. Then there's Lisa. Her mother didn't even set eyes on her. Poor little thing, she was. She's eleven now. And then there's Tyler. He was just about walking when he came to us."

"You have an extraordinarily big heart, Mrs Frost," Freya said, in total awe of the woman.

"God brought them into this world. It's down to us, his children, to look after them, be what it may."

"How lovely."

"Grant was altogether different. We weren't even looking to take on another child. But we were asked if we'd consider it. The boy just needed a home and some love, and, well, who are we to turn away one of god's creatures?"

"You said he's been through a lot. Can you tell me a little more about that?"

"Aye, well... Nobody really knows. Except for him, and whoever it was that did it to him."

"Did what to him?"

"That's what we've been asking ourselves. I told you. He doesn't speak. He's nice and all. To the others. Cares for them. Helps me out around the house. He just doesn't speak. You get used to it."

"And you have no idea of what he's been through?"

"I can imagine," she said, her voice grave. "He's been in the system since he was a nipper. Not all foster homes are like ours, Detective..."

"Bloom," Freya said. "Freya Bloom."

It was at that moment that Ben came into the kitchen and took the seat to Freya's left with a clear view through to the front door should the wanderer return.

"Aye, well. There's some awful places out there. Some terrible people. Shouldn't be allowed anywhere near children. Near people for that matter. No. I came to the conclusion a long time ago that whatever is in his past can stay there. I'm going to give that poor lad everything he needs."

"And you said he was in trouble. What was all that about?"

"Ah. I just picked up bits and pieces, you know? But there was a lad. From the next village. Him and Poppy."

Picking up on the suggestion, Freya nodded and found herself leaning forward, captivated by the boy's story.

"So Grant and Poppy aren't an item, then?" Ben asked, clearly a little confused.

"Ah, who knows. Teenagers, eh? And it's not like Grant confides in me."

"Because he doesn't confide in anybody?" Ben asked, by way of confirmation.

She smiled weakly and gazed elsewhere, distant and hurting.

"I've heard his voice twice in the two years he's been with us," she said. "The first time was when he arrived, and I can assure you, what he said is not something I would repeat under this roof."

"And the second?"

"Was two weeks ago. When we came home from the police station. After you lot had broken him."

"And what did he say?" Freya asked.

"That he was sorry. That was it. Nothing else. He was sorry."

"What was he sorry for?"

"Sorry for putting me through it all, I think. Sorry for letting me down, although he hadn't. He hadn't let me down at all."

"What did he do to the boy?"

"Beat him," she said immediately, and her attention drifted to the far side of the room. "He beat him to within an inch of his life."

"Was that jealously?" Ben asked. "Because this boy and Poppy had got together?"

"Who knows?"

"I want to help him," Freya said. "But he'll need to help us first."

"How? He doesn't say anything. He just disappears inside himself."

"Rose, I have to tell you something," Freya began, and waited for her to look her in the eye. "Poppy Gray was found dead this morning. She was murdered. We need to speak to Grant. He might be able to help us in our enquiries."

"Oh Lord," she said, and her hands instinctively held the collar of her blouse. "Oh, Lord no. Not our sweet Poppy."

"I'm sorry it's not better news."

"But who? Who would have done such a thing?"

"We're investigating, Rose. That's why we need to speak to Grant."

"You don't think it was him? Not our Grant. No. It can't be. Ah, Jesus, Mary and Joseph, what a terrible thing."

"Will you call me?" Freya said, slipping her a card. "When he comes back? We'll do our best to make it as easy as we can on him."

She nodded. "The children will be home soon. My husband has taken them swimming. I've still to make a pie for their dinners."

It was her way of inviting Freya and Ben to leave.

"Call me, Rose. We can help Grant. But we need his help in return."

"I will," she said.

"Thank you, Rose," Freya finished. "I'll send somebody to speak to him tomorrow. Perhaps it's best if we deliver the news."

She nodded, rested her heavy arms on the table, and sighed. "That poor lad."

CHAPTER FOURTEEN

Detective Constable Jackie Gold walked through the automatic doors of Lincoln Hospital. She explained who she was and who she was there to see to the woman on reception, and was advised to follow the blue lines through the corridor, past the cafeteria, towards the Rainforest Ward. The walk seemed to take an age and took her through parts of the hospital she hadn't seen before. The place was a maze and none of the signs seemed to make any sense. Eventually, she found the cafeteria, but from then on, none of the directions the receptionist had given her made any sense at all, and it was pure chance that she saw the sign for the ward down a branch of corridor she would never have thought to venture down.

Another reception desk greeted her when she entered the ward, and she almost expected the nurse to congratulate her for actually finding it. There must have been dozens of people wandering the corridors looking for their destinations.

According to the nurse, Lee Sanders was stable but unconscious in a room on the left-hand side, and only when Jackie had presented her with her warrant card was she allowed in to see him. The door closed behind her. The room was dark, drab, and exactly how she had imagined a hospital room to be. The curtains had been closed and the room was stuffy. Lee was lying in a bed with thin sheets covering him. His head was swathed in bandages, and a machine beeped every few seconds while a drip kept him hydrated. There was no sign of the boy's mother, so Jackie took a seat and checked her emails on her phone. She could wait a while, she thought, until she saw the message from Ben that they would be holding a briefing in an hour. The station was at least a thirty-minute drive from the hospital, so the mother better hurry up.

Thinking that she had probably passed her in the cafeteria, Jackie wondered if somebody should send out a search party to bring her back. Maybe she should do what they did in the cartoons her son Charlie liked to watch and feed a piece of string out to make retracing her steps easier.

The machine beeped and the boy's finger twitched. Charlie did that in his sleep. He was probably dreaming, Jackie thought, and then wondered what it was about. She'd spent hours watching Charlie, wondering what he thought, what he dreamed of, and if he was happy. He seemed happy. Content, at least.

The door pushed open, with no care for keeping the noise down, and a nurse stopped in the doorway. "Can I get you a drink?" she asked. "Tea? Coffee?"

"Not for me, thank you," Jackie replied. "I'll just hang on here for a little while until his mother gets back."

"She shouldn't be long. She left about an hour ago. Said she was picking up some clothes for them both."

"Will she stay here too, then?"

"Yes. We can't give her a bed, but most mothers would sleep on the floor if they had no other option."

"The floor?"

"We don't make them sleep on the floor," the nurse said. "We give them a chair with a footstool. I just meant–"

"It's okay. I get it," Jackie said. "I didn't leave my boy's side when he was in here."

"He was in this ward, was he?"

"No. Not this ward. I can't remember which one. But it was closer to the main entrance. Easier to find," Jackie explained. "But I stayed right there. Three nights. I couldn't leave him."

"I have a feeling Lee will be with us for a few days at least. He's had quite a hit on the head," the nurse said, and then leaned out of the door at the sound of approaching heels. "Ah, here she is now. I'll leave you to it. If you need anything at all, just come to the desk."

"Thank you," Jackie said, and waited in anticipation for the mother to enter.

The mother stopped in the doorway and realised who Jackie was before she saw the warrant card. Hanging from one shoulder was a sports bag presumably with clothes and washing kits for them both. In her other hand was a plastic bag filled with food and drink, presumably from the cafeteria.

"You're police," she said, setting the large sports bag down then laying the food bag carefully beside it. "Have you caught her yet?"

"Why don't you sit down, Mrs Sanders–"

"Miss Sanders," she corrected her. "I never married."

"We're here to help."

"I told your man everything I saw. The man in the uniform–"

"It helps to go over the details."

"She was driving too fast. That's what happened. Lee didn't stand a chance. Now look at him. Brain bleed, they said. Brain bleed."

"Let's go over what happened. Together," Jackie suggested. "My name is DC Gold. Call me Jackie. I've got a boy a little younger than Lee."

"I suppose he has a dad."

"No, actually. I've raised him myself," Jackie said proudly. "Let's go through it again, shall we?"

"Shouldn't you be out there looking for her?"

"There's a whole team of people out there, Miss Sanders."

The woman stared at Jackie as if making a decision.

"Teresa. Call me Teresa," she said eventually, and laid her hand on Lee's. "Where do we start?"

"At the beginning. Where was Lee?"

"He was with a few boys from the village. There's a field not far from the house. He's not allowed any further than that." She studied Lee's hand in her own, and a single tear rolled down her cheek. "Poor boy has been couped up all winter. With the longer days now, I thought maybe he'd be okay to go and play. You know? To burn off some of that energy. They know to stay together–"

"It's okay. Nobody's judging you, Teresa. I get it."

"There's a stile in the field. Kind of hidden behind the trees. The other boys go home that way. Toward the village. So Lee comes home alone. I always tell him to run, not to talk to anybody, and to check the road. He knows how to cross the road. He's a smart boy. But she was just going too fast."

"So you saw her? You saw the car coming?"

"No. But I heard it. Nobody ever comes down our road. It doesn't go anywhere. It's not even a shortcut. It's just a loop that connects our house and the fields to the village and the main road. But I heard the tyres. The screech. And I felt it," she said quietly, clutching the lower part of her stomach as if the very thought of it all made her feel sick. "Here. I felt it right here. I knew."

"What were you doing at the time?" Jackie asked.

"Washing up. Cleaning. Making the most of not having Lee around. That sounds bad, doesn't it?"

"No. I understand," Jackie said. "You get a lot more done when they're not making a mess behind you, don't you?"

"Yes. Yes, you do. I ran out. I ran up the drive and into the road. And then I saw him. He was lying in the road. He wasn't moving. He wasn't crying. He was still. Everything was still. Even the car."

"And you ran to him?"

"Not at first. I was in shock, I think. The car door opened and the girl got out," Teresa said, recalling the memory with a bitterness in her eyes. "And she looked at me, and she looked at Lee. Then she ran. She was scared. I saw it in her eyes. I called for her to stop. I shouted. But she ran."

"What did you say?"

"I told her, look what you've done. Look what you've done to my boy."

"You must have been tempted to run after her?"

"Yes and no," Teresa mumbled. "Lee was lying there. He needed me. He needed his mum."

"Did you recognise her, Teresa?" Jackie asked, and Teresa shook her head.

"No. I'd never seen her. But I know her face. I'll never forget her face. You put her in a line-up and I'll point her out just from the smell of her fear. I swear to god."

"What was she wearing?" Jackie asked.

"A dress, I think. A pretty one. Like a summer dress."

"And you're sure you didn't run after her?"

"Of course. How could I? How could I leave my boy in the road like that?" she said. "I should have. I should have got her and dragged her back and forced her to look at what she did to my boy. I hope she rots in jail. I hope she never sleeps a wink again."

"Where did she run to?"

"I don't know. Up the track towards the village, I think. I didn't exactly stand there and watch her. Maybe I should have got in the car and gone after her. Maybe I should have mowed her down."

"Teresa, you can't say that."

"Well," she said, "look at him. Just bloody look at him. He's never hurt anybody in his life. He doesn't deserve this. He might never be the same. She deserves something. She deserves to never be the same too–"

"She's dead, Teresa," Jackie said, ending the rant. "We found her body a little way from your house. She was murdered."

CHAPTER FIFTEEN

THE FIRST FLOOR OF THE STATION WAS PREDOMINANTLY MAJOR investigations, with the exception of Detective Superintendent Harper's office, who oversaw every faction in the building, from uniform, through CID, to Freya's major investigation team.

They took the fire escape stairs as usual, due to the lift and the main staircase being on the far side of the building. In the first floor corridor, Harper's office was the first door on the right, followed by DCI Will Granger's office, the little kitchen area, and the washrooms. Most of the left-hand side of the floor was taken up by the incident room, the doors to which were notorious for squealing like a wounded beast.

It was that squeal that announced Freya and Ben's arrival, and the team looked up from their laptops, except the youngest member, DC Gabriel Cruz, who was messaging his girlfriend – a particularly attractive female uniform – on his phone with an excited smile on his face.

Freya strode over to her desk, which she had positioned beside the white board, while Ben dropped his laptop bag on his desk and plopped down in his chair.

Leaving the team to carry on as they were for a few minutes,

Freya prepared her briefing, the way she usually did – by writing the name of the victim in the centre of the board. She didn't know why she bothered. After a few days of information coming in and avenues opening up, she rarely ever got the chance to add anything to it. She was always out on the road. Active police work, her old DCI would have called it. She preferred the term 'working like a dog'.

Poppy Gray, she wrote, in capital letters, then circled the name as if to make a point. She added Desmond Gray and Izzie Brand, and joined them to Poppy's name with two lines. Then she added Mr Harringer to one side and ran a dotted line towards Poppy. Hopefully, Gillespie could fill those dots in with what he'd found out in his interview. She then did the same with Teresa Sanders. She glanced around the room, noting that Jackie was still out, then added Grant Sayer's name to the board. At that point, she had exhausted their knowledge of Poppy's network.

"Can you call Jackie?" she said to Ben, when she was done with the board. "See if she's on her way back."

"Got it," he said, leaning back in his chair.

"How is everyone else getting on?" she asked nobody in particular. "Gillespie?"

"Aye, golden, boss," he replied. "Although, not as good as Cruz over there."

The team all turned their heads to Cruz, who blushed and fumbled for words.

"Had a date with the wee lass from uniform last night," Gillespie added.

"How the bloody hell did you know that?" Cruz began.

"Even splashed out on a steak for her. A steak? Mind you, if I still lived with my mum and borrowed her car, I'd be able to afford to buy a lass a steak."

"Aw, Gab," DC Nillson chimed in. "I'm pleased for you. She's a lovely girl."

"Aye, she's lovely now. Wait until his nibs over there starts rubbing off on her, and she'll be coming in late, snapping her laptop shut bang on the dot."

"I will not be rubbing off on her," Cruz interjected, then blushed again when he realised Gillespie's trap. "You're just a sad, old man, Jim. You're jealous because I have youth on my side. And how the bloody hell do you know about my date? I didn't tell anyone for this exact reason."

"For what reason?" Chapman asked.

"This. The ridicule. The taunting and the laughing. I kept it a secret."

"Well, you did a good job there then," Gillespie said. "I didn't hear of it. Did you, Anna?"

"No," Nillson replied. "I had no idea."

"Chapman?"

"I've got a hundred better things to be thinking about. That said, good luck to you, Gab."

"Boss? Ben?"

"Nope," Ben replied. "Didn't have a clue."

"Couldn't care less," Freya said, amazed that the conversation had gone from a brief update to see how they were doing with their enquiries to Cruz's sex life. But she was willing to let it go in the name of morale.

"See," Gillespie said. "Top marks on keeping your date secret. In next week's lesson, I'll be teaching you the art of not taking your date to the pub where your colleagues drink."

"Eh?" Cruz said.

"The Crown?"

"No," Cruz said, his expression dropping into a look of absolute horror.

"Table twelve?" Gillespie added.

"No."

"She had steak and roast veg, the rump steak, if I'm not mistaken."

"No, please–"

"You had a side order of fries and onion rings, and you told the waitress you were on a diet when she asked why you weren't having a main."

"You're a monster," Cruz muttered.

"She had two glasses of white wine. You had a single diet coke, which you made last all night."

"You were watching?"

"Aye," Gillespie said. "I couldn't believe my luck. I wasn't even going to go for a pint, but my milk was off. So I figured I'd have a liquid dinner."

"Why would your milk being off affect your dinner? What were you having? Cereal?"

"Aye. Crunchy Nut Cornflakes. You can't have them with off milk."

"That's your dinner?"

"It's a healthy option."

"Healthier than what? A bar of chocolate?" Cruz said, clearly identifying a gap in which he could move the topic of debate away from his date and back onto Gillespie's lap.

"Don't try that one with me, kiddo. I wasn't born yesterday. I've still got a story to tell."

"Oh God, no," Cruz said. "Please, Jim–"

"What story?" Anna said.

"It doesn't matter," Cruz interjected. "I want to hear about Jim's cornflake dinner. No wonder you look like you're dead already."

"Never mind my cornflake dinner, Gab. Why don't you tell everyone what happened when you went to the little boy's room?"

"I don't know what you mean."

"Aye, you do."

Then Cruz reddened even more. He glanced around at everyone and found the entire team waiting for an explanation.

"Jim, no," Cruz said.

"The bathroom?" Chapman said, intrigued enough to have turned her chair to face the conversation.

"Aye, Gab. Tell them about your little..." Gillespie left a pause for dramatic effect. "Accident."

"It was the sink."

"Tried to hide it, didn't you?"

"It came out too fast. I wasn't expecting it–"

"Went in with his shirt tucked in. Came out with his shirt hanging free."

"I was soaked."

"Wasn't expecting a detective like me, with eagle eyes, to be watching, were you?"

"I didn't pee my pants."

"Oh, come on, Gab," Ben cut in. "You did it before a few months ago. Remember?"

"That was different. I thought you were going to kill me–"

"Did she notice?" Chapman asked.

"No, thankfully," Cruz mumbled.

"Aye, she did."

"Eh?"

"I watched her. She was staring at your crotch, man."

"Oh, for god's sake."

"And we haven't even got to the best part yet," Gillespie said, then leaned forward into the group to deliver the line with emphasis. "The cheque."

"The cheque?" Chapman said.

"Oh, come on," Cruz whined. "How long were you there?"

"All night. Watched you. Followed you. Heard everything you said."

"Followed me?"

"Who do you think was in the next cubicle when you were stripping off your pants?"

"No. Not you."

"Who do you think passed you the loo roll so you could mop up your wee accident. Pun intended, by the way."

"Not you," Cruz said, holding his hand to his chest. He stared up at Freya, pleading for her to help. "I think I'm having some kind of heart attack, boss."

"What about the cheque?" Ben asked, clearly hoping to prolong Cruz's suffering.

"No, please. No more."

"Well, Ben, that's a good question," Gillespie said, and he leaned back in his chair, scratching at his beard, adopting the pose of an intellect, or a psychiatrist or philosopher. "Now, I know for a fact that you, Ben, aren't great at the wining and dining game. It's a fact, right?"

It was common knowledge that Ben wasn't the most romantically aware on the team and his idea of wooing a woman was a stroll along the river sharing a bag of chips. He nodded, keen for Gillespie to make his point.

"However," Gillespie continued, "if you were to, say, fancy the pants off a girl, and had finally plucked up the courage to ask her out, after three months, I might add, you would, I hope, at least make sure you had enough money in your bank to pay for said meal, so as not to make a complete, trouser-wetting fool of yourself."

"Of course," Ben replied, then his mouth fell open as all eyes once more fell on Cruz.

"Not this numpty," Gillespie added. "Three different bank cards. Three rejections. Three apocalyptic hues of red across little Gabby's face. I thought the wee lass was going to walk out on him. And if it wasn't for me, *she* would have had to pay for it. Imagine that?"

"You?" Cruz said, amid the hushed laughter. "It was you–"

"Aye," Gillespie said, clearly pre-empting where Cruz was going.

"The mystery payer. You paid for our dinner."

"I saved your bacon, sunshine, that's what I did."

"You paid for his and Larson's dinner?" Chapman asked, shocked at the revelation.

"Aye. I'm not a complete savage. No offence, Ben. I couldn't just sit and watch him go down in flames at the final hurdle, could I, eh? I mean, despite the urine incident–"

"It was the sink."

"And despite him having no money to pay for her delicious steak, he entertained me all night. It was better than going to a show, or one of those comedy nights where the comedian makes fun of the crowd. It was hilarious."

"So now he owes you money?" Ben said.

"I'll pay you back," Cruz added. "Every penny."

"No way. It was my pleasure, sunshine. I mean, the way I see it, I just bought the rights to that story. It belongs to me now."

"No," Cruz said. "Please. I'll pay–"

"And I'm going to tell it to everyone who'll listen," Gillespie stated triumphantly. "Every chance I damn well get."

CHAPTER SIXTEEN

"RIGHT," FREYA SAID, CLAPPING HER HANDS TOGETHER. "Enough chit-chat. Ben, where's Gold?"

He raised his hand, checked his watch, and counted down.

"Three, two..."

The incident room squealed open.

"Sorry I'm late," Gold said in a rush. "Had to wait for Lee Sanders' mum to get back."

A rush of cool air followed her and then ceased when the door had squealed closed, slamming with a noise like a shotgun.

Freya eyed Ben then noted the heeled boots Gold was wearing. He followed her gaze and smiled back at her, shrugging.

Freya pointed to the white board and spoke quietly, forcing them all to tune in.

"For those who were not at the crime scene, here's a rundown of events," Freya said. "I'll see if I can articulate everything we know. Poppy Gray is the daughter of Desmond Gray, who owns the Witham Valley Guest House in Stixwould."

"Oh, I know that one," Cruz said. "My dad used to stay there when Mum kicked him out. Is it still going?"

"This morning," Freya continued, eyeing Cruz to shut him up

and focus on what she was saying, "Poppy stole a car belonging to one of the guests."

"One Roy Harringer," Gillespie added. "Stays there once a month. Lives down in Norfolk, but comes up to see a client of his. Works with IT or something. Security stuff. Anyway, he was in the shower when he felt a cool breeze."

"That'll be the rotten windows," Cruz said. "I'm surprised they haven't fallen out–"

"And when he got out, he realised his car keys were missing. He got dressed then reported it to Mr Gray, who subsequently called us lot."

"Why did she steal it?" Chapman asked. "Do we know yet?"

"Not yet," Freya advised, trying to push on. "She rounded a bend about a mile from her father's guest house and, for reasons not clarified as yet, hit a small boy–"

"Lee Sanders," Jackie said. "I spoke to the mother at the hospital. She said she heard the tyres squeal and knew. You know, like a parent thing. She ran out. Saw the girl climbing from the car and then she ran."

"Did she go after her?" Freya asked.

"No," Gold said. "Her boy was lying on the ground. You can hardly blame her."

"She stopped, at least," Freya said, trying to hide the effect of the disruptions. "Which is more than some would have done. Uniform arrived on scene and closed the road. Then DS Gillespie arrived, followed by DS Savage and I. We split up. DS Savage and I followed the track opposite the house, while DS Gillespie and CSI searched the car."

"Michaela Fell?" Jackie asked, unable to stop her eyes from darting to Ben and back.

"Yes. Not that it matters."

"No. Of course not," Gold replied. "I was just wondering."

"Gillespie?" Freya said, inviting him to take over.

"Aye, boss. Well, Michaela and I were searching the car. She had the suit and all the PPE. Me? All I had was a pair of gloves. So I checked the back of the car. Found a holdall full of men's dirty laundry, which I've handed in," he said, then lowered his voice to a sinister growl. "Then I checked the boot. Popped it open, and what do you know?"

"Go on?" Chapman said.

"A body."

"A what?"

"Female, in her forties-ish. Looks like she's had an argument with a cricket bat and lost."

"Beaten to death?"

"We won't know the cause of death until tomorrow," Freya interjected. "But it does look that way."

"So the fella with the car, the shower guy," Cruz said, "he had a dead body in the boot of his car?"

"That's one possibility," Freya agreed.

"So why did he wait until he got dressed before calling the police?"

For all his bad habits and naivety, Cruz had actually just stumbled onto a valid argument. "Go on," Freya said, encouraging him to say more.

"Well, that's it really," he said. "I mean, come on. Serial killer rule number one, never leave the body in your car. Rule number two–"

"Don't wait to get dressed before you call the police?" Gillespie said.

"Something like that," Cruz said, nodding. "Picture it. She's probably a prostitute or something–"

"Whoa, hold on," Anna said, sitting forward. "I disagree. Why does she have to be a prostitute?"

"The fella's working away. He makes the most of his free time. There are countless stories of men having extra-curricular affairs while they're working away."

"Do you mean extra-marital?" Anna said.

"You know what I mean. Serial killers too. I've seen all the documentaries. They prey on prostitutes and homeless people because they're vulnerable and because nobody is going to notice if they go missing. It's the perfect crime."

"He's right," Freya added.

"Until somebody steals your car," Gillespie said.

"Yeah, well... That's my point," Cruz continued. "If somebody stole your car, Jim, what would be your first reaction?"

"I'd find them and break their legs," he said. "Then their fingers, maybe. I don't know. Whenever I think about it, my daydream kind of gets stuck on the first part."

A few of the team stared at Gillespie, a little concerned with his statement. But Cruz was on a roll. He wasn't going to let anything stop him from getting his ideas out there.

"You'd call the police is what you'd do. But he didn't. He went to the owner of the hotel–"

"Guest house," Ben corrected him.

"Right," Cruz continued. "What the bloody hell is the landlord going to do about it?"

"Come to think of it," Gillespie said. "it was Gray who called it in on his behalf."

"There. See? Harringer was hoping to find the car without having to involve the police."

Freya stared at the Detective Constable, seeing him in a new light. "That's a good observation, Cruz," she said.

"Ah, see?" Cruz said. "All we have to do is find the missing prostitute, catch him on CCTV, and that's a wrap, as they say."

"That is, of course, only half of the problem," Freya said, watching his elation fade.

"Eh?"

She tapped the board behind her.

"Poppy Gray?"

"What about her?"

"She was found dead around a thousand yards from the scene

of the accident."

"Dead?"

Freya nodded. "Two dead bodies. One injured boy. And a stolen car."

"Do you want to tell them about Grant, or should I?" Ben asked.

"No. I've said enough. You go."

"Poppy's stepmother, Izzie Brand, mentioned a boyfriend, or just a friend. We're not sure which yet. A boy named Grant. Lives in a home in Stixwould."

"A home?" Gillespie asked.

"Yeah, like a foster home or something. We spoke to the owner, Rose Frost. Grant was in some kind of incident two weeks ago. Seriously hurt somebody. Anyway, when he heard us at the front door, he jumped out of the window and legged it."

"Does it all the time, does he?" Gillespie asked.

"Yes, as it happens," Ben said, perplexed at Gillespie's insight.

"He'll be back," Gillespie said with confidence. "You want me to look into him, boss?" he asked Freya.

"If you could, Gillespie. Thanks," Freya said. "Chapman, you're on research. I want social media accounts, phone records, bank records of everyone. Gold, you're with the mother, Teresa Sanders. Make sure she's okay, and I want you at the hospital in case Lee Sanders wakes up. He might have seen something."

"At the hospital, ma'am?"

"Yes, is that okay?"

"Sure, yeah. That's fine."

"Just stay close to her. Make sure she doesn't feel alone, alright? Take your laptop. You can work from the hospital. Work with Chapman. Check missing persons. DS Savage has a file on the unknown. See if you can find a match," Freya said, then turned to Anna. "Nillson, I want you to look into whatever happened two weeks ago with Grant Sayer. Talk to Lincoln HQ. Also, have a look at the other guests in the guest house. Get

Gillespie's notes off him and take over. I want to know everyone who has stayed there in the past two weeks. Run the names by Chapman and let's see what we find."

Freya looked around the room. Chapman was already making notes, copying down the names from the board onto her pad, Ben was thumping his laptop waiting for it to do something, and Gillespie was deep in thought. Cruz, however, was leaning back in his chair, pleased with himself.

"Meanwhile, DS Savage and I will be visiting the pathologist tomorrow morning to understand the cause of death and anything else she might have for us. After that, we'll be meeting Izzie Brand to get a formal ID on Poppy Gray, and she might even offer us insight into our mystery lady. Is everyone clear on what they have to do?"

"Ma'am," Gold replied, always the first to reply. Freya imagined her at school, sitting up front. She was like an adult teacher's pet.

"Aye, boss," Gillespie growled in his thick Glaswegian accent. "I'll take care of our lad."

She gave him a knowing nod by way of thanks and found Cruz still smiling to himself, hands folded behind his head.

"You okay there, Cruz?" she asked.

"Yep."

"You seemed pleased about something."

"I just looked up the address on Google Earth," he replied.

"So?"

"It's the only house within half a mile."

"Right?"

"That means I won't have to go door to door," he said. "I always have to go knocking on doors. *Excuse me, I'm DC Cruz from the police. I was wondering if blah blah blah*. Ha. Not this time. There are no neighbours. Nobody will have seen a thing."

"No, you're right," Freya said. "There will be no door knocking for you, that's for sure."

"Sounds good to me, boss," he said.

"Especially after that insight into the habits of serial killers and how they choose their victims."

"And my mother said I waste my life on Netflix," he boasted.

"That was fine detective work," Freya said, seeing a smile creep onto Ben's face in her peripheral.

Cruz sensed something was coming.

"I don't know how you haven't made DS yet," she added.

Cruz's expression looked panicked. He sat forward and dropped his hands to his sides, waiting for it.

"You must be an expert profiler?" Freya said.

"No. It was just from documentaries."

"Still... I have a job for someone with your exact skill set."

His eyes widened and that childlike smile found its way back onto his face. "Really, boss?"

"Something special," she said.

"I'm game for it."

"Good. Tomorrow morning, I want you to see Sergeant Priest downstairs. Have him assign you a uniform."

"Another one?"

"Not Larson. This isn't a job you want to take your pretty little girlfriend on. It's far too dangerous."

"Alright. I'm sure she'll be disappointed, but she'll understand," Cruz said.

"See CID for a list of every known sex worker within ten miles."

"Eh?" Cruz said, and his smile waned once more.

"I want you to pay them all a visit," Freya said. "Every single one of them. See if any of their friends are missing."

"Prostitutes?" he moaned. "Me?"

"You'd better go and see the search and rescue boys while you're out," Gillespie said. "See if they can lend you a dry suit. If the thought of a night with PCSO Larson was enough to make you pee your pants then those girls will eat you alive, sonny boy."

CHAPTER SEVENTEEN

Freya had promised herself an early night and she had been secretly looking forward to it for a long time.

But by the time she had got home from work, slipped out of her new boots, and spent a good ten minutes rubbing her feet, she had cleaned up the broken mug she had kicked down the stairs earlier in the day, then to her horror, she had seen something she could never unsee and smelled something which would remain in her nostrils for eternity.

Filth.

A smattering of dust covered the parts of the dining table that weren't covered in paperwork. She slipped into her slippers, sighing with relief at the instant comfort they offered, then before she got her cleaning stuff out, she used the washroom.

She saw it there too, but only because she was looking for it now. The dust had been the catalyst, and she knew she would not be able to settle until she'd cleansed.

It wasn't often Freya did the housework. The way she saw it, she only used a fraction of the house, so she only really needed to clean those particular areas. The kitchen being one, plus the washroom, the bedroom, and the dining room table. Everything else should realistically still be clean since she last did it all. A month ago, she thought. Maybe more.

Of course, she knew this was just her own way of giving herself a reason to be lazy, but she felt she had earned it. There must have been two hundred pieces of paper on her dining room table, ranging from at least four different investigations. There were images of the body that had been found on the beach, Jessica Hudson. Then there were notes on the woman in the woods, Jane Blythe, the girl in the manhole, Abigail McGowan, and of course, Emma Blanch, the first victim of a shocking plot, and perhaps Freya's most testing investigation in Lincolnshire to date.

She pulled the papers together into one big pile and shuffled them to one end of the table, then sprayed the table with polish and gave it a rub. She wasn't really *cleaning* cleaning. Not how she liked to clean, in a pair of tracksuit bottoms, music on loud, and a bowl of searing-hot water with a sponge and some disinfectant. This was just a mask. It was the minimal effort required to remove the dust and make the place smell better than before. It was an opportunity for her to ponder the unknown woman and how she came to be in the boot of the car. She did the same in the washroom using a bathroom cleaner, and the same in the kitchen with a kitchen cleaner.

One day, she'd get around to giving the place a good seeing-to. Maybe. Not tonight though. Tonight was her night, and on that note, she was just about to switch the top light off when...

The hob caught her eye.

Not the hob itself, but the phantom stains and sauces and grizzly oils that seemed to appear out of nowhere. It always amazed her how it got so dirty. Whenever she used a saucepan or a frying pan, she was always so careful, to the point of being obsessive, about not spilling anything on the hob. Yet it always seemed to be covered in some kind of sauce, it nearly always had rice on it, and from where she was standing in the doorway, it resembled the hob in a student kitchen.

So she cleaned it. She pulled the big, heavy, iron things off, left them in a bowl to soak, and she scrubbed. When she was done with the cooker, she washed the big, iron things, replaced them on the cooker, and stood back to admire her handiwork.

Then she saw the little pile of rice and food she had brushed onto the floor while she had been cleaning. Huffing, she got the dustpan and brush from the cupboard and cleared it up, then tossed them back into the cupboard, closing the door before they had time to fall back out.

The last job was always to fold the tea towel. Folding the tea towel was the experienced kitchen cleaner's way of slapping their hands together after a good day's work, saying right, that's me, I'm done. She poured a wine, happy with her impromptu cleaning effort, and even wiped the worktop down when she was done. She walked through to the lounge to settle into her favourite – and only – armchair. There was a particular position she could sit in, with her feet beneath her, from where she could just reach her wine on the floor, and on the other side, reach her little nail kit. Her nail kit had grown somewhat over the years. There were bottles in there she didn't even remember buying and colours she wouldn't dream of using. But she kept them anyway.

Positioning her laptop on the arm of the chair, she opened it, logged in, and browsed to Netflix. Then, having watched the previews of nearly a dozen of the latest films and shows, she settled on one from about twenty years ago with Tom Hanks and Meg Ryan. Her wine had warmed and when she looked at the little clock in the corner of the screen, she noticed she had spent nearly twenty-five minutes deciding what to watch.

Twenty-five minutes of her precious me-time?

Agitated, she rushed to the kitchen, poured another wine, spilt some, wiped it up, then carried the glass back to the lounge. Then, on reflection, she went back to the kitchen, got the bottle out of the fridge, picked up a family-sized bag of Minstrels, and took those as well.

Finally, she had enough wine to last through the film, enough snacks, and twenty nails to paint.

She hit play and watched the opening credits while she selected a colour for her nails. A little bottle of azure blue caught her eye, and she held it up to the light to see if there was enough left for her to do her fingers and toes, or if she would have to select a different colour for her toes. Not that it was warm enough yet to wear open-toed shoes, but that wasn't the point.

She tilted the bottle, trying to gauge how much was left, then turned it to the window.

That was when she saw it. The face at the window. A man's face. Smiling and holding something up for her to see. He waved.

"Oh, Ben," she whined to herself, then called out to him. "I'm doing my nails."

"Eh?" he said. It was dark outside, and he moved closer to the window to look inside. "You're painting your nails?"

"I know," she said.

"You what?" he called, then disappeared. Moments later, there were three unmistakable raps on the door.

"Give me strength," she said to herself, as she put her nail kit down, paused her movie, pulled her feet from beneath her, and then ambled to the front door.

"I bought Chinese," he said, brushing past her and going straight through to the kitchen. "I haven't been shopping, so I grabbed some on the way home. Figured you'd be hungry."

He pulled two plates from the cupboard then set about distributing the food.

"I got some prawn crackers too," he said, splitting the plastic bag open, and a few little fragments of cracker seemed to jump out on purpose and spread out on her worktop. Opening the rice should have been a simple affair. Or so Freya thought. At least a hundred grains of rice were catapulted in all directions across her kitchen, and at least ten of those landed on the hob. He'd placed the empty plates on the far side of the hob due to the limited space. So he began spooning sweet and sour chicken from one side, where the bags were, to the other, tiny droplets of sauce landing on the big, heavy, iron things in the process.

Finally, he pulled two forks from the drawer, grabbed himself an empty wine glass, and then loaded her up with one of the plates and one of the forks. "Shall we eat in there?" he asked, pointing at the lounge. "Looks like you cleaned in here. I don't want to be the one who messes *that* up."

He turned sideways and edged past her, out through the hallway and into the lounge, from where she heard an exaggerated sigh, as he most likely plonked himself down in her armchair.

"What are you watching?" he called, then clearly he took it upon himself to have a look. "Tom Hanks? I love Tom Hanks."

She savoured the peace and quiet of the kitchen for a few moments until the grains of rice and sauce on the hob irritated her, then she took a slow walk through to the lounge. Exactly as she had thought he would, Ben had claimed the armchair, so she pulled one of the dining chairs out and set her plate down on her nice, clean table.

Ever the gentleman, Ben jumped up from the seat. "Take the armchair," he said. "I'll sit in the uncomfortable chair."

"No," she snapped. "It's fine. You sit. Make yourself comfortable."

But he set his plate down opposite her and pulled out another seat. Then he stared across at her, arms folded.

"You didn't come just to mess my kitchen up, did you?" she asked.

"I've been thinking about our unknown woman," he replied.

Well, if he's here, we might as well talk about the investigation, she thought, and she took a forkful of food. As much as she had been irritated by his arrival, the food was far better than the packet of minstrels she would have no doubt devoured.

"Go on."

"What Cruz said rings alarm bells. It pains me to say it, but he might have a point."

"He does have a point," Freya corrected him, and in that instant, Ben's presence was no longer a burden or an irritation. They were talking about the case. He came alive when he talked about the case. He glowed.

"I say we bring him in," Ben continued. "We've got enough on him. A body in his car. What else do we need? I say we bring him in and lean on him."

"I agree," she said, having considered the few facts they had while she had been cleaning. "In fact, we should ask Gold to broaden her missing person's search."

"To Norfolk," Ben suggested. "Good idea. He could have picked her up from there."

"Or on the way. It's only an hour or so away."

"It's two separate crimes."

"It's simpler, and more likely," Freya agreed.

"There was blood spatter on the front of the car."

"He could have hit somebody on the way up to Lincolnshire. Stuffed her in the boot, planning on dumping the body up here somewhere."

Ben forked the last of his meal into his mouth, set his fork down, and sat back. "Two bodies. Two crimes."

"Too much coincidence," Freya said. "I see it. I totally see it. But it's just too coincidental."

"Do you want to raise the stakes?" Ben said. "Double or nothing."

"You owe me a naked dinner."

"With an apron," Ben said. "We agreed on the apron."

"What do you have in mind?"

"If I'm right, not only do you cook me dinner naked–"

"With an apron," Freya added, confident that she was right anyway.

"But you wait on me hand and foot, all night."

"All night?"

"And not a week night either. A weekend."

She gave it some thought for a few moments, having already made her mind up that it would in fact be her sitting down all night, while naked Ben in his little apron would be fetching her whatever she wanted, stoking the fire, and pouring her wine.

"Deal," she said.

"That's that then," Ben said, looking far less confident than Freya felt. He collected the two plates and even picked up two stray grains of rice that had fallen onto the table, and he disappeared into the kitchen.

Freya remained seated. She thought about the bet, and as much as it amused her to think of Ben's awkwardness in a little apron, she couldn't help but wonder if it was a ploy to start something. She already knew he was awkward with women, having seen him ruin his chances with Michaela Fell on more than one occasion. Maybe he just didn't have the confidence to reach out and grab her. God knows she wouldn't put up a fight. She would strip him before they even got up the stairs.

There was a naivety about him. Something that suggested sex just wasn't a priority. In which case, the bet was simply fun. A means to humiliate each other. They had already seen each other naked, so there wasn't much more to hide.

He'd been gone for far too long and she could hear him doing something in the kitchen. Her mind immediately went to the hob, and all that effort she had made, and wondered if, for some unknown reason, he was making pudding.

She made her way through the hall and peered into the kitchen, only to find him lifting the big, heavy, iron things to wipe the spillage from the hob. He then gave the iron things a wipe down and set them back down into place.

Finally, he folded the tea towel and hung it over the cooker door handle.

"I best leave you to it," he said.

In the space of thirty minutes, he'd gone, in Freya's estimation, from irritating, to annoying, to intrusive, and now he had returned to his nearly perfect self. He had, after all, just bought her dinner, progressed the investigation a little, and had cleaned up after himself. There was still time to do her nails and have an early night.

He fetched his jacket then returned into the hallway while pulling it on.

"I'll pick you up tomorrow morning. We'll need an arrest warrant for Harringer, and to search his room," he said, half out the door.

"Already on it," she said with a smile. "I'm sending Nillson."

"I'll be seeing you then," he said, and disappeared around the corner, only to return a few moments later, leaning back to offer an afterthought.

"What is it, Ben?" she asked.

"The blue one."

"The blue what?"

"Nail stuff. The blue one."

"To match my eyes?" she said, pleased he had taken the time to notice.

"No," Ben replied. "To match your cold, cold, heart."

He winked and then disappeared until the morning.

CHAPTER EIGHTEEN

THE FOLLOWING MORNING, BEN REVERSED THE CAR INTO THE spot in the hospital car park, applied the handbrake, and then closed his eyes for a moment of peace.

"What are you thinking?" Freya asked, just as he knew she would. She had a habit of filling silences when he needed them and creating them when he needed her to speak.

"Izzie Brand," he replied. "It's a bit of an ask."

"It doesn't have to be, Ben," Freya replied. "I'll explain the situation, and who knows, she might even offer to have a look. Then it won't be an ask, will it?"

"Is it even allowed?"

"It's not standard practice, if that's what you mean. But there are no laws stopping her from looking under supervision, and if it helps us with our investigation, then I'm all for it. The worst that can happen is that she doesn't recognise the woman, which means she's at least probably not from Stixwould or the surrounding villages."

"Oh, that's okay then. That just leaves Norfolk, Essex, Sussex, Cornwall, Devon, London, Yorkshire–"

"Don't be facetious, Ben. It doesn't suit you."

He climbed out and leaned on the roof.

"Two bodies. Two separate crimes," he said, positioning what he said the previous night as his final standpoint.

"Two bodies. Somehow linked."

"There's a lot at stake."

"The reward will be worth it," she said. "Not to see you naked, of course. But to have you wait on me hand and foot for an entire evening would be an absolute delight." Freya closed her door and headed towards the hospital. She turned to look over her shoulder as Ben locked the car. "I'm sure the girls will love it too."

"Girls?" he said, and ran the few steps to catch her up. "What girls? You didn't mention anything about girls."

"I know. But you didn't mention anything about there being *no* girls."

"What girls?" he said. "I'm not bloody prancing around butt naked–"

"You'll have an apron."

"I'm not waiting on a bunch of you all night long. Naked or not, Freya. No bloody chance."

"I'm not saying you need to wait on us all. Just me. The girls will be there for the show."

"You bloody crook."

"Besides, what have you got to worry about?" she said, as the automatic doors switched open. "You're positive it's two separate crimes. How confident are you?"

"Well, pretty confident. But still..."

"Ah, so not so confident, then."

"The bet's off," he said. "The deal is that I cook dinner and wait on you all night, or vice versa. Or should I invite the boys round?"

"If that's what makes you happy?"

"So you'd be happy with Rob, Squawk, and Snowy all leering at your backside as you bring me dinner, would you?"

"Not really. But it won't come to that, will it?"

"Eh?"

"If you win the bet, somehow, and I have to cook you dinner–"

"Naked."

"With an apron. I know for a fact that you're too gentlemanly to invite others round to see. In fact, I'd be surprised if *you* even looked at my backside. Me, on the other hand? I'd have absolutely no problem at all enjoying a nice meal while my girlfriends watch you coming to and fro with your little backside hanging out. They'd love it."

"Hang on. You don't have any girlfriends up here. You only know me, and the team..." He paused as soon as he said it. "No. Not Jackie, Chapman, and Anna."

"They would very much enjoy seeing you prance around semi-naked," she said. "Feeling confident still?"

"Not really, no."

"Good."

They entered the long corridor that led them to the mortuary. It always struck Freya that the corridor seemed like a complete waste of space. It gave the visitor time to reflect on loved ones, which wasn't always ideal when they were about to ID a body, and it gave Freya time to think about Doctor Bell, or Pip, as was her preference, and that usually filled her with dread.

She hit the buzzer and waited, glancing at Ben, who was clearly in a bit of a quandary about the bet he'd so readily engaged in.

"Game face on," she whispered when she heard the internal door opening.

Doctor Pippa Bell spoke with a strong Welsh accent. She was naturally beautiful, tainted only by her passion for brightly-coloured hair and a face full of piercings. Freya tried to recall what colour her hair had been the last time she had seen her, as she seemed to enjoy it when Freya commented on a new colour. But in the four previous investigations Freya had worked on during her time in Lincolnshire, the pathologist had a different colour each time.

Bright green was the spring choice apparently. She looked like Grotbags from a kids TV show Freya had watched as a child.

"Well, well... If it isn't the dynamic duo. Lincolnshire's Cagney and Lacey, I see."

"They were both women," Freya said, and Pip rolled her eyes at Ben.

"Morning, Pip," he said.

"I suppose you're here for the young girl in the pretty dress?"

"We are, yes," he replied.

"Shame. Maybe I should start wearing dresses." She eyed Ben suggestively, then laughed and headed into the reception. "Come on," she said. "You know where the gowns and masks are. I'll see you inside in a mo."

She slipped through the insulated double doors.

"I should invite her as well," Freya said. "Now that's somebody who would appreciate seeing you naked."

Ben pulled two gowns and two masks from the little cupboard where they were stored and tossed her one of each. The throw wasn't great and she made no attempt to catch them. Instead, they fell to the floor in a heap.

"DI Standing," he replied, knowing full well that not only would Detective Inspector Steve Standing, Freya's adversary within the force, be more than happy to watch Freya dressed in just an apron, but that Freya would never ever forgive Ben for inviting him to do so.

The doors opened with a swish behind Freya and Doctor Bell stood there, her expression that of a bemused school teacher at her wit's end.

"Bickering, are you? Never stop, do you?" she said. "I haven't got all day, you know? I've got a viewing in thirty minutes."

"Yes, I know, Doctor Bell," Freya replied. "It was me who arranged the viewing."

"Oh, right."

Ben pulled his mask on and tied his gown as he walked into the room, feeling the cold air on his bare skin like he had stepped into another world.

Despite there being half a dozen stainless steel benches available, Doctor Bell usually only had one body out of the fridge at a time. This time, however, there were two mounds beneath two blue sheets on two of the benches.

"Poppy Gray," Doctor Bell said, as Freya came to stand at Ben's side. Even though she was wearing a mask, Ben could tell by her eyes that Freya was still grinning at their amusing little argument. "Asphyxiation."

"Strangled?" Freya said, and those lines around her eyes vanished with her smile. Ben couldn't help but notice that, for her age at least, her skin was smooth, taut, and, dare he think it, youthful. "Or was there some other means?"

"Oh no," Doctor Bell said, adopting her gravest of tones to convey the seriousness of the situation. "The killer used his bare hands."

Carefully, she pulled back the sheet and lay it on Poppy's chest, exposing the girl from her neck up. Incisions had been made from behind both of Poppy's ears to her chest, where they met to form a Y-shape, and from there, a single incision continued under the sheet, and would, Ben knew from experience, stop below her stomach. The cuts had been closed and the sutures were exposed.

"See here, now," the doctor began, as she pulled a pen from her breast pocket and waved a circle above Poppy's throat. "Heavy bruising. She fought. And see here and here," the doctor said, indicating the areas on the side of the girl's neck. "Finger marks. Dead bodies don't bruise."

"Can you tell how big the hands are from those bruises?"

"Not really. There's too much variation in the way the killer might have held her, I'm afraid. However, what I can tell you is the trachea has been compressed. The killer was in front of her. Maybe pinning her down? These marks here at the front? Thumb marks."

"She was found in a ditch."

"Was there room for two people?"

Ben thought back to Michaela lying beside Poppy's body.

"Plenty," he said.

"There you are then, you see."

"Fingernails?" Freya asked.

"I've scraped her and sent it to the lab, same with vaginal swabs, blood, and saliva, and before you go all stupid on me, Ben... No."

"No what?"

"No sign of sexual interference. Not recent anyway."

"What would you call recent?"

"In the past few days. But there was some tearing. Older wounds. But they weren't made yesterday."

"That's interesting," Freya said, nodding as she processed the information.

"Do you have somebody in mind?" Doctor Bell asked. "Sexual, was it?"

"That was one of my theories," Freya said, giving Ben a sideways look, and his confidence in the bet lifted a little.

"She was pretty," Doctor Bell said. "You know, some days I hate my job. I could have been a dentist or a surgeon, and I would never have to know that people like Poppy here die."

"I can't imagine you as anything else," Freya said honestly.

"Oh?"

"I think you're wonderful at what you do."

"Well now," Doctor Bell said, turning her attention to Ben. "Somebody's after one of my special sweets."

"Sweets?" Ben asked.

"For the children. When they're good."

"Children come here?" Ben asked.

"No. But if I were a dentist, I'd have special sweets for them, wouldn't I? Do keep up, Ben," she said, this time rolling her eyes at Freya. "It's a wonder you get through the day with him sometimes, Freya."

"Yes," she agreed, and those wrinkles around her eyes reappeared as she smiled beneath her mask. "It's a wonder indeed."

"Now then," Doctor Bell said, covering Poppy back over and turning on her heels military style. "This one wasn't quite so lucky."

She came to stop on the far side of the next bench and laid her hands on the sheet as if she was connecting on some spiritual level with the body below.

"Our mystery woman."

"Did you have any luck on the fingerprints?"

"No. She was a good girl."

"DNA?"

"DNA? I've only had her a day. Give me a chance, will you? How long do you think it takes? It's not like you see on the films, you know?"

"I know," Freya said. "But I wondered–"

"If I could fast-track it?"

"Yes."

"I have. But you'll still have to wait. Three days minimum, or so I'm told," she said, then returned to her calm posture. "Asphyxiation."

"Again?" Ben said, cocking his head to one side to listen carefully. He felt his stomach churn at the idea of Freya being right about the murders being linked.

"Crushed larynx," Doctor Bell stated, as a matter of fact. "This one fought hard. Harder than Poppy. Like she had something worth fighting for."

"Are you suggesting that Poppy didn't have anything to fight for?" Freya asked.

"Poppy had everything to fight for. She just didn't fight as hard. She was much weaker than her killer. But this one. Oh no. She gave him everything she had." She pulled the sheet down to reveal the Y-section that had been stitched back into place. Pip raised one of the woman's hands. "See these grazes? She was alive when those happened."

"I need to know who she was, Doctor," Freya said.

But Doctor Bell ignored her and produced her pen from her breast pocket once more. She circled the air above the woman's knees.

"Post mortem," she said, louder than anything else she had said that day, as if she was calling her professional opinion out to a distant audience, or perhaps just to get Freya's attention, who was staring at Ben with those laughter lines around her eyes.

"Sorry?" Freya said. "You're saying the grazes on the knees happened after death occurred?"

"I am. A conundrum, isn't it?"

"It is," Freya said. "But what about the strangulation?"

"Well, if you wait just one minute, I'll get to that," Doctor Bell replied, putting Freya effortlessly back in her box and circling the area around the woman's groin. "No sexual interference, Ben."

He nodded, embarrassed that the doctor felt she had to make the point to prevent Ben from asking the question.

"Now then, Detective Inspector Bloom..." The doctor circled the air around bruises on both sides of the neck again, and then a faint bruise at the front. "Deeper bruises, aren't they?"

Freya nodded and Doctor Bell waited for Ben to agree. He nodded his agreement.

"Want to know why?" she asked.

"I presumed you would tell us?" Ben said.

"And I will," she said, moving around to stand behind Ben. She put her hands on his neck and groped for position. "Feel my thumbs, Ben, do you? In the back of your neck?"

"Yes," he said, his voice a hoarse whisper.

"Different MO," she said, and she released him, then returned to her spot. "Then we have the injury to her face."

"I was wondering if you'd noticed," Freya said.

"Hard to miss, isn't it?" she said. "One blow. One hard blow with something blunt, curved, and hard."

"A hammer?"

"No, too small. The radius of the blow is at least six inches. Could be more. Something larger than a hammer."

"The bumper of a car?" Freya suggested.

"Oooh," Doctor Bell said with a smile. "The front of a car. Now there's a good one. But the fact remains."

"The fact remains what?" Ben asked, a little confused.

"Different MO."

"Different killer?" Ben asked.

Doctor Bell looked between them, then settled on Freya. "Could be."

"Could be, or is likely?" Ben said.

"Poppy was overpowered. She was strangled from the front. Our mystery woman here was attacked from behind. Our mystery woman was hit by something large and hard, could be a car. Could be something else. Who knows?"

"If you had to put money on it," Ben said.

"Like if you had a bet, or something," Freya added.

"What would you say?" Ben asked.

Doctor Bell smiled. She was intuitive, smart, and didn't suffer fools. She saw through their questions and drew her own conclusion.

"If I had to bet?" she asked.

"Yeah, you know?" Ben said. "If you had to follow a particular lead."

"Then I'd say they were killed by two people," she said, and Ben couldn't help but smile. Then the doctor added, just for good measure, "Or one killer who is still learning. Someone who hasn't quite got it right yet."

"Someone who hasn't got it right yet?" Freya said, like she was toying with the words. She looked at Ben. "But may strike again."

"Or two killers?" Ben said.

"Thank you, Doctor Bell," Freya said. "We'll wait in reception for our guest. I imagine you'll need some time to prepare."

CHAPTER NINETEEN

THEY SAID THE GUEST HOUSE WAS DECREPIT BUT THE BUILDING DC Anna Nillson was looking at wasn't far off the old Tulholme Abbey ruins a couple of miles away. She could get her fingers into the cracks that ran through the walls and, in places, her entire hand could have fit through the rotten window frame.

It was a shambles, and whoever paid to stay there, whether that be for one night, two, or for however long, should be pulled to one side and introduced to something called the internet. Anna knew of at least a dozen local Airbnb hosts offering anything from little, wooden shacks in secluded parts of their properties to full two-bedroom houses to rent.

Two uniforms accompanied her, waiting on the drive in case Harringer decided to bolt.

She had to make this count. During her first three years of working in major investigations, she had been under DI Steve Standing, who had claimed every arrest worthy of record, regardless of which member of the team had put in the hard work. But since his transfer to Lincoln HQ, she had been working under DI Bloom, and now was her chance to get a solid arrest on file.

Anna rang the bell. It wasn't a homely bell – a nice, pleasant *ding dong*. It was more of an angry buzz, loud and offensive. Through the glass, she saw a figure approaching the door and she readied her warrant card. It was a man who appeared to be in his sixties or seventies but hadn't slept since his forties. Dark rings framed his bloodshot eyes, and there was enough room in the bags beneath them for a week's supply of sleeping pills. His shoulders sagged like he was carrying the weight of the world and his expression suggested that he was expecting bad news but it might finish him off.

"Mr Gray?" she began, flashing him her warrant card. "I'm Detective Constable Anna Nillson. I'm looking for one of your guests. A Mr Harringer?"

"Oh, I see. Thought you'd be back." He stepped to one side and held the door open.

"Is he here?"

He flicked his eyes up to his left, gesturing at the stairs. "Heard him banging around this morning. Missed breakfast though. Not like him."

"I need to go up and speak to him. Is that okay?"

"I've got other guests."

"We'll be as quiet as we can," Anna said, and gestured for the two uniforms to follow her.

"He's in room five. He always has room five. It's up the stairs on the right," he advised. "Should I come?"

"Perhaps it's best if you stay here, Mr Gray. I'll find you if I need anything."

"I see," he said sadly.

"I'm sorry for your loss, sir," Anna offered, making it clear they weren't completely heartless. "Is your wife around?"

"No. No, she's gone to..." He paused, searching the room for a distraction, then let his eyes fall back to the black and white tiled floor. "She's gone to see my daughter. I couldn't face it, I'm afraid."

"It's not easy, sir. Is there anything we can do to help?"

"No. No, just catch the bastard that did it. That's what you can do," he said, and the use of the word *bastard* seemed alien coming from such a gentle man.

"We're doing everything we can."

"I suppose you want another statement from him, do you?" he said, as Anna was halfway up the broad staircase. She peered down at him. It would have given her great pleasure to announce that Harringer was their lead suspect in the second murder investigation, and that there was a chance he was also responsible for Poppy's death. But there were protocols. There were ways of doing things that often frustrated Anna.

"I just need to ask him a few questions."

"I see," he said, eyeing the two uniforms behind her. "Are they here in case he doesn't talk?"

In another situation, the comment may have been humorous. But neither Anna nor Mr Gray were in the mood for humour.

"You'd be surprised what people do when they're upset, sir," she replied, and then ascended the remaining stairs.

"That's it, turn right at the top," he advised her, as if she might get lost. "The door will be in front of you."

There was one door on the right marked by a brass number five. With the uniforms behind her, she knocked. Three raps, hard and distinct. "Mr Harringer?"

She waited, listening for movement. There was none.

"Mr Harringer, it's DC Nillson. I have a few questions about your stolen car."

She glanced back at the uniforms, who gestured they too could hear nothing from inside. So she knocked again.

"Mr Harringer, are you in there?"

Eyeing the first uniform, a man named Griffiths, she started imagining the worst.

"Is Gray down there still?"

Griffiths turned, looked down the stairs then back at Anna, and nodded.

"Mr Gray, do you have a key for this room, please?"

"Of course, but we don't usually go in when the rooms are occupied–"

"Mr Gray, may I please have the key or can you open this door?"

She moved from the doorway and came to stand at the top of the stairs, finding Gray making his way up slowly, using the handrail to steady himself.

"If he's not there, maybe you should come back. He's a private man," the ageing landlord said as he neared the top, breathless from the effort.

Anna retrieved a folded piece of paper from her breast pocket, unfolded it, and presented it to Mr Gray.

"It's a warrant for his arrest, Mr Gray, and to search the room. I'm sorry, I didn't want to give you any more stress after what you're going through."

"Arrest?" he said. "But he's a victim. It was his car..."

His voice cracked and he held onto the handrail as if he might topple at any moment.

"I'm sorry, but we have good reason. Can you open the door, please?"

He stared at her, then squinted and read the printed warrant she was holding out. Finally, he nodded.

"I see," he said, and he edged sideways to get past the now crowded space. He fumbled for his keys. It was a small bunch, Anna thought, for such a large house with so many locks.

"Is that a master key?" she asked, more out of interest than anything else.

He gave it a twist, then pulled it out, and stepped back. "Opens every door in this house," he said. "I've been here longer than I care to remember. Decades. That's the third time I've ever had to use it."

"Well, let's hope you don't need to use it anymore," Anna replied, with her hand on the handle making it clear that she wouldn't go in until he had stepped back and the uniforms were ready behind her.

They shuffled into place and Gray waited on the landing behind them. Only when she was happy he was out of harm's way did Anna give the brass handle a twist, and push the door open.

The room was much like Anna had imagined it to be. The same hideous, floral-patterned wallpaper covered the walls, and the same worn and tired carpet covered the floor. The light switch was Formica, yellowed and cracked, and aside from the fire escape instructions, the framed pictures on the walls were what she expected to find in the storeroom of a charity shop – the sort people put up to fill a space, rather than because they enjoyed the images. The curtains were thick, heavy, and the colour of red wine, and the furniture had already been old and out of fashion when Queen Elizabeth had been crowned. In fact, the only things in the room that had been bought new in this century were the bedsheets, which were bright white in comparison to the ageing decor, and the only thing missing from the room was the guest.

And his belongings.

Anna strode through to the ensuite, glanced inside, and felt the damp in the air, hot and musty.

"He's gone," she announced, stepping over to the window. She pulled one of the curtains back and stared out at the fields opposite the house, then instructed the uniforms. "Get on the radio. He doesn't have a car."

"Gone?" Mr Gray said, stepping inside, as Anna searched the fields for movement and looked up the road as far as the window would allow.

"There's no belongings here. The wardrobe is open and empty, the bathroom is empty. He's gone, Mr Gray. The question is why, when my colleague told him not go anywhere."

"Perhaps he had to get back. He has a family, you know."

"His car was also involved in a hit and run accident," she said, as a little, red Fiesta ambled by on the road outside. She studied the passengers and the driver – a female with two children in the back. The car pulled to one side of the road, then the driver flashed the lights once. The reason became clear moments later when a single-decker bus squeezed through the space between the hedge that bordered the field and the woman's car. Again, Anna searched the passengers through the large side windows, but none fitted Harringer's description. "You said he was here this morning. How long ago?"

Mr Gray shrugged. "Twenty minutes ago. The wife's out, like I said."

"Where's the nearest bus stop?"

"Bus stop?" he said, then pointed in the direction the bus was travelling.

Anna turned to Griffiths. "Stop that bus."

"He doesn't use the bus," Mr Gray said, as the two uniforms darted from the room and bundled down the stairs. Anna followed, then stopped in the doorway to give Mr Gray one last piece of advice.

"Don't clean this room. Leave it exactly as it is."

Then she ran. She took the steps two at a time, ran through the open front door, and leaped down the few steps. The liveried car with the two uniforms sped from the drive as she started her own car, and they hit the sirens, waking the sleepy village. She followed as fast as her little Toyota would allow, hoping they would catch the bus before it turned off the lane.

She rounded a bend too fast, venturing onto the grass verge, and a lady on a push bike coming in the other direction shook her head. Anna could hear the sirens in the distance and knew she would catch them soon, hopefully before they stopped the bus. She wanted to be the one to stare down at him, to read him his rights, and she wanted to be the one to hand him over to the custody sergeant. She slowed for the next bend and the tyres skidded a little on the loose gravel, but she held it, and when she emerged on the other side, she saw the reassuring flashing blues of the police Astra and the bright, red brake lights on the back of the bus. It was stopping.

Griffiths pulled the Astra in front of the bus, a textbook manoeuvre to stop the vehicle from speeding off. Where they had stopped, however, the bus was blocking the entire lane. Thankfully, there were no other vehicles coming, not yet. But if they hung around too long and oncoming traffic started to build up, they might have to start asking drivers to reverse up the road, never a good place to be in on fast country lanes.

She pulled up behind the bus, put her hazard lights on, and climbed from the car. The doors hissed open from the front and halfway down the bus, and Anna stepped on, flashing her ID to the driver. Then she turned to face the bewildered passengers. An old man with a little dog on his lap was nearest the front, dozing, and probably not even aware of what was happening. Two elderly ladies with concerned looks on their faces sat side by side halfway down, while nearer the back a handful of school kids started asking questions. But it was a gentleman who sat four rows from the back that caught Anna's interest. Having only a description of Harringer from Gillespie, she eyed him, and he averted his eyes, feigning interest in the world outside. He held onto the handrail of the seat in front, and Anna caught the shine of a wedding ring.

"Mr Harringer?" she asked, and slowly, he turned to face her. His eyes darted to the open rear doors, then back at her, and she felt a smile creep onto her face, daring him to try it.

He took the dare. Leaving his bag, he pulled himself up using the handrail in front for purchase and launched himself from the seat. In an instant, Anna was moving. He leaped out of the open door, landing on the grass verge, and less than a second later, Anna followed suit, rugby tackling him down to the grass.

The school kids roared with delight. Griffiths and his partner ran to her aid, and when she sat up with her knee pressed into Harringer's back, they cuffed him. It was a smooth operation.

Textbook, even. One that the school kids would remember for sure.

"Roy Harringer, I'm arresting you on suspicion of murder. You do not have to say anything, but it may harm your defence if you fail to mention something you later rely on in court. Anything you do say may be given as evidence. Do you understand?"

"I haven't done anything."

"I'll take that as a yes, then," she said, and she let the two men haul him to his feet before grabbing Harringer's bag from the bus. "Sorry about the disruption, everybody," she announced.

"Is he a murderer?" the schoolboys asked, eyes wide with excitement.

Entering into a conversation with the kids would be a recipe for disaster, so she thanked the driver for stopping then oversaw Harringer being loaded into the back of the Astra.

"I'll meet you at the station, Griffiths. I want to book him in," she called, then positioned herself to stare at Harringer through the rear window. "This bastard's mine."

CHAPTER TWENTY

As was the case with many hospital mortuaries, Freya found the room that was used to present the deceased to family to be less restful than it was clinical. But it was private, and through the use of partition curtains, they were able to give both Poppy Gray and the mystery woman a space of their own.

The makeshift chapel of rest was through a door in the reception, where Ben and Pip were talking. She left the two bodies, each covered with a clinical, blue sheet, and joined them.

"Thank you, Doctor Bell. It's the perfect little spot."

"We usually use the hospital's chapel of rest. But logistically, it's a bit of a nightmare."

"I think you've done a fine job, thank you."

"Just give me a shout when your guest arrives," Doctor Bell said. She had removed the smock she usually wore, and to Freya's horror, she was walking around in a pair of jeans with more holes in them than actual fabric, a faded Led Zeppelin t-shirt, and a pair of pink Crocs on her feet.

"Thank you, Doctor Bell," Freya replied. "I forgot to mention, by the way. Your hair. The green suits you."

"Matches my eyes, don't you think?" The doctor beamed.

Leaning a little closer to her, Freya gazed into the doctor's eyes. They *were* green. How had she never noticed that before?

"That's odd," Freya said. "I've never noticed you have green eyes."

"I don't. They're contacts. My real eyes are different."

"Yes well, I imagine they would be."

"No, I mean different, different. This one's blueish," she said, pointing to her left eye. "And this one's more of a grey-slash-hazel. Depends on the light."

Freya was about to raise the point that Doctor Bell had dyed her hair green to match her coloured contact lenses, or something to that effect, when Ben, who was standing behind Doctor Bell, gave her a look that screamed, *Just stop. Don't even go there.*

"It suits you," Freya said, with a practised smile. "I like it."

"Well, that's good to know. I'll inform my fashion adviser."

"Your fashion adviser?" Freya said, kicking herself for prolonging the conversation. Ben rolled his eyes in the background, shaking his head in despair.

"My mum," the doctor said with a smile. "Bless her. She comes up with these looks, you see. These ideas. And, well, it's not like *she* can go about with green hair and whatnot, is it? So I try them for her. I'm her model."

"How lovely," Freya replied. "But why can't your mum dye *her* hair? If that's what she wants to do, then she should do it. Who cares what other people think."

"But who'd see it? What would be the point?"

"Everyone. Everyone who saw her on the street, in the shops, wherever. It's a statement, and you carry it well. I'm sure she would too."

"In the shops? On the street?"

Ben shook his head and ran a finger across his throat.

"You do know, don't you?" Doctor Bell said.

"Know what? Am I missing something?"

The doctor stared at Freya as if she had just insulted her family in the gravest way possible.

"She's dying of cancer. Has been for some years now."

"Oh my god, I'm so sorry, Pip," Freya said. "May I ask where?"

"All over. Riddled with it, she is. Hasn't a hair on her body. I suppose she could get a green wig, but who'd see it?"

"That's terrible. So you dye your hair to please her?"

"It makes her smile. Anything I can do to make her smile is a win. No matter how short. She comes up with the looks and then uses it to raise money for her treatment."

"You're incredible, Pip."

"Ah," she said, but the discussion had clearly choked her a little. "Go on with you."

"I mean it. I can't believe you actually dress like that and dye your hair just to please your mum. It's so lovely."

"Dress like what?" Doctor Bell asked. "She doesn't tell me what to wear. I dye my hair for charity. To raise money for her treatment. I pledged to have a different colour hairstyle every month for a year. People love that stuff. Donations coming in from everywhere."

"Oh," Freya said, wishing the ground would open up and swallow her whole. "Then that's even more remarkable."

But the damage had been done.

"What's wrong with what I wear?"

"Absolutely nothing," Freya said. "If that's your thing."

"If what's my thing?"

"The ripped jeans. The faded t-shirt. And..." Freya nodded at the Crocs on her feet, which personally, she deemed as obscene.

"My Crocs?" Doctor Bell said, her voice rising. "What's wrong with them? They're the most comfortable shoes I've ever owned."

"Not really shoes though, are they?" Freya mumbled.

"You stand out there all day on your feet with your hands inside somebody's cavity." She peered down at what Freya was wearing, which just happened to be her new boots, which she was especially happy with. Granted, her feet had been a little sore the previous night, but they were new. New boots took a while to break in. "I suppose you think I should wear those, do you?"

"Well, these might be a little impractical for what you do."

"How much?"

"The boots?"

"Yeah. Eighty? Ninety pound?"

"A little more," Freya said, holding her finger and thumb an inch apart and feeling a little self-conscious.

"A hundred?" the doctor exclaimed, almost disgusted at the thought of spending that much on footwear. "A hundred pounds?"

"Try three," Ben said with a smile, and Freya glared at him.

"Three what? Three hundred?" the doctor said, then turned back to Freya, eyes wide and mouth ajar. "You spent three hundred pounds on those?"

"They're real leather."

"That's even worse."

"Don't tell me you're a vegetarian as well?"

"Vegan, actually."

"Oh, for god's sake. Not another one."

"Not another what?"

"Nothing," Freya said. "Look, all I wanted to say was that your green hair suits you and looks lovely, and somehow we're now discussing dietary choices. Eat what you like, Pip–"

"Doctor Bell," she said. "Only my friends call me Pip."

For some reason, the comment stung a little. Freya had always considered the doctor to be on her side.

"I expect you're busy," Freya said. "I meant no harm. Perhaps we can start again?"

"Perhaps. Another day maybe," she replied, then turned to Ben. "Call me when your guest arrives. I'll handle the viewings so she doesn't go and insult her."

The doctor slipped from the room and went about her business, and Freya slumped into one of the reception room chairs.

"How do you do it?" Ben asked.

"Do what?"

"Manage to upset nearly everyone you meet."

"You know what, Ben? I have no bloody idea."

The sound of heels on a tiled floor could be heard, and Ben peeked through the little window in the door.

"That's her," he said. Then he opened the internal door, and called out to Doctor Bell, "Pip?"

There was no reply and no indication that Doctor Bell had even heard him. So Freya moved to the main doors, spied Izzie Brand walking along the corridor, and opened them just as she arrived.

"Izzie, hi," Freya said, stepping to one side so she could come in. Ben nodded once, smiled briefly, and Izzie glanced around the reception, looking at the pictures and the ceiling, and anything else she could find to avoid eye contact.

"We're just waiting for Doctor Bell," Freya explained. "How was your journey?"

"Ah. You know?" she said. "I don't really remember it. It's been a strange twenty-four hours, Detective..."

"Bloom. Detective Inspector Bloom, and this is Detective Sergeant Savage."

"I'm sorry. I should have remembered."

"Don't worry. I'm sure you have enough on your plate. How is your husband?"

Izzie studied the floor and her feet, the way a scolded child might. Eventually, she found the words, and met Freya's gaze. "Not great. I won't lie."

"Well, hopefully we won't take up too much of your time."

The doors swished open and they all turned to find Doctor Bell standing in the doorway, her hands folded before her, and dressed in a crisp, white smock, minus the trademark pens and glasses she usually carried in her breast pocket. Freya glanced down at her feet, and even the pink Crocs had been replaced with sensible, lace-up shoes.

"Hello, Izzie," she said, her voice low and sombre. "I'm Doctor Bell. I'll be right there with you. Have you been offered tea or coffee?"

"No, actually."

"Perhaps you'd like a tea before we go through–"

"No. No, it's fine, thank you. I'd like to get it over with. If you get my meaning?"

"Of course," said Doctor Bell. "Would you follow me?"

The doctor led Izzie through to the next room, and just as Freya was about to follow, Ben caught her arm and gestured he would stay in the reception, which was probably a good idea as it would be a little overcrowded in the next room.

Freya followed the two women and closed the door behind her. Doctor Bell glanced up at her, then at Izzie.

"Take your time," she said. "Are you ready?"

Izzie nodded and Doctor Bell slowly revealed Poppy's face, pulling the sheet down to her chest, where she let it rest neatly.

"Oh, my poor girl," Izzie said. "Oh, my dear, dear, girl."

As if on cue, the doctor offered her a box of tissues and Izzie took one, holding it to her eyes. A few moments of silence passed and Izzie's expression never faltered. She wore the face of a grieving parent, regardless of the relationship.

"It's her," she said finally, and reached out to touch Poppy's forehead, but stopped, and looked at the doctor.

"It's okay. It helps sometimes," the doctor said.

Izzie touched her tentatively. Then she developed a little more courage, and lay her hand on Poppy's hair.

"He should have come," she said. "He'll regret it. I know he will."

"We can arrange another viewing," Freya said. "Will that be okay, Doctor Bell?"

"Of course," she replied, once more adopting a solemn expression, and even throwing in something between a nod and a bow.

Izzie gave her step-daughter one more look, stroked her hair tenderly, then pulled away and put her hand in her pocket, signalling she was done.

"Would you like a few minutes alone?" Freya asked, but Izzie shook her head.

"I've said my goodbyes," she said softly. "Thank you."

Doctor Bell replaced the sheet and Izzie's demeanour altered the moment Poppy was recovered. She exhaled, wiped her eyes, then took a step toward the doors and pushed her way out into the reception.

"I'll take good care of her," Doctor Bell stated, and Izzie gave her an appreciative nod.

"I know," she said. "But you shouldn't have to. She shouldn't be here in the first place."

CHAPTER TWENTY-ONE

Back in the reception, Ben stood as soon as he heard the doors open and smiled warmly when Izzie came through. Freya followed, feeling less than excited about the next few minutes than she had been before the chat about Doctor Bell's hair. She coughed once to clear her throat.

"Izzie, thank you so much for coming," she began. "I wanted to speak to you about something. Now is not an ideal time, but please hear me out. What I have to say is important."

Izzie stared between Freya and Ben, then settled on Freya.

"What is it?" she whispered.

"We believe Poppy stole Mr Harringer's car."

"You told me. I don't believe it. No, I *can't* believe it," she said. "But the facts are the facts, I suppose."

"I'm afraid it's worse than that. We searched the car at the scene, Izzie."

"Okay," she replied, visibly uneasy.

"We found somebody in the boot. A body."

"Oh my god," she whispered, pressing the palm of her hand against her chest. "Who?"

"We don't know. We were wondering if Poppy had an argument with anybody recently."

"An argument? Poppy? No. Was it a man?"

"A female. We believe whoever killed Poppy might be responsible for her death too."

"And you don't know who it is?"

"We were hoping you might have been able to help us there. We wondered if you'd heard anything. But not to worry–"

"She's here, isn't she?" Izzie said, and she peered back into the small room where she had shared a final moment with Poppy. "Behind the other curtain. I'm right, aren't I?"

Freya nodded.

"And you want me to look at her? You want me to tell you if I recognise her?"

"It crossed my mind, Izzie. But we felt it wasn't right to ask of you. With what you're going through–"

"No," she said, reading something in Freya's eyes. "I'll do it. If it helps you find whoever did this. I'll do it."

"Are you sure? It's a big ask, Izzie."

"Positive. If she's local, I'll know her. I want to help."

Freya turned to Ben. "Would you mind seeing if Doctor Bell could accommodate this?"

"Sure," Ben said, going along with the charade. Freya felt a slight pang of guilt at her underhand methods, but it was for the greater good, and it was times like these she forced herself to recall the far more questionable methods she had used to get results in the past.

It took less than ten seconds for Ben to enter the room, give Doctor Bell the nod, and for the curtain around Poppy's bay to be closed and the one around the unknown woman to be pulled open.

"We're ready," he said, holding the door open.

"You're sure?" Freya asked Izzie.

"I want him caught."

"In that case..." Freya said, sweeping her hand towards the room from which they had just come.

"Hello again," Doctor Bell said, a little less stiffly than before. "I must warn you that her attack was more brutal than Poppy's."

"Brutal?"

"She has a facial injury."

"Oh," Izzie said, and looked to Freya. "Thank you for the warning."

Carefully, Doctor Bell pulled back the sheet, again letting it fall neatly on the woman's chest.

"Oh dear," Izzie whispered. "The poor thing."

Interestingly, she didn't reach out to touch her. She gazed down with sorrowful eyes but kept her hands firmly in her pockets.

"Do you recognise her, Izzie?" Freya asked softly.

She shook her head. "She's not local. Not from Stixwould anyway. Not that I know."

"Thank you," Freya said, keen for Doctor Bell to cover the woman.

"But she has a family?"

"At this stage, I'm afraid we don't know anything about her," Freya said.

"I'm sorry I can't be more helpful."

"That's fine. It was lovely of you to offer. It's not an easy thing to do, is it?" Freya said, as Doctor Bell replaced the sheet.

They stepped back out into the reception and Izzie walked over to the main doors, pulling them open in her own little world. She turned back, as if remembering her manners.

"Thank you," she said, then lowered her head and disappeared back into the lengthy corridor.

"Two bodies. Two crimes," Ben said, hoping to raise Freya's spirits. But she just smiled briefly at the comment.

"Would you mind if I just had a word with Doctor Bell before we go?" she asked. "Alone."

Ben smiled, stretched, clicked his shoulder, and nodded. "Damage repair?" he asked, as he dropped into one of the chairs.

"Something like that," Freya replied, and she opened the door to the little room where they had left her. Doctor Bell was in the process of wheeling the unknown woman into her workspace via a door at the back of the room.

"Doctor Bell?" Freya said, as she let the reception door close. She checked to make sure Ben wasn't listening in at the door. "I was wondering if I could talk to you about your hair?"

"Is this the final insult?" Doctor Bell asked. "The final stab in the back?"

"I'd like to make up for my earlier mistake," Freya said.

"Go on."

"Your charity. I'd like to help."

CHAPTER TWENTY-TWO

THERE WERE SIRENS IN THE DISTANCE BUT CLOSE BY, AND DS Gillespie stood at the doors to Mrs Frost's home wondering if Anna had encountered any trouble. She was just the other side of the village going after Harringer. By rights, Harringer should have been his arrest. But he knew boys like Grant. And this was where he felt he could make a difference.

He rang the doorbell then stepped back to stare up at the window, through which he thought he had seen movement while he walked up the path.

The door opened and a plump lady opened the door, wiping her hands on a tea towel. She looked at him expectantly, waiting for him to introduce himself. So he flashed her his warrant card and her expression sank as if her face was made of goo.

"DS Gillespie, ma'am. I'm here to see Grant Sayer."

"You'd better come inside then, dear," she said. Then she called up the stairs, "Grant, dear, there's a man here to see you."

No reply came, so the woman turned to Gillespie.

"You can go on up if you want. It's the white door at the front of the house. You can't miss it."

"I'll wait," Gillespie replied.

"Wait?"

It took a few moments of silence, and for a brief moment, Gillespie thought his plan had backfired. But then he heard the sounds of grunting and struggling from outside. He opened the front door and found the uniform he had positioned there grappling with a lad matching Grant Sayer's description.

"Aye, lad. Boss said you'd try to run." He turned back to the lady, who clutched at her collars and wore a troubled expression. "Is this Grant Sayer?"

She offered him a bitter glare. "You know full well it is."

"Is there somewhere I can have a wee chat with him?" Gillespie asked, then peered past her into the house. The faces of two small children stared back at him from the kitchen doorway. "In private?"

"You won't hurt him? He's sensitive."

"Aye, I know all about him, Mrs Frost. It's just a chat. Man to man."

"You can use his room. He'll be comfortable in his own space. That's where the counsellor usually speaks to him. It's his safe place."

Gillespie spoke directly to the wide-eyed boy in the uniform's grasp. "Maybe it's time you and I had wee chat, Grant." He nodded toward the house. "I'll take it from here," he said to the uniform.

"Aren't you going to take him away?" the lady said, as Gillespie pushed the boy through the door. "Like last time?"

"He's done nothing wrong, Mrs Frost," Gillespie replied. "Though to look at him you'd think he was as guilty as sin itself. Relax, sonny. I'm on your side."

The boy stared at him, his expression a mix of fear and bitterness. Though the bitterness wasn't aimed directly at Gillespie. It was far broader than that. Society, maybe? Anybody outside his circle? The world, even.

"Up the stairs," Gillespie told the boy, in as friendly a voice as he could muster. Then, before he followed him, he turned to Mrs Frost. "Mine's a tea. One sugar," he said with a wink. "And make it a big one."

In the safety of his room, Grant dropped into the corner where his single bed had been pushed against two walls. He pulled one of the pillows up to his chest and brought his knees up to hold it there, hugging himself and refusing to look Gillespie in the eye.

"You okay, Grant?" Gillespie said softly. "Listen, I'm not here to hurt you. I'm not here to arrest you. I'm here because I need your help, sonny."

Grant said nothing. He didn't even look Gillespie's way.

"Do you mind if I sit?" Gillespie asked, and he perched himself on a little chair beside a computer desk. "Listen, son. I know you don't say much, and I'm not going to make you speak. Not if you don't want to. But if I say something and it's upsetting you, you show me, okay? You show me if something I say touches a nerve, and I'll stop right there. Like I said, I'm on your side."

Grant's eyes darted to Gillespie for the briefest of moments, then returned to a bookcase. Gillespie followed his gaze, studying the books. It was mostly fiction and ranged from action adventure books set in places like Africa to crime novels set in Britain. Gillespie recognised a few. There was a series set in Yorkshire, just north of Lincolnshire, one set in Scotland, and one set in Wales. A few other books were dotted about among the series, but as a habitual reader, Gillespie was impressed with the collection.

"You're friends with Poppy, Grant," he said, not as a question, but as an opener to gauge Grant's reaction. But there was no reaction. Not a hair moved on the boy's head. "Grant, I've got some bad news for you. I'm sorry to be the one to tell you, but we found her body yesterday. She's dead."

If he had been made of stone, he would have moved more.

The only sign that he had even heard Gillespie say those words was the glint of moisture that formed in his eyes.

"I'm sorry, mate. Really, I am. It's a terrible thing to lose someone. I'm told you were best friends. Thick as thieves, they said. That's why I need your help. I need you to help me catch whoever did it."

With no reaction from the boy, Gillespie glanced around the room. There were no posters on the walls and no dirty laundry on the floor. There were no computer games or consoles, or whatever they were called these days. There was nothing to suggest this was a kid at all, except his age. He'd been forced to grow up fast, and the sentiment resonated with Gillespie.

"I heard you got yourself into a wee bit of bother. A fight or something?" Gillespie said, hoping to stir some kind of reaction. Anything would be useful. "I heard it was because Poppy met somebody. Is that right, Grant? Nod if you want."

Grant did not nod.

"I know how you feel. I fancied a girl for years when I was a lad. Absolute crushed me when she met somebody else. Someone older and who had a job, which meant he had money. What was I to do? Little Jimmy with nothing in his pockets except a spent tissue and a boiled sweet I'd pinched from the shop. Don't tell anyone about the sweet, though. That's between you and me."

Adding humour into the mix didn't stir any kind of reaction at all. The lad was rock solid. Impenetrable.

"Anyway... It didn't last. Between them, I mean. She came back to me. Friends, like, nothing else. But she came back. Aye, it's tough being young. Best thing I did was to get old. Now I'm old, I wish I had my time all over again. I'd show him, if I did. I'd show her too," Gillespie said, then heard himself venturing onto a tangent. "Anyway, what does all that matter? The fact is that you did show him. I mean, aye, you'll have to face what's coming, but if you ask me, you've no previous offences, you'll get off just fine. Slapped wrist. Maybe a fine. But as long as the boy's alive and not disfigured, you'll be grand. He is okay, isn't he?"

Grant's eyes darted to Gillespie and back to the row of books. Then he did something new. He nodded. Once. Slight. But it was a nod.

"You'll be fine," Gillespie said, to close off the conversation. He settled into the chair, pulled his leg up onto his knee, and leaned on the desk.

"It's a pretty nice house, eh? I mean, I've seen a thousand worse. Looks like you fell on your feet. The old lady is pretty sweet too. She's got her arm around you, son. She wouldn't let anything harm you. You know, when I was a kid, and I mean a kid, a baby, my parents decided they weren't ready for me. I haven't a clue what I did wrong. Nothing any other baby wouldn't have done, I'm sure, but I was too much for them. Packed me off to a place like this. A home. It was dire. A right hole in the arse end of Glasgow. I was there until I was six or seven or something. Then they decided they didn't want me. That's where it all began. My journey. From one home to another, then another. Always the new boy. Always the butt of the jokes. Ah, it's all history now, like. But it was hard. I mean, real hard. Stuff happened I'll take to my grave with me. Nobody needs to know about it. Found myself in bother most days in the hope that somebody would send me away again. To a new place, you know? Somewhere nice. They did send me away. But it was never anywhere nice. Not like this. Not like Mrs Frost. They were terrible days, Grant. And I used to bottle it all up. Every day, the torment, the abuse, all of it, I'd bottle it all up until the bottle couldn't take any more. Then it would burst, of course. It would burst and spew all the crap I'd bottled up everywhere. It would be carnage, Grant. I'd scream and shout and lash out. I'd break stuff. People too, sometimes. Aye, that did me no good. No good at all."

Grant turned his body to stare at Gillespie. He appraised him, studying Gillespie from his boots up. But he said nothing.

"Did me no good at all, Grant. Best thing I ever did? Turned eighteen," he said, making a cut in the air with the blade of his hand with an accompanying swishing sound. "Got the hell of out there. Glasgow, I mean. Upped and left with just a wee bag and bugger all else. Now look at me."

He looked himself up and down, and noticed the paunch he had been developing over the past few years.

"Aye, well, don't look at me as such. My point is, it gets better, son. You've got it good here. One day, you'll be out there on your own too. You can make a difference to people's lives. Like me. Now, I'm telling you stuff I haven't told anyone in years. Why? Because you need to know it. You need to know there's light at the end of the tunnel. You can turn what's happened into something good. And you can start right now, if you want. If you don't want to, then that's fine. But if you want to help us catch whoever murdered Poppy, then hey, I'm here for you. Nobody needs to know you spoke. I won't tell a soul. You won't have to stand up in court either. There are other ways. But if you do know, kid, if you do know if someone wanted to hurt Poppy, then call me. Text me even, if you don't want to say it. We just need a name."

Gillespie stood and tucked the chair under the desk. From his pocket, he withdrew one of the cards DCI Granger had dished out with Gillespie's name and number on. It even had his email address on – no doubt the reason why he kept receiving emails for Viagra and male enhancement pills.

"You're alright, Grant. You've got a bright future ahead of you," Gillespie said, as he reached for the door. "You can make a difference. Think about that. I'll be back tomorrow. I've got something you might like."

CHAPTER TWENTY-THREE

A few heads turned as the spoon DC Jackie Gold was using to stir her coffee rattled against the mug. That was how quiet it was in the hospital cafeteria. And she wasn't surprised. The cakes were dry and boring, the flapjacks set like concrete after being chewed for a few seconds, and the sandwiches were unbuttered. Who doesn't butter a cheese sandwich? It was the second day she had spent in the cafeteria, and she could navigate her way to it from the main doors with ease now. She could also navigate her way to the Rainforest Ward where Lee Sanders was, and as a result, she felt like a hospital veteran. She had poked her head into Lee's room when she had arrived, but the mother hadn't been there. The nurse said that she'd popped out to get some more bits, as Lee had needed assistance in the night. Jackie was slightly unsure what exactly that meant, but was quite sure it wasn't a good thing.

She had sampled the cakes, flapjacks, and sandwiches, and had decided from that moment on that all she would buy was the stuff the hospital bought in rather than trust the woman behind the counter, Doris, to make herself. Crisps, chocolate bars, and fruit.

Although, so far, there had been more chocolate bars and crisps than fruit.

Coffee was the only other exception, despite how bitter it was. A Starbucks would have been good, but no. Little pop-up cafeterias all seemed to think that women like Doris who, when faced with a queue of three people and was run off her feet, could handle a coffee machine. Somebody in management thought that she could grind coffee, foam milk, and deliver an exceptional latte, despite the fact that she couldn't even be bothered to butter sandwiches. She couldn't multitask either. Talk about letting the side down. While somebody's coffee was being made, she could take the payment, or even ask the next person in the queue what they wanted, but no. She was a one task at a time woman.

And as for the chalkboard that read, 'Our coffee has been hand-selected,' Jackie thought, *From what? A list of one? A selection of sand from B&Q?* She'd had better coffees from the kitchen on the first floor of the station, which was famous for having terrible coffee that came in a jar, labelled simply, *coffee*, with a bar code and some legal stuff in tiny writing.

From where Jackie was seated, in the corner out of the way, she would be able to spot Teresa as she walked by. She thought it was time to really get to know her. The first question on her mind, which she had yet to ask, was if anybody else had ever made the connection to her both being a mother and being called Teresa. There was a joke in there somewhere that Gillespie would nail, but Jackie would probably just somehow make it sound offensive. She just thought it instead. Even the nurse on the reception desk at the Rainforest Ward hadn't picked up on it, when Jackie had said, "I'm looking for Lee's mother, Teresa."

Instead, she had just received a blank expression in return and a shake of the nurse's head.

And that was about the sum of DC Jackie's Gold's great hospital adventure – waiting for a boy with a massive head injury to wake up, to see if he had seen anything.

She opened her laptop, connected to the hospital wi-fi, and began the laborious task of scanning through the missing persons records, shortlisting the names by demographic and region. Thirty to forty years old. Female. Lincolnshire. Missing.

There were three, and the whole exercise had taken her just fifteen minutes. She opened each of the files in separate tabs, then found the photo Chapman had sent through. It was both grim and upside down, and every time Jackie turned her phone up the other way, the display somehow adjusted the image. It took Jackie a good five minutes to find the little button to freeze the orientation of the image, and when she had done it, she wished she hadn't. It was a grim sight.

She had a quick look around to make sure nobody could see her laptop, then memorised the unknown woman's features and opened the first of the three tabs to reveal the first contender. The voice played out in her head like a game show host. *First up, we have Deborah Dickinson!* Thirty-three years old from Boston, and if the photo was anything to go on, she had spent at least fifteen of those thirty-three years either sniffing something or injecting it. It was sad, and Jackie felt for the women who were in those positions, but drugs were a steep spiral, and for some people there was no getting off the ride.

She binned the contestant off, allowing Deborah from Lincolnshire to go home emptyhanded, or as the case was most likely to be, not go home at all.

The next contestant, a slightly larger lady named Elaine, with tattoos reaching up from her chest, across her neck, and disappearing behind her head, also went home emptyhanded.

The third contestant, however, seemed to fit the bill. She was the right age, had the right colour hair, and seemed to be the right build. Joanne Fitzpatrick. She was pretty too, although it was hard to say if the mystery woman had been pretty from the photo. She read the missing report a little more to see if she recognised anything. Joanne Fitzpatrick. Born in Scopwick. Moved to Metheringham. Divorced.

Jackie looked up from her laptop at the oblivious people eating and drinking at the other tables. Doris must be doing something right. Whatever her opinion of the food, people were always eating there. She stared down at the report again and thought about the location. Metheringham was fairly close to Stixwould. Five miles, maybe? It could be her. She carried on reading, her heart racing at the thought of being able to call DI Bloom with the good news.

Was a hairdresser. No tattoos. Transgender.

She read the line again to make sure she had read it correctly.

Yep, it definitely said transgender. Not that somebody's gender identity was a problem for Jackie, but it did pose a few questions. The woman was found wearing a dress, which suggested that she was, indeed, presenting as a woman, as Joanne.

Ben would have said something. He'd seen the body, and the pathologist – the weird girl with the crazy hair and piercings – would have picked up on signs of gender reassignment surgery. If, that was, Joanne had undergone any.

Confused, Jackie closed the lid of her laptop and sat back. She took a sip of her bitter coffee thinking that if all these people kept coming back for more food and coffee, then maybe it was Jackie's tastebuds that were off?

That was when she saw her. Mother Teresa. Although she had to force the name to the back of her mind in case she accidentally let it slip.

"Teresa?" she called, as Lee's mother walked past, her head somewhere far off. Jackie waved to catch her attention, and Teresa found her on the back table, but didn't seem too pleased. "I'll shout you a coffee," Jackie said, seeing the queue of four people all on their phones, clearly wasting away while Doris watched coffee pour through the grounds.

"No need," Teresa said, and she edged her way between the

tables. "I, erm..." She glanced at Doris then back at Jackie before taking the seat opposite and leaning forward to speak quietly. "I'm not a fan of the coffee here, to be honest." She held up her handbag and opened it to reveal a little can of instant. "This is much nicer. There's a kettle on the ward for the nurses. They've been letting me use it."

"I don't blame you," Jackie said, smiling at her and grateful for the company. "How have you been anyway? You holding up, love?"

Teresa nodded and faked a smile. "He had a bad night. Alarms and beeps went off. Nurses rushed in. Then the doctor was called, who said there was nothing wrong with him. Nothing *wrong* with him? Then what are we doing here? And why isn't he running around like he normally is?"

"You gave them what for then?" Jackie asked.

"Yeah, I did. It's not their faults. The nurses, you know? But what's the point of having those machines if some fella from the other side of the hospital has to run over when they go off only to say he's okay. I swear they don't tell me everything. Do you ever get that? Like you're surplus, or... or that because you're not a doctor, you won't understand?"

"I know what you mean–"

"I'm not bloody stupid. That's what gets me. Granted, I don't work in a hospital, but I still went to uni. I can understand what they say when they bloody say it. I tell you. It's like it's a big secret in there and I'm the ugly duckling."

"It's just the way they operate," Jackie said. "I had the same thing with my boy. Not the head injury, mind. But he was sick. And nobody told me what was going on. I was so frustrated. I felt like crying."

"Oh, I know," Teresa said. "I've been here two days now, and I still couldn't tell you exactly what's wrong with Lee, except that he has a noggin the size of a golf ball on his head and he's been asleep. Of course, the sleep is induced. They told me that much."

"Induced?"

"Yeah, they have to do that until he's had all his scans and whatnot. Don't want him running around until they know there's no serious damage. Then there's the bleeding, but they said that's manageable."

"It's a wonder what they do, isn't it?" Jackie said. "I mean, how do they know what's happened inside his head? And if they do find something, it makes you wonder if they'd actually tell you, or just send you both home."

"Oh, I know," Teresa said again. She sat back in the chair, and glanced around her. "It's not just me though, you know? See her over there?" She nodded towards a middle-aged lady who had been there since before Jackie had arrived, and who was so engrossed in her little Sudoku book that she hadn't looked up since, except for when Jackie had stirred her coffee. "She's here every day. Every time I walk past, she's here. I don't even think she's visiting anyone."

"You don't think she just comes here for the coffee, do you?" Jackie suggested, and they both laughed, then settled into an uneasy silence.

"Why are you here, DC...?"

"Gold. Call me Jackie," she said with genuine affection for the woman. She felt like they had connected on some level. Maternal, maybe?

"Why are you here, Jackie?"

"I told you. Lee might have seen something. My boss wants me to be here in case he wakes up," Jackie explained. "The longer the delay after a crime like this happens, the less chance we have of finding them. That's a fact. If Lee remembers something, anything, it might give us half a chance."

"But why you?" Teresa asked, as she flicked a strand of stray hair from her forehead. "Why you in particular?"

Jackie shrugged.

"Don't know, really. I always seem to get these jobs. It's

normally me that has to go and deliver the bad news when somebody dies as well. Not pleasant, let me tell you."

"I can imagine. But you must be good at it. And I think I can see why. Your boss, is he a good boss?"

"She. It's a woman. DI Bloom. She's lovely. Don't get me wrong, I wouldn't want to cross her. She's up from London. Moved here last year. There was a bit of resistance at first. But we soon got used to her. She's awesome. Really knows how to bring a team together."

"I imagine she clocked you for being the gentle type right away," Teresa said. "That's a good thing, by the way. Not an insult."

"I know. Yeah, you're right. I'm not really one for the arguments. I find talking to people far more effective. I guess it's who I am," Jackie mused. "How about you? You said you were a nurse."

"HR," she said, then leaned forward again so as not to be overheard. "It's like being a mum to two hundred kids you don't love."

"They okay with you being off work?"

"Yeah, they're great. Very supportive."

Another one of those silences crept in, and after a few moments, Teresa collected her bag, which she raised up for Jackie to see. "I bought a few books to read. I should probably go and see how he's doing."

"Not that they'll tell you much, right?"

She smiled a smile that wasn't really a smile, and Jackie returned the sentiment.

"I'll be here," Jackie said. "I'll just finish my delicious coffee and I'll stick my head in before I go."

"Thank you, Jackie. It's been lovely talking to somebody. It can get quite lonely."

Jackie fished in her handbag for a card. She usually had one or two floating around in there, along with all her other junk. She found one and slid it across the table.

"Call me," she said. "If you want to, that is. It's nice to have other mums to talk to."

Teresa smiled at the gesture and collected the card from the table. "I might just do that."

CHAPTER TWENTY-FOUR

It was late afternoon by the time Freya and Ben got back to the station. They climbed the fire escape stairs in silence then entered the corridor and heard the dull hum of voices and laughter. They stopped, looked at each other, then approached slowly.

Of all the voices they could hear, and all the laughter that filled the spaces between, Gillespie's was the loudest on both counts. But he wasn't just shouting, and he wasn't just laughing, he was hysterical. Taking a door each, Freya and Ben peered through the windows into the incident room and watched in amazement.

Gillespie was doubled over, and if she didn't recognise when he was laughing, Freya would have said he was having some kind of fit. He banged his hand on the table, clutched at his stomach, and issued a wail, telling somebody to, "Just stop. Stop it, will you? You're killing me."

They craned their necks to see what was happening and found both Chapman and Nillson, of all people, with red faces, wiping their streaming eyes with tissues, and Chapman clutching at her bladder as if she was about to wet herself.

The focus of their attention though, as if they had to even

guess, was Detective Constable Cruz. He was standing in the centre of the room; his shirt was torn and untucked, and his trousers bore a dark patch down one of the legs. To top the look off, his hair, which was usually flat and combed forward as if his mother had licked her hand and smoothed it forward before he left for work, was sticking up in all directions. There were dark smears across his face, and Freya thought she saw a trail of blood coming from one of his nostrils. The boy looked like he had been beaten up, electrified, then put out with a fireman's hose.

The team, of course, was offering him their greatest sympathies.

"It's not bloody funny," he stated. "I could have been killed."

But the statement only served to send Gillespie into another round of hysterics. So much so that he dropped to the floor, bleary-eyed, and groped for the nearest chair to rest on.

"Tell me again," Gillespie said when he had collected himself. "This time, I'll try not to laugh."

"Which bit?" Cruz said sulkily.

"Start at the beginning," Chapman called out, clearing her throat and trying to be serious.

"I did what the boss asked. I did a bit of research and found one. You know?"

"A what?" Anna asked, her voice rising in pitch as she held the laughter at bay.

"A prostitute."

They erupted once more.

"Ah listen, if all you're going to do is laugh then I won't bother–"

"No, no, no," Gillespie begged, teasing him back onto the story. "We won't laugh. You found a prostitute. Then what?"

"Well, I found loads. Once I worked out how to find them, I built a list. Thought the boss, would recognise my efforts, and all that. After that, I put them all on a map and worked out a route. Figured I'd go from one to the other without wasting time."

"Very efficient," Gillespie said.

"Well, I thought so. So, I went to the first house, knocked, and suddenly thought to myself, I can't just ask if A, you're a prostitute, and B, are any of your mates missing? So I had to lie a bit. You know. Get in there. Get her talking."

"Go under the covers, you mean?" Anna said, and they all hissed as they tried to control their laughter.

Glancing across at Ben, even he was finding it all very amusing. Freya, however, felt for the poor lad. She'd give it a minute or so then break it up. Thankfully, DCI Granger was out, and Detective Superintendent Harper hadn't been in for weeks.

"So she answered the door. What a mess she was. Drugged up to the eyeballs. Stank of fags and booze. Hair was all over the place. And her makeup? It would have been like paying the joker to lay there and fall asleep. Not only that, everything you can imagine and more was hanging out," he said, eyeing Gillespie. "And I mean, hanging out."

"What did she say?" Chapman asked, not interested in what he saw.

"Well, she kind of leaned on the door frame. Sleazy like. Asked me what I wanted."

"And what did you say?" Gillespie said, readying himself for an eruption.

"I asked if I could come in for a chat."

It happened again. The three of them giggled like school kids and, once more, Cruz had to be talked down off the ledge and convinced to carry on.

"What did she say?" Anna asked.

"She said it'll cost me."

"Did you ask how much?" Gillespie asked, wiping his eyes.

"Well, yeah. Bloody fifty quid."

"You didn't pay it, did you?" Chapman asked.

"Did you get a receipt?" Gillespie said. "You might be able to claim it back."

"I told her I hadn't got any money. Which I haven't. I mean, you saw, Jim. I'm bloody skint."

"Then what, Cruz?" Chapman said, clutching her bladder. "Come on, before I explode."

"I asked if I could have it for free. I meant the chat, not the other thing," Cruz said, as if it was obvious what he had meant. "I told her it's not like she's busy, is it? I might have suggested she sorts her makeup out. Then she whacked me."

"You gave makeup advice to a prostitute?" Anna asked, incredulous.

"Not advice, as such. I just pointed out that it might be a bit smudged, and it might be a bit off-putting for the punters. You know? Like when someone has food on their face. You can't help but stare, can you?"

"So that's the nose," Gillespie said, panting from the effort of holding it together. "How did you rip your shirt?"

"That was the next house," Cruz explained. "I'm telling you, I've been through it all today. The next place was like some kind of bedsit. There was loads of them."

"Them?" Chapman asked.

"Prostitutes. They had like a front room where they all sat. Disgusting place, it was. Smokey and stinky. Anyway, when one of them gets a job, they go to their bedrooms and, you know? Do the business, like."

"And did you do the business, Gab?" Anna asked.

"No. But they let me in, so I got further than the first house. I told them who I was this time, and that we've found someone. A body, like. Asked them if any of their colleagues were missing."

"And were they?"

"No. Problem was, they wouldn't let me go. Said I should stay a while seeing as I was so young and pretty. Started grabbing me and kissing me and that. I couldn't get away. They pinned me down. Three of them, there were, tearing and clawing at me. I don't know which one of them it was, but she had my belt undone and my trousers down in seconds. One-handed too."

"How did you get away?" Anna asked.

"The bloody uniform I was with heard me screaming from the next house. She had to come in and save me."

"So how did you get the stain on your trousers?" Chapman asked, slightly disgusted that he had not only been into one of those places but had been touched and kissed by them.

"No," Gillespie said, his face turning serious. "No. You didn't. Tell me you haven't–"

"I couldn't help it."

"No way."

"Oh, leave off. I was terrified."

That was it. Gillespie was done. All his powers of control had been spent and he burst into tears of laughter. The knock-on effect was that Anna, who had until now been fairly controlled, erupted, and Chapman ran from the room, taking the smallest steps she could. She tore open the incident room doors, and Freya stepped into the room.

She glared at Gillespie who, despite her presence, was inconsolable, blinded by tears and doubled over in hysterics. She eyed Anna, who had at least managed to control herself, and winked slyly. Then she turned her attention to Cruz. She studied him from his feet to his dishevelled hair. "Enjoying yourselves, are we?" she said eventually.

"No, boss," he mumbled. "Not really."

CHAPTER TWENTY-FIVE

"Cruz, go and get yourself washed and changed," Freya said. "Tidy yourself up."

"Yeah, you look you've been dragged through a brothel backwards," Gillespie added.

"I'll have to go home," Cruz whined. "I haven't got any clothes here."

"My gym bag is in the locker room upstairs," Anna suggested. "There's a pair of tracksuit bottoms in there you can use. We're about the same size. There's a clean t-shirt as well. But you can take them home and wash them. I don't want them back until they're clean."

"Thank you, Anna," Freya said. "Cruz, go and sort yourself out. Gillespie?"

Cruz walked out of the room bow-legged. Gillespie was recovering, slowly.

"Gillespie?"

"Aye, boss," he said.

"Are you back with us?"

"Aye. Sorry. But that has to be the funniest thing I've heard in years, boss. Can we send him back tomorrow? He's got a whole list to get through."

"Do you want to know what else is funny?" Freya said, her voice low. "Two women are dead, and it's down to us to find the killers."

He dropped the smirk that was on his face and sat up in his seat. "Killer, you mean, boss? You said *killers*. Plural?"

"It depends on your point of view. For the time being, we'll be treating the enquiries as separate, looking for any crossover of information along the way. But yes. It is my opinion that we're dealing with one killer."

"What did Doctor Bell think?" Anna asked.

"She gave a very good analysis. Poppy was strangled to death. The killer was in front of her. Perhaps even kneeling on her. Our unknown was also strangled, but from behind. Very different MO. Plus, there's the facial injuries to consider. Sadly, when I asked Doctor Bell if she thought the killer was the same person, she sat on the fence. So, we're treating the two murders as individual cases for now, but we'll run them alongside each other. If you're working on the Poppy Gray investigation, keep the other investigation in mind, and vice versa."

The incident room door squealed open, and a rather sheepish-looking Chapman crept back in and took her seat.

"Feel better for that?" Freya asked.

Blushing, Chapman lowered her head.

"Look, I'm all for having a laugh. God knows, we need a laugh with what we do. I'm not angry. I'm not disappointed. In fact, I find it quite funny. But do me a favour, will you? Just keep in mind that we could hear you all the way out by the fire escape stairs. If that was DCI Granger, he'd have had a lot more to say about it. You're all smart. So bear it in mind. If I get dragged into his office, I won't hesitate to pass the sentiment down. Is that clear?"

"Aye, boss," Gillespie said, just as the door opened once more. This time, the squeal was prolonged. The squeal was more of a creak, and they all turned to find Cruz standing in the doorway with a very nervous look on his face.

Freya eyed him for the second time in less than ten minutes. He was wearing Anna's post-gym t-shirt, which was his size and actually showed his hips. But the slogan – *Let's Get Sweaty* – did very little to help his look. Especially when Freya's gaze was drawn to what he was wearing on his legs. A pair of pink and grey, disruptive patterned yoga pants, which didn't fit as well as the t-shirt, left very little to the imagination. To top the look off, Cruz had put his work shoes back on – a pair of dirty, slip-on dealer boots.

Gillespie was gone. He was in a different world, from which there was no bringing him back. Chapman buried her face in her folded arms on her desk and was physically jolting with the suppressed laughter.

Anna, however, was appalled.

"They're my yoga pants," she screamed at him.

"Eh?"

"Yoga pants, Gab. They aren't bloody tracksuit bottoms."

"Oh, really? I thought they were tight."

"Tracksuit bottoms are baggy. You know? Loose fit. Casual. What I wear on my way home from the gym. Those are yoga pants and quite clearly are not loose fit. I can see everything, Gab. I feel violated."

"What?" he said defensively.

"Gab," Ben said, the voice of reason, calm, collected, but clearly suppressing the desire to burst, "it's not a good look, mate. Honestly, I don't know whether I should be disgusted or buy you a drink. What do you think, Jim?"

He turned to Gillespie, who had tears streaming down his face. He tried to speak, but his throat was so constricted from the laughter, all that came out was a high-pitched squeal. And then he erupted again.

A door slammed somewhere further down the corridor. Freya

guessed it was the fire escape. A few moments later, DC Gold appeared.

"What's going on?" she asked from the doorway, and Gab turned to face her. "Oh my god, Gab. Put it away."

"It is away," he whined.

"Where's the rest of it?" she asked, trying to edge past without touching him. "You're like a life-size Gym Barbie."

"Oy!" he said.

If there was an edge that Gillespie had yet to be tipped over – that was it. He got up from his seat and stumbled into the far end of the room, where DI Standing and his team used to sit before transferring to Lincoln HQ. Although he was very much out of sight, they could still hear his childish giggles and whimpers, and the occasional "Gym Barbie?" or "I don't know if I should be disgusted or buy you a drink." Both of which were followed by more suppressed laughter and choking sounds.

"DC Cruz," Freya said, loud and clear, and the room silenced, save for Gillespie's incessant whimpers at the back of the room. "Either go home or get changed. You can't stay here like that. I'm trying to run a murder investigation here."

He looked across to Anna. "Mind if I have another look in your bag?"

"Be my guest, but don't you dare put those yoga pants back in there. You can take them home and wash them. In fact, no. I want a brand-new pair. I'll send you a link to them. I don't think I could ever wear them again, knowing what's been running down your leg."

Cruz took the hint and made his way back through the incident room door, and down toward the stairs to the second floor locker room. The room silenced and Freya searched the team, waiting for them to get their laughs and giggles out of their systems.

Apart from Gillespie, who would need some kind of opiate to calm him down, the team was pretty much ready to listen, when from upstairs, even through the thick, concrete slab, they heard the CID team erupt into laughter, wolf whistles, and cheers.

"Poor bloke," Ben said. "You have to hand it to him. I would have just gone home and never come back, I think."

"You and me both, Ben," Freya said, then called up the end of the room. "Gillespie! We're waiting for you. We have murders to solve, remember?"

They waited for Gillespie to either reply or stand up. The lights were off at that end of the room, and they could see him seated at his old desk with his head rested on his arms.

"Gillespie?" Freya called, then glanced at Ben.

Intrigued, Ben made his way to the other end of the office.

"Hey, Jim. You okay, fella?" he asked. He crouched beside Gillespie then immediately stood and made his way to the team's end of the room, and addressed them all. "Do me a favour. Give us a bit of space, will you?"

"Is everything okay?" Freya asked, while DCs Gold, Nillson, and Chapman all looked on, adopting concerned expressions.

"I'm not sure. I'll call you in five or ten minutes," he said quietly, as he made his way to Gillespie. Then he called over his shoulder, "And keep Cruz out of here too. The last thing we need is Gym Barbie walking back in here."

CHAPTER TWENTY-SIX

BEN TOOK THE SEAT OPPOSITE GILLESPIE, BUT SAID NOTHING. He waited a few moments for Gillespie to collect himself, and enjoyed a rare moment of peace in the office.

"I'm sorry, Ben," Gillespie said, then sniffed loudly. "Have they all gone?"

"I asked them to give us some space," Ben said, leaning over to grab a box of tissues from the desk behind him. He set them down in front of Gillespie.

"Aye, well. There was no need–"

"It's fine, Jim. But you need to talk to me, mate. One minute you were in high spirits, laughing your backside off. And the next minute? What's this? What's happened?"

"Ah, I'm a mess, Ben. A right old mess. It was that wee lad."

"Grant?"

"Aye, him. Poor fella."

"It reminded you of something?"

"Ah, listen, Ben. I can't talk about it. Chokes me every time. I can't help it. It's like, it's like I've learnt how to store all those memories at the back of my mind somewhere. You know? Like in a dark corner of my brain. And, I don't know how, but I've somehow managed to keep them there. In the dark. Been there for years. I always know they're there. It's like... How do I explain it?"

"You don't have to explain if you don't want–"

"It's like a pair of old trainers in your cupboard. You know you'll never wear them again, right? You know they stink, and that you should probably throw them out. But you can't. You can't throw them out. You try. You try to get rid of them. You walk them out to the bins and you dump them in there, and you swear you'll never ever wear them again. But the next day, they're back. Somehow they've walked by themselves all the way back inside your house and set themselves down in your cupboard. So, you try to move on. Every day, you go to the cupboard to get your new trainers out and you don't even see the old ones anymore," he explained. "But you know they're there."

"But you can't throw them out?" Ben asked, keeping the terrible analogy going.

"Aye. I've tried. Went through it all when I joined up. Therapy and stuff. I just cracked on in the end. Pushed it all to one side, you know? Easiest way."

"But do you think talking to Grant has stirred up old memories, then?"

"It's like I was looking in the mirror, Ben. At myself. Fifteen years ago. And that fight he got into last week? That was me every bloody week."

"Why? You're so placid now. I had no idea you were like that."

"Ah, you don't want to know, Ben. I grew up in homes, right?" he said. "I told you that before?"

"Yes, a few times. But you've never really said much about it."

Gillespie sucked in a long breath and closed his eyes.

"When I was young, there were good homes and there were not so good homes."

"And yours was one of the latter?"

"All of them were."

"All of them?"

"About a dozen, I think. It's hard to remember them all. I was just a wee nipper when... you know? My parents gave me up. I remember from about four or five onwards. Terrible times, Ben. Terrible times. But the thing is, I was talking to this kid–"

"Grant?"

"Aye, him. The lad. And I just saw myself. It didn't really hit me at first. But then I looked closer. The books."

"I saw those. He's an avid reader."

"More than that. He's created himself a world, Ben. In his room. He gets lost in the books. I did the same. Read all sorts. It's the only bloody reason I can read and write now."

"I think Chapman might contest that, mate," Ben said.

"Well, *I* can read my writing. That's all that counts. But if I hadn't had all those books, and my own little world, I'd have been a right old mess."

"Instead of the mess I see before me today, you mean?"

"Ah, you know what I mean. I want to help him. I know what's in front of him and, you know, I don't want him to be sitting right here in fifteen years' time wondering why that big, mad, Scottish copper didn't warn him all those bloody years ago."

"You can't help them all, Jim. You know that. You're seasoned."

"Aye, but I can help this one. And I will," he said, stabbing the desk with his finger. There was strength in how he said it. The old Jim was showing himself. Ben just had to coax him back gently. "He didn't say a word. Do you know that?"

"Yeah, Mrs Frost said he'd only spoken twice or something since he's been there."

"That was me, Ben. Not that bad. But the only time I'd talk was when I was in my last home, when I'd been through it all. The abuse, the bullying, the beatings. The only words that ever left my mouth were vile expletives, telling the whole world where it can go. Either that or book stuff."

"Book stuff?"

"Aye, you know? If somebody asked me about the books I'd read, I'd come out of my wee hole just long enough for the social worker to assess me, mark me down as healthy, then bugger off to the next poor wee bastard."

"How are you going to help him? I'm guessing you don't need to talk about what happened to you?"

"Ah, Ben. I had stuff happen to me, stuff I was forced to do, and stuff I wouldn't wish on my worst enemy. I'll take all that to my grave. He's had it too, you know? The abuse. The beatings. He's had it. I can see it in his eyes. He doesn't need reminding of that, just like I don't."

"Sorry," Ben said. "I'm trying to empathise."

"No need, Ben. It's okay. It's just one of those things that, unless you've been through it, there's no way you'd understand. And that's a good thing. The fewer people who have to go through it, the better, in my opinion. And if you *have* been through it, then you know the other person is trying to forget it."

"The trainers?"

"Aye, the trainers," Gillespie whispered, his voice hoarse, but he was in far more control of his emotions now. "What that boy needs is the light. He needs to see it, right there in front of him, at the end of the dark and lonely tunnel. I can't lie to the boy. The tunnel is dark, Ben. It's a terrible place to be. But he has to move toward the light. If he can't see the light, he can't move towards it. And if he can't find the light, then I need to show him how to find it."

"You're going to see him again?"

"Aye, yeah, I am. Tomorrow. I told him I'd be back. I'm not going to let him down, Ben."

"Do you think he can help us?"

"With Poppy Gray?" he asked, then shrugged. "He was close to her. So maybe."

"Do you think we need to question him?"

"Maybe. But he didn't do it," he said, shaking his head. "No way. When you're in that place, and you have a friend like Poppy, there's no bloody way you'd kill her."

"Even if she betrayed you?"

"No. Not a chance."

"We can't rule him out, Jim."

"Aye, I know that. I just have to prove it wasn't him."

"Do you think you can get through to him?"

"Eventually, aye. Tomorrow? I don't know. But I won't give up."

"That's admirable, Jim."

"It's human is what it is," he replied.

"Do you want to take some time? Go home, maybe? I think Freya wants a debrief to make a plan."

"I'll stay up here out of the way. I don't want to bring the team down."

"Well, join us when you're ready," Ben said. "Can I get you a coffee or something?"

"Coffee? I've just ridden an emotional roller coaster, Ben. I need a bleeding sedative."

"No can do."

"Aye, well," he said dismissively.

"I'll leave you to it, but if you ever want to air those old trainers..."

"Thanks, Ben," Gillespie said. "And hey, it goes without saying that this is between you and me. I don't want everyone to know–"

"About your stinky, old trainers?" Ben said, leaning forward and slapping his old friend on the shoulder. "You can keep them to yourself, Jim."

CHAPTER TWENTY-SEVEN

On the stairwell, Freya, Chapman, Anna, and Gold were waiting for Ben to give them the go-ahead to return.

"She's just a bit lonely," Gold said. "So I gave her my number."

"Are you offering counselling, Gold?" Freya asked.

She laughed it off. "No. We're just two single mums. We've got a lot in common. It's bloody hard work, and I don't think anybody really appreciates how hard it is. If I didn't have my mum helping me, I'd have no chance. What with picking Charlie up from rugby, football, piano, and all the other afterschool stuff. I'd have to leave my job. Lee Sanders' mum, Teresa, doesn't have any help at all. I don't know how she does it."

"I don't know how either of you do it," Anna said, pulling a face. "I don't think I'll ever be a mum."

"Ah, come on," Freya said, enjoying the girl time more than she had expected.

"I'm serious. Keiran wants kids. I don't think I do. I don't see why I have to pause my career to look after a baby while he gets to move up. It's not right."

"There's plenty of relationships where that isn't the case," Freya said. "Mum delivers the baby, takes a few weeks to recover and bond with the baby, then the dad takes over. She goes back to work. It's quite normal now."

"I can't see Keiran going for that. He can barely wipe his own backside, let alone be responsible for a baby. No. If it happens, it'll be me who has to take care of it."

"Listen, while I've got you all here. I'm planning a little get-together for when we're through with this investigation. Nothing huge. It'll just be us four and maybe one or two others. At my house. I can't say too much, but trust me, I think you'll like it."

"Alright," Chapman said.

"Yeah, that sounds nice. Just girls?" Gold asked.

"Mostly, yes," Freya said, trying to hide the smirk that was itching to creep over her face. "Anna?"

"Count me in. I feel like I've been hiding away all winter."

"Good. No need to bring anything. I'll have wine and there will be food. Just bring yourselves."

"Ah, that's lovely, thanks, ma'am," Gold said.

"Promise me you won't call me ma'am though, Gold. Not at my house."

"That'll be a hard habit to break," she replied. "I'll try."

"What will be a hard habit to break?" a voice said from behind them. They turned to find Cruz at the top of the stairs. He still looked ridiculous with Anna's *Let's Get Sweaty* t-shirt, jogging bottoms, and work shoes, but at least he wasn't doing his best Barbie impression. "What are you lot planning?"

"None of your business," both Anna and Chapman replied.

He stared down at them suspiciously. "You lot are up to something."

"You're paranoid, Barbie boy," said Anna, just as Ben poked his head around the corner.

"All good," he said.

"Is he alright?" Gold asked.

"He's fine. He's sitting in Standing's end of the room. Leave him be, eh?"

"Yeah. What's wrong with him, though?" Gold asked.

"Actually..." He replied to Gold but stared at Freya while he spoke. "Nothing. He's good. He just needed some time. Nothing to worry about. Let's do this briefing, shall we? It's been a long day."

The six of them filed into the incident room, and the door squealed closed, then slammed. They all took their seats except Freya who claimed her spot beside the white board, where she waited for them to settle.

"Alright. Here we go," she began. "You all know how I work by now. I want bullet points. No lengthy monologues. Keep to the facts and we can speculate after. Nillson, you first. Talk to me about Harringer."

"He's downstairs," she replied. "Arrived at the guest house. Had to ask Mr Gray to unlock the door. Room was empty. No belongings. Nothing. He doesn't have a car, so I figured he must have taken the bus."

"Could have got a taxi?" Gold suggested.

"Unlikely. He needed a quick getaway. Taxis take ages around there. They have to come in from the city."

"But you found him?" Freya asked.

"Yeah. Uniform stopped the bus. He tried to run, but I nailed him," she said, punching the flat of her hand. "That's one on the file for me."

"Have you spoken to him at all?"

"No, his solicitor is due in any moment now. She's coming up from Kings Lynn. Besides, whoever goes in will need something concrete on him," she said, and glanced at Chapman hopefully.

"Other than a dead body in his car?" Cruz said.

"The car was stolen. It was reported. He wouldn't even need a lawyer to walk away from that."

"Nillson is right," Freya said. "Chapman. What do you have on him?"

DC Denise Chapman took a deep breath. "Well, we were right to bring him in. But we're going to have to work hard to keep him here," she began. "Roy Harringer is an IT security specialist. Lives in Kings Lynn, Norfolk, with his wife and two kids. I've had a look at his financial statements, and it seems he travels frequently. Domestically, I mean. Not abroad. He was recently in Oxford, Dorset, and then went home to Norfolk for a few days. Then he came here. His records show that he visits these places regularly. So I spoke to someone from his company's HR department. All his trips are valid business trips. He has regular clients in those specific locations."

"IT?" Freya said. "Can't that all be done remotely now?"

"He's a Pen Tester," Chapman replied, then waited for one of the blank faces in front of her to say something. Of course, it was Cruz who stated the obvious.

"He tests pens?" he said, looking confused. "Is that actually a job? What is he, freelance?"

"Penetration tester," Chapman explained.

"Those girls you met earlier would be good at that, Cruz, eh?" Ben said.

"A penetration test," Chapman explained, "is when a security specialist attempts to hack a business to identify holes in security. They'll act out the exact same methods as a real hacker, and then suggest actions that can be taken to mediate them."

"Right," Ben said. "So he's an ethical hacker?"

"Kind of."

"Which means that his laptop will be of no use to us."

"We can try. But the chances are he'll either have a different machine or has done something to get rid of any evidence. A lot of hackers use virtual machines now, alongside VPNs. Which means if he did any research on the victims, he could have done that on a machine in Russia, and we wouldn't even know he'd connected to it."

"It's worth a try though. Did we get a laptop?" Freya asked.

"I've submitted it already," Nillson said. "Along with the rest of his belongings. It's all in the lab being black-lighted."

"Good. What else, Chapman?"

"He was in Oxford two weeks ago. The same time a woman named Anita Carter went missing. Same demographics as our mystery woman."

"You what?" Ben said.

Chapman smiled. "I thought you'd like that."

"Has she been found?"

"Dorset police found her a few days ago, when Harringer was back in Norfolk preparing for his Lincolnshire trip."

"You think he took her from Oxford and dumped her in Dorset?" Freya asked.

"To slow down the identification process. By the time they worked out who she was, he was long gone."

"There's something you're not telling me, isn't there?" Freya said. She knew when Chapman had made a breakthrough. It was written all over her face.

"Another girl, Katy Southgate, went missing from Long Sutton three days ago."

"Same demographics?" Freya asked.

"To the tee," Chapman said with a smile.

"Where's Long Sutton?" Gold asked.

"Just outside of Kings Lynn," Cruz said. "It's on the A17. He would have had to go through it on his way up here. It's an old market town, if I'm right. That's where Wisbech Castle was, until the great floods in the thirteenth century, of course. Wiped it out completely."

The team stared at the young man who had made such a fool of himself only an hour ago but once more demonstrated his unique general knowledge skills.

"What?" he said.

"Nothing," Anna replied.

"So this Katy Southgate could be our mystery woman?" Freya

asked. "I need photos of her. And the other woman. Anita something."

"Carter, ma'am."

"That's it. Get me everything you can."

Chapman, smiling, as ever was fully prepared. She held up a blue file for Freya to take. "Should be all you need in there."

"You're a rock star. Did you know that, Chapman?"

"Thanks, ma'am. I got lucky."

"Yes, of course. It always amazes me that the people who work the hardest seem to get the luckiest," she said, and gave her nod of appreciation. "Any other guests?"

"Nobody I'm concerned with, ma'am," Chapman replied. "An old couple who stay there every year. Other than them and Harringer, the place was dead."

"That doesn't surprise me," Freya said. "Gold, missing persons?"

"None local, ma'am," she said.

"None?"

"Not that match the demographic," she said. "Apart from one but, erm..."

"But what? Do we have a name?"

"Joanne Fitzpatrick. Right age. Right hair colour. Born and raised in Lincolnshire."

"But?"

"Well, Joanne used to be John."

"She's transgender?" Freya said, and Jackie nodded.

"I figured if Doctor Bell had seen something, then she would have said something, ma'am."

"Indeed," Freya said. "Keep her file open. You're right, Doctor Bell would have mentioned any major surgery. Cruz?"

"Eh?" he said, looking up from his phone.

"Progress?"

He shrugged. "Don't make me tell the story again, boss."

Freya sighed, then laughed once and shook her head. "Right,

that's our mystery woman making progress. What do we know about Poppy Gray?"

"Gillespie has made good progress with the friend," said Ben. "A Grant Sayer. Looks like he had a run-in with another lad two weeks ago. Chapman, can you check with Lincoln HQ? See if you can get a name of the other lad. It seems Poppy Gray slept with this other kid and Grant took a disliking to it. Maybe he thought more of Poppy than she did of him. Anyway, Grant beat the hell out of him. I'd like to check to see if the other lad had reason to go after Poppy."

"Good call," Freya said. "What about Grant?"

"I'm dealing with him," Gillespie said. At the sound of Grant's name, he had walked from the far end of the office, and stood there, his hands hanging by his sides. "I'm seeing him tomorrow. I'm making progress, boss."

"It's not too close to home, Gillespie?" Freya asked, recalling a moment they had shared a few months ago when he had revealed a glimpse into his troubled childhood.

"It doesn't matter, boss," he replied, and stared at Ben. "The way I see it. Even an old pair of trainers have their uses."

CHAPTER TWENTY-EIGHT

INTERVIEW ROOM TWO LOOKED ALMOST IDENTICAL TO interview room one. Even the tables had the same names of re-offenders scratched into them and the same posters on the walls, warning visitors of the effects drugs had on families, and how drink driving was responsible for more than six hundred deaths last year. That was the one that always got Freya. That's nearly two people per day for a year, despite the government spending an absolute fortune on advertising campaigns, despite the law clamping down on offenders, and despite the fact that the culture had at least shifted to the point where people were more likely to grass an offender up now than ever before. To the majority, drink driving was a heinous crime and drink drivers were now looked down on in disgust by society. They were now the minority. A tiny percentage of the population large enough to cause more than six hundred deaths per year. The tide was turning, but by Christ was it slow in happening.

But the man seated at the table in interview room two was not there for drink driving. He was there for crimes far worse, but he belonged to an even smaller percentage of the population than drink drivers. Murderers. Freya recalled seeing the death statistics for the previous year while waiting in Granger's office recently. Eighty-five thousand people were caught drink driving, while, as the poster eluded to, more than six hundred people died from it. However, when that statistic was put next to the homicide rate of just over six hundred, the imbalance became clear.

The same number of people were murdered as the number of people who died as a result of a drink driver. That was an appalling statistic.

Ben took his seat opposite the solicitor, and Freya faced Roy Harringer. He was a charming looking man, lean, dark features, with two days' worth of greying growth on his square jawline framing his thin lips. But it was his eyes that were startling, to Freya at least. She doubted Ben would notice, but they were an ice-blue. The type of eyes women fell for. The type of eyes women were drawn to like moths to a flame.

Ben announced the date and time on the recording and glanced at Freya, handing over to her.

"We'll go around the table," she began. "Please state your name clearly for the recording. Detective Inspector Freya Bloom."

"Detective Sergeant Ben Savage."

"Lucy Shaw. Solicitor."

"Roy Harringer. Victim."

"Thank you," Freya said, ignoring Harringer's closing comment. "Mr Harringer, I must remind you that you are under arrest on suspicion of murder. It may harm your defence if you fail to mention now something you later rely on in court. Anything you do say may be given in evidence. Do you understand?"

He nodded. "Yes," he said.

He had a deep voice. Not one of a leader. He carried no authority in his tones. But there was an arrogance there. A confidence in his own intelligence. That was going to be Freya's challenge. The man was clearly smart, being an IT security professional. She would need to prove she was smarter.

"Mr Harringer, can you please confirm your home address for me?"

"Home address?" he said. "Seventy-one Old Farm Road, Kings Lynn, Norfolk. Want the postcode?"

"That won't be necessary. But could you please state your reason for being in Lincolnshire? You were staying at the Witham Valley Guest House in Stixwould. Why?"

"Work."

"In IT security?" she said. "Is that correct?"

"Yeah."

"And what is the name of your client here? Who are you here to see?"

"I think that's confidential. GDPR or something."

"I think you'll find, Mr Harringer, that when you're facing the charges you are, we're more than within our rights to ask the name of your client."

He glanced across at his solicitor, who nodded.

"Tyrone Group," he said reluctantly. "They manufacture animal feeds."

"I see. And as part of your role, I understand you try to gain entry into their systems? Is that correct?"

"Yes, it is, but I don't see what that has to do with anything–"

"It doesn't, Mr Harringer. But I am keen to build an accurate picture of you for the benefit of a jury, who may or may not be required to listen to this interview."

"A jury?"

"You were in Oxford two weeks ago. Is that right?"

He nodded, far more unsure of his position than before.

"What were you doing down there? Who were you seeing?"

"Private school. I'm not giving names. They're my biggest client. If you want the name, you can go through my company."

"That's fine. And how long were you in Oxford for?"

"Three days. Always three days."

"Always?"

"One to breach the security. One to simulate control of the network. You know? Deliver a ransom warning. Put the fear of god into them. And one to show them how I got in and what they can do about it."

"And you do this regularly, do you?"

"Yeah. Monthly for Tyrone. I give them a month to fix their security, then try again. Find a new way in. It keeps their security tight."

"And from Oxford, you travelled down to Dorset. That's a long way to go, isn't it?"

"Yeah. I don't usually do Dorset. I was covering for somebody."

"Three days?"

"Always."

"And then back to Kings Lynn?"

"Yeah. Had a few days with the family before coming up here."

"Must be hard on your family? All that travelling?"

"Pays well. If the wife wants to keep her Range Rover and all her shopping accounts open, then there's no point in her moaning about me going away. She gets it. She understands."

"And from Kings Lynn to here, which road did you take?"

"Which road?" he said, glancing at his solicitor again. "What does that bloody matter?"

"Which road, Mr Harringer? Please."

"The A17. Always the A17. It's the quickest way."

"And you always stay at the Witham Valley Guest House, do you?"

"Always. It's a bit grubby. But the breakfast is good and I like the peace and quiet. I always have the same room. It helps. You know? When you travel. It helps to form habits. Going to something familiar feels more like home. Easier to relax."

"I get that," Freya said, nodding. She opened her file and slipped out three images that Chapman had prepared. She presented him with the first image. "I wonder if this person is also familiar to you, Mr Harringer?"

Harringer stared at the photo, straight-faced.

"For the benefit of the recording, I'm showing Mr Harringer a photo of Anita Carter taken from a social media account," she announced. "Do you recognise her? Do you know her?"

He shook his head. "No."

She slipped the second photo in front of him. "For the benefit of the recording, I am showing Mr Harringer a photo of Katy Southgate. Also taken from a social media account. Do you recognise her, perhaps?"

"I don't know who that it is. I don't know either of them."

Freya separated the images, so they sat side by side. "This woman is Anita Carter. She was reported missing from Oxford two weeks ago. Dorset police discovered her body earlier this week."

"What?" he said, and gave his solicitor a panicked look.

"This woman," Freya continued, "is Katy Southgate. She was reported missing from Long Sutton two days ago. Right about the time you were passing through on your way up here."

"I do not know that woman," he stated.

"Tomorrow, your DNA and fingerprints will be analysed against those found in Anita Carter's home and in Katy Southgate's home. So, I'll ask you again. Do you know either of these women?"

He shook his head. "No. No, you've got it wrong. It's a coincidence."

"I'm sure it is, Mr Harringer. We'll find out tomorrow, won't we?" she said, placing the images back in the folder and snapping it shut. "The body found in the boot of the car you reported stolen is Katy Southgate, isn't it?"

"What? No. A body? In my car?"

"I don't have time for games, Mr Harringer. I'm going to be one hundred per cent transparent with you. I think you picked

Katy Southgate up from Long Sutton. I think you brought her up here to get rid of the body. Just like I think you killed Anita Carter in Oxford and took her to Dorset to get rid of the body. We checked your phone records," she said, withdrawing a printed map from the folder, which showed Harringer's movements during his stay in Dorset by way of a red line that resembled the path of a drunk man on the way home from the pub. Another printed map showed his movements from Kings Lynn to Lincolnshire, his only stop being in Long Sutton. "You stopped in Long Sutton."

"For diesel. It's cheaper than in Kings Lynn. I always stop there."

"And then there's Poppy Gray," Ben said, speaking up for the first time. "We found her just a short way from where she crashed your car. Strangled."

Freya laid the crime scene photos of Anita Carter, the unknown woman, and Poppy Gray on the table before him.

"How was Poppy involved, Mr Harringer?"

"I don't know."

"Why did she take your car?"

"I don't know."

"Did you kill her? Did you kill Poppy Gray?"

"No. No, I bloody didn't–"

"How about Anita Carter? Did you murder Anita Carter?"

"No."

"You're under caution. Remember that. What you say will have a bearing on how the jury perceives you."

"I didn't kill any of them," he said coldly. "I was there. Yes. In Oxford. And I was in Dorset. And yes, I stopped in Long Sutton. But did I kill any of them? No," he said, with a look of disgust. "I suggest you look elsewhere, Detective."

"Why did you run?" Ben asked, as he leaned forward to study the man's eyes. "DC Nillson, the arresting officer, said they had to stop the bus you had caught, despite DS Gillespie telling you not to leave the guest house. She also said you tried to run from the bus when she boarded and she had to use force to restrain you. Doesn't sound much like the actions of a man with nothing to hide, Mr Harringer."

Harringer peered at his solicitor, who had been making notes as the interview had progressed. She gave a slight shake of her head, and Harringer returned his attention back to Ben.

"No comment."

It was as Freya had expected.

"Mr Harringer, we are working with the constabularies in Oxford, Dorset, and Long Sutton. We have your car, your financial records, and your phone records. We've taken your DNA and fingerprints, and by this time tomorrow, we'll very likely have enough to charge you with the murder of Anita Sutton. Do you understand what that will do?"

"No comment."

"I'll tell you anyway. That will give us the time we need to look further into Katy's murder, and Poppy's murder. You could be looking at three life sentences here."

"No comment."

"You'll be taken from here and returned to your cell. I suggest you..." Freya pointed a finger at the solicitor. "Find a local hotel. If I have to wait another half a day for you to join us, your senior partner will be hearing about it. And you," she said, turning her finger towards Harringer, "I suggest you use the time tonight to consider your statement. Make it as easy on yourself as you can. You're not getting out of this one, Mr Harringer."

CHAPTER TWENTY-NINE

THE HOUSE WAS COLD AND STILL. FREYA DROPPED THE LITTLE bag of shopping on the kitchen counter and flicked the kettle on. She always boiled water when she got home from work, gasping for a nice cup of tea. She almost always poured herself a glass of wine while the kettle was boiling too, and tonight was no different. The kettle would boil, then it would cool, and she'd probably do the same thing tomorrow, she thought, as she sipped her Chianti.

A couple of months ago, she would have stayed in her coat and work clothes, swapping her boots for slippers and then curling up beside her log burner. But now spring had arrived; the temperature had warmed to just a few degrees cooler than comfortable, instead of resembling the arctic tundra. It was warm enough for her to kick off her boots, find her most comfortable pyjamas, and curl up in her dressing gown beside the log burner.

She collected the Grant Sayer file from her dining room table, then walked through to the kitchen where she tipped the contents of the plastic shopping bag onto the worktop. A bag of one-minute rice with vegetables, a jar of pesto, and a block of cheese. It was an odd collection of items to buy, but while picking the items up, she had fancied cheese on toast, or pasta with pesto – and cheese, of course – or, if she really couldn't be bothered to wait, rice.

Checking the food cupboard, she found her bread to be past its best, so she tossed it into the bin. She searched for pasta but remembered she had finished the little bag of penne a few nights before. So, with her scissors, she snipped the corner off the sachet of one-minute rice, chucked it in the microwave, slammed the door, and set it for one minute.

She hooked a finger into the file Chapman had prepared and studied the first page. It was just notes on Grant Sayer, including his date of birth, parents, a brief summary of the various homes he'd been in and names of the carers, and then a brief summary of his criminal record.

The list of homes he'd been in was far longer than his criminal record, which amounted to a caution for ABH against a boy who, according to Chapman's notes, had a criminal record longer than Grant Sayer's list of care homes.

The second and final entry on Grant Sayer's record was for GBH and took place just two weeks before Poppy Gray was found dead. Chapman's notes were an objective summary of the events, presented in a format that was easy for Freya to digest and interpret. Danny Osborne and Poppy Gray had sex. Grant had found them and beaten the living daylights out of Osborne. He'd beaten him so badly that Poppy had made an anonymous call to the emergency services giving them his location. With three broken ribs, a fractured femur, and a broken nose, Danny Osborne was in no fit state to walk. His parents had then pressed charges on their son's behalf.

The next page told an objective account of Danny Osborne's criminal record. One warning for possession of a class B drug, cannabis. One formal charge of possession of a class B drug, cannabis. Two shoplifting charges, one from Halfords, the other from Tescos. The list of petty crimes went on. He was clearly no angel and wasn't exactly unfamiliar with breaking the law, and in Freya's experience, the charges against Sayer were indicative of parents who, for the first time, had actually been on the receiving end of a crime as opposed to being dragged to the local nick to collect their unruly son.

If Freya was looking for some kind of reason behind the minor crimes Osborne had been charged with, she had to look no further than the boy's father, who trumped his son's efforts with a drink driving ban, four counts of possession of a class B drug, cannabis, and one count of possession of a class A drug, cocaine. He had served a six-month sentence in HMP Lincoln for aggravated burglary, and a further ninety day sentence for handling stolen goods. To top it off, the father, Jeffrey Osborne, had a note on his file stating he was part of a group of local men under ongoing surveillance. Any decision to question him, or bring him into an investigation, even as a tertiary witness, would need sign-off from Lincoln HQ. Quite the role model.

Sadly, in Freya's experience, the parents would push as hard as they could for a conviction. Perhaps in the hope of compensation? Or more likely, an opportunity to demonstrate their knowledge of the law and get their own back on society. Bizarre, Freya thought, but that was how many of these people's minds worked.

The microwave pinged. She retrieved the red-hot bag, snipped the top off, and in an effort not to make a mess, she began forking her meal directly from the bag into her mouth.

She had taken just three mouthfuls of the tasteless mush when there were three raps on the front door.

"Evening," Ben said, when she opened the door and stared out at him. He held up a bag. "Dinner?"

Freya held up the sachet of rice. "Too late. What is it?"

"Jacket potato."

"Cooked?" she asked.

"Well, yeah. Otherwise, it would just be potato," he said, as if the answer was obvious. "Just add cheese and beans."

She glanced down at the muck she was eating, then without saying a word, walked back into her kitchen, dropped the sachet in the bin, slung the fork into the sink, and got out the cheese she had bought from the fridge.

Ben closed the door behind him and carefully pulled the two foil-wrapped spuds from the bag. Seeing him about to make a mess, Freya gave him two plates, then passed him the cheese and a grater.

"Beans?" he asked.

"Just cheese for me. I don't eat beans."

"I do."

"In the cupboard by your head."

"You've been reading, I see?" he said without looking up, and he flicked to the front page of the file, then put it down to continue preparing dinner. "How's our silent friend looking?"

"Anger problems. Not a bad kid though."

"And the other one? What's his name?"

"Danny Osborne. He has previous for possession and shoplifting. And a few other petty crimes."

"Troublemaker, eh?"

"His role model isn't exactly a saint."

"Ah, right. One of those families?" Ben said, passing her a bowl of baked beans. "Microwave, two minutes, stir, then put on again for two more minutes."

The microwave was behind Freya, so she turned, put the bowl inside, and set it for four minutes. When she turned back, Ben was reading while he grated the cheese. "My guess is that mum and dad will push as hard as they can. First time the law has been on their side."

"Yep."

"Injuries are quite severe. They'll seek compensation."

"Yep."

"Grant has a record for ABH. He'll get three to six months

with a tough judge, or a few weeks with a big fine if he gets a lenient judge."

"Yep. Might put him on the straight and narrow."

"Gillespie won't like it."

"Gillespie shouldn't be getting close."

"He wants to help the boy."

"Whatever Grant Sayer did two weeks ago has been done. Nothing Gillespie says to him will alter the boy's future. If Gillespie somehow sees himself in Grant Sayer, then he needs to be prepared for the worst. As you said, Ben, depending on the judge, Grant Sayer is looking at one to six months."

"What if Danny Osborne attacked Poppy?" Ben asked.

Freya stared at him, searching for some kind of logic, but found none.

"Osborne might be a rogue but he doesn't have a history of violence. Grant Sayer does."

"But what if Poppy did something to him? She and Grant were close. She obviously cared for him on a friend level. And Grant very clearly cared about her. What if she was protecting Grant? What if she said something? Threatened to expose Osborne?"

"Or his father?"

Ben nodded. "How about this? Poppy had a relationship with Osborne. He told her things. Things that perhaps even he shouldn't know. Grant Sayer caught them at it, beat the living daylights out of him, and the family press charges. Poppy goes to Osborne, tells him to drop the charges or she'll reveal whatever it was he told her."

"Wow, you've got it all mapped out. Tell me, Ben. Is this an effort to find Poppy's killer, or to help your friend by proxy?"

"This is about Poppy Gray. Gillespie is a big man. He can deal with the consequences."

"So?" she said. "We have Harringer. As long as we can tie him to the death of Anita Carter from Oxford, then we can detain him. CPS have already given us the go-ahead based on those facts."

"We bring Osborne in."

"The son? We can't touch the father."

"It's a start. And let's face it, regardless of Gillespie's efforts with Grant Sayer, the boy isn't exactly going to wake up singing in the morning, is he?"

"Two killers," Freya said, as the microwave pinged.

Ben turned and unhooked an old apron Freya had hung on the back of the kitchen door. "I'll try not to gloat," he said, holding it out for her.

Smiling, she stepped forward, took the apron from him, and closed the gap between them, so she was looking up at him, their faces just inches apart. She hooked the apron on the back of the door while holding his gaze, teasing him to lean forward. "I won't be needing that just yet," she said. "Your beans are cooked."

CHAPTER THIRTY

The investigation was getting deeper, as was often the case. In just a few days, they had gone from having no witnesses or suspects to having Harringer in custody, and Danny Osborne and Grant Sayer as key components. As such, Freya had driven herself to work, suffering the inadequacies of her little rental car for the journey, aware that she and Ben might very well be required to work independently.

She parked in her spot, noting Detective Superintendent Harper's empty space, DCI Granger's occupied space, and the remaining spaces allocated to the Major Investigations Team, all empty. It was six forty-five, early for Freya. But as much as she enjoyed seeing her new team working together, laughing and joking, she needed some headspace. Time to reflect on the scenarios and the consequences.

She took the fire escape stairs as she usually did, then entered the corridor. She was just about to wake the squealing beast of a door when Granger called out from his office.

"Bloom?"

How the bloody hell does he do that?

"Guv?"

"A word?"

She stopped in his office doorway and found him wearing casual clothes. He wore a hooded sweatshirt with tracksuit bottoms and when she glanced down at his feet, she saw him sporting a pair of running shoes.

"How did you know it was me?" she asked.

"I can smell your perfume and I know your walk. Just like I know DS Savage's giant strides, DC Chapman's elegant steps, and even DC Cruz's lazy shuffle," he said, finishing writing whatever it was he was writing. He looked up. "I've started using the gym upstairs. I'm not getting any younger, Freya, and I'd like to go into my sixties a few pounds lighter than I am now."

"Wouldn't we all," she said, for want of anything better to say.

"You were wondering why I'm dressed like this," he said knowingly.

"Either that or you were planning on breaking into a rap, guv," she joked.

He stared at her.

"Not the rapping type?"

He smiled eventually.

"Would you like to sit?" he asked, presenting the guest chair with a sweep of his hand.

The two of them had come to an arrangement a few months back that Will Granger, despite his senior rank, would not force Freya, who hated being told to sit when she preferred to stand, to take a seat. The gentle invite didn't go unnoticed and Freya took him up on his offer. Time with the boss, when it wasn't in the form of a grilling, was usually productive. Any insight into the man's mind and plans was beneficial to a strategist like Freya. She had her mental pen and her mental pad ready to take notes.

"Update?" he asked, handing the reins over to her. "You have a man in custody, I hear."

"Roy Harringer. He's staying at the guest house that Poppy

Gray's father owns. A regular. Works in IT security and does a fair amount of domestic travel."

"And it was his car that Poppy Gray stole?"

"It was, yes. With the body of the unknown woman in the boot. We've since learnt that another woman, Anita Carter, was reported missing from Oxford. Her body was found in Dorset a few days later."

"Don't tell me. Harringer went to both places?"

"We've got his phone records, bank statements. He was there. No doubt about it."

"He was just in Dorset, or he was actually at the spot where the body was found?"

It was a good question to ask and was the only hole in Freya's plan, but one that was easily answered.

"His phone records and bank records both confirm he was in Dorset. He travelled from his client's office to his bed and breakfast, according to his phone records."

"But not to the crime scene?"

"He's an IT security specialist, guv. He'll know we can trace that information. All he had to do was leave his phone in the bed and breakfast."

"That's a hole."

"We're working with both Oxford and Dorset police, plus we have local CSI going over his car. With any luck, there'll be evidence of Anita Carter inside."

He sighed but nodded. "So you want to nail him with Anita Carter to buy time to prove he killed the other girl? The unknown?"

"That's about the size of it, guv. He came to Lincolnshire three days ago. Does so regularly. Stays in the same guest house. Takes the same route from his home in Kings Lynn to Lincolnshire."

"A17?" Granger suggested.

She nodded. "Passes through Long Sutton, where three days

ago a woman by the name of Katy Southgate was reported missing."

He cocked his head to one side. "And you think our unknown woman–"

"Is Katy Southgate. Yes, guv."

"That'll take time to prove."

"Hence the focus on Anita Carter."

"You've got the means. What's the motivation?"

"We need to know more about him. We need to know what drives him and we need to find a link."

"And if there isn't a link?"

"Then we could be looking at a serial killer."

"A serial killer? That's a bit of a leap."

"It's the only alternative. If there's nothing Anita Carter or Katy Southgate actually did to him, then we can only assume that they fit his particular criteria."

"Both single?"

"Demographics are a perfect match, guv."

"What about Poppy Gray? She was much younger."

There it was. The other hole.

"For the time being, we're treating it as two independent investigations. I've got DC Gold waiting for the boy to wake up. I've got DS Gillespie trying to get through to Poppy's friend, Grant Sayer."

"The quiet kid?"

She nodded again. He'd read the file notes and seemed to be on board with her decisions so far, which was always a plus.

"He had an altercation with another boy two weeks ago. Somebody Poppy was having relations with."

"Sex, Freya. You can say it. They were both consenting adults," he advised. "I take it our boy Sayer got a little jealous?"

"Yes, guv. It looks like he thought more of Poppy than she did him."

"And he attacked the boy, marking him as aggressive, which of course makes him a suspect in the Poppy Gray investigation?"

"No, guv."

"No, what?"

"I don't have him down as a suspect."

"Why not?"

"Because he loved her. Because she was all he had. His only friend."

"And she betrayed him."

"I haven't ruled it out entirely, guv. But he's not a focus right now. The other boy is."

"Who's the other boy?"

"A Danny Osborne. Petty criminal. He's got a few charges against him, possession, shoplifting."

"And now he's a killer, is he?"

"His dad's name is Jeffrey Osborne, guv," she said, hoping the name might ring a bell or two.

"So?"

Clearly it hadn't.

"He's served time for various offences. Again, a petty criminal–"

"Bad influence."

"Agreed. We have a theory that Daniel Osborne mentioned something to Poppy during their relations."

"Pillow talk?"

"Something like that. We think that when Daniel's parents decided to press charges, she might have used that information against them. To protect her friend."

"Plausible," he said, nodding. "I'm sensing quite a large *however*."

"There's a note on Jeffery Osborne's file from Lincoln HQ. Under no circumstances are we to question him or bring him into any investigation without sign-off from Lincoln HQ. He's under twenty-four-seven surveillance."

Granger pondered the position they were in for a moment. He leaned back in his chair and swept his grey hair off his forehead to form the parting that seemed to be chiselled into his head.

"So, you don't want to bring *him* in. You want the boy," Granger said, studying Freya's eyes. "But you think there may be a repercussion if you bring the boy in and the father gets involved?"

"Exactly."

"And you want me to seek approval to bring Daniel Osborne in?"

"Correct, guv," Freya said. "I was wondering if you could have a word with Detective Superintendent Harper for me. He might have some clout with Lincoln HQ."

Again, he stared at her, as if debating something, then relented.

"I suppose you should know," he said, then leaned forward on his desk, twiddling his pen in his fingers. "Detective Superintendent Harper hasn't been here for some time. I'm sure you've noticed."

"Guv."

"And the team?"

"There's been a few suggestions as to why he hasn't been around."

"Such as?"

"Promotion, mainly. Speculation, that's all it is."

"He's sick, Freya. I need you to keep this to yourself. Not even DS Savage can know."

"How bad is he?" she asked.

Harper had been affectionately nicknamed Arthur by the team, due to his uncanny ability to start a task then delegate it to somebody halfway through. Hence, 'Half-a-job Harper' had become Arthur. The naming had taken place long before Freya had been seconded to the station and was used with the utmost affection. He was a good man, coming to the end of his tenure, and his retirement was looming. It had been Arthur who had brought Freya up from London. His peers in the Met had suggested she would be a good temporary resource to fill a space in the team.

"Bad," he said.

"Anything we can do?"

"Your jobs, DI Bloom," he said. "And keep it to yourself. I'm picking up most of what he was doing, so if I'm not here, you know what I'll be doing."

"No worries, guv. We can handle it."

"That's why I'm telling you," he said, fishing a file from the pile on his desk, a subtle hint that the conversation was over. Freya stood and made toward the door. "I'll talk to HQ about Osborne. In the meantime, I suggest you bring the quiet lad in. I want to see progress and that means more than one line of enquiry, Bloom, whether the team have befriended him or not."

CHAPTER THIRTY-ONE

THERE WAS NO NEED TO POSITION A UNIFORM AROUND THE corner this time. Of that Gillespie was sure. Although Grant hadn't actually uttered a single word during their last chat, Gillespie was sure he would make some progress today. Positive, in fact. But that didn't stop him checking the first floor window from which he'd jumped before. It was open slightly, but he wasn't waiting for his chance.

Gillespie rang the doorbell then stood back, as was polite, and searched up and down the street. It was a quiet village. So quiet that the only vehicle he'd seen during the few minutes he'd been there was a bus passing through, a few early morning commuters staring into space as their days began.

The door opened and Mrs Frost stared up at him, tying a knot in her apron strings.

"You?" she said.

"Aye, it's me. Good morning, Mrs Frost."

"Don't you give me good morning. What have you said to him?"

"Eh?"

Not expecting to come under attack so soon, Gillespie started to fear the worst.

"You. That wee chat you had with him," she said, doing that thing with her fingers to demonstrate speech marks.

"What's wrong, Mrs Frost? Has something happened?"

"Has something happened? Yes, something has happened. He's gone, hasn't he? God knows when he'll be back. Been gone all night. I called him down for supper and he didn't come. I went up there to get him, he wasn't there. Window wide open, and not a Grant to be seen anywhere. What did you say to him?"

"I think maybe I should come in–"

"I think maybe you should be out there looking for him. Never mind coming inside."

"Mrs Frost, please. May I have a word with you? I'll go look for him after. He can't be far. He does it all the time, right?"

"I wouldn't say all the time, but yes, he's done it before. A few times," she said, re-tying her apron strings. Two faces appeared in the kitchen doorway behind her, giggled, then disappeared.

"Then he won't have gone far. I need to talk to you. It'll help me find him."

"Well..." she muttered.

"Please, Mrs Frost. I'll go out there and find him. But I need to talk to you first."

"You'd better be quick. I've a pie in the oven and it won't do for being burnt."

She stepped aside and Gillespie entered the house, peering up to the first floor landing at Grant's door. It was closed, and he'd expected nothing else. Perhaps some part of him hoped to find the boy staring down at him. Waiting for him. Pleased to see him, even.

"You'd better come through here," Mrs Frost said, leading him through to the kitchen.

The smell of home baking was better than any other smell in the world, as far as Gillespie was concerned.

"What is it?" he asked, nodding at the oven.

"The pie? Beef and ale. Grant's favourite."

"Well, if he catches scent of that, he'll be back in no time," Gillespie said, hoping to lighten the mood. But it was a long shot, and if Mrs Frost's scowl was anything to go by, he well and truly missed his mark. The two youngsters both ran from the room laughing and Mrs Frost called after them the way nobody had ever done to Gillespie.

"You'd better get washed up, you two. Breakfast soon, then we'll go to the park."

She returned her attention to Gillespie, eyebrows raised in anticipation for what he had to say.

"How much do you know about Grant's past, Mrs Frost?"

"Well, as much as anybody else. More, I'd like to think. But no doubt there's something I haven't been told."

Spying the kitchen table, Gillespie pointed at a chair. "Do you mind if we sit? It'll just take a moment."

He sat without waiting for an answer and Mrs Frost eyed him with suspicion. Then, after a moment of deliberation, she took the seat opposite him.

"Do you know something I don't, Detective...?"

"Gillespie. Call me Jim. And no. Well, not about Grant. But I can empathise. I was like him. Troubled, I mean. I, erm... I don't want this to sound like a sob story because, honestly, it's not. I was a wee bairn when I was sent off. Obviously, I didn't have a clue then. But when I grew up, when I was, I don't know, however old you are when you start to realise your surroundings, that's when I realised things weren't quite right. I had a shocking time of it, Mrs Frost. I just wanted to make sure you had an idea of what Grant has probably been through."

"He hasn't had an easy start in life, I'm sure. I've accommodated him as well as I can."

"And you're doing a great job. I'm not just saying that. If I had been sent to a home like this, I'd have been a very different lad.

But I wasn't. And Grant wasn't before this. You see, Mrs Frost, not all homes are like this. Not all homes have a few wee nippers bounding around and a cheery mummy in the kitchen cooking up delights like steak and ale pie, which, by the way, smells delicious. Some of them have other boys who would have been Grant's age or older. Some of them boys do things. Horrible things. Things that men like me, like Grant, and like a thousand others out there can never ever talk about. And they do it because they're angry, they do it for power, for control, and they do it because nine times out of ten someone further up the line did it to them. Do you understand?"

"I think I know what you're talking about, Detective. I've always told Grant he can come to me–"

"Aye, and that's grand, Mrs Frost. I wish I'd had someone to go to. Someone like you. You're lovely. But I wouldn't have. I wouldn't have come to you. Just like Grant will never come to you. Because nobody truly understands, and he doesn't want to talk about it. He's trying to forget it, but he can't. When he walks out that door there in the street, he thinks people know what he did. What they made him do. Those other boys. He thinks people are disgusted by him. By those things he was made to do. He'll go one of two ways, Mrs Frost. He'll either stay in his shell and be that person that can't get a job, that signs on every week, and lives in a poky, wee flat provided by the council. Because one day he'll have to leave here. One day, he'll be out of your care and he'll have to stand on his own two feet."

"The alternative?"

"He can do what I did. Start afresh, someplace nobody knows him. But it's hard, Mrs Frost. I was lucky. Not everyone is that lucky."

"Why are you telling me this? Do you honestly think I haven't wondered what he's been through? Do you honestly think that I took him on, sent him to his room, and just got on with life? How many nights do you think I've lain awake at night wondering if he's in there hurting himself, or just hurting? How often do you think I wonder what his voice sounds like? I've heard it twice, and both of those times, he's been in a rage or upset. Don't you think I'd love for him to come down and help me with dinner? Or even just sit there and tell me about his day? Or what he'd like to do with his life?"

"I don't doubt that for one minute, for a second even," Gillespie said. "But I think he needs a little encouragement, and with your permission, I'd like to be the one to help him. Tell me where he is, Mrs Frost."

"I don't know."

"Of course you know. You just spent the past five minutes demonstrating how lovely you are. You don't think for a minute that I believe you could just carry on baking pies if you didn't know he was safe, do you? You're far too good at being a mum for that nonsense."

"And how would you know what I'm like behind closed doors?"

"Because while I was in care, in the dozen or so homes that took me in just to get the government benefits, not to help kids like me, I never once came across anybody like you," he said, feeling his bottom lip tremble at the memories. "If I had, there'd be a very different me sitting right here right now, Mrs Frost. Now tell me where I can find him. Let's get him on the right road, eh? What do you say?"

CHAPTER THIRTY-TWO

DC Jackie Gold stood in the doorway of Lee Sanders' room. He was alone, asleep, and blissfully unaware of the world around him. Yet, since yesterday, another machine had been hooked up issuing yet another tone in the chorus of beeps.

"Beautiful, isn't he?" a voice said from behind her. She turned and found Teresa walking towards her carrying a little wash bag. She held it up. "Just been to do my morning ablutions. This place makes me feel so dirty. I haven't had a shower for three days now."

Jackie was taken aback by the honesty and it must have shown on her face.

"I've been strip washing," Teresa explained. "That and a hell of a lot of deodorant."

"Why don't you go home?" Jackie suggested. "I'll stay, if you want. I'll call you if he wakes up."

Teresa shook her head and stood beside Jackie, looking at her boy.

It was heart-wrenching. If the tables had been turned and it was Charlie lying there, there was no way Jackie would let someone she hardly knew keep an eye on him. But she pressed it further, seeing the effects of the last few days in the bags beneath Teresa's eyes.

"I mean it, Teresa. Go and get washed up. Or at least let me go to your house for you. I can grab you a few things."

"I thought you had to be here the moment he wakes up."

"I'll only be an hour. I can go. Honest, it's fine."

"No," Teresa said, adamant. "No, I'll be fine. But thank you. Honestly, thank you, Jackie."

They exchanged smiles, and Teresa rested her head on Jackie's shoulder briefly. A short display of affection and gratitude, from one single mother to another.

"No, I've got enough to get us by for a day or two still."

"How was last night?" Jackie asked, as Teresa stepped into the room and put her wash bag in her little holdall.

She sighed and averted her gaze to stare out of the window.

"Didn't the nurses tell you?"

"Tell me? Tell me what?"

At the window, Teresa turned to face her. Her expression was grim and her eyes shone with suppressed tears. "He had another fit, Jackie," she said, her voice rising in pitch. "The doctors came. They even asked me to leave while they worked on him."

"What? Why?"

"I don't know. They won't say. Or they don't know. Remember?"

"Oh, Teresa," Jackie said, and she went to her, wrapped her arms around the woman, and held her.

That was when the dam broke. She seemed to jolt in Jackie's grasp, as everything she had held back for the last few days came flooding out.

"I'm going to lose him. I know I am."

"No, you're not," Jackie said, pushing her away to hold her at arm's length and stare into her eyes. "Be positive. You have to be positive. You're tired. That's all. He's fighting. Look at him. He's fighting. Whatever it is, his little body is young and fit, and he can beat it."

"I wish I could see it like that," Teresa whined, and she came back for another hug.

"The lump on his head is nearly gone," Jackie said, trying to encourage her. "He's on the mend. Just a day or two more, and I bet he'll wake up and wonder where the bloody hell he is."

Teresa gave a little laugh, but it was weak and constrained by doubt.

"I hope so, Jackie. I really do. I can't lose him. I don't know what I'll do if I lose him. I mean, we've come this far. Everything I do is for him. For his future. If he dies..."

"He won't die–"

"If he dies, I'll have nothing left to live for."

"You've got everything to live for. He needs you to be strong, Teresa. Come on. Pull yourself together. You need sleep."

"I can't leave him."

"Maybe I can have a word with one of the nurses. Get you a bed or something. It can't be doing you any good sleeping in that chair."

"I'm fine," she replied, and sniffed loudly. "I'm fine. I'm sorry. I just have these moments of doubt. He'll be fine. You're right. He'll be okay."

"Teresa, you need to take care of yourself too."

"I know, I know. And if he's still here tomorrow, I'll go home for some sleep. You'll be here though, won't you?"

"Of course I will. I can't sit in that cafeteria all day," Jackie said. "I swear, that woman you pointed out to me, I think she thinks I'm watching her."

Teresa laughed, genuinely this time, and she held a tissue to her nose and gave it a blow.

"Thanks, Jackie."

"That's okay," Jackie replied, rubbing the woman's arm. She gave it a squeeze. "I brought you something."

"For me?"

"Yeah. I wanted to show you something. Thought it might pass the time."

Teresa's face brightened a little.

"Come on," Jackie said, and she pulled up a chair close to the one Teresa had been sitting in. From her bag, she produced a photo album and laid it on the little table. "I want you to meet my Charlie."

CHAPTER THIRTY-THREE

WITHOUT GILLESPIE IN THE INCIDENT ROOM, THE PLACE WAS quiet, save for the incessant humming from Cruz and the tapping of Chapman's fingers on her laptop keyboard.

Freya considered her meeting with Granger and stared at the board, as if something might jump out at her. Some vital clue that she hadn't seen before. But it didn't. It never did. Which was usually a sign they needed to talk to more people.

"What is that? The Harry Potter theme tune?" Ben asked Cruz, when the young DC had hummed the same part for the seventh or eighth time. "Don't you know the next part?"

"It's the Jurassic Park theme song. It's nothing like Harry Potter," Cruz said. "And yes, I know the next bit. But I've got the main bit stuck in my head."

"Well, do you mind not sticking it in our heads?" Anna asked. "It's bloody irritating."

"I can't help it. It was on the telly last night. Been humming it ever since. It's a sign of an active mind, you know?"

"What? Humming theme songs?"

"Just humming anything," Cruz explained. "All the greats do it. It's also a sign of happiness."

"Who told you that?"

"I can't remember now. I read it somewhere, I think."

"Okay, then, Cruz," Freya interjected. She sat back in her chair, tapping her pen against her desk while she thought. "Let's tap into that odd but somehow fertile mind of yours."

"My what?"

"Serial killers."

"What about them?"

"You seemed to be very knowledgeable on them before. What if Harringer was a serial killer?"

"Harringer?" he said, and he squinted one eye as he considered the alleged crimes. "Israel Keyes."

"What's Israel Keyes?" Anna asked.

"Not what, who," Cruz said.

"Who what?" Ben asked.

"Israel Keyes. He was a serial killer in the States," Cruz said, as if everybody should have known it. "From what we suspect Harringer of doing, I'd say he was using the same thinking as Israel Keyes, which doesn't really work over here. The UK is too small."

"Whereabouts in the States was he?" Ben asked, taking interest in what Cruz had to say.

Freya enjoyed moments like this. The young DC deserved a chance to demonstrate why he was an asset to the team. He might not be the brightest, but he certainly added his value at the most unlikely of times. And after his performance yesterday, this was his chance to claw a few brownie points back.

"That's just it," Cruz said. "He was everywhere. I can't remember exactly, but I think he lived in Alaska. Somewhere near Anchorage. But he'd fly to Utah, for example, and then rent a car. He'd drive that car to another state, murder somebody, drive to another state to bury them, then do the trip in reverse. It was convoluted but it worked. He'd even plan the places where he knew he would kill at a later date and bury boxes with everything he needed inside. Stuff like gaffer tape, rope, or whatever. It was so clever. If the police ever found a body, they wouldn't know who it was as the victim would be from a different state. The various police factions weren't connected back then. But, even if they did manage to work out who the victim was, there was no way of connecting them to a rented car from another different state, and then back to a flight back to Alaska. It was genius. Most successful serial killer, in my opinion."

"Most successful?" Ben said doubtfully.

"Yeah. The only reason he got caught was because he did something that was unplanned. Acted on the spur of the moment. Think about it. Harringer lives in Kings Lynn. Drives to Oxford. Kills Anita Carter. Drives her to Dorset. Buries her. Then goes home," he explained, turning back to Freya. "If you're asking who he reminds me of, it's Israel Keyes."

"So you think he was emulating a known serial killer?"

"No. But it does raise a serious question," Cruz said, leaning back in his chair, apparently pleased with his response.

"How many others have there been?" Freya said. "Chapman, how far back did you go when you looked into Harringer?"

"A few weeks," she said, shrugging. "You didn't ask for anything further back than that."

"That's okay. Cruz, sit with Chapman. Work together. Find out where he's been, and match that to unsolved cases that fit the demographic. Make that a priority, I'm sitting with Harringer later today. I want to hit him with something he can't get out of."

Cruz got up from his seat, picked up his phone, and edged his way through the desks towards the door. "No problem, boss," he said, just as the incident room door opened.

"Where are you going, Cruz?" Freya called out.

"I just need to use the bathroom. Won't be a minute."

He stopped when he saw a woman standing in the doorway, and edged past her, looking her up and down quizzically. A slightly disgusted look spread across her face when she heard Freya call out Cruz's name.

"Michaela," Freya said. "We weren't expecting you."

"No," she said, taking a step into the incident room. She came to a stop behind Ben, who closed his eyes and muttered something to himself. "I was passing. I thought you might like to see what we found."

"Sounds ominous," Freya said with a smile. "Let me introduce you. This is DC Chapman and DC Nillson. You know Ben, of course, and that was DC Cruz who just passed you."

She offered Chapman a wide-eyed nod, clearly remembering Freya's fictitious appraisal of the team's professionalism.

"Shall we use this table over here?" Freya suggested, and she moved to a round breakout table with five seats.

"It won't take long," Michaela insisted. "But I thought the results were interesting."

She retrieved a file from her tote bag and placed it on the table, then took a seat with a view of the team. Perhaps so she could keep a wary eye on the apparent misfits.

"We've analysed the car, inside and out. We have the DNA of the subject found in the boot, however, we can't find a match on any database."

"How up to date is the database?" Freya asked, thinking of Katy Southgate. "Chapman, any ideas?"

"I know local police have been searching for a match too. But if she hasn't been arrested or volunteered her DNA, then she won't be on there."

"Who are you talking about?" Michaela asked.

"A missing person from Long Sutton. We think our man picked her up on his way up here," Freya explained. "Chapman, can you share the records with Michaela for me? Just in case you stumble across anything else."

Michaela nodded then turned to the next page.

"We found traces of blood on the front of the car," she said, introducing the next topic. She shook her head. "No match to either Lee Sanders or the unknown with Doctor Bell."

"No match?" Freya said. "What about Anita Carter?"

Michaela, clearly playing catch up, shrugged. "Who?"

"Dorset police found a body a few days ago. It's a girl from Oxford who was reported missing."

"Hold on, hold on," Michaela said. "You think the unknown woman is from Long Sutton, at least an hour from here, maybe more. And you think the blood on the front bumper belongs to a woman who went missing from Oxford and was found in Dorset?"

"That's about the size of it. Chapman, talk to Dorset police and have them send the DNA results to yourself and Michaela. If it's a match, then we've got him. How quick can you do an analysis, Michaela?"

"If it's just a like for like, we can turn it around it around pretty fast."

"I need it faster than that," Freya said. "Chapman, scrub what I just said. Call Dorset. Make the introductions to Michaela's team. I need to know if the blood belongs to Anita Carter by two o'clock."

"Two o'clock?" Michaela said.

"That's when I'll be conducting the interview. If we don't have it. We might have to let him go. Is there a problem?"

"We've digitised our records. As long as Dorset have done the same, we'll be able to get it done."

"Chapman, over to you."

"Ma'am," she replied.

Freya turned to Michaela, who was staring at Chapman, looking her up and down.

"Professional enough for you, Michaela?" Freya asked with a smile.

"We'll see," she replied, then stood to leave. "I hope this was beneficial. Like I said, I'd normally call but I was passing, and well..."

Freya raised her eyebrows, waiting to hear the real reason for Michaela's impromptu visit.

"I wonder if we might have a word?" Michaela said.

"Sure," Freya replied, and leaned on her folded arms.

"In private."

"Ah, I see. Then follow me," Freya replied, and led her to the incident room door.

"Thanks, all," Michaela said, glancing around at the team. "Enjoy your day."

Ben said nothing. He hadn't moved, spoken, or even given an indication that she had been there, other than his initial reaction.

Freya pulled the door open for her, just as Cruz came through, wiping his hands on the sides of his trousers.

"Ah, you off?" he said, holding out his hand for her to shake. "I'm DC Cruz. I've seen you. A few months ago, in Dunston. You're the CSI girl Ben talks about, aren't you?"

She baulked at shaking his hand, but her reaction was somewhat distracted by his mention of Ben.

"Michaela," she said. "Michaela Fell."

"Nice to meet you anyway, Michaela," he replied, and edged past her to get into the incident room. "I'll just squeeze through. Don't worry. No need to move."

She looked as if she might be physically sick at his touch.

"This way," Freya said, as Michaela recovered from her interaction with Cruz and gave the back of Ben's head a final stare.

She led Michaela to the fire escape stairs, held the door, and followed her inside. Then, leaning on the handrail, she peered down to check they were alone and stared at Michaela, waiting to hear what she had to say.

"Here?" was all Michaela said.

"We can use an interview room if you'd prefer," Freya said. "But this is where we come for informal discussions. Off the record, as it were. You're safe in here, plus, this is a rank-free zone, so say whatever it is you have to say."

Appearing slightly bemused, Michaela put her hands in her coat pockets and stared Freya in the eye.

"I wanted to apologise," she said.

"Ah," Freya replied. "I see."

"I might have been a little harsh earlier. It's no reflection of you, or your team. I'm afraid I got a little defensive. You know? With Ben and me, and the whole incident at his house."

"Incident?" Freya said.

"You know what I mean. I've been harsh on him. I know I have. But DS Gillespie said something to me. It didn't really hit home until much later, when you'd all left the crime scene."

"What was that?"

"I can't remember word for word. But it did make me reconsider how I'd reacted."

"Reacted to seeing me at his house?"

"Having stayed the night," Michaela explained, and Freya nodded her understanding.

"And then seeing Ben half-naked on the stairs?"

"That didn't help."

"I didn't exactly do a lot to stop your imagination running wild, did I?" Freya said. "We're good friends, you know? Ben and I. But that's all it is."

"Do you want more from him?"

"If you're asking if you would be stepping on my toes by seeing him, which I think you are, then you should know that I value his friendship. I want him to be happy," Freya said, non-committal.

"I see," Michaela replied, and an awkward silence ensued.

"Truce?" Freya suggested, and Michaela beamed shyly.

"I'd like that."

"Good," said Freya. "What are you doing this Saturday? I'm planning a little get-together. Just us girls. A few glasses of wine and some live entertainment. How does that sound?"

A door below them opened and a figure bustled onto the

stairs. It was DCI Granger, taking each step rather gingerly, clearly suffering from his gym session.

"Ah, Bloom," he called out, without losing momentum. Using the handrail for assistance with each step, he hobbled onto the midway landing where the stairs turned and he saw Michaela. "Thought I could hear your voice. I'm afraid that's a no-go with Osborne. Lincoln HQ have twenty-four-seven surveillance on him. Spent too much money on him to have it all wasted on something his boy may or may not have done. Sorry, but you'll have to find another way."

"What about the boy? Can we bring him in?"

"Find me proof. Something concrete. I'll see what I can do. No promises," he said, as he heaved himself up the final step, shuffled past them, breathless, and through the door into the corridor.

"Sometimes I feel like even the powers that be don't want us to solve anything," Freya muttered to Michaela, who smiled back at her, understanding her frustrations.

"Saturday?" Michaela reiterated.

"About three p.m.? I'll send you the location."

"I'll be there," Michaela said, as she started down the stairs Granger had struggled to climb. "I'll be looking forward to the live entertainment."

CHAPTER THIRTY-FOUR

From Mrs Frost's home, Gillespie had crossed the road and worked his way along the lane to a little sign that marked a footpath through the fields. From there, he could see the forest in the distance where Poppy Gray had been found, and he traced the route back to the Sanders house, a tiny dot on the far side of open farmland, small clusters of trees, and a network of dykes.

He made his way down the footpath, leaving the quiet village behind. It was times like this he enjoyed his job. There was no abuse, no crowds, no noisy cars, and nobody to interfere with his thoughts. It was just him, his overactive brain, and the fresh air. The footpath led to a track, and adhering to Mrs Frost's directions, he followed the track to a field, where on the far side was a style, which he climbed over, and a tree, which he walked beneath, and then he saw it, and all of a sudden he knew why Grant liked the place so much.

There was so little sound, other than the birds, that the path behind him seemed almost deafening in retrospect. There were no buildings to be seen in that little natural dip in the ground, and no sign of mankind at all, save for the white scars that planes had left in the blue sky above him.

A small and gentle river flowed by, which Mrs Frost had called a beck, and had then had to explain that it was like a small stream. No doubt if know-it-all Cruz had been there, he would have explained it in depth. But he wasn't. It was just mother nature, DS James Gillespie, and sitting by the edge of the beck, Grant Sayer.

"Your mum said you'd be here," Gillespie said, by way of a greeting. But the boy didn't flinch. No doubt he'd heard Gillespie coming, like a small elephant traipsing across the grass. He walked up behind him and found Grant staring out at the water. "Mind if I sit?"

Of course, Grant said nothing, so Gillespie sat, keeping his distance. The water was mesmerising, but that wasn't why he was there. He looked about the surrounding area, noting a small, spent fire near to the tree he had ducked beneath.

"You slept here?" Gillespie said, expecting no reply. "Christ, Grant. You must be starving, sonny." Then Gillespie remembered the smell of Mrs Frost's home baking. "I hope you took one of those wee pies? Aye, that'll keep you going alright. That and a flask of tea, and then you sit back here and watch nature's TV."

Grant moved. It was just his arm, as his hand found a small pebble in the soil. He rolled it in his fingers then tossed it into the water, admiring the splash. Then he returned to his distant gaze.

"I ran away once, you know?" Gillespie continued with his monologue. "Well, more than once. Loads of times actually, but I think it was the first time I'd run away and meant it."

Grant glanced sideways at him then averted his eyes when Gillespie tried to meet his stare.

"There were these three lads. In the home I was in, you know? A wee bit older than me, but not much. I was the new kid, and thinking back, they were probably just trying to see who I was. Whether I was okay or if I didn't belong. If they'd have asked me, I'd have told them straight. I didn't belong anywhere and certainly not there. It was the oldest one that started it. Came into my room after lights out. The other two kept watch outside the door while he did what he had to do. Kept the bruises to below my shirt and bloodied my nose. Tore my books up. Then, when I thought he was done, just when I thought I'd escaped, I heard his belt buckle."

Gillespie coughed to clear his throat, and hated himself for dragging the memory out of that dark place. But it needed to be aired. He needed Grant to hear it. Of all the people to hear it, to share it with, it had to be Grant.

"Ah, who cares, right? I didn't even fight back. I'd had bigger and harder boys than him force my face into the pillow. If anything, it just made my mind up for me. He did what he had to do, spat at me, and left me there. I was gone before the sun came up, in the back streets of Glasgow's east end searching through the bins for something to eat, begging the wee baker shop for yesterday's buns. I didn't care. Not then. Not now. You do what you have to do, right? They can't get to you," he said, tapping the side of his head with his index finger. "Not here. They can't reach inside you. They can beat you, and hurt you, and sodomise you, but they can't break you. Not if you keep it all locked up. Not if you have your own world. That's what you do, aye? Lose yourself in your own world? Ah, ya don't have to tell me, kid. The world," he said, tapping his head again. "Far better than most of this world, aye. Anyways, I was out the back of this wee book shop. In the bins, as normal. Looking for something. You know? To while away the lonely days and nights. Something to take me away to a new world. Found a wee bag left by the back door of the book shop. Curiosity got the better of me and I looked inside. That was when I met him. Josh Conroy. Do you know him? Came up behind me and blocked my exit. You sure you haven't heard of him?"

Grant's eyes narrowed, and he turned his head to stare at Gillespie's hands. Not his eyes. But his hands were progress.

"Crime writer," Gillespie explained. "Bloody marvellous, his books are. I didn't know him, of course. He could have been just another bloke looking to have his way. So I insulted him. Told him what I thought of perverted old bastards like him. And I backed up. I remember it. I was clutching this old book. A paperback I'd found in the wee bag. The cover looked okay and it had all the pages. That's all I needed. But he walked up to me, not afraid and certainly not menacing. And I let him. I let him take the book from my hand. And can you guess what he did next?"

Slowly, Grant looked up and, for the first time, met Gillespie's stare. He shook his head.

"He signed it," Gillespie explained. "Bloody signed it. Turns out he'd bloody written it. Worth a wee fortune to a wee lad like me. Not that I sold it, mind. No way. I kept it. Read it all. Read all his books over the years, and I'll never forget that time."

Gillespie silenced to allow Grant a few minutes to imagine the encounter. He wondered if the lad had ever had to beg for his food. Or if his running away had never gone any further than sitting by a wee stream in a field with a stolen homemade pie and flask of tea.

"You're wondering what happened next, aren't you?" Gillespie said. "Aye, well... The local rozzers picked me up. Police, you know? Took me back to the home. Ah, what did I care? I had a signed book by Josh Conroy. I had my own world to live in. And I did. Live in it, you know. Until the boys came back the next night."

Grant averted his gaze again at the mention of the trauma.

"Ah well. Who cares, right?" Gillespie said. "I beat the living hell out of him, took my book, and I was gone," he said, flicking his own stone into the water. "Anyway... That's all water under the bridge now, eh? Look at me now. Did alright for myself, eh?"

Grant said nothing. He just stared. Gillespie wondered if he was having an imaginary conversation in his head. Like telling Gillespie to just go away and leave him the hell alone. That's what he would have been doing.

"Thought I'd leave you this," Gillespie said, reaching into his inside pocket, watching to see if Grant's eyes moved. They didn't.

He slid out an old paperback, titled *Say No More* by Josh Conroy, and set it down on the grass beside Grant.

"We've all got our own worlds, Grant. If you ever want a hand in this one, I'd like to help," Gillespie said, and he climbed to his feet and turned to leave him to enjoy the book in peace. "Just let the old lady know you're alright, Grant, eh? She's worried sick."

He left Grant there and ducked beneath the tree, and he had just put a boot on the style and was ready to climb over when a voice called out. It was Grant. By the time Gillespie had stepped back down and turned around, he was there, standing beneath the tree with the book in his hand.

"She didn't want to," he said, his voice deep like that of a man, and somehow fitting for a boy of Grant's stature. "She told him to stop."

CHAPTER THIRTY-FIVE

Ben stared at his laptop waiting for the little, blue, spinning circle thing to stop, and for his emails to open. It wasn't a difficult request, he thought. Open emails. Everyone else seemed to manage it just fine and they had almost identical laptops. But Ben's had never been right. It took about five minutes to actually turn on, then another five to ten minutes to be usable. Sometimes. Sometimes it was just never usable. Like today. And so began the rigmarole of restarting the machine, waiting five minutes for it to turn on again, and another five minutes for him to be able to actually move the cursor. On the occasion, like today, that still didn't work, keeping his finger on the power button until the screen turned black and the little fan stopped spinning sometimes did the trick.

So he tried it. The screen turned black. The little fan stopped spinning. And he was about to turn it back on when he considered taking it up to IT. But he knew what would happen. It would be like taking a sick child to a doctor, and none of the symptoms he had experienced would happen. The laptop would behave normally. Maybe he should move desks and go and sit near IT, using fear as a tactic to trick the laptop into actually working for once.

He closed the lid and shoved it to one side. Most of the important stuff was sent to the entire team anyway, and they were bound to have announced anything if it had come through.

He pulled the file across for Poppy Gray. The theory was that Poppy had stolen the car from the guest house, knocked Lee Sanders down, and then run up the little track. There, she had been killed. Removing Harringer from the mix, that left Mrs Sanders, who quite rightly had been tending her injured boy. And if it wasn't Mrs Sanders, then who was it? The Osborne kid? His father?

"What if Mrs Sanders hadn't been alone when the accident happened?" he said out loud, and Freya looked up from her desk.

"Go on," she said, and Ben stood and made his way over to the white board for no reason other than, without a working laptop, his desk seemed pointless and infuriating.

"Think about it. We take Harringer out of the equation. Which means we take the unknown woman and the car out of the equation. We're left with Poppy knocking the kid down, and Teresa Sanders. Until now, we've been sure Teresa Sanders stayed with her boy, and it makes sense. I don't know of any parent who could leave a child as injured as Lee Sanders was and run off after someone, regardless of what they had done. But what if Teresa hadn't been alone? What if she had somebody with her?"

"And that somebody was the one to give chase."

"He or she then did something terrible, something unforgivable."

"Then took off?" Freya asked. "Gold is getting close to her. Give her a call. See if Teresa Sanders has said anything about a boyfriend, or a friend. Anybody. She might have mentioned somebody in passing. But there is another alternative. Something we haven't discussed yet."

"What's that?" Ben asked.

"What if Poppy wasn't alone? What if *she* was with somebody, and Teresa Sanders just didn't see them. What if Poppy ran up that track after somebody?"

"Why would she do that?" Cruz asked. "You don't run towards a killer. You run away from them. Always away."

"Not if you trust them," Freya said. "This is good. Let's keep this going. We've got Harringer, let's focus on Poppy Gray. Who could have been with her?"

"Grant Sayer," Ben said. "Gillespie won't like it. But we have to consider him." He paused, thinking. "Or the Osborne kid."

"He's a no-go. That's straight from DCI Granger. HQ have surveillance on the father. We can't touch them. Not without something he can take to the powers that be."

"It's a bloody murder enquiry," Ben said. "The boy is potentially a key player."

"Maybe the father is up to something even worse?"

"Like what?" Cruz said, adding his two-pennies worth. "What's worse than murder?"

"That depends on your point of view, Cruz," Freya replied. "If, say, you've deployed a surveillance team on a team of individuals, and we're talking monitoring phones, watching houses, and mobile teams, you're looking at a pretty big bill. Are you going to let that all go to waste just because some jumped-up has-been detective in the sticks has a little murder she needs solving?"

"Probably not," Cruz replied thoughtfully.

"Exactly," Freya said. "So, until we have something solid to take to Granger, Osborne is off-limits. We focus on Grant Sayer."

"Gillespie is with him now," Ben said. "We'll know more this afternoon."

"We've got something," Chapman said. "I think, anyway." She moved from one of her screens to the other, checking her facts, and she held her hand up just to keep Ben and Freya interested.

"Oh, Christ," Cruz said. He was in the seat beside her and

could see exactly what she was looking at. "Israel Keyes eat your heart out. Not literally, of course."

"Chapman?" Freya said, and Ben felt her glance at him to make sure he was paying attention.

"Harringer," Chapman replied. "We've been through his travel records and developed a map and timeline of all his travels over the past three months. It's mainly from his phone records and his bank statements. He gets about a bit. Must be in high demand."

"While Chapman did that, I pulled together a list of all missing persons and unknown bodies found across the various police factions. Oxfordshire, Derbyshire, Dorset, Essex. Wherever he's been in the past three months, we know who's gone missing from those locations," Cruz said. "And if there are any unclaimed deaths."

"Can't be many," Nillson suggested, looking up from her laptop and entering the conversation.

"More than you think. It's frightening when you think about it," Cruz said.

"Anyway," Chapman interjected, before Cruz went off on a tangent, "Sarah Cooper. Reported missing from Luton nearly four weeks ago. Turned up dead in a field just outside of Romford in Essex."

"Nobody knows how she got there and local police are due to hand it over as a cold case. Expended too much resource on it."

"Do we have DNA?" Ben asked.

"Yep, we've got the lot. Romford nick made the data available nationwide, hoping for someone like us to come along," Cruz said proudly.

"I'm sitting with Harringer in an hour," Freya said. "Any later than that and he walks. Get the DNA to Michaela. Let's see if we can't match Sarah Cooper to his car. We need something to hold him."

The phone on Ben's desk rang, and while the team discussed

the latest breakthrough, he strolled over and answered the call, not recognising the number that flashed up.

"DS Savage," he said.

"Ben?"

He recognised the voice but couldn't put a face to it.

"Can I ask who this is please?"

"Don't be like that."

And then he realised who it was.

"We were just talking about you," he said quietly. The last thing he wanted was for the team to realise who he was talking to and listen in.

"All good, I hope? I didn't feel my ears burn."

"It was work-based. You know us. Professional."

"Is that a dig? If it helps, DC Chapman didn't look like a dogger, but I'd be wary of that little bloke. Cruz, was it? Spent far too long in the bathroom. And why does he take his phone?"

"You didn't call to talk about the team, did you? If it's about what you saw at my house, I honestly didn't mean to flash you. It was the towel–"

"I'm not sure what you're on about, if I'm honest. I wanted to say I'm sorry. For the way I treated you. Do you want the good news?" she asked, the excitement evident in her voice.

"You found a signed confession in the glove box?"

"Close," Michaela replied. "It's about the blood on the front of the car."

Ben felt his face light up. He waved his hand to get Freya's attention, and then hit the loudspeaker. "Say that again. What you just told me."

"You mean the bit about you flashing your penis at me? Or what DC Cruz does in the bathroom?"

"Eh?" Cruz said, both confused and annoyed.

"The blood, Michaela," Ben said, silencing Cruz's outburst with a single raise of his hand. "The bit about the blood."

"Am I on loudspeaker?"

"We can all hear you, Michaela," Freya said. "Thanks for getting back to us."

"The blood on the car bumper. It's not Anita Carter's. We had a video call with Dorset lab to save time. It's not a match."

"Damn and blast," Freya snapped. "Okay, thank you, Michaela. Will you keep looking, please? I need something to hold Harringer."

"I'll call if I find anything else," Michaela said, bringing the call to a close.

"Hang on," Ben said. "We've got another one. Another body. A girl from Luton. Found in Romford, Essex. Maybe the blood is hers?"

"It could be her. What's the name?"

"Sarah Cooper. Romford nick were due to hand it over to cold cases. I'll have Chapman make an introduction."

"The dogging girl, you mean?" Michaela asked.

"The bloody *what*?" Chapman called out, clearly not taking the comment as well as Cruz did.

"That's her," Ben said, seeing the funny side. "Can you turn it around fast?"

"I can try," she replied. "But I wouldn't pin your hopes on it."

"Thanks for calling, Michaela. Take care, yeah."

There was a pause, which signified that Michaela was either dying inside for not thinking before she spoke, or that she wanted to say more.

"You too," she said, in a far more friendly tone than she had used in recent conversations.

Ben hit the button to end the call and stared up at the team.

"Dogging girl?" Chapman said, her face twisted with disgust.

"What I do in the bathroom?" Cruz said, adopting Chapman's expression.

DC Anna Nillson, who had until now been listening in while she worked, burst out laughing.

Freya scooped her file from the desk and sauntered over to the door wearing probably the biggest smile Ben had ever seen on her face. "Come on, Ben. This is our last chance to scare the hell out of Harringer. With any luck, he'll confess, but somehow I doubt it," she said, as her phone began to chirp.

She was halfway through the door and stopped to answer the call.

"Gillespie. Give me some good news," she said, and Ben watched her smile fade, then return with even more vigour than before. "Bloody good work, Gillespie. Brilliant."

She ended the call just as DCI Granger came out of his office, clearly overhearing the team's shouts.

"What the bloody hell is going on out here?" he asked, his face reddening. "I'm on a call with DCI Harper, and all we can hear is you lot. You especially, DI Bloom."

"Sorry, guv. Just had some good news," she replied. "Gillespie managed to get Grant Sayer talking."

"So? Is that a reason to shout in the corridor?"

"It's Danny Osborne, guv," Freya started.

"The boy who had relations with Poppy Gray, you mean?"

"He may have had relations with *her*. But she didn't exactly consent to it."

"He raped her? Is that what you're saying?" Granger said, making sense of the information his own way.

"Enough to bring him in, do you think?" she asked, and there was no concealing the smugness on her face.

"How sure are you?"

"The witness has spoken twice in the past two years. This is the third time. He's not one to waste words, guv."

Granger nodded. "I'll see what I can do. We'd have to work with the surveillance team and go in when the father is out of the way. He's eighteen, so we won't need a parent present. But we need to take their direction." He nodded again, considering the calls he would have to make. "Good work. Leave it with me. I'll call HQ now."

Leaning into the incident room, Freya caught Anna's attention. "That's one for you, Nillson. When we get the all-clear, you can bring him in."

"Osborne?" she said. "Me?"

"Yes, you. You're my go-to girl for all the rough stuff. Talk to Sergeant Priest, you'll need uniforms. Get an arrest strategy together. You know what to do," Freya said. "And take Cruz with you. Show him how it's done. He might learn something."

CHAPTER THIRTY-SIX

The route back to the Rainforest Wing was so easy now, Jackie could have navigated it purely by smell – the cafeteria and its bitter coffee, the long corridor where the open windows let the scents of flowers into the building, then the smell of stale sweat and bodily functions as she neared the wards. The whole route was, of course, layered with disinfectant, which was stronger in the corridor, where for some reason the guy with the mop and bucket seemed to spend most of his time.

This time, however, that was where the familiarity ended. She hit the buzzer to be allowed onto the ward, and when, after about twenty seconds, the door hadn't clicked open, she peered through the little window and found the nurses' station empty. She gave a little tap on the glass, just as a nurse ran past. The nurse stopped running, glanced down the ward, then hit the buzzer to open the door.

"Can I help you?" she said, with urgency in her voice.

"DC Gold. I've been sitting with Lee Sanders."

"Come on," she said, turning on her heels. "You can help us with his mother."

"What's happening?" Jackie asked, struggling to keep up with her. But she didn't answer, and by the time Jackie got to Lee's room, it was obvious. There were at least five nurses in there, all busy following protocol. Two doctors issued orders and conferred with each other. None of what either of them were saying could be heard, though, above the wailing of Teresa Sanders.

She was standing just inside the door being restrained by a nurse, who was fighting to get her out of the room.

"Teresa," Jackie called, and the boy's mother launched herself into Jackie's arms, her face burning and sticky with tears pressed on Jackie's neck. "What's happening?"

"He's crashed," the nurse explained, grateful to have Teresa out of her arms. "Get her out of here."

"Teresa, let's go," Jackie urged, trying to lead her from the room. But the mother was adamant. The flat soles of her trainers gripped the lino floor, and she dug in.

"No," she shouted, pulling from Jackie's grasp. "I'm not leaving, not now. He needs me."

Grabbing her around the waist, Jackie pulled Teresa out of the way of a nurse who was trying to get past with a trolley carrying some kind of machine.

"Now, Teresa. Come on, let's go. They know what they're doing."

"He needs me. He needs me."

Finally, Jackie managed to link her hands around the woman's waist, hoist her into the air on her hip as far as she could, and drag her out. But Teresa wasn't giving up that easily. Her arms flung out and she gripped the door frame. She kicked out at Jackie's legs, catching her on the knee, and then when Jackie released her, she sprang forward to be by Lee's side.

"Get her out of here," one of the doctors ordered, and two of the nurses managed to drag her kicking and screaming back to the door, where Jackie took over, managing to get in front of her and force her backwards.

"He's gone," she screamed at Jackie, her face bright red with anguish. "He was fine. Then the machine...the beeping..." she blubbered, gesturing at the devices that had been surrounding Lee for the past three days. "They all started."

"Let's go," Jackie said, spying a few visitors chairs to one side of the doorway. "Let's sit here. We'll be close by. Nothing is going to happen. Let them do their jobs, Teresa."

"He needs me," she whined, and Jackie had to get up close and personal, so that her face was just inches from Teresa's. "I mean it, Teresa. He's going to be okay. You're here. He knows it. He can hear you. I'm sure he can. And if he's fought this long, he's not giving up just yet. Come on. Sit."

Teresa didn't budge and another nurse came tearing down the ward, barging them out of the way to get into the room.

"Look," Jackie said. "There's about ten of them. He's going to be fine."

Slowly, Teresa relented and allowed Jackie to coax her towards a seat. Positioning herself between the mother and the door, Jackie prepared to grab hold of her if she tried to intervene again.

"Tell me what happened," she said. "I was only gone ten minutes."

"He just..." Teresa began, then faltered. "I don't know. He just. The machines. It was chaos. The nurses, they came in and told me to leave. Then more came. They said he was okay. But then the doctors came. They ran. Doctors don't run. Even I know that."

Offering her a tissue from her bag, Jackie could do little but imagine it was Charlie in there, and there was no way she'd let some copper she didn't know stop her from being by his side.

"Oh, Teresa," she said, and pulled her in for a hug. "I'm here. I'm with you. But you need support. Is there no one I can call? Family? A boyfriend maybe?"

"There's nobody," Teresa muttered through the tissue, and she blew her nose, just as a male voice called out from the room.

"Clear."

"Oh god, no."

"Teresa, stay," Jackie said, holding her close. This time, she wouldn't let go. Not until it had finished. One way or another.

The defibrillator recharged with a high-pitched whine, and Jackie felt Teresa's body jolt just as if she'd been the one on the receiving end of the shock.

"Think of a good time," Jackie suggested. "Think of a time when it was just you and him. Playing. You said he likes football. Think of a time, Teresa."

"I've done it. I've tried. I wasn't there for him. I wasn't good enough," she said. "I was always busy."

"Don't say that–"

"I was. I'm a terrible mother. I can't remember a single good time. Always me moaning at him, or him whining. But he can whine. Oh god, I want to hear him whine, Jackie."

"You will. Have faith in them–"

"Clear."

Another recharge of the machine, and Jackie glanced along the ward. The open door meant the few patients and visitors that were present could hear everything. But Teresa hadn't noticed. She had her face buried in Jackie's neck, and Jackie couldn't tell if she was holding her or keeping herself from collapsing onto the floor.

"He'll be okay," she whispered into Teresa's ear, rocking her gently back and forth. In Jackie's mind, she was remembering Charlie's face when her mother had taken him swimming, and he'd come back elated and wild with energy, and had told her all about the slides. In fact, every memory she recalled of Charlie coming home elated, it had been after her mother had taken him somewhere. "He'll be okay. Just think of a time."

CHAPTER THIRTY-SEVEN

DC Anna Nillson pulled the car up behind a van that was parked on the side of the road. She killed the engine and sat back, and she heard the chatter over the radio as the marked transport van found a place to hold up less than a mile away. The surveillance teams had made it clear that under no circumstances was the van to come any closer until they had confirmed Jeffery Osborne was out of the area, and, according to his movements, he was due to head into Lincoln in under ten minutes.

"This is bloody mental," Cruz said from the passenger seat. "I haven't done anything like this since I was in uniform."

"You haven't been on a raid since you joined DI Bloom's team?"

"Well, yeah, there was that old bloke in Nocton that time. But he was dead anyway. And then there was that kid who sold all the war memorabilia."

"He was dead too, though, right?"

"Yeah."

"Well, hopefully this one's alive, and you can watch me nick him," Anna said, then held her hand up as a call came over the radio, giving them the all-clear. The next call confirmed that the transporter was on its way carrying six burly uniforms, and Anna repeated her plan to them for the third time. Two men around the back. Two to wait in the van. And two to provide back-up for her and Cruz.

"You mean we're not sending uniform in?"

"No, Gab. He's a boy. He's hardly going to fight back. Besides, we don't want to be too heavy-handed. It's all about Daniel Osborne. We can't let it be known that we know anything about his dad at all."

The transporter cruised by and Anna pulled out behind it. There were no screaming sirens, no fuss whatsoever. Two of the uniforms made their way to the back alley while Anna and Cruz got out. It was a council house, a little rundown but otherwise a decent sized family property. The grass could have done with a mow, but it was spring, and most people hadn't got around to the first cut of the year just yet.

"Stay behind me," she advised him, as she knocked on the door. Three raps, just like DS Savage. She waited a few seconds, listening for movement from inside, then rapped again, triggering an angry response.

"Alright, I'm bloody coming."

The front door was white UPVC with three frosted windows set into the plastic, and through it, Anna saw a figure approaching slowly. Then the door opened.

"Daniel Osborne?"

The young man's hair was short and heavily gelled, and though he barely needed to shave, he had grown what he clearly regarded as a beard but was little more than a few lengthy whiskers sprouting from his chin and a layer of soft down across his upper lip.

Between the gelled hair and the laughable beard, however, a wide plaster covered the bridge of his nose, and the remnants of two black eyes were evident in the form of two dark but yellowing rings.

Clearly in some discomfort, he stood unnaturally straight, held up only by the assistance of two crutches. With a broken femur and several broken ribs, the boy wasn't running anywhere.

"What?" he said, seeing the transporter van outside and rolling his eyes. "I ain't done nothing."

Anna revealed her warrant card. "I'm Detective Constable Nillson from Lincolnshire Major Incident Team. This is Detective Constable Cruz."

"So?"

Anna paused. She could see it in him. She could see the cruelty in his eyes; whether by nature or nurture, the blood that ran through the boy was bad. She would have loved nothing more than to cuff him and drag him to the transporter. But this one, this one was for the team. It was for Poppy. She turned to Cruz, who was staring at the lad, eyeing his filthy tracksuit bottoms in disgust.

"Cruz," she said.

"Eh?" he looked up as if he thought he had missed something. Like he hadn't been paying attention.

She nodded at Osborne. "He's yours."

"Me?"

She gave him a wide-eyed stare as if to say, 'Hurry the bloody hell up though'.

"Oh, right," he said, clearly unprepared. Then he stepped forward. "Daniel Osborne, I'm arresting you on suspicion of rape. You do not have to say anything, but it may harm your defence if you later rely on in... No, wait."

"Is this a joke?" Osborne said. "Am I being arrested by a schoolboy? I ain't putting up with this."

He shoved the door closed and Cruz stuck his boot out, kicking the door open. Turning on his crutches, Osborne made a sucking noise with his mouth, presumably something he'd seen in a film.

"Get out my house, boy. You ain't coming in here."

"Boy?" Cruz said, and to Anna's surprise, Cruz stepped into the hallway and seemed to grow with the indignation. "Boy?"

"Might as well be," Osborne muttered, his confidence waning.

And Cruz spoke, every word articulated clearly as if reciting his own name.

"Daniel Osborne, I'm arresting you on suspicion of rape. You do not have to say anything. But it may harm your defence if you do not mention now something you later rely on in court."

"Shut up, bitch," Osborne spat, but the deep voice he had used before had risen in pitch. "I ain't going nowhere. Rape? How am I going to rape anyone? I can barely make a cup of tea, fool."

Cruz leaned in close to him, so close that Anna thought he was going to headbutt the suspect. But he didn't. He stopped there, staring deep into Osborne's dark eyes.

"Anything you do say may be given in evidence," Cruz finished, and in one deft movement, he cuffed the boy's wrist to his own. "How do you feel about that, boy?"

CHAPTER THIRTY-EIGHT

Roy Harringer was a handsome man. He wore a flannel shirt with a check design. He had rolled his sleeves up and loosened his collar, presumably, Freya thought, due to the temperature in the cells which was often uncomfortable by design.

Ben made his way to the desk and set the recording up while Freya loitered beside the door waiting for Harringer's legal representative, who arrived five minutes late and chose to defend her tardiness with a scornful look aimed directly at Freya.

"A little more notice next time wouldn't go amiss," she muttered.

"I'm confident there won't be a next time, Miss Shaw," Freya replied. "How does that sound?"

"Doubtful," Shaw muttered, as she took her seat beside Harringer and opened her files.

As before, they went around the room to introduce the present parties, then, as a wild cat might, Freya went straight for the jugular, and to coin one of Gillespie's phrases, she did not pass go and she did not collect two hundred pounds. She maimed, hoping to break Harringer with hard facts.

"We finished the previous interview, whereby you denied any knowledge of both Anita Carter or Katy Southgate, Mr Harringer, despite, and for the benefit of the recording, our researchers placing you in Oxford when Anita Carter was reported missing, in Dorset, at the time she was found, and passing through Long Sutton when Katy Southgate was reported missing. Have you used your time effectively, Mr Harringer? Would you like to amend your statement at all, or do you wish to continue as you were?"

"I've never heard of her."

"Who?"

"Anita Carter."

"And Katy Southgate?"

He shrugged, and held his hand to his chest. "Hand on heart. Never heard of her."

He glanced across at his solicitor, who finished making her notes, then gave him the nod.

Freya laid her hands flat on the table. "Perhaps you could tell me a little about Katy Southgate?"

"I don't know her. I just told you."

"Long Sutton. You said you stopped for petrol. Was she filling up as well, maybe?"

"No–"

"Maybe hitchhiking. Do people still hitchhike?" she asked Ben.

"Yeah, still happens," he said.

"So maybe she was hitching a ride, Roy? Maybe she was going your way?"

"No. I told you–"

"Or maybe she had broken down. Although, there was no mention of her car being found. How do you normally find your victims, Roy?"

"I don't have victims–"

"Is it you that makes the first move? A good-looking man like you. They must flock to you. Man alone. Wedding ring. Girls love a married man. Frequent travel. They must be queueing to climb into the boot of your car."

"Can we keep this to the facts, please?" Miss Shaw said. "You are fast running out of time, so I suggest you use the remaining..." She checked her watch. "Hour effectively."

"I know you did it, Mr Harringer."

"You know nothing–"

"Talk to me about Sarah Cooper," Freya said, and watched his expression change. When she had first mentioned Anita Carter and Katy Southgate, his expression had remained as impassive as the day she had first seen him on the stairs at the guest house. But now, at the mention of Sarah Cooper, he demonstrated some kind of recognition, though he quickly tried to hide it. "You know her."

"I do not–"

"Then I imagine learning that she was recently found dead in a field in Essex will mean very little to you."

This time, he was unable to hide his emotions. His face pulled back to form a grimace, revealing his incisors as a predator might threaten its prey.

"What?" was all he managed to mutter.

"Sarah Cooper. Lived in Luton. Was reported missing four weeks ago. Turned up dead in a field in Romford, Essex, shortly after," Freya said, stating the facts with absolutely no hesitation whatsoever. "And for everybody's benefit, we checked your bank and phone records. It seems you too were in Luton at the time Sarah was reported missing. And guess what, Mr Harringer?"

He seemed to wobble on his seat, like his neck had turned to elastic. But he said nothing.

"You were in Romford the day before her body was found. Imagine that."

"Isn't this simply pure coincidence?" Shaw suggested.

"Coincidence?" Ben said, speaking up for the first time. "Your client was in Luton when Sarah Cooper was reported missing, and then travelled to Romford where her body was found. He was then in Oxford when Anita Carter was reported missing and travelled to Dorset where her body was found. Now we have Katy Southgate, who, for fear of overstating what we've already mentioned a dozen times, was reported missing from Long Sutton right about the time Mr Harringer was travelling through. It's her, isn't it? In the back of your car, Roy–"

"I wouldn't hurt anybody–"

"With a woman's body in your car, Roy," Freya said, taking the reins from Ben, "we may not have enough to charge you yet. But we have enough to continue an investigation centred around you and your family."

"What have my family got to do with this?"

"Right now, nothing. But we will obviously have questions. Your wife will need to be interviewed. Your house will be searched."

"Or?" he said.

"Or I can spare them. Your family. I'll give you a little insight into what could happen if you come clean, shall I? People tend not to get bail on a murder charge, so we'll keep you here until you attend the magistrates court for your first hearing. From there, you'll be held on remand, in prison most likely. HMP Lincoln. Then a date will be set for your appearance in the crown court, by which time we will have progressed with the murders of Sarah Cooper and Katy Southgate. You could be looking at three counts of murder, Roy. Thirty years plus. What will that make you? Eighty something when you get out? How old will your children be? They'll probably have kids of their own by then. You may or may not have met them. Through the glass in the visitors area. But they won't really know you. You won't really know them. Either way, your family will find out. It's just whether or not you want to put them through the heartache now, or when you're safely behind bars."

He stared at the floor, slowly raising his gaze to meet Freya's eyes.

"I didn't kill them," he said.

"Then I'm afraid you're in for a rough ride. As are your family. Think about your kids. Think about their lives. And your wife? Is it worth it, Roy?" she asked, shaking her head. "Is it really worth putting them through all that? Tell me what happened. The more you tell us now, the better the light in which a jury will see you. But lie to us, hide information from us, and it won't just be you that suffers."

He cleared his throat and whispered in Miss Shaw's ear, who did her best to hide some kind of surprise. Then he turned back to Freya and shifted his attention to Ben.

"My wife can't find out."

"I'm sure the papers will be careful not to let her see their articles," Freya said facetiously.

"No. I mean... What I'm going to tell you, it stays between us, right?"

"I'm afraid this is a police interview. The recording may or may not be used as evidence. Just like everything you've said."

"It can't," he said, and he began rocking back and forth, clutching at his stomach. "She can't know. It wasn't me who killed those women, but..."

"But?" Freya said, seeing the light in his eyes brighten.

He took a breath, choosing his words, summoning the strength to reveal his dark secrets.

"I know her."

"You know who?"

"Sarah," he said. "Sarah Cooper."

Freya and Ben exchanged glances. It was coming.

"And you saw her, one month ago when you were in Luton?"

He nodded.

"For the recording, please."

"Yes. I know her. I saw her. But I didn't kill her."

"We're going to need a little more than that if we're going to help you prove your innocence, Roy," Freya suggested.

"I didn't kill her," he said, and slammed his hand down on the desk. Then he said it. Those three words that made no difference whatsoever. "I loved her."

Freya glanced at Ben, who waited for the rest of it to come. The flood gates were open. It was only a matter of time.

"I loved them both," Harringer said.

"Them both?" Ben asked.

"Sarah," he said, looking between Ben and Freya. "And Anita. I loved them. I wouldn't hurt them. Why would I hurt them?"

"And Katy Southgate?" Freya asked.

"I don't know her. Honest to god, I don't know Katy Southgate," he said, tears streaming down his face. "And I certainly wouldn't kill her either."

The room was silent, save for Harringer's tears and soft whines, as he buried his face in his hands. Shaw wrote her notes, devoid of any emotion, and clearly quite angry that her client hadn't revealed the truth to her from the outset.

Ben nodded at Freya in response to a question she had only thought, not voiced.

"Do you realise what will happen next, Roy?" she said. "You will be released. You may go home, but you may not travel from there while this investigation continues. Your home will be searched, your family questioned. The lives of your wife and children will be affected, but I dare say not as much as the life of that poor boy who now, three days after your car knocked him down, is still in critical condition."

Harringer stared at her, his eyes a burning red.

"Last chance," she said.

But Harringer said nothing.

"That's time," Shaw said, collecting her notes into an orderly pile. "Will you be charging my client?"

Freya stared at her, then at Harringer.

"Not at this time," she said. Then Freya muttered under her breath, as she stared Harringer in the eye, searching for something, a sign, a clue, "God help you."

CHAPTER THIRTY-NINE

Teresa Sanders sat with her head resting on Jackie's shoulder. She had long since stopped sobbing, but a steady flow of tears ran from her eyes and, occasionally, she blew her nose, working her way through Jackie's supply of tissues.

Another sound that they hadn't heard for a while was the defibrillator recharging. Even the controlled but anxious voices of the nurses and doctors had died down to a gentle lull. A few of the nurses had left, along with one of the doctors, hurriedly making their way out of the ward to see another patient with another set of problems. By Jackie's count, though she hadn't looked inside the room for a while, she estimated there to be one doctor and two nurses remaining. She could hear their hushed voices, but that was all.

It was hard not to imagine the worst. But the reality was that Lee had crashed several times in the last few days, and despite everything she had said to keep Teresa from breaking down, she hadn't believed a word of what she had told the young mother. She hoped, of course. But hope was just a torment when it came to a sick child. A poor, defenceless boy who had only been out crossing the quiet lane outside their home.

Life could change in an instant.

She'd seen it so many times before. Especially while she had still been in uniform. So many road traffic accidents. So many split-second decisions. So many lost lives and broken families.

The door opened and Teresa opened her eyes but stayed where she was, as if she was hiding behind Jackie.

"DC Gold, isn't it?" the nurse said, and she pulled the door closed and nodded once at somebody inside.

"That's me, yeah. Is–"

"Would you care to come with me?" the nurse said. She was what her mother might have called a robust woman with the face of an angel. But clearly an experienced nurse. A resilience had formed like a protective shell.

"Is Lee..." Jackie started, hoping the nurse would fill in the rest. But she turned and eyed Jackie, revealing nothing through her stare.

"We can talk in one of the rooms," she said, and walked on, expecting Jackie to follow.

"I'll just be a minute, okay?" Jackie said, easing Teresa's head from her shoulder.

It was like the woman was drunk. Dog tired. Emotionally drained. She barely had the strength to keep herself upright. But Jackie positioned her against the wall and looped her arm through her handbag, an old trick she had learnt sleeping in airports during her younger days, when all-inclusive holidays in Majorca were booked as soon as she and her mates had enough cash. It had become a twice-a-year affair. Three times, one year. But it was always the journey home when they could barely stand, let alone walk to the plane, when they would loop the handles of their luggage around their limbs and find a quiet corner of the airport to crash.

"I'll just be a mo, alright?" she whispered, and brushed her hair from her face.

Teresa was a pretty lady. She didn't deserve this. Her future was uncertain. On one hand, the rest of her years might very well be spent alone in that house in the middle of nowhere. On the other, she could have a severely disabled child to look after well into his adult years.

Following the nurse, Jackie approached the front desk and caught sight of her in a small room. She waved, signalling she was coming, but the smile she offered was weak and filled with anxiety.

"Is he alright?" Jackie asked, as she entered the little consultancy room and closed the door behind her. She waited with bated breath while the nurse unfolded her file and beckoned for her to sit.

So Jackie sat. Perched on the edge of the seat, hands clasped together in prayer, she waited. It was as if the nurse was teasing her. As if she was prolonging the agony.

A few moments later, they were joined by a doctor in a white jacket. He nodded a greeting, unsmiling, and took the nurse's file from her, sliding it across the desk like he was an estate agent perusing the portfolio with a client. He pulled off his glasses, folded them, and then stowed them in his breast pocket. Then he linked his fingers, leaned on the desk, and stared at Jackie. It was a practised move. Clearly perfected to instil the utmost confidence in grieving parents.

"Lee pulled through," he said finally, and Jackie could have just fallen to the floor right there, had it not been for what the doctor followed up with. "But we don't know for how long."

"What do you mean? You said he pulled through. He did it once. He'll get better, won't he?"

"Detective, how much do you know about head injuries?"

He was a handsome man. Or at least he had probably been in his day. With benefit of a full head of grey hair, his blue eyes were like marbles. And he was lean. So lean and muscular that even the muscles on his hands were toned.

"Not much. I've seen plenty, but once the paramedics get them in the ambulance, that's the last I see of them. Why?"

"Well, that's the easy bit, I'm afraid. We get to deal with the repercussions. It's rarely a pretty sight. But in this instance, it's not the head injury we're concerned with."

"I don't understand. He was hit by a car. He had a lump on his head like a golf ball."

"And we're quite happy that his head injuries are well and truly on the mend. That's why he's in this ward and hasn't been referred to a full-time neurologist. There's something else. We're not sure what. But we need to keep him in, maybe long-term."

"What? Why? If his head is okay then–"

"Something happened in the accident. It triggered some kind of underlying illness. It's his blood. We'll be performing a transfusion. But, I'm afraid, he could experience the effects for the rest of his life."

"Oh God–"

"And it might not be a long life, I'm afraid."

"Wait..." Jackie said, getting to grips with the root of the conversation. It was like interviewing a suspect who was leading you down the garden path. The trick was to understand the reason why. Not the how. Not the who. The why. "Why are you telling *me* this? Why aren't you explaining this to the boy's mother?"

"She doesn't have any family. She doesn't have any friends. We were hoping you could..." The doctor paused, clearly hoping Jackie would fill in the blanks.

"Break the news to her?" Jackie said. "Are you kidding me?"

"No. No, not break it. Of course, I'll do that. I was hoping you would be with her. Help her understand it."

"Like an appropriate adult? Aren't there people who do that?"

"You're close to her. We've seen you. We've seen nearly as much of you as we've seen of her. And if I'm honest, Detective, I'm concerned for her well-being. She needs to go home. She needs proper rest. There's nothing anyone can do now until we perform the transfusion. But she refuses to leave his side. There's something not quite right with her."

"Her son is in intensive care."

"No. It's more than that. I'll be keeping an eye on her. But if I'm honest. I think she might do something stupid. I don't quite trust her state of mind."

"Do you have children, Doctor?"

"Yes, I do, and this is not the first time I've witnessed a distressed parent. I'm reporting her state of mind to you. Her son is my responsibility. I wouldn't be doing my job if I failed to report what experience tells me is a fragile mind."

"You want me to be with her when you tell her?" she said.

"Is that too much to ask?"

The request required little time for consideration. In a flash, Jackie put herself in Teresa's shoes, and the decision was made in a fraction of a heartbeat.

"Of course," she said. "Whatever she needs. I just need to make sure that if he does come around, then you'll call me. I also have responsibilities."

"Of course," the doctor replied.

"Of course," Jackie whispered to herself.

"There's one other thing."

"Go on," Jackie said, preparing herself for another blow.

"There's no certainty that the boy who was hit by that car will ever show his face again. He could be very different. His brain is active. We've scanned him. But there is always that possibility. Such matters are rarely black and white."

"That's what I thought," Jackie said, clearing her throat. She wiped a rogue tear that had broken free of her defences and steeled herself for the doctor.

"We have your number, thank you."

Considering his professional and courteous manner, his method of ending a conversation needed a little fine-tuning.

Jackie left the room, leaving them to talk between themselves. She wandered down to Lee's room, wondering how she would approach the conversation. And more importantly, how she would get Teresa to go home and rest.

But when she turned the corner, Teresa was gone. Hurriedly, Jackie half-ran and half-walked down the ward, spying Lee's open door, and then when she finally reached it, she nearly fell into the room, only to find Teresa standing beside Lee's bed, lying across his legs with her face buried in the sheets.

Wondering if she should leave her to have a few moments alone with her son after his narrow escape, or if she should pull her away, Jackie put herself in Teresa's shoes once more. Those few moments with him might be her last. Besides, what harm would a few moments do?

She closed her eyes, feeling like a voyeur, and was just about to step out of the room when Teresa spoke, her voice muffled by the sheets and the tears, and the three days of fragmented sleep.

"I'm sorry," she said. "I'm so, so sorry this is happening to you."

Whether she sensed Jackie was there, or if she had heard her come in, Teresa raised her head, and everything the doctor had said rang true. She wasn't fit to take care of a child even if he did wake up.

The woman needed rest.

"I'm taking you home," Jackie said. "No arguments."

CHAPTER FORTY

Over the years, Gillespie had walked hundreds of people through the rear doors of the station into, what he liked to call, the custody suite – a one-star hotel offering warm water and stale sandwiches by way of lunch and a receptionist who rarely smiled.

But this time it was different. This time, he felt a sense of pride, privilege even, as he led a wary Grant Sayer inside, through the hallway and to the custody desk. Sergeant Priest, a heavy-set man from the wilds of Yorkshire, who by his own admission had worked the uniform longer than anybody he knew, and who when he had made Sergeant needed nothing else from life. The next step up the ladder doubled in paperwork and lacked the parts of the job he enjoyed, and the step down the ladder involved actually going out and dealing with the public, something he felt a little too long in the tooth and cynical for these days.

"Who do we have here then, Jim?" he called out, when he saw Gillespie leading Grant through, holding his arm gently for encouragement rather than force.

"This is Grant Sayer. But it's okay, Michael. You can put your pen back in your pocket. He's on our side."

Priest cocked his head and studied the boy, who, by Gillespie's admission, wore the sour look of a guilty teenager, and even the trademark hooded sweater. Then his eyes fell on the book in his hand.

"Do you need an interview room?" Priest asked. "I believe DI Bloom has finished in two."

"Won't be needing that either. I'm taking him up. I thought I'd bring him in this way so he can meet you. So he can see we're not all bastards," Gillespie said. Then he leaned towards Priest and spoke quietly, although still loud enough for Grant to hear. "Had a bit of a rough ride with the boys over at Lincoln HQ recently."

"I see, well, you'd better take him up then. Show him how we do things around here. Nice to meet you, Grant," Priest said, and to Gillespie's surprise, he leaned over the desk to shake Grant's hand.

It was an odd moment that neither Gillespie nor Grant had been expecting, and he watched as Grant stared at the proffered hand, looked up into Priest's eyes, and made an internal judgement call. Then he took the hand but said nothing.

"Come on then, Grant. Let's go. I'll introduce you to the team, get you a coffee, and we'll go from there."

He led Grant through the corridor, past the interview rooms, and then into the fire escape.

"It'll be nice and quiet upstairs. We can sit and chat," Gillespie said, stopping on the stairs and turning to face the lad. "I'd like you to tell my boss what you told me, okay? It's going to make a difference, Grant. Honestly. A real difference."

Clutching the book in both hands, Grant followed Gillespie up the stairs, where they were met with a roar of noise from the incident room.

"It's okay," Gillespie said, encouraging Grant to follow him. "Come on."

He pushed open the door and held it there, standing in the doorway. Inside, Ben, DI Bloom, Chapman, Anna, and Cruz were in a heated debate. The mood was clearly fractious. The noise died when they heard the incident room squeal open and one by one they turned to face Gillespie.

"Harringer's bloody gone," Cruz said, despite Gillespie's wide-eyed warning glare. "Bang to rights. Body in the car. A trail of destruction. She broke him, Jim. Had him in tears, and still the CPS wouldn't go ahead."

While Cruz rattled off an account of what Gillespie presumed was the Harringer interview, the others sensed from his demeanour that he was trying to shut him up.

"Cruz," Anna said, and she jabbed him with the point of her elbow.

"Eh? What was that for?"

"I've got a friend with me," Gillespie announced. "I hope you don't mind?"

"Of course," DI Bloom said, and she flipped the white board to hide the spread of names and links to Poppy. "We'd love to meet him."

Turning to Grant, who stood tentatively a little further down the corridor, Gillespie beckoned him forward. "Come on, son." He nodded to tell him it was okay and offered him a warm smile, although he could feel the boy's trepidation. Grant moved forward, looking to Gillespie for some kind of support. He was putting all his faith into Gillespie, and Gillespie damn well knew it. One wrong comment from someone like Cruz could send the boy back into his own world for months.

He stopped beside Gillespie and took a furtive glance at the team and the room, then lowered his gaze to the floor, as if he was ashamed of who he was.

"This is Grant," Gillespie said. "We're going to sit up at the far end of the room where it's quiet. Boss, if you could join us?"

DI Bloom nodded and welcomed Grant into the room, then clapped her hands once. "Right, party over. Let's get back to work. You all know what to do."

Most of the team were both professional and empathetic enough not to stare at Grant as he worked his way through the room then into the much darker and quieter end of the room where DI Standing's team had once been located.

"You'll be fine up there," Gillespie said, urging him to go and take a seat. "I'll be with you in a minute or two, alright? Go on, lad."

Grant stared at the book in his hands then up at the ceiling, where at that end of the room the lights were usually kept off.

"You want light? To read?" Gillespie asked, turning to Ben, who from his seat, and due to his long arms, could simply lean back and flick the switches. The lights buzzed and flickered, then came on. "That alright for you?"

"Would you like a drink, Grant?" Freya asked.

But the boy refused to look at her.

"Aye. He's had a right night," Gillespie said on his behalf, and then turned again. "Gab? Three teas, eh?"

Cruz, who had heard the mention of drinks and knew what was coming, had feigned interest in a document he was reading and pulled his most practised charade of appearing busy from his hat of transparent charades. Then he looked up, this time with his best, *Are you talking to me?* expression.

"Oh, for god's sake," he whined, holding his hand out toward his laptop, as if to say *I'm right in the middle of something here,* until DI Bloom shared with him her own practised expression – a glare that cut through to the young DC's very soul. "Alright, alright," he said. "Three teas coming up."

"I'll have one too if you're making," Ben said, and winked at Gillespie with a smile.

"Ooh, please," Chapman added, while Anna simply held her mug out for Cruz to collect as he passed.

"Expensive round, Gabby," Gillespie commented, and he sulked through the incident room door and out into the corridor.

"Probably best if we keep him outside for as long as we can," DI Bloom said. "Just in case he says something he shouldn't."

"Aye, boss. We could always send him for cake. That wee coffee shop does an awesome carrot cake."

"I'll send him up there," DI Bloom suggested.

"Thanks, boss," Gillespie said, then lowered his voice. "He's a wee bit fragile. Maybe let me do the talking? At least until he's comfortable?"

"Do you think an interview room will be more appropriate?"

"No. Absolutely not, boss. The lads at HQ, they didn't exactly give him the experience of a lifetime, if you know what I mean. We need to show him we're not like them, or he'll just clam up."

"What did they do?"

"Nothing wrong. Nothing illegal, if that's what you mean. But they didn't exactly demonstrate any empathy either, by all accounts. Grilled him for what he did to Osborne like he's some kind of criminal."

"Okay. Let's do this," she said. "Is his mother, or carer, coming?"

"She said she'll get the other bairns together and meet us downstairs when we're done. The truth is, boss, he won't utter a word if she's around. Besides, he's eighteen and he's volunteering."

"He's eighteen? Why's he still in care? I thought he was a minor?"

"Not anymore. He's free to go wherever he wants and whenever he wants. But what's he going to do? Where's he going to go? He can't get work."

"And Mrs Frost is okay with that?"

"Aye, of course. She's the closest thing he's got to a mother. What would you do?"

"I guess. I mean, it's not uncommon for kids to stay with their parents until they can afford to move out. Why should a care home be any different?"

"Aye, and it's not like he's under arrest. I had a wee word with her before I brought him here. She trusts me. She's lovely. If I'd been put in a home like that when I was a nipper, I'd probably still be there too."

"Well, thank god you weren't," she said, in the nicest possible way. "Let's make it work for us. Go on, I trust you. You lead."

CHAPTER FORTY-ONE

"How are you doing, Grant?" Gillespie said, as DI Bloom took her seat opposite the boy. She was putting a lot of trust in Gillespie. He couldn't let her down. "How are you getting on with the book? It's good, eh?"

Grant nodded then returned his attention to the yellowed pages.

"This here is Detective Inspector Bloom. She's my boss. She's alright. Going to help us. But I need you to tell her what you told me. Do you remember? Down by the river, Grant? It's important. It's important we get the facts right if we're going to find out who hurt Poppy. Do you understand that, Grant?"

He looked up from his book, met Gillespie's eye, and nodded.

"Will you help us?" Gillespie asked. "Will you tell Detective Inspector Bloom what you told me?"

Grant glanced across at Bloom, who found herself forcing the scorn she usually wore from her brow and opening her expression into something a little more welcoming. Something must have worked, because the boy nodded again.

"That's great, Grant," Gillespie said, as somebody coughed behind him.

He turned and found Cruz standing there holding a tray with three teas on and a handful of sugar sachets.

"I'll be mum, shall I?" Gillespie said. He distributed the drinks then collected the sachets of sugar. "You know what would go well with a nice cup of tea?"

Cruz's expression plummeted.

"Cake?" Bloom suggested. "Do you want some cake, Grant?"

He eyed them both, then Cruz, and then finally, he nodded.

"Couldn't grab us a few slices of the carrot cake, could you, Gab?" Gillespie asked.

"What carrot cake? There's nothing in the kitchen except the biscuit tin, and there's only Rich Tea in there. You ate all the decent ones."

"I meant the carrot cake in the wee coffee shop down the road."

"You what? I'm not... I've got work to..." he started, unable to find a reasonable argument.

"There's some cash on my desk," Bloom said. "Get everybody a piece. They deserve something."

He carried the tray back to the team, collected the twenty-pound note from Bloom's desk, then, grabbing his duffel coat from the back of his chair, he pulled it on as he yanked on the incident room door a little over-zealously. It squealed open, slammed against the wall with a bang, and then collided with the heel of his shoe as he left the room, tripping him up. The sounds of him cursing could be heard down the corridor, and then the room was silent once again, as had been the plan.

"Shall I get you started?" Gillespie suggested. "You were telling me how you climbed from your bedroom window and went looking for Poppy. Remember?"

Grant nodded, a little more enthusiastically than before, but said nothing. It was as if he wanted to speak but words failed him.

"She had told you she was meeting Danny and that she didn't want to see you. You remember, Grant? You said you knocked at her house in case they were there. But they weren't, were they? You told me that her stepmum sent you on your way. Told you she'd gone out with her boyfriend?"

At the mention of the stepmum, Grant pulled an involuntary sneer, which Bloom noticed but let slide for the time being.

Again, Grant nodded. "Yeah," he said softly.

It was a magical moment. A moment that Gillespie had prayed for during the drive to the station. It was the loosening of the dam, which was soon to break.

"Tell us what you did after that," Gillespie suggested. "How did you know where to find them?"

He shrugged. "The stream. We always went there. She did. Always there."

"She was always at the stream?" Gillespie asked, for clarity.

"Or the house," Grant replied. "She liked it there."

"So you took a wee walk down there, eh?" Gillespie said, hoping to keep the momentum going.

But Grant just nodded.

"You found them there?"

Grant said nothing.

"Come on, Grant. You were telling me earlier. You're not in any trouble, son. Not with us. This is about Poppy, remember? Eh? You found them there."

"He was hurting her," Grant said suddenly, and louder than before, as if the emotion had freed up his vocal cords. "I heard her. Screaming."

"Screaming?" Bloom said, speaking up for the first time. "Definitely screaming?"

"Like an animal. Crying. Hitting him. But he wouldn't stop. He wouldn't get off."

"Can you describe the position he was in? Danny Osborne? Where was he in relation to Poppy?"

"Lying on her," Grant said, and his breathing became faster as he remembered the time. "He held her down. Her arms. Pinning her down with his hand."

"And his other hand?"

"In her hair. Pulling it. Like she was a doll."

"And she was in pain?"

"When he held her hands back, she couldn't hit him. She was trying. Rolling this way and that. But..."

"Go on, Grant. You're doing well, mate."

"He was too strong. She saw me, though. She saw me under the tree watching."

"What did she do?" Bloom asked.

He shrugged again and shook his head. "Called my name, she did. She called me for help."

"And that's when you went over and stopped it, was it?" Gillespie asked, and he received a curt nod in reply. "Listen, Grant. We don't want to go into what happened afterwards. After you stopped him. But we need to know if maybe Danny Osborne is the type of boy who would have sought revenge."

He stared at Gillespie with those vacant eyes.

"Do you think he could have attacked Poppy, Grant? Do you think that maybe he was scared she would tell on him?"

Grant lowered his head. His demeanour shifted. He was withdrawing, and Gillespie saw it too.

"Grant, has Danny Osborne's father been in contact with you?"

His eyes widened and he wiped away a tear.

"He has, hasn't he? Has he threatened you, Grant?" Bloom asked. "You're safe here. You're safe with us. Nobody is going to know anything you say."

"He stopped me. He was driving. He stopped his car."

"And what did he say exactly? Grant?"

He shrugged again. "I can't say. Mrs Frost. The kids," he said, shaking his head and biting down on his lower lip. "I shouldn't have said anything–"

"No, you're doing the right thing. It's okay. We need to know though, so we can stop him from hurting people. Do you understand that, Grant?"

"Yeah," he mumbled, or something to that effect, but he was interrupted by DC Nillson coughing herself by way of an entry.

"Sorry," she whispered, as she slipped Bloom a folded piece of paper. "Thought you should see this."

She gave Grant a sorrowful look then retreated back to the busy end of the room. Bloom opened the note, read the contents, then folded it and placed it in her jacket pocket.

"I tell you what I'm going to do, Grant," Gillespie started. "Your hearing is next week, aye? The magistrates court?"

He nodded.

"I'll tell you what. I'll be there, son. I'll stand up if I have to. A character witness. Do you know what that means? Of course you do. You've read more crime novels than I have. I'll do it, Grant. I'll make a difference. Remember how I told you I wanted to help you? But you need to make a difference too. You need to help us. Who killed Poppy?"

"I don't know. I don't know who did it," he shouted, then immediately sank back into himself.

"Alright, alright. Don't worry. I'll still be there. How about this? We'll have what you said typed up," Gillespie said, and glanced at Bloom to check his idea would be enough. She nodded once then returned her attention to the boy. "You can sign it, and we'll nail Danny Osborne for what he did to Poppy, eh?"

Grant said nothing.

"Grant, there's something I have to tell you," Bloom said, thinking of those three words on the slip of paper. "I have to choose my words carefully. I can't divulge sensitive information. But if I said to you that as of thirty minutes ago, you need not ever worry about Danny Osborne's father again, would that help?"

He glanced from Bloom to Gillespie and back again.

"I mean it. Nobody is going to get hurt anymore. I promise you that."

He opened his mouth to speak, and the words were there, just ready to be spoken. But he faltered. Afraid.

Bloom leaned forward to whisper, "He's not going to be able to hurt anybody for a very, very long time," and winked at him.

"All you have to do is tell us it was him, Grant. That's all you have to do," Gillespie urged.

But Grant shook his head. A sorrowful smile formed on his lips, as if he was disappointed.

"Danny Osborne raped Poppy," he said. "I don't know who killed her. I wish I could say. I wish it was him," he said, looking straight into Bloom's eyes for the first time. "But it would be a lie."

"Okay, mate," Gillespie said, seeing that Grant was reaching the end of whatever had been holding his emotions intact. "Let's go and see Mrs Frost. Get you home, eh?"

He nodded, for the last time.

"Grant..." Bloom said, as Gillespie helped him to his feet. He looked up at her, fear in his eyes. "Thank you. What you did was very brave. We'll do everything we can to help you."

CHAPTER FORTY-TWO

When Freya walked back to the white board, weary and tired, she locked stares with Ben, who said nothing but held two fingers up in the universal peace sign. Then he lowered them before doing the same thing again. He was clearly not a hippy. Nor was he re-enacting Churchill's famous *V for Victory* gesture.

He was gloating.

Two murders, two killers.

She had little left inside of her to argue, or smile, or anything except flip the white board back over and stare at the names.

The incident room door burst open, and she turned hoping to find Gillespie, to tell him what an incredible job he had done with the boy. But it was Cruz. He plopped a bag down on the nearest desk.

"Cake," he said, looking around the room, but it was evident that Freya's mood had worked its way through the team, and nobody reacted at all. "Doesn't anybody want a piece?"

"I'm not hungry anymore," Freya said. "You can have mine."

"Yeah, I'm not feeling it, Gab. Take mine as well," Ben said.

"Yeah, and mine," Anna piped up. "Actually, leave it. I'll take it home for Keiran."

"You've got to be kidding me. I just walked to the other end of the village to get these," he whined. "Chapman? Come on."

"I'll take mine home. Might have it later," she replied.

"Bloody marvellous," he said, opening the bag and taking a wedge for himself. "Well, I'm not going to miss out just because you lot are sulking. What's happened anyway? It's like a bloody morgue in here."

"Terrible analogy," Anna said, shaking her head at him in disgust.

The door opened once more and Gillespie entered, his shoulders sagging with the weight of the bad news.

He stopped in the doorway, eyed Freya, then took a few steps closer.

"I'm, erm... I'm sorry, boss. I really thought he'd open up and..." he started. "Well..."

She stared at him, bowing slightly to see that usually cheery face of his, and he met her gaze.

"What?" he said.

It was all Freya could do to shake her head at him. "You are a man of such extraordinary talents, Gillespie. And not only that, but you have a heart. A big, dopey, wonderful heart," she said, finding the resources to offer him a smile. "I have never seen such a wonderful display of police work."

"Eh?"

"They can't teach you that in training, Gillespie," she said. "The way you connected with that boy. Honestly, it blew my mind."

"Aye, well. It was nothing, really–"

"It was everything. We might not know who killed Poppy, but we can damn well put Danny Osborne away."

"What? We'll need more than his word, boss–"

"Chapman, get Doctor Bell on the phone. Put her on loudspeaker."

"On it," she replied, leaving Freya staring at Gillespie.

"I mean it. That was incredible," she said, and nodded at the bag on the desk. "Have some cake."

"Ah, to be honest, I'm not hungry anymore."

"Oh, for god's sake," Cruz cried out.

"Hello, Doctor Bell speaking," the doctor answered, slightly breathless, and somehow her Welsh accent was stronger than ever before.

"Doctor Bell, it's DI Bloom. Freya."

"Oh, hello, Freya, I was just thinking about you, and our little–"

"You're on loudspeaker, Pip. The entire team is listening," Freya said, feeling the burn of multiple stares.

"Oh, I, erm..." she began, before entering professional mode. "How can I help you, Freya?"

"When you showed us Poppy Gray's body, you mentioned signs of sexual intercourse."

"Mmm hmmm," she replied, agreeing.

"You said there were scars. Inside her."

"Not scars. Scar tissue. Fairly recent. Not old, but not new, if you get my meaning. Do you want me to look into it? I can have it analysed."

"Yes," Freya said. "But in the meantime, I need your professional opinion."

"Oh, well, I don't know about that."

"Is it credible to suggest the damage to Poppy could be as little as two weeks old?"

"Her vaginal scar tissue?" the doctor repeated. "Yes. Yes, I'd say that was quite accurate."

"You'd be willing to testify to that effect?"

"I would, yes."

"Then please do look into it further. I think we have the culprit."

"You found her killer?"

"Sadly not," Freya said. "But we found the man who raped her. It's a start. Thank you, Doctor. I'll see you–"

"When I see you," the doctor finished cryptically, and Freya imagined her placing a finger to her nose and winking.

The call ended and Freya made a show of shuffling papers, while inside she forced her emotions back down inside her. Torn, she desperately wanted to be able to walk down those stairs, pull Osbourne into an interview room, and hit him with a murder charge. The rape charge, as cruel and beastly as the act itself was, seemed not to even scratch the surface of what he deserved.

"Ma'am," Chapman called out, just as Freya was trying to collect her senses and continue with the briefing. She looked up and found Chapman finishing a call and replacing the handset.

"If it's bad news, I don't want to know," Freya said, but of course she was lying. She just wasn't ready to deal with it.

"Katy Southgate has been found."

"What?"

"That was the local CID. South Holland. He said they found her less than a mile from her home."

"Murdered?"

Chapman shook her head, knowing exactly what the repercussions of the call would be. "She killed herself. Hose pipe. They found a note in the car."

"Damn it," Freya snapped.

Suddenly, there was an energy inside her that wanted to lash out, to swipe the papers from every desk in the room and to tear those bloody doors off. The rage was wraith-like inside her, like it was bouncing off her internal walls seeking a way out. And she calmed it, though it was a temporary fix.

"Get Michaela on the line. Put her on loudspeaker," she said, seeing her last possible way of securing at least a murder charge on Harringer.

"What are you doing, Freya?" Ben asked.

"Closing it down, Ben," she said in a tone that he didn't deserve. "We've come too far to let Harringer walk."

"Hello," came Michaela's voice, loud and clear.

"Michaela, it's Freya. Freya Bloom."

"Oh hey, Freya," she started, then an intake of breath came over the loudspeaker. "Not another one? Tell me you haven't found another."

"No, you're safe. Don't worry. I was wondering if you managed to get any clue that Sarah Cooper was in the car? Hair, fingerprints, DNA. Whatever you've got. They found Katy Southgate near her home. She's not our girl."

"Nothing. We do still have one hair sample that is yet to be identified. But nothing on Sarah Cooper."

"In the boot?"

"Nope. Oddly enough, it was on the driver's seat."

"Not Poppy Gray's?"

"No, sadly. The only hair samples we have from Poppy are what Doctor Bell gave us."

"So we have nothing on him at all."

"I just report what I find, Freya. I wish it was better news."

"I know. Thank you. Thank you for all your help."

"Anything else I can do?" Michaela asked.

"No. No, you've been great. I'll see you."

Chapman ended the call, steepled her fingers, and waited for Freya to continue.

"So, our current sad state of affairs are we managed to solve two murders that we're not investigating, but we can't prove it, we still have a dead body that we don't know who it belongs to, we've managed to solve a rape that we're not investigating, and we still don't know who murdered Poppy Gray." When she said it like that, she felt absolutely useless.

"We've still got Osborne," Nillson spoke up.

"Osborne is barely able to walk. Whoever killed Poppy Gray climbed in and out of that ditch, as well as struggled with Poppy while she fought for her life. Chapman, get onto HQ. Grant Sayer mentioned Jeffrey Osborne paying a visit to Grant to warn him off. See if he paid a visit to Poppy as well, and while you're talking to them, see where he was when Poppy was killed. They've had round-the-clock surveillance on him, they should at least be able to tell us if he was at home, or out, or whatever."

Chapman picked up the phone and set to work.

"Ben, where's Gold?" Freya asked.

Leaning back in his chair, staring at the board, Ben roused himself from his thoughts. "She's still at the hospital, but I did ask her to come back for the briefing."

"Call her. Get her on loudspeaker. Let's have an update."

Freya paced three steps to the board, but the names and dotted lines meant nothing. She turned on her heels and paced three steps back, just as Ben put the call on loudspeaker for all the room to hear.

"Jackie, it's me," Freya called out.

"Hi, ma'am," Jackie replied, sounding tired but doing her best to sound enthusiastic.

"What's the latest from Lee Sanders?"

There was heavy road noise coming over the call and Gold's voice was distant, like she was having to shout to be heard.

"Not good, ma'am," she said. "He crashed again. While I was there."

"Is he alive?"

"Yes, but barely. The doctors are doing a full blood transfusion. It'll be a few more days yet."

"I don't understand. You said he was recovering when we spoke to you yesterday."

"He was. He is. I don't know. They say his head should be fine, but somehow the accident has triggered something. Something in his blood maybe. They aren't sure. But they're keeping him in while they investigate. Could be long-term, ma'am. He might never fully recover."

"Oh, poor kid," said Freya, voicing her thoughts. "How's the mother?"

"Distraught. I've taken her home to get some sleep, finally. She's been sleeping in a chair, ma'am. She's like a zombie. I made her promise me she'll get some sleep before she goes back."

"And Lee is unconscious?"

"They think he'll come around after the transfusion. But what he'll be like is anybody's guess. They want to do more tests. Poor kid. Makes you wonder if he knows what's going on. He was just walking home. Just crossing the quiet, little lane outside his house. Everything changes so fast," Gold said, leading somewhere but then catching herself.

"What about a boyfriend, or a friend? Was she definitely alone when she heard the accident?"

"She's got nobody. If she loses Lee, then she's on her own," she replied, and she sniffed, the emotion clear in her tone.

"It's okay," Freya said reassuringly. She turned to look at Gillespie. "This is turning out to be quite an emotional investigation by all accounts. You're doing a great job, but we need you back here. If he's not going to come around today, then there's no point you being there."

"I'm on my way to the station now. Be there in ten minutes."

"Good. It'll be nice to have you back."

Freya nodded for Ben to end the call. He picked up the handset and finished the call privately. Freya wasn't listening, but knowing Ben, he would have added his own words of wisdom, trying to reassure Gold she had done well.

For some reason, Freya tuned into the sound of Chapman finishing her call, who replaced the handset and found Freya staring at her when she looked up. "They've arrested Jeffrey Osborne," she said. "Him and several others are all involved in some kind of drugs ring. Big time. Thousands of pounds worth."

"What about Poppy?" Freya asked.

"He wasn't even in Lincolnshire when Poppy was killed, and

neither were his accomplices. They were in Hull, in a cafe, planning."

"Damn it. Are they sure?"

"They had a man wired sitting at the next table. Irrefutable, ma'am. Although, yes, they confirmed he visited the guest house a few days before, as well as the foster home."

"So he made threats."

"But he didn't act on them, ma'am. Sorry."

It was Gillespie who spoke up, coming out of the daze he'd been in since arriving back from dealing with Grant Sayer. Sadly, what he had to say was far from useful.

"That doesn't leave us many options, boss," he said.

"No, Gillespie, it doesn't."

"I mean. We've got the boy's mother, who we agreed wouldn't have left her boy dying by the roadside to give chase. And according to Jackie, she has nobody else to turn to."

"Are you going somewhere with this, Gillespie?"

"Aye, boss. So if it wasn't the wee lad's mother, then we have to look at Poppy's family. The father and the stepmother. Where were they?"

"The father can barely walk up the stairs, Gillespie."

"Which leaves the stepmother."

"Izzie," Freya said, for no reason other than to remind herself of that chat they had a few days before. "She was at home, cleaning. I want to talk to Danny Osborne. Cruz, call down to Sergeant Priest. Ask him to take Danny to the cells. We're interviewing him. And get him a duty solicitor. I don't want to give him any wiggle room on this."

"Me?" Cruz replied. "Interviewing? With you?"

"That's right," Freya confirmed. "You were the arresting officer, were you not? I'm quite sure you can handle a teenager with a broken leg, three broken ribs, and a broken nose. We might not have Poppy's killer, but I'll feel a damn sight better if we can put the man who raped her away, and give Grant half a chance."

CHAPTER FORTY-THREE

Sergeant Priest had given them incident room two, and Cruz prepared the recording while the duty solicitor set his notes up and familiarised himself with the investigation.

Freya watched him. Over the years, she had met and interacted with hundreds of duty solicitors, and as in any profession, some were better than others. This one, a man named Carl Gordon, seemed professional enough. He dressed well, he was punctual, unlike others, and he waited to be spoken to, instead of trying to get a head start before the recording had begun.

The door opened and a uniform entered, holding the door open for Daniel Osborne, a sullen looking individual, to follow him in. His crutches tapped on the hard floor and he refused to make eye contact until he had taken his seat. He set his crutches to one side, and then stared at Cruz.

"Are we ready, Cruz?" Freya asked, noticing that he was averting his eyes from Osborne.

He hit record then waited, allowing Freya to lead. She announced the date and the time, and then introduced herself, before requesting the other attendees to follow suit.

"Detective Constable Cruz."

"Carl Gordon, Duty Solicitor."

"Daniel Osborne."

"Daniel, I'm obliged to reiterate the reason for you being here. You are under arrest for suspicion of rape. You do not have to say anything, but it may harm your defence if you do not mention something you later rely on in court. Anything you say may be given in evidence."

"So help me god," he said with a sneer.

"Are you religious, Daniel?"

"Devout Christian. In fact, I'm supposed to be at a bible reading right now."

"Shame," Freya said, opening her file. "Talk to me about Grant Sayer."

Osborne gave a laugh but said nothing.

"For the recording, Mr Osborne has a broken leg and a broken nose. His eyes are blackened, presumably from the broken nose, and I suspect that beneath his t-shirt, he has some kind of compression bandage for his broken ribs," Freya said, more to buy time than for any other purpose. "How did you get those injuries, Daniel?"

"I was attacked. You should know. I'm prosecuting."

"Attacked? Who by?"

"A loser?"

"A loser? I imagine he must be in a worse state than you are?"

Osborne said nothing. He sat uncomfortably, trying his best to find a posture that didn't hurt, while also demonstrating his arrogance.

"Who was it?"

"Read the files. You can read, can't you?"

"Yes. But I'd like you to state who it was that attacked you."

"Grant Sayer."

"And Grant is a loser, is he?"

"Just some weird kid in the village."

"And he just attacked you for no reason?"

Osborne inhaled loudly and exhaled slowly as if the whole affair was tedious and he'd much rather be elsewhere.

"Why did he attack you?"

"Because I got what he wanted."

"That's vague, Daniel. Come on, you just said you're prosecuting him. You must have a story to back that up."

"He caught me shagging the girl he wanted to shag."

"And the girl's name?"

"Poppy. Poppy Gray."

"And where was this?"

"Oh, come on. You must have the file," he said, and reached out for Freya's notes, but his broken ribs denied him, and he cried out.

"I want you to tell me," Freya said. "Where did this attack take place?"

Breathless from the sharp jolt of pain that no doubt soared through his chest, Osborne took a deep breath. "Down by the stream. Near the village."

"And you were there with Poppy, were you? Just the two of you?"

"Yes," he said, sounding bored.

"You went there together? Or did you meet her there?"

"I met her there."

"Was that arranged?"

"Eh?"

"Was the meeting arranged? Or was it by chance that you saw her? And one thing led to another?"

He eyed Freya, then Cruz.

"Arranged."

"So if we looked at Poppy's phone, we'd find some kind of record? A text message or WhatsApp? In her call history maybe?" Freya asked, knowing full well that her phone had not been found.

He was considering his answer carefully now. The responses were slower to come.

"I met her. In the village."

"And you just arranged to go down to the stream to have sex, did you?" Cruz said, then glanced at Freya apologetically. But it was a valid question, just phrased a little differently to how Freya might have phrased it.

"Oh, look. Boy Wonder's woken up."

"Answer the question," Freya said.

"No. We got talking. That's it. I like her," he said. "And she likes me."

"So you got talking. When was this?" Freya asked, and if she was honest, she was a little surprised she wasn't being met with a series of *no comments*.

"A few days before."

"A few days before what?" Cruz asked.

"Before I saw her at the stream," he said, as if Cruz was a child, or was finding the explanation hard to follow.

"So you didn't actually arrange to meet her at the stream?" Cruz said, and his irritation was showing, something Freya would have to guide him on later.

Osborne shook his head.

"So when you told us you had arranged to meet her, that was, in fact, a lie?"

"I'm just...upset. That's all."

"You don't look very upset," Cruz said.

"That's subjective," Carl Gordon stated. "That could be construed as misleading for the benefit of the recording."

"Right, so let me get this straight," Freya said. "You met Poppy in the village. You got talking to her. You liked her. You went your separate ways?"

Osborne nodded. "Yeah, but she liked me as well."

"She told you that, did she?" Cruz asked, and Freya noticed he was on the verge of sounding like an overbearing mother, scolding him rather than delivering emotionless questions.

"No. Of course she didn't tell me that. I don't suppose you'd know, little boy. But when it happens, there's a chemistry. You feel it. One day, if you live long enough, you might experience it yourself."

"But then, a few days later, you happened to bump into her down at the stream," Cruz asked. She had to hand it to him, he allowed the insults to slide off him like he was made of Teflon.

"Yeah. It was nice. You know? Just me and her," Osborne explained.

"What were you doing there? You live in the other side of the village."

"Out walking, weren't I? Nice day and all that."

"That was Poppy's favourite place. I suppose you knew that, didn't you?"

He shrugged again. "No."

"Seems a coincidence that with miles and miles of countryside all around, you happened to bump into her there."

"I heard her. From the track. She was crying."

"Crying? Poppy Gray was crying?"

"You can go there. See for yourself. I was walking along the track when I heard her. I saw it was her and I went to see if she was okay."

"Right, of course," Cruz said, his voice filled with sarcasm. "And I suppose you pulled the silver tongue out, did you? Somehow managed to convince her to stop being upset long enough for you to have your wicked way?"

"You have got no idea about women, have you?"

"And you have, do you?" Freya asked, eyeing the scruffy teenager up and down. "I think the question is rather pertinent. Firstly, though, I'd like to understand why she was upset."

"I don't know," Osborne said.

"You don't know? Or you won't tell us?"

"Her parents. Her dad, or something. I can't remember."

"No," Cruz added. "You were too busy filling your head with what you wanted to do."

"That's out of line," Gordon interjected.

"What about her dad?" Freya asked. "Do you know why she was upset? The real reason?"

"No. Why don't you go and talk to him about it? I'm not a bloody counsellor, you know?"

"Well, you must have said something right, if you somehow managed to stop Poppy being upset," Freya said. "What did you say to her?"

"I don't know. It was ages ago–"

"It was two weeks ago, and if you can remember the details you've given us so far, then you can remember what you told her to calm her down, and you can remember why she was upset in the first place."

"I don't know what I said. I don't–"

"That's because you didn't calm her down, did you?"

"What's that supposed to mean?"

"She wasn't upset. Grant Sayer caught you and Poppy having sex. Is that correct?"

"I told you. Yeah."

"What I don't understand, Daniel, is how the situation went from Poppy being upset to you two having sex right there."

"Passion," he said. "Emotions will do that."

"Until a man like Grant Sayer comes long? And catches you?" Freya said. "You see, not only is the transition from one emotion to the other hard to believe, but I also can't understand why someone as well-mannered as Grant Sayer would interrupt the pair of you having sex, and then attack you."

"He's not well-mannered. He's a nutter."

"I've spoken to him. He's very polite. In fact, when I gave him the opportunity to lie to implicate you, he said he couldn't lie."

"He doesn't even speak. That's rubbish."

"Oh, he speaks alright. I had a very pleasant conversation with him only an hour ago."

"Grant Sayer? The kid from the foster place?"

"You see, Poppy had arranged to meet him by the stream. Just like she always did. Because they were friends."

"Were?" he said, his expression altering slightly.

"I can place you by the stream, and I even have an eyewitness to prove you were raping Poppy. It wasn't consensual."

"That's a lie."

"And I have medical records from Poppy's post-mortem to correlate with forced sex, at least two weeks ago."

"Her what?" Osbourne said, and the colour that had built up with his anger drained from his face again.

"Her post-mortem, Daniel. Didn't you know?"

"She's dead?"

"We found her body a few days ago. We're treating it as suspicious. You *were* a suspect, until we realised you're in no fit state to have done what was done. But there's no escaping the fact you raped Poppy Gray two weeks ago. And the reason for your broken bones is not due to the jealousy of Poppy's only friend, but because he caught you raping her. You can prosecute him all you like, Daniel, but I'm afraid you'll have a hard time walking away from this one, if you pardon the pun."

"She's dead?"

"I'm sorry you had to find out this way," Freya said, for the benefit of the recording. "Do you have any further questions?"

He shook his head in disbelief.

"I'm going to ask a question, and I want to make it very clear, your answer will be taken into consideration when you stand before a jury. Did you, two weeks ago, rape Poppy Gray?"

He looked up, wide-eyed and suddenly very frightened. "No."

"Thank you, Daniel. Despite your claims, I'm arresting you for the rape of Poppy Gray. You do not have to say anything, but it may harm your defence if you fail to mention something you later rely on in court. Anything you do say may be given in evidence."

She turned to Cruz, who was staring at Osborne with what could only be described as hatred in his eyes – a complete reversal of the scene at beginning of the interview. "Take him away and charge him, DC Cruz."

CHAPTER FORTY-FOUR

"SO?" BEN ASKED, AS THEY WOUND THEIR WAY THROUGH THE country lanes towards Stixwould.

Freya was deep in thought about the Osbornes. There wasn't a chance in hell that Daniel Osborne could have murdered Poppy Gray, and as for the father, the information from HQ surveillance was just as solid as she could have hoped for. Except that she would have hoped for a small window when surveillance might have lost him, a change of shift or something. But no. It wasn't him. It was something she had come to learn years ago. No matter how hard you wanted somebody to be guilty, sometimes they just weren't. She may have learnt it years ago, but that didn't mean it got any easier.

"What else did he say?"

"He tried to tell us that Poppy consented, despite being upset about something."

"And what was it she was upset about?"

"I don't think she was, but we can find out while we're here," Freya said, as Ben pulled the car into the small car park outside the Witham Valley Guest House. "Maybe the reason Poppy was upset and went to the stream is the same reason she stole the car?

If it is, then Desmond Gray or Izzie might be able to shed some light on the situation."

"You seem tense," Ben said. "Not worried about the bet, are you? I mean, it's just a bit of fun–"

"If you think I'm even remotely worried about that, Ben, then you really don't know me at all. We're running out of suspects, which means we either missed someone, or we've overlooked them."

She climbed from the car, and exactly as she had expected, Ben met her over the car roof. "You think Harringer had something to do with Poppy's death, don't you?" he asked. "That's why we're here."

"Well, it's a bit of a coincidence that the daughter of a guest house owner is killed while a serial killer is living under his roof."

"We can't classify Harringer as a serial killer," Ben hissed, keeping his voice low in case any other residents overheard them.

She leaned on the car, met his stare, and waited for him to start listening. "You don't honestly still believe there are two killers, do you?"

"We agreed we'd treat them as individual cases. The MO. The way the bodies were found."

"Ben," she said, silencing him again, "we've got the murder of Anita Carter, as well as Sarah Cooper. That's the opportunity. In the next few days, his life is going to be turned upside down. He's already admitted to having affairs with them both. It won't be long before we find the motivation. What we don't have is the motivation for him killing Poppy, other than for stealing his car, and that, quite frankly, is a bit far-fetched. One killer."

She winked at him, mostly because she knew he hated it when she did that, then turned and made her way toward the front door.

"You can't just leave it there."

She rang the bell, then stepped back.

"Freya?"

A figure appeared behind the frosted glass and made its way slowly toward the entrance.

"Freya?"

The door opened to reveal Desmond Gray leaning on a walking stick. The past four days had clearly taken their toll on him. He looked at least a decade older.

"Mr Gray. How are you holding up?"

He stared back with sunken eyes and mumbled something unintelligible. Then he moved out of the way, making a show of inviting them in.

"We were wondering if we might have a few words with you and Izzie," Freya said, as they stepped inside. Ben closed the door while Desmond Gray took a moment to consider what Freya had said. His reaction time was slow, like he hadn't slept for a week, which in light of his daughter's death was probably accurate.

"Have to be quick," he said, pointing toward the rear conservatory where they had spoken before. "Plenty to be getting on with."

"Never ends, does it?" Freya agreed, as she moved through the hallway and pushed open the door. "I was wondering if you could tell me about your guest Mr Harringer."

Gray followed, and then Ben. Instead of taking a seat in the uncomfortable, wicker furniture, Freya elected to remain standing. But the effort was clearly too much for Gray. He dropped into an armchair and set his stick to one side.

"What about him?" he asked eventually. "Upped and left without paying, he did."

"That may be our fault. We arrested him."

"You did what? I thought you just questioned him. His car was stolen."

"It's a long story. One which I won't burden you with. But I'd like to know how you found him? Is he a good guest?"

"Suppose so. Haven't really got a cause to complain. Pays on time, usually. Comes regularly."

"And his room?" Freya asked.

"How he left it. That's what you said to do. You said not to touch the room."

"That's right. We'll have his belongings collected so you can use the room," Ben said. "How regularly did he come?"

"Oh, I'd have to check the books. Izzie does it mostly, when she's around. I haven't been myself lately. Keep making mistakes. Age, I suppose."

"How old are you? If you don't mind me asking, that is."

"Sixty-seven," he said proudly. "Feel about eighty, mind."

"So you had Poppy when you were forty-eight?" Ben said.

"I did, yes. I know, I know. I was fitter then. Younger wife," he said, smiling fondly at the memory. "Wouldn't change a thing. Marvellous, it was. Poppy. My best years."

"And you met Izzie when?"

"Izzie?" he said. "Five, six years ago now. Saved me really. Not easy raising a teenage girl. You know, what with all the girl's stuff, and that. Izzie was a godsend."

"Sorry, where is Izzie now?"

"Working. Another godsend. If it weren't for her job, we'd be out on our ears," he replied, glancing around the old place.

"Are things really that bad? The guest house doesn't pay for itself?"

"Barely. Some months are better than others. Izzie's salary helps out during the bad months. The thing is, there seem to be more bad months than good recently."

"Why don't you sell up?" Ben asked. "This place will be worth a small fortune to the right buyer."

"And do what? Rattle around in a little bungalow? That's what Poppy used to say. She said she would help me, you know? I wanted one last stab at getting this place going again. If it didn't work, then maybe I would sell up. Spent too many years working at it to just give up."

"I'm sure," Freya said. "And you said Izzie helps too?"

"I can't do the stairs anymore. Some days are better than others, but recently it's been tough. My head wants to, my brain, that is. Wants to get up there and clean. A lick of paint here and there. But my body doesn't share the vision, I'm afraid."

"I know the feeling," Freya said. "Especially in the winter months."

"Winter, spring, summer. You name it."

"And when is Izzie due back?"

"Oh, I don't know. It'll be a late one. Short-staffed or something. Somewhere over in Boston. I told her, you need to find someone to manage that place. You can't keep going over there for days on end. Not while I'm like this."

"Like what?"

"Open your eyes, Detective. I'm nearly seventy going on bleeding ninety years old. Whatever it was I did when I was younger has caught up with me. Smoking, no doubt."

"And your wife leaves you here to manage this place alone?"

"What choice do we have? Can't turn people away just because I'm having an off-day."

"Is today an off-day, Mr Gray?"

"About as off as they get," he admitted.

"And Izzie is at work, is she?"

"That she is," he replied with a sigh. "Though, ironically, she's normally here when I have a bad day. She normally helps me to bed. It's a blessing nobody's staying right now," he said, then leaned forward. "Some days, I dread new guests coming while she's away. Means I have to get up and down those blasted stairs. Ah, maybe Poppy was right. Maybe it's time to pack it all in. Not much point to it now she's gone."

"Have you been to see Poppy?" Freya asked. "I did ask one of my team to call and arrange a time."

"Ah, I couldn't. Wanted to. But no," he said sadly. He tapped a finger to his temple. "I've got her here. Last time I saw her, she was wearing that little dress. Always loved a dress, Poppy did.

Especially when she had a tan. She's been to see her mother, over in Spain. Marbella or Majorca or something. One of those places. She often went, Poppy did. Who am I to stop her? It was a hard winter, this year. I suppose she was dying to get out of her big jumpers."

"Tell us about it," Freya said. "That last time you saw her. If you don't mind sharing, that is. You said she was home early?"

"No. I don't mind. Yeah, she was early. Only by an hour or two. But it was a nice surprise. She was there. Right there in the doorway. I was here. Sitting right here in this armchair. That was a bad day for me. You know? I could barely stand, let alone get up and down those stairs. Said she'd just drop her case off, then make me a tea, she did. I remember it because I heard Izzie calling down to her. Must have been a nice surprise for Izzie, seeing Poppy. She made a lovely brew. In the pot, you know? Proper tea."

"It's always better in a pot," Freya said, offering him an encouraging smile.

"Yes," he said, then the smile on his face that Freya had worked so hard to get faded. "That was it."

"That was the last time you saw her?" Freya asked.

"That's when everything changed. She ran upstairs to put her case down. Then I think I had a nap. Roy came down. You know? Mr Harringer. Shouting and swearing, he was. Said his car was missing. I called up for Izzie, but I figured she was wearing those headphones. Always has them in, she does. Music blaring. So I called up for Poppy, but she couldn't hear me either. Figured she was in the loo, like. You know? Flying does that, doesn't it?"

"It can do, yes," Freya agreed.

"So, I called the police myself. That must have been around eight. Roy went back upstairs."

"And then we arrived around ten?"

"Yeah," he said. "I never did get that tea from Poppy, but by god, was she something." He tapped his head again. "I'll keep her there. Nobody can take her from me there."

CHAPTER FORTY-FIVE

"We'd like to have a quick look in Poppy's room, if we may?" Freya said. "Just in case we missed something before."

Gray was staring across the room at the doorway, perhaps remembering that last moment he'd spoken to his daughter, and Freya's words seemed to drag him back to the now.

"As long as you don't expect me to come with you," he said, pointing to a small box behind the door. "Key's hanging up just there."

"We know the way," Freya said, and taking the bunch of keys, they left him there with his memories.

They were halfway up the stairs, walking side by side, when they heard the old man downstairs sobbing. They stopped, and Ben glanced at Freya, as if he was deciding if he should go down and just be with him. For a no-nonsense type of guy, Ben had a big heart. That was one of the things she liked about him the most.

"Sometimes it's best to leave them to grieve," Freya said. "As hard as that is."

He shook his head. "Poor sod. Where's his bloody wife?"

"Earning the money to keep this place going by the sounds of it."

They reached the top of the first flight of stairs and, using the key Gray had given them, unlocked Harringer's door. It was exactly as it had been before.

Almost.

The bed was made and the bathroom still looked exactly as it had when Freya had first visited – unused. Not even the towels were out of place. The large towel hadn't been hung up on the radiator or left on the floor, as most hotel users would leave them. It had been folded, and the smaller hand towel was sitting on top of it on a shelf near the bath.

"He didn't even have a chance to shower," Ben said, making the same observation as Freya.

"He'd been here for at least two nights," she said, pulling a face. "And he didn't shower or use the bed?"

She peered inside the wardrobe.

"There are no clothes. Nothing," Freya said, as she stepped over to the wardrobe and slid open the door. Ben watched her, drawing his own conclusions, but before he could announce them, Freya had an idea.

"I need to check upstairs," she said, and marched from the room.

"What for?" Ben replied, and hurried after her. She was already at the top of the stairs on the threshold of Poppy's bedroom when he arrived. "Can you talk to me?" he said. "At least share your ideas."

"That's all it is right now, Ben," she said. "An idea. But there's something there. A thread to pull, as it were."

She pushed open Poppy's door, and unlike Harringer's room, Poppy's was exactly as Freya had last seen it. Immaculate.

"No," she said, shaking her head. She stepped back and ventured further along that narrow hallway into the family's living space.

"Freya? We can't just go wandering around. We don't have a warrant."

"Just give me a second, will you?" she replied. "Keep an eye out in case somebody comes."

"You mean like the old man? I can hear him now, running up the stairs."

"Just keep an eye out. Give me a minute to think," she said, then waited for him to leave the suite.

The space was as Freya had imagined. The old servant quarters were small but functional. A small bathroom, a modest lounge area, and a room adjacent to Poppy's which Freya assumed to be where Mr Gray and Izzie slept before he began sleeping downstairs. Freya pushed open the bedroom door. Inside, a large double bed took up most of the space, while a wardrobe and a chest of drawers took up the rest. A narrow space approximately one-foot wide provided a space around the bed to move about. Freya stepped inside and edged around the bed to peer through the window, and as she pulled back the curtain, she realised she was standing on something. It was pair of men's briefs with the branding around the waistband. Not the type a man of Desmond Gray's age would have worn.

There was just enough space for the door to open and she had to either lean around the door to peer inside, or climb on top of the bed. The sight that greeted her reminded her of a hundred teenagers' wardrobes she had peered into before. Clothes that had once been folded were now all a mess on the bottom of the wardrobe. A few clothes were hanging up still, but not many. There were shoe boxes, and jewellery boxes, bags and receipts, and on the bottom shelf, tucked to the back so that Freya had to crouch to see it, was a paper bag. She pulled it forward, fingering the gap to see inside.

She saw the type of packaging drugs came in – white with limited graphics and large volumes of small text.

"Ben?" she said, as she pulled the bag onto the bed and carefully tipped it upside down.

He stepped into the room, glanced around, and found her crouching in the small space on the far side of the bed.

"You rang?" he said, as if he were a servant, but then his face straightened when she held up one of the bottles the little boxes contained. "What's that?"

"Benzodiazepine," she replied, then followed his gaze down to the dirty briefs on the floor. "Harringer's."

"Harringer?" he said. Then he made the connection and hissed, "And Izzie?"

"You heard him. He said he loved them all."

"Yeah, but–"

"But what?" she said. "Anita Carter, his Oxford girl. Sarah Cooper, his Luton girl. Not Katy Southgate. He doesn't stay there. He just passes through."

"But Izzie Brand? His Lincolnshire girl? I guess it makes sense. And those?" He collected one of the bottles and studied it. "What's it for? Athletes foot? Piles?"

"They're Benzos. For anxiety, sleeping, and restlessness," she replied. "Seizures as well, I think."

"She works in a care home. She's bound to have stuff like this knocking around."

"Not that. That's controlled. Signed in and out type of controlled. Controlled enough that you wouldn't stash them in a wardrobe under a pile of old clothes."

"So? She's the manager. You heard what the old boy said. She goes around to all the different homes. She must have to keep a supply. They might even be Desmond Gray's?"

She stared at him, wide-eyed, unable to believe that he hadn't made the connection.

"Oh, I have no doubt they are for Mr Gray. But I'd be willing to bet he doesn't know about them," she said, coaxing him on. "If they're prescribed, which I very much doubt they are, why are they stashed beneath a pile of old clothes?"

Then the penny dropped.

"He just said, she's usually around when he has his bad days."

Freya stared at him while she pondered the facts.

"You're about to make a huge leap, aren't you?" he said.

"She's drugging him," she said, ignoring what he said. "She goes to work, comes back for a few days, gives him a few doses to keep him tired, then goes away again."

"Yeah, but come on. You saw her. She's not a killer," Ben argued.

"I'm not accusing her of being a killer. But she can make him sick enough that he can't get up the stairs, that he thinks his body is giving up, or that he'd have to go–"

"Into a home," Ben finished. "Which she could arrange quite easily, and keep him dosed. And all the while, she's having her fun with Harringer."

"She wasn't meant to be home. Do you remember? Izzie said that when we first came here. Gray just said it too. Poppy was supposed to come home later. She just got home, went to see her dad, ran upstairs to get changed and make him a tea, and then heard them."

"So she saw them, and they saw her," Ben said, almost as a question. He paced the little corridor outside the bedroom, the way he did when he was figuring something out.

"Maybe she cried out in surprise," Freya suggested. "Or maybe Harringer heard the car start?"

"Would you recognise your own car starting?" Freya asked.

"I would. It's a subconscious thing."

"We're three floors up and the window is closed. The bins," Freya said, feeling the excitement grow. "Do you remember the bins had been knocked over?"

Ben nodded. "So she stole Harringer's car as payback. To punish him. And he heard the bins being knocked over, looked out of the window–"

"And then went after her, knowing what he had in the boot," Freya finished, and added a smile. It was a special smile, one she kept in reserve only for when she had outsmarted Ben. "One killer."

She paused.

"Where's Harringer?" Freya asked, and Ben's moment of elation as they pieced the crime together came tumbling down as he realised their mistake.

"He's being released," he said. "We're too bloody late."

CHAPTER FORTY-SIX

Seldom did Ben use the lights in his front grille or the siren that had been fitted. But in this instance, he did. He sped through the lanes while Freya frantically searched his phone for the number. She hit dial and clutched the phone as the call came over the speakers.

"Custody desk," came the answer, when the big, friendly Sergeant Priest picked up the phone.

"Michael, it's Freya. DI Bloom."

"Ah, good evening, ma'am," he began, his voice baritone and lazy, like he had all the time in the world for speech.

"Harringer," she said. "Have we still got him?"

"Roy Harringer,' he replied, as he checked his system. "He was released an hour ago. Couldn't hold him any longer. Is there a problem?"

"Yes. A big one. Get all units on the lookout for him. You have his description. We've got him."

"We don't have anything on him," Ben added. "Other than a pair of dirty pants."

"I'll get right on it," Priest said, and put the phone down without saying goodbye.

"Damn it," Freya hissed, as she searched for another number and hit dial.

Ben navigated the bends in the road, using the gears to slow down, and then accelerating out of the bends. There were few people whose driving Freya truly trusted, and Ben was one of them.

"Chapman," came the next voice on the phone.

"It's me," Freya said. "They let Harringer go."

"Yeah, I spoke to Sergeant Priest. Time's up apparently–"

"I think he killed Poppy Gray," Freya began. "Bring his bank records up. He doesn't have a car. How is he getting home?"

"I'm on it now," Chapman said.

"None of this is concrete, Freya," Ben said as he came to a T-junction and then gunned the engine onto an A-road. "We still don't have anything on him. He was in Oxford, Dorset, Luton, Romford, and now here, and yes he was sleeping with women from all of those places. But there's absolutely nothing on the car or the bodies to incriminate him."

Ignoring Ben's pessimism, Freya waited for Chapman to come back.

"He's used his card twice in the past hour. The florist up the road, then paid a taxi firm," she said, keeping her language short and sweet. "Lincoln Private Taxi. Paid for it a few minutes ago. He must have ordered it as soon as he left the station."

"Any idea where they took him?"

"I'm calling them now," Chapman replied. "I'll call you back."

"Put me through to Cruz," Freya said, before Chapman ended the call. A few moments of silence passed, then Cruz answered.

"Boss?"

"Get on the phone. We need to find Izzie Brand. She's the manager of a chain of care homes. Forest something," Freya said, unable to remember the exact name.

The sound of Cruz tapping on a keyword came over the phone. "East Forest?" he asked. "They've got a home in Woodhall

Spa, Navenby, and one in Boston. Want me to take a drive over there, boss?"

"That's it. Get Boston nick on the case. Call them, tell them to bring her in. We'll arrange transport."

"What's the charge, boss?" he asked, quite rightly too. "They can't just go in and arrest her, can they?"

"I don't want her arrested, Cruz. I want her in protective custody. I think Harringer is going after her."

"Eh?" Cruz said, and she could imagine his gormless expression as he did.

"She's the last one on his list, Cruz."

"Jesus," he said, never one to refrain from announcing his true thoughts. "I'll get onto them now. Hold on, Chapman wants you."

The line went dead for a few seconds as the call was transferred.

"He got a taxi to Lincoln Hospital, ma'am," she said. "Want me to get uniform there?"

"The hospital?" she said, turning to Ben. "What's he–"

"Finishing the job," Ben said, before she could complete the sentence. "What if Lee Sanders saw him? What if Harringer went after Poppy, then went back for Lee–"

"But the mother was there," Freya said. "So he ran back to the guest house and asked Gray to call the police. That's why he got Desmond Gray to call 999."

"To give him an alibi," Chapman said, joining in the *finish other people's sentences off for them* game.

"We'll be there in ten minutes," Ben said, as he overtook a slow-moving Toyota.

"What about Jackie, ma'am?" Chapman suggested. "She said she was going back."

"Okay, talk to Priest. Get uniform there," Freya said, forming a plan as she spoke. "I want Anna on standby. I'll call Gold now."

She ended the call and began searching Ben's phone for Gold's number.

"I hope you're ready to lose a bet," Freya said, as the call connected.

Gold's voice sounded tired and croaky. Her heels echoed through what sounded like a corridor or a large hall. "Ben?"

"No, it's me," Freya said. "I'm on Ben's phone because it's connected to his car. Where are you?"

"The hospital called. They said Lee woke up. The transfusion worked, ma'am."

"That's brilliant news, Gold."

"I'm just going to pop in to see how he and Teresa are doing."

"Are you close?" Freya said.

"Not far. I've just got us a coffee each from the cafeteria."

"Run, then," Freya said.

"What?"

"Harringer has been released. We couldn't hold him anymore. We think Lee Sanders saw Harringer at the scene. He's on his way there now."

The sound of Gold's heels grew louder and faster, as the young DC sped up.

"I don't get it," she said as she ran. "Why would he have been there?"

"We think he was sleeping with Poppy's stepmum and she caught them. She stole the car in spite, or... I don't know. But Harringer chased her. If Lee was conscious when Poppy ran from the car, he might have seen Harringer go after her."

"Oh Christ," Gold said, as she ran full pelt along the corridors, only her breathing and heels coming across the line. "I'll call you back."

"Two minutes out," Ben announced as the call ended. "Do we have enough to bring him in?"

"No, but that's never stopped me before. He has absolutely no reason to be here. We might even catch him in the act."

Ben brought the car to a stop at the entrance to A&E, and

they both jumped out, flashing their warrant cards at the security guard who came out ready to tell them to move on.

"This is an emergency," Freya explained.

"This is a hospital, sweetheart. It usually is," he replied, his voice thick with cockney charm.

"Has anyone been through here in the past five minutes?"

"Only about seventy people. Like I said, it's a hospital."

"Damn it," Freya said, refraining from cursing more than that. She kicked the car instead, and then ignored Ben's glare. "Male. In his fifties. Grey hair, blue eyes, six-foot," Freya explained. "He would be wearing a black jacket with a check shirt and he might have come through here in the past hour."

The security guard rubbed his chin, lifted his radio, then bit down on the aerial in deep thought.

"In the past hour, you say?" he muttered using only four syllables to pronounce the entire sentence.

"Maybe more recently. The last half hour perhaps?"

"Six-foot? Grey hair and blue eyes? Nobody's come through here looking like that," the guard stated matter-of-fact.

"He'll be carrying flowers," Ben added, remembering what Chapman had said.

"Black jacket," Freya repeated, hoping to stir his memory.

But the guard stared past them into the car park. "What about him over there?" He pointed at a man who matched the description. He was hurrying along the footpath towards the main entrance, carrying a large bunch of flowers.

"That's him," Freya hissed, as Harringer strolled briskly towards the hospital around three hundred metres away. She turned to the guard who, despite having spent the past ninety-nine per cent of his security career being bored stupid, and now actually had something to do, froze. "Shut the place down."

"I can't just shut it down," he said, as Ben began to run after Harringer.

"Well, what can you do?" Freya hissed. "This is a bloody emergency."

"We usually call you lot."

"Fat lot of good you are," she muttered, then turned, and was about to run after Ben when her phone vibrated in her hand.

"Michaela," she said. "Give me some good news."

"Are you sitting down?" the CSI asked.

"I don't have time to sit."

"The hair I found in Harringer's car," Michaela said. "I know who it belongs to."

CHAPTER FORTY-SEVEN

"Who the bloody hell designed this place?" Freya spat, when they reached the end of another corridor and were faced with an identical choice of left or right. She searched the signs that were fixed to the wall. None of them even suggested the existence of a Rainforest Ward. She studied the floor where blue and red lines had been painted. The red one went right and the blue line turned left. "Blue or red?"

"There are more signs pointing right than there are left."

"Right it is," Freya said, and they ran on, not stopping until the red line had somehow been re-joined by the blue line. "This doesn't make sense," she said, just as the security guard she had insulted ran past the end of the corridor ahead of them. He slid to a stop then waved them on.

"This way," he called out, then ran on ahead of them. By the time they reached the end of the corridor, he was nowhere in sight.

They ran on, bursting through doors and sliding around corners. Twice they had passed the cafeteria and Freya was ready to give up and call Gold for directions when they rounded a corner, and there, twenty yards ahead of them, was a man wearing a black jacket walking away from them. He had grey hair and he was carrying a large bunch of flowers.

"Roy Harringer, stop there," Ben called out.

The man stopped as requested, but when he turned, he wasn't wearing the angered expression of a cornered killer; his expression was one of confusion.

He may have looked the part with his hair, jacket, and the flowers, but he did not have blue eyes, and he was certainly not Harringer.

Freya hissed a curse.

"Are you talking to me?" he said, with a quick glance around him to make sure he hadn't been mistaken.

"We thought you were somebody else," Ben said.

He stared at them both, nodding, but just as he was about to turn and carry on with his day, he asked, "Any idea where the Rainforest Ward is?" His accent was clearly Northwestern, somewhere close to Newcastle, Freya guessed.

"That's the children's ward, isn't it?" Freya asked.

"Aye, pet. Supposed to deliver these. I'm bleeding lost, I am. Girl on the front desk said to follow the blue line, but it doesn't make sense."

"Are they for Lee Sanders, by any chance?" Ben asked, and he opened his warrant card for the man to see. "Detective Sergeant Savage. This is Detective Inspector Bloom."

The man held his free hand up. "Hey now. I'm just a cabbie, like. I've done nowt wrong."

"Who are the flowers for?"

"Erm, Teresa Sanders," he said, reading the little card. He gave a shrug again. "I don't know her."

"Who paid you?"

"I don't know. Some fella flagged me down. I had a drop in Woodhall and was heading back to base, like. That's when he stopped me. I'll give the money back, like. I'm not supposed to do pickups, you know? I knew I shouldn't have stopped."

"What did he look like?" Ben asked. "The man who stopped you?"

"The bloke? Upset, he was. Said he needed to get these to some lady. Said to say how sorry he was. Looked like he'd been crying."

"And where is he now?"

"How should I know? I left him there. I'm sorry. I shouldn't have–"

"You weren't to know," Freya said, turning to walk away before the urge to scream got the better of her.

"So do I deliver them or what, pet?" the cabbie asked.

"Give them to your wife," Ben said, leaving the man. "At least something good might come of it."

"Eh?" he said, clearly bemused.

Then Freya remembered something the man had said. She turned and took a step towards him, and he backed up a few steps, eyes wide.

"How much did he pay you?"

He shrugged for the third time and pulled out a wad of cash. For a moment, Freya thought he was going to count out a few notes, but he just held it up for her to see. "I haven't counted it yet."

"He gave you all that?"

"Emptied his wallet," the man said. "I thought he was bananas, myself. But I weren't going to turn that down."

Freya glanced at Ben and found his expression to match her own thoughts.

"How upset was he? You said he was crying."

"Oh, Jesus. Like he was about to end it all..." The man stopped mid-sentence. "Oh no. No, no, no."

"Where was he going?" Ben asked.

"He told me not to say anything if anybody asked."

"This is important. The man you spoke to is unhinged. Where?"

"Metheringham. The station."

"Metheringham train station?" Ben asked, then he looked at Freya. "There's a rail crossing there. High speed. Freight."

"Have I messed up?" the man asked. "I didn't know. Honest, I didn't know."

Leaving the man behind shouting questions at them, Freya turned and followed the blue line. She pulled out her phone, dialled Gillespie, then waited for him to answer, praying that it wasn't too late.

"Aye, boss," Gillespie said, sounding chirpy when he answered his phone. He spoke loudly, to be heard over the noise of the road in his car.

"Gillespie, where are you?"

"Just heading back to the wee lad's house. Had the statement typed up and I was going to have him sign it. Should be enough to nail the Osborne lad along with the scars Doctor Bell found."

"I need you to stop that. I need your help and need it fast."

"What's the trouble?" Gillespie asked. "You sound like somebody just died."

Unable to think of anything to say to such an off-hand comment, Freya said nothing.

"Oh no," Gillespie said. "Is it Harringer? Chapman said he'd been released. Has he done it again? Who's he killed?"

"Himself," Freya replied. "If you don't get a bloody move on."

CHAPTER FORTY-EIGHT

When DS Gillespie reached the rail crossing at Metheringham station, he had expected to find chaos, or a queue at least. But there was nothing, and worse of all, there was no sign of Harringer. He parked in the car park, locked his car, and then checked both platforms. Platform one, for trains heading towards Lincoln and beyond, had just three people waiting, none of which matched Harringer's description, and on platform two, there was just one person, a fifty-something-year-old female.

The digital sign on platform one told him the next train was due in eight minutes, while platform two was a full eleven minutes. He wondered if the long wait was because he had just missed a train, and maybe Harringer had got on, but the trains out in that neck of the woods were infrequent. There was no barrier to swipe tickets, as the station was one of those unmanned, rural types that relied on ticket inspectors on-board. But not being a public transport type of guy, Gillespie didn't know if a ticket could be bought on the train.

Resigning to the fact that, had Harringer actually boarded a train already, owning a ticket was the least of his concerns, he headed towards the railway where it intersected with the road. Glancing right, then left, he saw nobody. A few cars crossed the line, then there was silence. Nothing. Pulling his phone from his pocket, he dialled DI Bloom and peered up and down the railway waiting for her to answer.

"Gillespie," she said, after just one ring. Her voice was urgent, and then silenced while she waited for him to give an update.

"Absolutely nothing, boss. He's not here. Either he got on the last train out of town or..."

"Or?"

"Or I don't know where else he could be."

"Damn and blast. We spoke to the cab driver who dropped him there. He definitely said Metheringham," Bloom said. "When was the last train? He might have got on it."

"Not sure. There's no timetable, but there are people on the platform, so I assume there hasn't been one for a wee while. There's nothing here. Nowhere to even buy a ticket."

"I don't really think getting a ticket is the top of his priorities right now, do you?" Bloom said, as Gillespie peered up the track towards Lincoln. The trains in that neck of the woods were diesel, so there was no third rail to be cautious of, yet, through the leather soles of his shoes, he felt the faintest of vibrations.

"Gillespie?" Bloom said.

"Hold on, boss."

"What is it?" she said, her frustration evident in the speed at which she spoke.

But Gillespie wasn't concerned with Bloom's frustration, or her temper, for that matter. What he was concerned with was the pathetic excuse of a man that ambled from the tree line two hundred yards up the track. If Gillespie had a checklist with which to indemnify Harringer, he would have checked the box for the short, neat, grey hair, and he would have checked the box for the smart, dark jacket. But the boxes for arrogance, confidence, and arrow-straight posture would have remained decidedly unchecked. Harringer walked with his shoulders sagging, like the weight of the world was resting on them. Even from a distance, Gillespie could see his mouth hanging open as he stared vacantly at the rails.

"I've got him," he said quietly. "I need an ambulance, and I need someone to stop the trains. And I need both of those quick."

He lowered the phone to his side, ending the call without waiting for Bloom to reply, and he took a moment to study Harringer, to be certain of his ambition. But, although Gillespie searched for some kind of ulterior motive, he knew in that deepest, darkest place in his heart, that there was only one reason a man would stand where Harringer was standing, positioned so he could witness his own ending charging toward him. An unstoppable force. Certain death.

Gillespie stepped off of the road and onto the tracks, placing each step on the railway sleepers to avoid the crunch of gravel alerting Harringer. After just ten metres, Gillespie crouched and felt the rail. It was hard to tell for certain, but he was sure he felt a vibration. The train was way off, but closing in fast.

The time for stealth was over. He needed Harringer off the tracks, and fast.

Gillespie stormed up the track, breaking into a run. The only plan he could think of was to grab hold of Harringer, drag him off the track, and hold him long enough for the train to pass. It might just give him time to talk some sense into the man. But the self-condemned man ahead must have heard or sensed Gillespie amidst his turmoil. He turned when Gillespie was just twenty metres away.

"Get away," he said, edging further up the track.

With both his hands held up, palms out, Gillespie slowed to a walk, matching Harringer's backwards steps one for one.

"Let's talk about this," Gillespie said. "What are you doing, man?"

"It's over," Harringer called back. "Ruined."

"You've got a wife and kids, for god's sake. Nothings over."

"They're better off without me. After what I've done, I won't even be allowed in the house," he said, shaking his head. "I can't face her. I can't bear to see the disappointment and hurt–"

"You did this, Roy. You. Not her. You did this, and you can fix it."

"How? How am I supposed to fix this? My face will be all over the news."

"Just stop," Gillespie said, and he came to a stop himself. "There's no evidence against you. You're a free man."

Harringer stared back at him and the rail beneath Gillespie's boot suddenly began to shiver.

"Do you understand what I'm saying, Roy? We can't prove a damn thing."

"But you think it. You think it and you'll carry on looking. You'll turn our lives upside down."

"Aye, yeah, we will. Just like we carry on trying to solve other crimes. But if you're innocent, you've got nothing to worry about."

"I'm not innocent though, am I?" he shouted, as he turned to glance up the track. The train was yet to round the corner in the distance, but it was getting closer, building speed. By Gillespie's reckoning, the eight minutes he'd seen on the platform display was way off. This would be a through-train. No slowing. It would pelt through the station at top speed.

While Harringer was turned, Gillespie took the opportunity to close the distance by a single step, keeping his movements slow and steady.

"Talk to me about it, Roy. Talk to me about Anita Carter. You were sleeping with her?"

Harringer stared at him. He wore the expression of a man who hated himself and dared anybody else to despise him more.

"It was more than that," he said, and Gillespie prepared to close the gap a little more. "Much more than that."

"You loved her?"

"And she loved me. She loved me, and I let her down. I let her family down as well as my own."

"How did you know her?" Gillespie asked.

"She ran a bed and breakfast," he said wistfully, and was distracted long enough for Gillespie to take another step. But he looked up just as Gillespie had moved. "They all did. Both of them. Anita and Sarah. Do you see? Do you see what's happening?"

"See what?" Gillespie asked.

"I've killed them. I've ruined my own wife's life. And my girl. My baby girl?" he said, breaking into a sob, just as the train rounded the bend perhaps a kilometre away. Vibrations thundered beneath Gillespie's boot now. He stepped closer, not caring if Harringer saw him.

"Stop," Harringer cried out, backing away with tears streaming down his face. "Don't you see? How can I go on? How can I go on knowing I destroyed all those lives?"

It was a freight train, long and heavy. Even if by some miracle the driver could see them ahead, there would be no chance of stopping it. It held hundreds of metres of container carriages containing tons and tons of cargo. And the mighty diesel engine that pulled the load would be in excess of a hundred tons, bearing down on them at well over fifty miles per hour.

Behind them, the sirens rang out for the crossing barriers to come down and stop the traffic. The driver pulled on the horn three times, but still, the train bore down on them.

Gillespie stepped off the track and edged closer along the gravel. But Harringer saw him and crossed to the other side, keeping the rails between them.

"We can talk about this, Roy," Gillespie said.

"The time for talking is over," he replied. "This is the only way to stop it."

"Roy, come on, man. What do you mean? Stop what?" Gillespie urged him from the side of the tracks, glancing at the oncoming train, gauging the time he had left. Less than a minute.

The driver sounded the horn three more times, louder now, and somehow with more urgency.

"Roy?" Gillespie called.

But Harringer just shook his head. He stepped onto the tracks and turned to face the train once more.

"Roy, did you kill those women? Did you kill Anita and Sarah?"

"They died because of me," he called over the rising noise of the train. He turned to stare at Gillespie. "And Poppy too."

"You're lying," Gillespie said, as the driver sounded the horn three more times and the squeal of brakes pierced the air. "You're lying, Roy."

But Roy's attention was lost to the oncoming train.

"Roy?" Gillespie called. But the time for speaking was over. Gillespie leaped onto the track and grabbed Harringer around his waist. Harringer spread his feet, digging his heels in.

"No," he screamed. "Get off me."

There were just seconds left now. Fifteen at the most, and Gillespie wrestled Harringer to one side. Another two steps and they'd be clear. But Harringer sank lower to escape his grip. Low enough that he could grip the rail, leaving Gillespie hanging onto the man's waist, pulling him with everything he had.

The noise was deafening, a cacophony of a thousand tons, merged with Gillespie's raging heartbeat pounding in his ears, every sense screaming at him to leave Harringer to his fate. But, unable to wrench his grip from the track, Gillespie bent lower to scream in his ear.

"You can fix this, Roy. You can make a difference."

The driver of the train sounded the horn one more time, this time, a long, relentless, and deafening roar. Harringer pulled Gillespie down further. Then he let go of the rail and stood, allowing Gillespie to stand for them both to meet their makers.

"You can make a difference, Roy. Come on," he shouted. "Only you can fix this. Talk to me. Why did Poppy die? Why did she steal your car?"

He had no idea if Harringer heard him above the racket. The noise around them was ear-splitting, like they were brawling in the eye of a tornado.

Then, at the final moment, with barely a second to spare, Harringer grimaced and pulled Gillespie's face close. "Poppy didn't steal my car," he shouted, and there was the hint of a smile on his face, like he had been relinquished of the weight of the secret. "If I don't do this, more will die," he said, while Gillespie was still reeling from the first statement. Then, with every morsel of strength that remained in his body, a last act of humanity, Harringer shoved Gillespie out of the way.

He landed on the hard gravel, rolled, then clawed his way to the brush that lined the railway, as the screeching train slid past as if the rails were made of ice. Where Harringer had been standing, a thousand tons of steel roared past in a blur, but all Gillespie could see was the pain in Harringer's eyes, as if the moment had been etched onto his vision for all time. He lay there on his back, popped up on his elbows, and watched in utter dismay at his failure. The only distraction was his vibrating phone in his hand.

It was DI Bloom, and he answered the call but said nothing. He just stared at the slowing train.

"Gillespie?" she said, then raised her voice to be heard over the background noise. "Gillespie, I need an update."

"He's gone," he said, hearing his own voice break. "I couldn't stop him."

"Gillespie, it's not your fault," Bloom stated. "You can't save them all."

"I had him, boss. In my hands."

"What did he say? Focus, Gillespie. What did he say?"

The train was slowing and the end was drawing near. Gillespie thought back to those few brief words, confusing as they were.

"Poppy didn't steal the car, boss," Gillespie croaked, his jaw trembling from the surging adrenalin. "He said if he didn't finish it, more will die."

CHAPTER FORTY-NINE

Freya didn't even have to utter a single word, and Ben knew. She felt her shoulders sag, and the dull ache that had taken root in her back had reached up to take hold of her neck.

"How's Gillespie?" was all Ben asked.

"Coping," she replied, letting the phone drop to her side. It was there a fraction of a second before it rang again, and on instinct, she hit the button to answer to call. "DI Bloom."

"Ma'am, it's me, Chapman."

"What have you got, Chapman?" she said, using her name for Ben's benefit.

"It's Izzie Brand. She hasn't worked at the care home for over a month. She was fired."

"Fired?" Freya said, and she turned to face Ben, hoping he would be able to put the fragments of one side of her conversation together. "For stealing?"

"Yes. How did you know?"

"Drugs. I'm right, aren't I?"

Chapman was clearly bemused. "Yes."

"Benzos?"

"Benzodiazepine, yes."

"I found them in her bedroom. She's been drugging her husband," Freya explained. "Any idea where she is?"

"I've got an ANPR alert set up. As soon as her car passes through a camera, it'll flag it. I suppose we just have to wait."

Freya digested the information, processed all the pieces like a blurred puzzle.

"Do me a favour. Get Cruz down to Metheringham train station. Gillespie is down there. He needs help. And Chapman?"

"Yes, ma'am?"

"Tell him not to cock about. Gillespie just witnessed a tragedy."

"Harringer?"

"Yes. He couldn't stop him."

"Oh, Christ. Okay, leave it to me."

Freya ended the call, leaned back against the corridor wall, and sighed.

"Let me guess. Izzie Brand is missing?"

"Correct."

"And Harringer's dead?"

"Correct."

"That's our lead suspect," Ben said. "Why would he do that? Why would he come all this way, then do that?"

"Guilt? Shame? Regret? Take your pick," Freya suggested.

"Ma'am? Ben?"

They turned to find Gold at the far end of the corridor running full pelt towards them. In the past six months of working with the woman, Freya had never seen her run, and she was doing so with conviction.

"You don't think Harringer killed any of them, do you?" Ben asked, as Gold ran toward them.

"He's a lover, not a fighter."

"So, who then?" Ben asked, but there was no time to reply.

"It's Lee," Gold explained, as she drew nearer, then came to a sliding stop before them, breathless, but keen to spill her news. "It's Lee Sanders. He's missing."

"Missing?" Freya said. "He's been unconscious for three days."

"Where's the mother?" Ben asked, then turned to stare at Freya, finally getting where she was heading. "Teresa Sanders?"

"That's just it. It's her who's taken him. The girl on the desk said she must have slipped out without anyone seeing. That was over an hour ago. I can't find them anywhere."

"Have you checked security?" Ben asked.

"I've spoken to a guard. He's checking CCTV. He said he'd call me."

"What does she drive?" Freya asked.

"I don't know. A people carrier type thing. A Galaxy, I think. Silver with dents in front wing."

"Let's go," Freya said, snatching a glimpse of what the completed puzzle might look like, only for it to blur at the edges. She set off in a run without waiting for Ben or Gold.

"Where are we going?" Ben called out from not far behind her.

"She's going home," Freya said, then ignored him until they had run from the hospital, across the road, into the car park, and were climbing into the car.

Breathless, Ben unlocked the car, climbed inside, and started the engine, while a very confused Gold climbed into the rear seat.

"What's happening?" she asked, in that childlike tone of hers. "You don't think she would hurt him, do you?"

Freya was pulling on her belt, waiting for Ben to come up with his interpretation. He set off, and for the second time that day, he switched on his blues and twos.

"You were right," he said, and he stole his eyes from the road for one moment to glance at her. "One killer."

"Give me your rundown of events," Freya said, as much for Gold's benefit as her own. "From the top."

Ben pulled onto the main road heading towards Lincoln's

outer ring road and overtook a queue of traffic at the little roundabout.

"Harringer was a bigamist."

"What do you mean *was*?" Gold said, and Freya turned to find her staring at her.

"He took his own life," she explained. "Gillespie witnessed it. He tried to stop him, but..."

"Oh my god–"

"Go on," Freya said, urging Ben to finish his own puzzle.

"A girl in every port, as it were. Anita Carter in Oxford. Sarah Cooper in Luton. But he got greedy in Lincolnshire. He had two. Izzie Brand and Teresa Sanders."

"What?" Gold exclaimed. "That's not right. She had nobody. She told me–"

"Michaela found Teresa's hair in Harringer's car, Jackie," Ben said. "How would it have got inside the car if all she did was run out of the house and tend to her boy? She'd been inside the car. Maybe Teresa found out about the others? All of them. Maybe she was jealous?"

"Is that motive enough?" Freya asked.

"We've seen people murdered for weaker reasons. Let's face it. She's clearly unhinged. She's taken her own son from hospital."

"Harringer said more will die if he didn't do what he did," Freya said, adding weight to Ben's story.

"She's not like that," Gold argued.

"Her husband vanished," continued Ben. "There's no trace of him. And she's committed to Harringer. She sees a future with him, somehow. But Harringer can't let go of the others. Anita and Sarah, and whoever else there was. He can't end it with them."

"So Teresa does it for him?" Freya said.

"She's not like that. No way," Gold said, her voice lacking the conviction it had only moments ago as she came to the realisation that the past few days had all been a charade. She had fallen for a pack of lies. She sat back in her seat in disbelief. "She was so lovely."

"Then Harringer comes to Lincolnshire," Ben continued. "Katy Southgate was nothing to do with him. She wasn't one of his girlfriends. He just stays at the guest house. Poppy's not home. Desmond Gray is downstairs. Him and Izzie are upstairs. Poppy comes home early, finds them in bed. Then she runs," Ben said. "She can't face her dad. She can't see the disappointment in his face. It would probably kill him."

"So what does she do then?" Freya said knowingly. "This part is crucial."

"She takes Harringer's car, crashes into the bins, and Harringer hears her. He goes after her. He chases her down the lane."

"Who is in the car?" Freya asked. "Who does he have in the boot?"

"It must be one of the others," Ben said. "It has to be."

"But he's not the killer. Remember?" Freya said, smiling as he fought with the facts and the hypothesis. "Who put the woman in the boot? Who is she?"

"Poppy hits Lee Sanders and runs up the track. She's scared. She's trying to get away," Ben said, trying to get back on track with his theory.

"So why didn't Teresa see Harringer run after her?"

"Maybe she did? Maybe she did see him? But she loves him. She wouldn't tell us if she saw him," Ben suggested, then changed his mind. "Or maybe it was Teresa that chased her? Maybe Teresa chased her up the track after all?"

"She killed Poppy," Gold said, as if it all suddenly made sense. "Not Harringer. Not Osborne. Teresa Sanders. It was easy for her–"

"Because she'd already killed Anita and Sarah," Ben finished.

"So what's she doing now?" Freya asked. There were several obvious flaws in Ben's hypothesis. But that was okay, the basic idea was there. Details could be added in later. "Why did she take Lee from the hospital?"

"Because he saw something," Gold said from the back seat. "Oh my god. He saw everything. I was with Teresa in the hospital. The doctor. He said something was wrong. It was like he was suspicious of her, or something–"

"Stop," Freya called out, holding her fingers to her temples. All the pieces were slowly falling into place in her mind, like the fog was lifting to reveal the truth. It was like seeing the answer to yesterday's crossword in that day's edition, and kicking yourself for not being able to spot it. "You're both right. And you're both so terribly wrong."

"Could you try to be a bit more cryptic?" Ben said.

"You're both right," she said, with all the clarity of hindsight. "It wasn't Poppy who stole the car and hit Lee. It was the only other person with access to his keys. And it wasn't Harringer who chased Poppy up the lane."

"What are you saying, Freya?" Ben said, a little dubious.

"I'm saying that it's funny that all the time we've been working on this investigation, only Jackie has had a chance to meet Teresa," Freya replied. "Jackie, what did you say to Teresa the first time you met her at the hospital?"

"What do you mean? The usual, I guess."

"You introduced yourself?"

"Of course. I showed her my warrant card."

"And what else did you tell her?"

"Only what you told me to, ma'am. That I'd be there a lot. That I'd been assigned to Lee. So that when he wakes up I can talk to him."

"And there we have it," Freya said. "That gave her all the time she needed to finish the job."

"Gave who all the time?" Jackie said. "Teresa? I don't understand."

"No. Not Teresa. We found *her* dead in the boot of Harringer's car," Freya said, and she found Jackie in the rearview mirror. "She's played us. She's played us like fools. She knew that as long as it was only Jackie who went to the hospital, she could get away with it."

"What are you talking about, Freya?" Ben said. "Teresa isn't dead."

"Oh, she's dead alright," Freya said. "The real one, at least. Izzie stole her identity."

CHAPTER FIFTY

From the outside, the Sanders house appeared empty, devoid of life. But it was exactly as Jackie had imagined it to be. She had read the reports, and from what Teresa had said over the past few days, it was exactly as she had described it. Peaceful.

The spot where Harringer's car had been dumped was marked with a hole in the hedgerow. She could see it in her mind's eye. The activity. CSI, traffic police, and the ambulance. But now there was nothing. An empty road, a lonely house, and a track, seemingly harmless.

But on the driveway, if you could call it a driveway, a bare patch of grass that hadn't been paved or concreted over, bearing two bare patches worn from being driven over repeatedly, was a silver Ford Galaxy with a few small, careless dents in the front wing.

"She's here," Freya said, then pointed to where the car had been dumped in the hedge. "Park over there. Out of sight."

Ben stopped the car where she had asked, applied the handbrake, and unclipped his seat belt. He stared at Jackie in the rearview mirror, and Freya turned to face her.

"This is where we need you," Freya said.

"Me?"

"You have a relationship with her."

"She's a murderer–"

"You don't know that. Not as far as she's concerned. She just thinks you're a lovely young DC with a big heart. I need you to knock on her door, Jackie."

"Alone?"

"We'll be here. Nothing will happen. We can't do anything until we know the boy is safe. We can't go charging in there. She might do something stupid."

"She might have already done it," Ben added.

"Don't say that," Jackie said.

"Are you okay to do this?" Freya asked. "It's okay if you're not."

"She was so lovely," Jackie said, remembering how she had laid her head on her shoulder. How they had shared tears.

"Gold?" Freya urged. "We're not here to judge her personality."

"Okay, okay," she said, and she fumbled for the door release.

"We just need to know that Lee is okay. We'll be right behind you, okay?"

"Right," Jackie said, as she climbed from the car. She took a tentative step towards the entrance to the drive. The tall hedges that surrounded the property were unkempt with thick thorns that jutted out. Peering back at Ben's car, she found Freya coaxing her on, watching her every move. She reached the end of the hedge and peered around the corner, hearing a car door slam. She saw the woman who had deceived her all this time. She was about to climb into the driver's seat when she caught sight of Jackie.

She paused with one foot in the car, her eyes darting to the back seat and then back to Jackie.

"Jackie," she said, forcing a smile. "What are you doing here?"

"The hospital," Jackie began. "They said you left. They said you took Lee. Is that right, Teresa?"

Jackie hoped that by using her false name, she might not realise the game was up.

"So?" she replied casually. "He's *my* son. He's on the mend."

"They need to keep him in, Teresa. They need to observe him. He could be seriously ill."

"They've done all they can do for him. It's down to me now."

"Can I see him?"

Suddenly dropping the faux-friendly expression she had worn, she allowed a bitter sneer to evolve. "See him? You don't believe me? You think I'd hurt my own son?"

"I just want to see he's okay, Teresa. I don't doubt you at all–"

"You do," she said, and she stepped away from the car for a moment. "He's fine. Not that he's any of your business."

"Actually, he is. Our business, I mean. He's involved in a crime that we're investigating. He's a victim."

"And I'm his mother, and I'm telling you he's fine," she said, and she stepped back to the car and climbed inside.

"Teresa, please," Jackie said, just as she slammed the door.

The engine fired up as Jackie took a few steps towards the car, and the reverse lights flicked on almost instantly. Moments later, the car lurched backwards, forcing Jackie to step to one side to let it pass. She ran to keep up a few steps, peering through the tinted rear window to see Lee, but all she could see was a child's hand lying flat against the glass.

"Stop. I mean it," Jackie shouted, and she ran to stand in front of the car as Izzie brought it to a stop facing the opposite direction to Ben's car.

The imposter stared at Jackie through the windscreen, her eyes wide with fear, her mouth hanging open as if she couldn't quite believe what she was doing. She glanced in the rear-view mirror, where Ben was slowly turning around. Jackie saw her expression alter, like she was witnessing the decision process taking place.

Then she gunned the engine.

The front end raised a few inches and Jackie moved out of the way just in time, and as the car passed, Lee's face appeared at the glass.

Ben brought his Ford to a skidding stop beside Jackie and she jumped in, lifting her feet just as Ben accelerated away again. Freya had dialled somebody and the call rang out over the speakers.

"She's got him in there," Jackie said, as Ben hit the switch for the flashing lights on his dashboard and in the front grille.

"It's okay, we heard everything," Freya replied, just as the call was answered.

"DC Chapman."

"Chapman, it's me. I need uniforms and traffic in the Stixwould area. Silver Ford Galaxy, dented front wing, currently heading towards..." She glanced across at Ben.

"South," Ben said, as they followed her speeding Galaxy around a small roundabout. "She's heading toward the river on the B1191. Current speed seventy-five miles per hour. That's seven five," he repeated for clarity.

"There's a child on board," Jackie added. "Lee Sanders is in the back seat."

"Did you get that, Chapman? No TPAC manoeuvres," Ben advised.

"Leave it with me," Chapman advised, ending the call.

Ahead of them, Izzie overtook cars, heading into oncoming traffic to do so, and twice she clipped the pavement, barely managing to keep the car straight.

"She's going to do something stupid," Freya said. "We need to get in front of her."

"I saw her," Jackie said. "I saw the look in her eye. She looks bloody terrified."

Ben followed where he could, finding safer moments to pass traffic, keeping them behind Teresa's Galaxy.

"We can stop after Kirkstead Bridge," Ben said. "There's a long straight."

"I can't believe I've been so stupid," Jackie said. "I've been with her all bloody week. I haven't even seen a photo of Izzie."

They powered onto Kirkstead Bridge, the rise in elevation forcing Ben to put his foot down harder. He leaned to one side trying to see past the Galaxy, vying for a chance to overtake.

"Don't take it personally, Jackie," Ben said, glancing in the rear-view mirror to look her in the eye. "If there's one thing I've learnt about this job, it's full of surprises–"

"Look out," Jackie screamed, as Izzie slammed on the brakes and skidded to a stop, narrowly avoiding a little, red Vauxhall heading in the opposite direction. Ben braked hard, steering away from the now stationary Ford in front. All three of them were out of the car in a heartbeat, but Izzie was faster. She had wrenched Lee from the backseat and half-carried and half-dragged him toward the edge of the bridge. Below them, the River Witham idled by. A few little boats were moored to a jetty and the surrounding scene was a picture of serenity.

But the scene atop the bridge was one of fear, guilt, and anger, and Izzie hoisted the boy up. "Don't come any closer," she shouted.

"Stop," Jackie pleaded, then felt Freya's hand on her shoulder as she positioned herself to spearhead the three detectives.

Izzie stared at her, her top lip curling in hatred as she fought Lee's flailing arms. He was crying. Frightened. Terrified. And he stared at the woman without an ounce of recognition. "You stay right there."

"Look what you're doing to him. Don't do this. We can help–"

"Oh, shut up, you whining little bitch."

"Eh?" Jackie said, feeling the tug of emotions in the pit of her stomach. "If you were truly a mother, you could never do this."

"She doesn't care about the boy. She only cares about herself. He saw something, didn't he? He saw what you did," Freya said, loudly and in a tone that demanded unrivalled attention. She stared at the woman with Lee's life in her hands, her expression calm and composed. "I'm right, aren't I, Izzie?"

CHAPTER FIFTY-ONE

"YOU DIDN'T HONESTLY THINK YOU WERE GOING TO GET AWAY with it, did you, Izzie?" Freya asked, shouting to be heard over Lee's cries. "Where were you going to go?"

Izzie said nothing. She tightened her grip on the boy, threatening to push him further over the edge.

Seeing the oncoming traffic slow to a stop precariously on the bridge, Ben ran ahead to warn the drivers.

"Or were you going to see Roy?" Freya continued. "Were you going to finish what you started? Is that it? And what about the boy? What about Lee? Were you just going to dump him in the river?"

"I don't know," she screamed.

"You don't have a plan?" Freya said, her tone sarcastic. "That's not like you. I think you had a master plan. I think you had a master plan but it all went wrong when Poppy came home early."

"What?" Izzie snarled, but she offered no argument.

"Do you want to know what I think? I think you set Roy up. I think you killed Anita Carter. I think you killed Sarah Cooper too. I'm right, aren't I?" Freya stated, taking a step towards her, chancing a quick glance down at the river below. "You followed him around the country. From Luton to Romford. From Oxford to Dorset. You set him up."

Izzie shook her head, but it was more disbelief than denial. Disbelief that her plan had been uncovered.

"You couldn't have him to yourself. He didn't keep his word, did he?" Freya said, edging closer and closer. "*You* kept your word. You were drugging your poor husband, weren't you? Drugging him to keep him away. Biding your time, until the day came that he had to give it all up. His life's work. Cash it all in. But Poppy came home early, didn't she, Izzie? She heard you and Roy arguing. She heard you tell Roy everything you'd done. How you'd got rid of all his problems for him, and if he didn't leave his wife, all you had to do was make a call to the police. Anonymously, of course. But they'd believe you. They'd look where he'd been. Just like we did. And there's bound to be some evidence somewhere. But Poppy heard it. She heard it all. It wasn't Poppy that stole Roy's car, was it? We found one of your hairs in the driver's seat. With a root, too. That's rare. Our CSI team matched the DNA to what we took from you at the hospital."

"Get away," Izzie said. "Don't come any closer. I'll drop him. I swear I'll drop him."

Verbalising the threat did little to calm Lee, who thrashed in her grasp, both clinging to her and pushing her away.

"You chased her, didn't you, Izzie?" Freya said, despising the woman before her. "You took Roy's car because his keys were beside your bed. You knocked the bins over in your haste. You chased her down the lane and you were going too fast, you were too scared of her getting away, of her saying something to her father, that you failed to stop in time. You hit him. You hit Lee, and you were so set on stopping Poppy that you left him there. You left a small boy dying by the side of the road while you went after Poppy. It was easy for you, though, wasn't it? It was easy for you to put your hands around her throat. It was easy for you to squeeze the life from her. Because you'd done it twice before."

"You didn't know her. You didn't know how she treated me–"

"She didn't deserve that, though, Izzie. Of that I'm certain," Freya said, just five steps away now. Izzie backed up as far as she dare. The water loomed beneath her and the boy, and all she would have to do is let go and he'd fall. "But when you got back to the car, his mother was there. It wasn't part of the plan. It shouldn't have happened. But you could deal with it, right? You could handle another one. After all, it wasn't you that would have to pay the price. You killed her. You saw an opportunity to pin another one on Roy. Another murder. That'll teach him. That'll teach him for letting you keep your end of the bargain while he went gallivanting around the country sleeping with his mistresses. You killed Teresa and stuffed her into the boot of his car. Then you went into her house through the open front door. You took her handbag. You took over her life."

Lee screamed and kicked out at Izzie, who momentarily lost her grip. He slipped through her flailing hands and she caught him, pulling him back up the handrail. She turned to Freya, who smiled at the demonstration of Izzie's weakness.

"You can't do it, can you?" Freya said, refraining from laughing but allowing a vindictive grin to creep onto her face. "You can't kill him now just like you couldn't kill him a few days ago. That's why you're in this mess. It's one thing to murder Roy's other girlfriends. It's another thing to murder an innocent teenager who could have exposed you. But you can't kill a small boy. Not with your bare hands, at least. That's why you stayed in the hospital, isn't it? That's why you pretended to be his mother. That's why Lee nearly died. You were feeding him Benzos. The same Benzos you were feeding your husband. Why? Because it's easier. Because you wouldn't have to physically touch him. Because you can't do it. You were just lucky that I sent DC Gold to the hospital and didn't go myself. That gave you the time you needed. Time enough to finish him with the drugs."

"No, stop," Izzie said, hanging onto the boy, realising her only bargaining chip had gone. "You have no idea what I'm capable of–"

"Oh, I think I do, Izzie," Freya said, closing the distance a little more. "Go on. Push him. Let go of him."

Lee stared at her, horrified. He clawed at Izzie's clothes, trying to pull himself over the handrail. But Izzie neither helped him nor pushed him away. She held him still, despite his agonising cries for help.

"Go on, Izzie. There's only three of us. What are we going to do? Leave him to die, like you did? No. We're the police. We'll help him. We'll dive in and get him if we have to. You could get away. You can run to Roy. You can start that new life together. That's your plan, isn't it? You and him. Someplace new. So, go on. Push him. Prove me wrong."

Izzie glanced at the boy for just a second, as if she was contemplating it. Deliberating. She glanced back at Ben to gauge his distance. He was too far away to stop her.

"Come on, Izzie. Show us. Show us you can do it."

"Freya, what are you doing?" Ben called out. "She's mad. Just stop her."

"I want to see," she replied. "I want her to prove me wrong."

"Look at him. He's bloody terrified."

"And so is she," Freya shouted. "Terrified because she knows she has nowhere to run."

"You're wrong," Izzie snapped. "You don't know me."

"Then come on. Push him. Show me what you can do, Izzie," Freya shouted, taking the final few steps until she was just in reach. "You can't, can you? You thought you could. You thought you could finish it. What did he see, Izzie? What did he see that you're so ashamed of?" Freya inched forward, locking stares with the desperate woman. "He saw you run after Poppy and then he saw you kill his own mother."

Izzie stared up at her, tears streaming down her face. But she was resolute. She hung on for a few moments longer until Freya delivered the final blow. Leaning in, until their faces were just inches apart, Freya smiled.

"Roy's dead, Izzie."

Izzie's eyes widened. Her mouth opened as if she might say something. But Freya wasn't going to let her have that pleasure.

"He never wanted you. You were just another girl in just another town," Freya said. "It's over."

She buckled at her knees, as if the weight of Freya's words had been too much, and Freya caught hold of Lee, pulling him over and handing him to Gold.

"Izzie Brand, I'm arresting you on suspicion of murder," Freya began. "Do you want to know what Roy's last words were?"

On her knees, now, Izzie stared up at her, a broken woman. She blinked away the tears and fixed Freya's gaze with her own vacant stare.

"If I don't do this, more will die," Freya said, and she leaned down to whisper in her ear. "Think about that while you're rotting in prison."

CHAPTER FIFTY-TWO

"WHAT WILL HAPPEN TO HIM?" JACKIE ASKED, AS SHE HANDED Lee Sanders to a uniform.

"Do you want the truth, or a nicer version?" Freya replied.

"The nicer version."

"I don't know," Freya said, as she leaned on the handrail of the bridge. Traffic police were on scene, allowing the long queue to disperse. But the whole affair had taken its toll on Freya. "Maybe Gillespie could tell us?"

"He'll go into the system?" Jackie asked. "It's so unfair."

"It's better than it used to be. You did well, Jackie. Really bloody well."

"I don't feel like it. I feel like a fool–"

"What, because Izzie managed to lie to you? How were you to know?"

"I should have checked the files. I would have seen a picture of her or something."

"I don't think so. I should have investigated her sooner. It is what it is. We can't change the past."

"How long do you think she'll get?"

"If she's found guilty of four counts of murder, then I doubt she'll ever breathe fresh air again."

"Are you suggesting she might get off?"

"Not with Poppy or Teresa, no. But Anita Carter and Sarah Cooper might be a little harder to prove."

"When did you know it was her? Izzie, I mean?"

"I don't know. Something wasn't right about her," Freya said, leaving an explanation into how her mind worked vague. "Do you know how many people were killed in drink-driving-related accidents last year, Jackie?"

"Eh? Erm... six hundred and something, isn't it? There's a poster on the wall in the station."

"Very good. How many people are murdered?"

Jackie pondered the question, shrugged, and shook her head.

"Six hundred," Freya said. "Funny, isn't it? How there are so few murderers compared to drink drivers, yet the number of deaths is the same?"

"Erm, I suppose so, ma'am."

"It's okay. I'm not going mad. But look at it like this. If there are so few murderers in Britain, what are the odds of two of them being in the same tiny little village, like Stixwould?"

"So you knew it was the same person?" Jackie asked, as Ben strode up to them, hands in pockets.

"I knew it was one killer," she said, eyeing Ben with a wry smile. "But for the life of me, I couldn't put it all together. Not until Michaela told me about the hair being matched to Teresa. That didn't make sense. Why would Lee's mother be in the driver's seat? At that point, we still didn't know who the unknown woman was. Until you told me the doctor had said something about her. Doctors are quite intuitive. The woman in the car needed an identity. She had to be someone local. It's funny how a tiny little detail can make all the difference sometimes."

"There's something niggling me, though," Ben said. "How did the hospital not find the Benzodiazepine in Lee's blood?"

"Simple," Freya replied. "Why would they look for it? They would have to run tests, and let's face it, testing for something that's normally prescribed to the mature generations just wasn't on their radar."

"Okay, so why didn't the lab connect Lee's DNA with the woman in the boot of the car?"

"Again, simple," Freya said. "Why would they even look? As far as we were concerned, Teresa was still alive. There was no connection between Lee and the body in the car."

"So there was only one killer, after all," Ben said, looking a little disappointed.

"One killer indeed, Ben. What do you have to say about that?"

Jackie stared between them, looking more than a little confused.

"I'd say it was time I put my apron on."

CHAPTER FIFTY-THREE

THREE DAYS HAD PASSED SINCE IZZIE BRAND HAD BEEN TAKEN away in handcuffs, and since Cruz had found Gillespie down by the train tracks and had managed to talk him back to the real world. The here and now.

Three days, as far as Gillespie was concerned, was a long time. Time to think. Time to reflect. Time to make a difference.

He pushed the doorbell and heard the welcoming chime from inside. A rotund woman came to the doorway, her figure appearing in the frosted glass before she opened the door.

"Mrs Frost?" Gillespie said. "Is it a good time?"

She studied his face for a moment, glanced up the stairs, then relented with a smile as welcoming as the chimes. "Of course it is."

She stepped to one side for Gillespie, then closed the door behind him.

"He's just upstairs. Do you want to go up and have a wee chat?" she said, putting on her best Glaswegian accent. She leaned onto the staircase and inhaled, ready to call out, but Gillespie stopped her.

"I want to talk to you both, if I may?" he said, and she looked at him quizzically.

"Me?"

"Aye, you both," he said. "You and the lad."

She clutched her collars with one hand and smoothed her hair. Then, slightly unnerved at the thought of what Gillespie could possibly say, she called up.

"Grant? Mr Gillespie is here to see you."

No reply came, of course. Gillespie had been expecting that. But he held up his hand for her to wait, and they listened. Together. Coming to stand at the top of the stairs, Grant Sayer stared down at Gillespie, and for a moment, there was a hint of warmth in his eyes.

"Hey, son," Gillespie said. Then, leaning onto the stairs and in true pantomime style, he whispered, "I don't know about you but I quite fancy having a wee chat over a nice, wee pie."

The smile that followed was rare. It was genuine. And above all, it was the best thing Gillespie had seen for years. Grant made his way downstairs and Mrs Frost managed to get a little flustered. Probably hiding her tears of happiness, the way people did. She bustled past into the kitchen mumbling something about putting the kettle on.

But Gillespie didn't hide his. He let his eyes well up and couldn't care less if Grant saw them, or Mrs Frost, for that matter.

"You doing alright?" Gillespie asked, noting the book in the boy's hand. It was another Josh Conroy. A brand-new book with barely a crease in the jacket. "You enjoying the series?"

Grant nodded. "The best," he said. Two words. So easy. So... Gillespie searched for the right word. But the trouble was there were so many. He settled on *perfect*. The words. They were so perfect.

"I thought so too," he said, and nodded at the kitchen. "Fancy a bit of pie?"

Grant nodded, still smiling, and led the way. Mrs Frost, who always seemed to be cooking for an army, was flustered. She had clearly dabbed at her eyes with a tea towel as her eyes were red but bone dry.

"Now then," she began, looking up at Gillespie. "Sugar, dear?"

"Aye, two for me, Mrs Frost."

"It's Rose," she said. "Please. Call me Rose. You're a guest in this house, and you'll always be welcome. So you might as well drop the formalities."

"Aye, two then please, Rose. Strong and sweet. Just like my women." He winked at Grant, who beamed at him.

"Grant, dear, can I make you a tea?"

He nodded, tearing his eyes from Gillespie long enough to be polite.

"Do you take sugar, Grant?" Gillespie asked, out of curiosity more than anything.

"No," Rose answered for him. "He's sweet enough."

"Actually, I thought I might have some this time," Grant said, the words flowing from him. Not stuttered or fragmented as they had been at the station. But flowing, like a stream.

Rose peered up at him, a little surprised to hear him talk, and to hear that he now wanted sugar.

"Two, please," he added, and then he returned his gaze to Gillespie, beaming.

"Two sugars coming up," she said, as she set a tray of pies down on the kitchen counter and fetched the sugar bowl from the side.

"Those look incredible, Mrs Frost... I mean Rose," Gillespie said, inhaling deeply. "Ah, pastry. Beef. And what's that?"

"They're steak and ale. Grant's favourite," she said, eyeing the lad fondly. Although a large woman, Rose's reflexes were sharp. The moment Gillespie reached out to take one of the pies from the tray, she whipped the tea towel from where it hung over her shoulder and snapped it against the back of his hand. "Wait. We're not animals in this house, Mr Gillespie–"

"It's Jim," he said. "I'm going to be popping round more often than I thought, so you might as well drop the formalities."

Rose smiled at his play on her earlier statement. "Good," she said, and reached for two plates. She handed them to him, leaving no room for objection. "Well, Jim, seeing as you're going to be here frequently, you might as well get used to laying the table. The mats are on the shelf. You'll need some coasters too. Can't bear ring marks on my table."

A few moments later, Rose had set the tea things on the table and they'd each taken a seat. Grant took a place opposite Gillespie, seeming to watch his every move.

"I'd, erm..." Rose began, then prepared her tea towel, ready to wipe her eye. "I'd like to thank you. For what you did. You know?"

"Ah, it was nothing, Rose," Gillespie said, brushing the comment off.

"I mean it. The way you stood up in court and said what you did. I know Grant won't say it himself. But you should hear it. So I'll say it for him. We're so grateful, Jim. So very grateful."

"Ah, he would have got off anyway–"

"That's beside the point. To have somebody like you. A policeman. Saying all those nice things. It meant a lot. You're a good man, Jim Gillespie."

Gillespie eyed them both. Then he eyed the pie, making sure that Rose caught his wandering eye. She put a piece on a plate then set it before him.

"The truth is," Gillespie began, "I've been thinking. About you both, actually. And well, it's like this. There's a man I know. Police, but he's nice. He runs the recruitment. There's places available, and listen, Grant, if you don't want to, I understand–"

"I want to," Grant said without faltering.

"I mean, it's not everyone's cup of tea," Gillespie continued, pulling a leaflet from his pocket.

"I'll do it."

"And it's bloody hard work–"

"I want to do it."

"The pay isn't great–"

Grant held out his hand and took the leaflet from him, and Rose dabbed at her eyes, finding a sudden interest in something on a shelf.

"Thank you," Grant said.

"Aye, well. Don't thank me. You haven't got in yet."

"Not for this. Well, yeah, for this, and the other day. In court. You made a difference."

"Aye, no bother, lad. I'm just glad to see you out of trouble. That Osborne kid will get what's coming to him. You mark my words."

"I'm sure of it," Grant said, winking at Gillespie then reading the leaflet like it was the latest Josh Conroy novel.

"There's, erm, one more thing I'd like to say," Gillespie said, taking a bite of the pie. Damn, it was good. How the bloody hell Grant wasn't twenty-five stone, he had no idea. If he had grown up in a house with a foster parent like that, he wouldn't have left the kitchen. "Rose?"

She cleared her throat and dabbed at her eyes again, eventually turning to face him.

"Yes?" she asked. "Is the pie okay?"

"The pie's perfect."

"Oh good," she said, although she seemed a little sad. The elephant in the room was that, should Grant get through the interview stage with the force, she could lose him. Gillespie saw it. He read it in her eyes even though she didn't say it. And she'd only just heard his voice. "I'm glad."

"You feel like you're going to lose him?" Gillespie said, sure that Grant wouldn't have wanted him to have the conversation behind his back.

Her lip trembled a little and she averted her eyes.

"I wish I had a mother like you, Rose. You don't know how good you are. How nice it is to see a place like this. I know, I saw some bad places. But there are nice places out there. I was just unlucky, and Grant, he was unlucky too. Until he found you."

"That's so nice of you to say."

"The thing is, Rose," Gillespie continued, making it clear he hadn't finished, "there's this wee lad, you see. Local boy. He just lost his ma. He'll be sent away somewhere. Somewhere different. Somewhere new and strange."

"Oh, how sad," Rose said, and that perfect example of humanity was evident in her eyes. "What's his name?"

"It's Lee," Gillespie said, meeting Grant's stare. "Lee Sanders."

CHAPTER FIFTY-FOUR

A SENSE OF TREPIDATION WASHED OVER BEN. HE DIDN'T THINK she would actually do it. But she had. She had called his bluff and he could hear them downstairs, giggling like schoolgirls. Freya had put some music on and he could still hear them over Madonna's *Material Girl*. He wondered at what point he should mention what had happened the last time he had heard that song. He wondered if he could somehow shift some of the attention off him and onto her, as he described the moment, lost in her own world, Freya had descended the stairs, fully naked, and found Ben in her kitchen. But they were girls. They would stand together. They would probably just criticise him for being in her house without her knowing, regardless of his argument.

He sat down on the bed, kicked off his shoes, and slowly pulled his socks off.

If it had been him that had won, if there had been two killers, he wouldn't have invited the boys over. No way. And if he had, no doubt Freya would have kicked off about how he'd betrayed her trust. About how he was making a mockery of her. Or something along those lines.

But he was where he was. There was no backing down now.

He would face the music, get it over with, and let them feel the embarrassment. That was it. The trick was to go with it.

He stood, dropped his trousers and his boxers, and unbuttoned his shirt, donning the apron as fast as he could. It was smaller than he remembered. He was sure he had tried it when he had brought Freya a Chinese takeaway. He was positive, in fact.

Although, it was hard to tell. It was just a plain, white apron. She could easily have switched them. But who has two aprons? He was sure that when he had left Freya in the lounge, he had tried the apron on and it had come to his knees, with enough around the sides to protect his modesty.

But this one he was wearing seemed shorter; it reached halfway up his thighs, and it barely wrapped around his legs. He was also sure that the strings had been long enough to wrap around his back and tie at the front, but these strings were so short, he had to try and tie a knot behind his back. He'd need to be some kind of contortionist to get it tight.

She'd bloody switched them. Devious cow.

"Ride it out, Ben," he said to himself. "Go with it."

There was a loud cackle of laughter from downstairs and a series of whoops, as a cork was popped from a bottle. It was Doctor Bell's voice that drowned out the music – that sing-song rhythm she had when she spoke, and her energy. Surprisingly, Chapman was loud too. Usually quiet and reserved, it seemed that out of work, she let her hair down. Good for her. This'll give her something to talk about.

He slapped his face a few times, took five fat and deep breaths, and rocked his head from side to side to warm up his muscles, as a fighter might before entering the ring.

"You've got this, Benny boy. You've got this."

But he couldn't leave his clothes like that. Not on the floor. He collected them up and folded them to the vocals of Tracy Chapman coming from downstairs.

"Do you think he'll really do it?" Pip asked, her voice travelling up the stairs as if the comment was really for him.

Her question was met with mixed responses. An even mix of yes and no. But the one he was listening for amidst the cacophony of female frivolity was Freya's. And he heard her as clearly as if she was standing at the foot of the stairs.

"Oh, he'll do it, alright," she said knowingly, like she knew he was listening. "I've never seen him back down from anything."

"Right, no more procrastinating," he said to himself quietly. He took one more deep breath and opened the bedroom door.

The music seemed so loud that he could barely make out their individual voices. Somebody walked through to the kitchen and he froze at the top of the stairs until they had poured themselves a wine and returned to the living room.

The living room was good. Knowing they were all in there was good. Perfect, in fact. It meant they couldn't loiter at the foot of the stairs and see up his apron. He thought about that for a moment, then descended as fast and quietly as he could.

Safe in the hallway, he peered through the gap into the lounge. From where he was standing, the angle was acute. He could see Jackie in the armchair holding a glass of wine.

"Right, come on then," Pip Bell called out. "Enough waiting. Let's drag him down and get this over with."

He glanced up the stairs for an escape, then at the front door. The kitchen would be no good; he would be trapped. But there was no time. They poured from the lounge like five girls on a hen night, and Freya was the hen, bringing up the rear with a wry and knowing smile on her face.

The rest of them – Pip, Jackie, Anna Nillson, and Chapman – stopped and stared at him. Four mouths hanging open in a mixture of disgust and amusement.

Ride it out, he told himself. *Go with it.*

He smiled, leaned on the banister, and winked at them. Then, as a final act of bravado, he placed his foot in the first stair, leaned on his leg, and teased the hem of his apron up.

Jackie was horrified.

Anna was fit to burst.

Chapman was as red as a beetroot but clearly, after half a glass of wine, was enjoying it.

Pip was frowning in confusion.

And Freya, the matriarch of the event, leaned on the doorway as if all her Christmases had come at once. The master plan. She savoured every second with pure delight. She fed off the girls' reactions and seemed to bloom in the moment.

"What are you, Ben?" Pip asked.

He glanced down at his apron, his pose, and then back at her. "Naked servant," he said.

Right at that very moment, when he thought things couldn't get much worse, there was a knock on the door.

"Answer it then, servant," Freya said from the back.

Slowly, Ben turned toward the front door to a chorus of laughs and whoops as the five females behind him got a direct view of his backside. He closed his eyes, told himself to go with it, then opened the door to a familiar face.

That was when he caught the joke.

"I'm sorry I'm late, I..." Michaela began, spying the five girls crammed in the hallway. She turned her attention to Ben, then stared him up and down in total disgust, meeting his nervous gaze and shaking her head in utter dismay. "What the bloody hell is wrong with you?"

There was a pause. A terrible pause, during which time the world did not open up and swallow him as he was hoping it would. He spoke the first words that came to his mind.

"Naked servant?" he suggested, knowing she wouldn't have a clue what he was talking about. He turned back to the gaggle of girls behind him, wide-eyed and lost for words.

But of all the girls, it was Doctor Pippa Bell who answered his question. Slowly, she raised a hand in the air. She was holding something. She flicked the power switch, allowing everyone to hear the angry buzz of a pair of battery-powered clippers.

"We're going to shave your head, Ben," she said. "For my mum's charity. Remember?"

"Shave my head," Ben repeated quietly. "Charity."

"Yeah. What's with the naked servant thing?"

Slowly, Ben's gaze shifted from Pip's look of incredulity and focused on Freya's winning smile. She was standing behind them all, beaming, and raised her glass to him in a silent toast.

"Gotcha," she mouthed.

The End.

NEVER TO RETURN - PROLOGUE

"It's freezing," Simon gasped, as one of his new trainers sank into the mud at the shallow edge of the River Witham. His mum was going to go bananas. He would be grounded for sure, and for a week at least. However, if he voiced that thought, Gavin would hear it, and then Simon's life wouldn't be worth living. Plus, Julie Lansbury was watching, so he couldn't back down now.

"Come on, Simple Simon, you big girl. I thought you said you'd done this before?" Gavin called out from the safety of the bank.

Simon stared up at Gavin, the largest of the three boys, who flicked a lock of blonde hair from his brow and took a pull on the joint he had rolled. He stared back at Simon, defying him to argue, daring him to voice his complaint. Because he knew Simon wouldn't. He never fought back. Until now, that is. Now he'd show them.

"I have done it before," Simon protested with one foot resting on the paddle board and the other sinking deeper and deeper into the stinky, brown mud. If it wasn't for the paddle, which he had jammed into the river bed, he would have toppled over, much to their delight. "I did it when we were in Saint Lucia last year. But the water was clear and warm, and I had sand between my toes. Not freezing cold filth and this muck all over me."

"Just get on with it," Gavin said, taking another pull, and Julie smiled. "You told us you can do it. So, show us."

"I can prove it. I've got photos. My mum took loads."

"Is your mum in them?" Dave asked, sitting up from where he lay on the bank, his hair being tended by Tess Mitchell, the quieter of the two girls, but just as pretty as Julie Lansbury.

"Some of them, I suppose."

"Is she wearing a bikini?" Dave asked, braving a playful slap from Tess.

"Oh, leave off, Dave," Simon mumbled.

"You mum's well fit," Dave continued. "I have absolutely no idea how a woman of her pedigree could conceive an imbecile like you. I bet she wears a thong, with her tight bum all hanging out as well."

"Dave, stop it," Tess said, and she shoved him away, much to the delight of Gavin, who picked up where Dave left off.

"I've seen her topless," Gavin said.

"You what?" Dave said.

"You have not," Simon argued.

"I have. She sunbathes topless in your garden. I saw her last summer, lying on the lawn behind that old greenhouse in your garden."

Simon wanted to argue. He wanted to contest it, but he knew the only time his mum ever sunbathed in that particular spot was when she wanted to get rid of her tan lines.

"There. See?" Gavin said, lying back on the grassy bank beside Julie. "He hasn't got anything to say. I can picture her now–"

"I'll tell them," Simon said, hearing the venom in his voice and regretting the threat before he'd even finished speaking the words.

"What did you say?" Gavin said, sitting up and shoving Julie out of his way. He climbed to his feet and strode towards Simon with purpose, his eyes narrowed and dark. He stepped into the water, then lowered his voice to a pre-pubescent growl that only the two of them could hear. "You won't tell anybody anything, paddle boy."

Gavin Forkes was a lunatic. His whole family was. He wouldn't think twice about getting wet or muddy, and he certainly wouldn't think twice about hitting Simon, especially if Julie was watching. Then again, maybe if Gavin punched him, it would work in his favour. But the idea of being hit was not a pleasant one.

"I might," Simon said, and he took another step back into the water, nudging the paddle board out with him. But the river deepened and he lost his balance, letting go of the paddle, the only thing that was keeping him upright. The water splashed as Gavin surged through the shallow water behind him, leaving Simon with only one escape route – the paddle board.

He clambered on and lay as a surfer might, paddling with his hands to get away. He was freezing. The winter had been hard, and everyone was talking about the joys of spring. But the bloody water was still cold enough that his body began to shiver.

"What did he say, Gav?" Dave called.

"He said something about my mum," Gavin lied, glaring at Simon, daring him to contest it. "Why don't you come here and say it again?"

But Simon was already too far from the bank for Gavin to reach him. The current caught the tail end of the board and began to turn him, pulling him further out into the middle of the river.

As if in victory, Gavin raised the paddle Simon had dropped into the air. "Oy, Simple. You forgot your paddle, you loser."

Then he tossed the paddle away into the long reeds.

For a fleeting moment, Simon saw them all stand. They were laughing. He turned to see where the river was taking him with the sudden dread that follows a very bad idea. And by the time he looked back, they were running along the riverbank. He'd gladly suffer a beating from Gavin if they could help him get to land. He peered into the murky water, wondering if he should jump in, but cowered at the thought.

That was when he realised, he'd made a terrible mistake.

The river dragged him further away, so fast they couldn't keep up.

"Help me," he called out. "Call someone."

But they didn't shout back. To his utter dismay, they all came to a stop, breathless, some of them doubled over to catch their breath.

And then they slipped from view. He passed beneath Five Mile Bridge, spying a man walking across. No, he wasn't walking. He was running. He stopped to peer down at Simon and stared in dismay.

For a brief moment, Simon was worried the man might recognise him, and try to help. But he didn't. He just ran off towards the little car park, rendering Simon completely alone.

The riverbanks bore tall reeds, impenetrable. He was moving now. Really moving. He clung to the board, searching ahead for one of the little boats that often cruised the waters. But it was late. It would be dark soon, and anyone who had been out on the river would have returned by now.

He brought himself up onto one knee, adopting the stance a surfer might just before they'd stand and carve the waves. He shook with fear at the task ahead, and the cold, and hot tears streamed down his face.

He saw nobody. No movement at all. Ahead, the river turned towards Bardney. Everything was exactly how he'd planned it.

But he didn't make it to Bardney. The weight of the board and his body combined, along with the momentum he had built up, took him out of the current and into the swirling waters on the inside of the bend. He managed to grab onto some reeds, and the board turned and came to a stop. If he let go, the river would take Simon around the bend and into the faster water.

Here, he thought. *This is where it happens.*

He peered up over the tips of the reeds, gauging the distance to the bank. Twenty feet at least. It was the perfect spot for what he needed to do. The weeds would tangle around his feet, and he knew the water was deep enough. He would drown and they would never find him. He pictured the board floating on without him. All the way past Bardney and on to Boston. It must be fifty miles. Fifty miles of meandering river for the police to search. They would never find him in time.

It was perfect.

Tying a few reeds into a knot, Simon managed to create a loop to slip his hand through. He lay with one arm outstretched and the current tugging at the board. It was all he could do to hold on and keep his balance, finding that if he lay flat on his front with his arm in the reeds in the water, he could get comfortable while he contemplated his final moments.

But the water was cold and dark, and the thought of slipping into it terrified him into submission. He could do nothing. It was the final hurdle, and he hadn't the courage to do it.

As the huge sky above him paled, then darkened, and the birds that had soared above returned to their nests, sleep took him. It came in fitful bursts. Sometimes he woke in a panic and called out. Other times, he would come around knowing exactly where he was, how helpless his situation and how much of a failure he was.

Twice, he woke and nearly lost his balance, but the fatigue that had been brought on by fear and tension soon took him again. He shivered and shook with the cold, and his arm was numb, though he dared not let go.

"This is it. There's no turning back now," he said aloud, but to himself. He sobbed, stared up at the sky, and shouted in anger, "Why me?"

"Simon?" somebody whispered in the darkness.

"Hello?" he called out weakly. "Is somebody there?"

With no nearby towns to pollute the sky, the night was as dark as he had ever seen it. Darker, he thought. The darkest night. There was no moon, or if there was, it was elsewhere. He would have given anything to see the moon. To have some light, albeit weak.

A shape appeared, or so he thought anyway. He blinked into the gloom in the direction of the gentle lapping he could hear. "Is anybody there?"

A bright torch light flicked on and swept across the water, blinding him so that he had to raise his free hand to shield his eyes.

"Help me," he called out, resigning to being rescued. "I'm over here."

"Simon?" a voice said. The hand that grabbed his arm felt familiar. Bewildered by the ordeal and the thought of being saved, he couldn't even speak. He was safe.

But then the hand tightened on his arm and forced him off the board.

"Help," he said, as his face plunged into the water. He pushed up for a gasp of air. "Help me, please."

But the hand found the back of his neck, and the next words Simon Bird uttered were lost to the freezing cold water of the River Witham. He screamed and thrashed for all he was worth, fighting the urge to breathe, holding on for just a moment longer. *There must be a mistake.* He reached up to pull the hand from his neck, but it was strong. Stronger than he was.

And then it came. This was it. This was how it was meant to be. His miserable life was over. He wouldn't have to endure his mother's bitter tongue any longer, or his father's pitiful cries. He wouldn't have to put up with the random beatings from Gavin, or the vindictive sneers and laughs from the girls.

This was it.

He fought it, but that was just instinct. That was his body in its fight for survival. His mind fought a different battle. His mind had come to terms with its fate. Where his body saw death, his mind saw escape. An end.

Peace.

ALSO BY JACK CARTWRIGHT

The DCI Cook Murder Mysteries

A Winter of Blood

A Secret to Die For

The Wild Fens Murder Mysteries

Secrets In Blood

One For Sorrow

In Cold Blood

Suffer In Silence

Dying To Tell

Never To Return

Lie Beside Me

Dance With Death

In Dead Water

One Deadly Night

Her Dying Mind

Into Death's Arms

Join my VIP reader group to be among the first to hear about new release dates, discounts, and get a free Wild Fens novella.

Visit www.jackcartwrightbooks.com for details.

VIP READER CLUB

Your FREE ebook is waiting for you now.

Get your FREE copy of the prequel story to the Wild Fens Murder Mystery series, and learn how DI Freya Bloom came to give up everything she had, to start a new life in Lincolnshire.

Visit www.jackcartwrightbooks.com to join the VIP Reader Club.

I'll see you there.

Jack Cartwright

AFTERWORD

Because reviews are critical to an author's career, if you have enjoyed this novel, you could do me a huge favour by leaving a review on Amazon.

Reviews allow other readers to find my books. Your help in leaving one would make a big difference to this author.

Thank you for taking the time to read *Dying To Tell*.

COPYRIGHT

www.ingramcontent.com/pod-product-compliance
Lightning Source LLC
LaVergne TN
LVHW041527040425
807752LV00001B/48
* 9 7 8 1 9 1 6 9 8 6 0 4 6 *